HINT OF RAPTURE

"You are correct about my brother. Gordon has everything: the title, and the family—"

"Lands!" she finished for him, her eyes flashing. "So ye went after mine instead, Garrett Marshall," she spat. "I'll have ye know 'The Honorable' doesna suit ye at all. Try Bastard, or Royal Spy! Aye, now that has a fine ring to it!"

It happened so fast, in a blink of an eye. One moment Madeleine was seated, then the next she was in his arms. His eyes were ablaze with fury, burning into hers.

"You will not call me that again," he grated. "I'm not the king's spy, Madeleine."

"Liar! I dinna believe ye," she answered hoarsely.

"Maybe you'll believe this, my lady wife," he said as his mouth suddenly came down hard upon her lips.

A HINT OF RAPTURE

MIRIAM MINGER

AVON BOOKS ◬ NEW YORK

AVON BOOKS
A division of
The Hearst Corporation
105 Madison Avenue
New York, New York 10016

Copyright © 1990 by Miriam Minger
Inside cover author photograph by Priscilla E.M. Purnick
Published by arrangement with the author
Library of Congress Catalog Card Number: 89-92493
ISBN: 0-380-75863-6

First Avon Books Printing: July 1990

AVON TRADEMARK REG. U.S. PAT. OFF. AND IN OTHER COUNTRIES, MARCA REGISTRADA, HECHO EN U.S.A.

Printed in the U.S.A.

RA 10 9 8 7 6 5 4 3 2 1

To my beloved parents,
Conrad and Ann Walker,
whose joyful romance has always been
and always will be, my inspiration

The luvely Lass o' Inverness,
    Nae joy nor pleasure can she see;
For e'en and morn she cries, Alas!
    And ay the saut tear blins her e'e:
"Drummossie moor, Drummossie day—
    A waeful day it was to me;
For there I lost my father dear,
    My father dear and brethren three!

Their winding-sheet the bluidy clay,
    Their graves are growing green to see;
And by them lies the dearest lad
    That ever blest a woman's e'e!
Now wae to thee, thou cruel lord,
    A bluidy man I trow thou be;
For mony a heart thou hast made sair
    That ne'er did wrang to thine or thee!"

                                    Robert Burns

Prologue

Farraline, Strathherrick
Inverness-shire, Scotland
May 1746

"**M**addie, wake up, wake up!" Glenis pleaded, rushing toward the bed as fast as her old bones would carry her. " 'Tis the redcoats, hinny, come to burn the house! Oh, God, protect us!"

"What are ye saying, Glenis?" Madeleine Fraser said drowsily, jarred from her sleep. Dazed, she sat up, her eyes adjusting to the faint light in her room. It was near dawn, and the murky gray world outside her window was blanketed in thick fog.

"Redcoats, Maddie, comin' up the road!" Glenis exclaimed. "Angus Ramsay just brought the news. He near scared the life from me, poundin' on the kitchen door as he did. He's gone now to wake the villagers in Farraline." She tugged urgently at Madeleine's arm. "Hurry, ye must get dressed and flee before they get here. They'll not want the likes of me, a wrinkled old woman, but ye're young, lass, and as pretty as they come. Oh, hurry, Maddie, for yer own sake!"

Madeleine did not hesitate. Fully awake now, she threw back the coverlet and vaulted out of bed, wrenching her white nightdress over her head. She shivered, her skin prickling with goosebumps. The early morning air was still chill this time of year in the High-

1

lands. She brushed by her servant and ran across the room to the massive wardrobe.

She flung open one door and grabbed the first gown she touched, a plain frock of blue muslin. She dressed quickly, donning first a chemise and linen drawers, but rejecting her stays. There was no time. She took a brief moment to fasten a light woolen shawl around her shoulders, then she was flying out the door with Glenis at her heels.

"Yer shoes, Maddie. What about yer shoes?" Glenis cried frantically. "Ye can hardly run barefoot into the mountains."

"I winna need them," Madeleine said over her shoulder. She crossed the carpeted hallway to the narrow side stairs near her room and took them two at a time, her hands braced against the whitewashed walls.

"What do ye mean, ye winna need them?" Glenis called shrilly from the top of the stairs.

Madeleine spun around and looked up at her terrified servant. Her deep azure eyes shone with fierce determination. "I'm not leaving my home, Glenis. The devils will have to burn Mhor Manor around me."

"Maddie!"

Ignoring Glenis's shocked expression and sputtered protests, Madeleine hurried through the drawing room to the main hallway. She could hear raised male voices growing louder and the nervous neighing of horses. With her heart hammering in her chest she threw open the front door and stepped outside.

Raw fear cut through her, and her knees felt suddenly weak. There were at least two hundred English soldiers advancing along the dirt drive toward the manor house, some marching, some on horseback. Many of them held smoking torches, the bright orange flames like beacons in the swirling fog.

"Courage, lass," Madeleine whispered under her breath. "Dinna let the bastards see yer fear."

She took a step forward, planting her feet on the damp flagstones leading to the drive. She pretended not to hear the wolfish whistles and lewd remarks, and she overlooked the leering grins. Her eyes were fixed on the silver-haired officer riding at the head of his men. She guessed he was a colonel from the abundant gold lace which adorned his scarlet coat. Clasping her hands tightly to keep them from shaking, she waited until he drew up on the reins and stopped just twenty feet from the house.

"I know why ye've come, and I ask ye to leave us in peace!" she stated loudly, but her words were drowned out by the raucous din. Quelling her apprehension, she tried once more, and again she was shouted down. To her surprise, the commanding officer held up his hand, and the rowdy soldiers gradually fell silent.

Madeleine drew a deep breath, her gaze meeting his narrowed one. "I know why ye're here, colonel, and 'tis a dirty business ye're about," she said in a clear, strong voice. "I appeal to yer sense of decency and honor, as a gentleman. Spare my home, and the homes in the surrounding villages. Most of our men are gone." She paused, swallowing against the sudden lump in her throat. "We're mainly women and children here. We canna fight ye, so we ask for yer mercy."

"Let me have at her," a strapping soldier called out, laughing coarsely. "When I'm between her legs, she'll not cry out for mercy. She'll cry out for more!"

"Aye, and I'll have her next!" another shouted eagerly, shoving his way to the front. "I've never had a wench so fine. Just look at 'er, with that wild mane o' chestnut curls and those ruby lips!"

Madeleine stepped back as the soldiers shook their torches threateningly. The air resounded with crude laughter and obscenities until the officer commanded their grudging silence once again.

The colonel studied her sharply, his expression grim. "I cannot do that, young lady. I have orders from the duke of Cumberland that must be followed—"

"Orders!" she blurted, cutting him off. The mere mention of Butcher Cumberland filled her with rage she could barely control. "We've already lost our cattle herds, our sheep and our goats, to yer duke's orders, driven off for slaughter to feed the lot of ye English. And our newly sown crops, our food for next winter," she emphasized, "were ruined when the soldiers drove the animals over the fields. We've only our homes left to shelter us. If ye burn us out, we'll have nothing left!"

"My orders are plain and cannot be altered," the officer insisted, shaking his head. "Now, if you have servants in the house, you'd best see that they stand clear—"

"Surely ye have a good wife at home, sir," Madeleine cried out desperately, trying another tack. "Children of yer own, aye, and grandchildren!" Emboldened, she swept her defiant gaze around the tight line of soldiers. "All of ye! Have ye not wives yerselves—sweethearts, children? What if 'twas yer loved ones in this miserable plight? Would ye not wish mercy to be shown?"

The hardened faces of the soldiers, faces that had grown immune to death and suffering, stared at her with little pity or remorse. Fighting a wave of despair, Madeleine turned back to the colonel. "Please, sir, I beg of ye. Dinna let yer men loose upon us. If ye do, I swear 'twill haunt ye to yer grave."

The officer looked down for a long moment, his fingers worrying at the reins. When he glanced at her again, Madeleine breathed an inner sigh of relief at the flicker of compassion she saw in his eyes.

"Very well, young lady. Your home and those in the surrounding villages will be spared," he said, ignoring his men's disgruntled mutterings. "Though I cannot promise you another officer will do the same in the future."

"Ye have my thanks, sir," Madeleine said.

"You might wish to save your gratitude," he replied cryptically. "There is one order I cannot change." He turned abruptly in his saddle and addressed his soldiers. "Strip everything of value from the house!"

A great cheer went up from the soldiers, and the

colonel had to shout above them. "Hear me well, lads. If any of you should take it in your heads to harm this lady or her servants, I'll hang you this very day. Now get on with it. We have the entire valley to cover before sunset."

"No!" Madeleine gasped in disbelief as the soldiers dropped their torches and rushed toward the house. Fighting and kicking, she was swept into the house by the human tide until a burly soldier plucked her to safety and deposited her in a dining room chair.

Madeleine tried to stand up, but the soldier held her firmly by the shoulders, forcing her to remain seated. All she could do was stare wide-eyed while the red-coats swarmed into the adjoining rooms and up the center flight of stairs, leaving a path of wanton destruction in their wake.

"No, keep yer filthy hands from that vase!" she heard Glenis scream from the drawing room. There was a crash of china, then a loud wail as the old woman was carried into the dining room and dumped unceremoniously in another chair. Glenis began to cry piteously.

Madeleine had no words of comfort to offer her. She watched in impotent fury as her mother's sterling silver was snatched from its cabinet, polished furniture was hacked to bits, portraits were slashed and gilt frames were carried off, rugs were soiled by muddy boot prints, and family heirlooms were stolen. She remained silent through it all, unshed tears brimming in her eyes, while her captor's callused fingers stroked her neck.

Ten minutes later the rampage was over. The soldier released her, but not before he pulled her head back roughly and kissed her full on the lips. His fetid breath made her gag, and she wrenched her mouth away.

"Devil!" she spat and wiped her mouth with the back of her hand. He merely grinned at her, his laughter echoing in the hallway as he followed the last of his triumphant companions from the house.

Madeleine started when the colonel suddenly strode

through the open door. He glanced first in the drawing room, then where she and Glenis sat in the dining room, as if to ensure his orders had been carried out. He did not meet her eyes. Then he was gone, his horse's hooves pounding along the drive as he rode away. She listened dully as the soldiers withdrew, the sound of their marching feet fading into the distance.

A hush like the silence in a tomb settled over the house. Madeleine could not find the strength to rise for a long time. She felt numb. Glenis's sobbing finally spurred her into action. She had to escape it or crumble herself.

She stood up and walked slowly into the entryway, stepping over bits of furniture and a smashed mantel clock, and shut the front door. Then she made her way in a daze to the drawing room.

She needed to be alone. She would survey the damage later, but not now. Not now.

Madeleine closed the door behind her, righted an overturned armchair, and slumped down on the soiled brocade. Her thoughts began to roil and pitch, heated outrage gradually sweeping away the numbness.

Why had this happened? Why? Had the Highlands not suffered enough? Would the horrors that had begun a month ago never cease?

She leaned her head back on the padded cushion, recalling Glenis's sorrowful words that wretched day in April.

"Come away from the window, hinny. Ye know yer da winna be comin' home. Come away, Maddie. 'Tis a hopeless thing ye're doin'."

Yer da winna be comin' home . . . Her father . . .

Madeleine's hands clenched into tight fists as fresh pain assaulted her, a jagged ache centered just over her heart. Her palms stung where her nails bit into the smooth flesh. Tears glistened from spiky dark lashes and spilled down her cheeks, staining the bodice of her gown.

She didn't care. She surrendered to the grief, angèr

and frustration tormenting her, in this silent room where no one would see her cry.

Yer da winna be comin' home . . .

The haunting words were so vivid, it could have been yesterday when Glenis bid her to stand away from the tall window. But today was the sixteenth of May, one month to the day since the Battle of Culloden was fought on rain-swept Drummossie Moor, a scarce twenty miles from the valley of Strathherrick. One month since she had learned from a kinsman that her father had fallen in the bloody mire, never to rise again. One month since she had run to the window in anguished disbelief, searching the muddy road that wound past the estate for any sign of her father among the retreating Highlanders.

Madeleine sighed raggedly, her blurred gaze staring straight ahead. Out of the many bold, strong lads who had rallied to the Jacobite cause, fewer than half of her kinsmen had survived the merciless slaughter at Culloden.

The fiery cross—the ancient signal to rally clansmen for battle, formed by two yew branches that were first set alight, then doused in goat's blood—had been carried to Strathherrick on a gray, misty morning last autumn. It was the call of Simon Fraser, Lord Lovat and the chief of Clan Fraser. He had finally decided to come out for Bonnie Prince Charlie in the young Stuart's bid to regain the throne of England, Scotland, and Ireland for his father, the exiled King James III.

Her father, baronet Sir Hugh Fraser of Farraline and cousin to Lord Lovat, had immediately taken up the call, summoning his tacksmen and tenants from their warm hearth fires. The entire valley had participated in a frenzied flurry of activity as the clansmen wholeheartedly prepared to join the Jacobite prince and his burgeoning forces.

Madeleine smiled faintly and wiped the hot tears from her face, tasting salt on her lips. She recalled the brave sight of the Frasers of Strathherrick as they readied to march, wearing the clan badge of freshly cut sprigs of yew in their bonnets. Her handsome father had been resplendent in his kilt and tartan plaid of red and forest green, a bonnet sporting a white cockade, the symbol of the Jacobite cause, atop his shining auburn hair.

How proud her dear mother, the bonnie Lady Jean, would have been if she had lived to see that day. How fervently Madeleine had wished at that moment that she had been born a son. She had cursed her sex and the skirts she wore which forced her to remain behind in Farraline with the rest of the women, instead of riding into battle at her father's side. Only his last words to her had helped soothe her angry frustration.

"Ye're the mistress of Farraline now, Maddie, whilst I'm gone to war. Tend to the needs of yer people in my stead. The women, wee bairns, and men too old for battle depend upon yer care and good judgment. Now give me a kiss and one of yer bonnie smiles, lass. We're off to fight for the Stuarts!"

Enveloped in her father's fierce embrace, Madeleine had never felt so honored or so trusted. Mistress of Farraline! Aye, she would make her father proud, and more than live up to his faith in her.

Her slim shoulders were squared, her back was straight, and her chin was held high as Sir Hugh Fraser walked proudly to the head of his men and mounted his fine roan gelding. The skirl of bagpipes soared on the whistling wind and resounded from the Monadhliath Mountains flanking the broad valley, stirring the blood of all who heard it, as the men of Clan Fraser began their long march toward Edinburgh.

With a rampant pounding in her breast, Madeleine had stared after the heroic parade of clansmen until their tartans faded into the distant slopes. She would never have believed it would be the last time she would see her father.

During the months that followed, news was carried often to Strathherrick on the progress of the Highland army under the command of Prince Charles Edward Stuart. Madeleine hung on to every word.

There was the long victorious march into England as far south as Derby, the cities of Carlisle, Preston, and Manchester falling under the Jacobite standard. But instead of pressing on to London, the army decided to retire to Scotland due to the massing of Hanoverian forces under the duke of Cumberland, William Augustus, the corpulent third son of King George II. There the Jacobites would make a stand on home ground.

Upon returning to Scotland, the army's hopes were raised once again after the victory at the Battle of Falkirk in January and the successful routs of English forts scattered throughout the Highlands. Then no more was heard until news was brought that Bonnie Prince Charlie and his forces were quartered at Inverness until spring, while the duke of Cumberland remained in Aberdeen.

All seemed quiet until early April, when a large company of men from Clan Cameron passed through Farraline on their way north to Inverness and a rendezvous with the prince. Madeleine's excited inquiries discovered nothing more than that Cumberland and his troops were on the move toward Drummossie Moor, a barren, soggy plain to the west of the River Nairn.

Drummossie Moor. Why Madeleine felt a sudden chill seize her at that news she would only understand a few days later, when word arrived that the Battle of Culloden, from beginning to end lasting only an hour, had been lost to the government forces.

"Damn them, damn them," Madeleine whispered. She had only to think of the bastards who had mowed down the Highlands' finest sons with their cannon, bayonets, and grapeshot, and she was filled with rage.

How she hated them. Englishmen. Redcoats. The devil's own spawn. Murderers!

Since that bloody day Butcher Cumberland and his men had wreaked their revenge on the Highlands, their brand of "justice" to right the treasonous wrongs perpetrated against the Crown by the rebellious clans. It was a reign of terror that still showed no signs of abating.

It had begun when the Butcher granted the fallen clansmen no quarter on the battlefield. Both the wounded and the dead were stripped where they lay, then those still alive were bayoneted or shot or clubbed to death. Only a few were reserved for public punishment. A barn filled with wounded who had dragged themselves from the field was locked and set on fire, the unfortunate men inside suffering a grisly death.

It was several days before the dead were finally buried in mass unmarked graves, denied the dignity of being laid to rest in their own lands. How true Glenis's words had been. Her father would never come home again.

Fleeing clansmen were pursued by dragoons all the way to Inverness, the fearsome horsemen cutting down Jacobite soldiers as well as innocent bystanders who chanced in their way, including women and children. Only the Highlanders who fled in the opposite direction, south toward Strathherrick and beyond into Badenoch, lived to become fugitives in their own land, and they were hunted like wild beasts among the craggy hills.

Dougald Fraser was one of these desperate fugitives. A distant cousin and childhood friend, he was the man her father had intended for her to marry when the war had been won. Now there would be no wedding for a long time, if at all. If Dougald or any other fugitives, including their Lord Lovat, were caught, they faced imprisonment, deportation to the Colonies, or hanging.

Their bonnie prince was also a hunted man, with a price of thirty thousand pounds on his head. Madeleine knew in her heart that no Highlander would betray him, even for such an outrageous sum. Although a proclamation had been issued that anyone caught aiding the royal fugitive faced certain death, tales abounded of those who had risked their lives harboring the prince and his companions during the past four weeks.

All the atrocities had done little to curb the Butcher's insatiable thirst for blood. He turned next on the Highland people who had been left at home while their men fought the war. Operating from his newly regained headquarters at Fort Augustus, south of Loch Ness, he ordered his soldiers to strike out across the countryside and harry the glens.

Madeleine had heard horrible tales from fugitives passing by night through Farraline; tales of cold-blooded killings and the rape of young and old. Chieftains' houses were plundered and burned to the ground; Lord Lovat's beloved Dounie Castle in Beauly was one of the first to be laid waste. Even the rough, one-room cottages of the peasants were rarely spared the torch.

Madeleine's gaze swept the scattered wreckage in the room. After the senseless ferocity she had witnessed this morning, it was a miracle that Mhor Manor had not been burned. She could only hope the colonel would keep his word and spare the neighboring villages.

Bitter tears scalded her eyes, and she rose from the chair to pace angrily.

As if this day's injustice and devastation were not enough, what of the news that had come to Strathherrick only last week? The estates of chieftains who had participated in the uprising were being confiscated for the Crown, and Lord Lovat's lands were already forfeited and being administered by a royal commissioner. It seemed the English were wasting no time in their efforts to subdue the Highlands.

Worst of all, every Highland male was being forced to swear an oath that he would never again wear the belted plaid, tartan or any Highland garment—unless in a king's regiment—never possess a weapon, not even a dirk, or play the bagpipes, now considered an instrument of war by the government.

''If I were a man, I'd die before I'd swear that cursed

oath," Madeleine whispered vehemently. "And I'd wear the kilt to my grave!"

She pulled aside a slashed curtain and looked out across the weed-strewn lawn and disheveled garden. The fog had lifted, revealing a pale blue sky streaked with shafts of golden sunlight. The beauty of it did little to soothe her aching heart.

An unsettling thought struck her. Would the English seize Mhor Manor as well?

The estate in Strathherrick had been in her family for over a hundred years, deeded to the Frasers of Farraline by the tenth Lord Lovat, the father of old Simon the Fox, their chief. Though he was the heritable head of Clan Fraser, the land belonged not to him but to her father.

Madeleine sighed heavily. No, the land now belonged to her. She was the mistress of Farraline.

Her attention was suddenly drawn to a mother and three little boys, their heads bent, their clothing dirty and bedraggled, who hurried along a footpath that cut across the estate. She recognized the woman as Flora Chrystie, the wife of one of her father's tacksmen who had died at Culloden. She guessed the young widow, who was seven months gone with child, had been alerted to the soldiers' approach and was fleeing for the safety of the mountains.

She watched as Flora turned her face, pinched and pale, toward the manor house. The woman bowed her head slightly in respect, then urged her children onward. Instead of scampering down the path, the boys clung listlessly to their mother's skirts, lacking the energy to run. They suffered, like so many others, because the plundering of their cattle and the destruction of their crops left little food to appease the gnawing hunger in their bellies.

Madeleine's throat constricted painfully at the pathetic sight, and defiant indignation seized her.

If something wasn't done soon, her people would starve! Even if their homes were spared, what good were roofs over their heads if they had no food to sustain life?

Her father's last words came back to her in a rush, reviving her flagging spirit and giving her strength:

Ye're the mistress of Farraline now, Maddie. . . . Tend to the needs of yer people. . . . They depend upon yer care and good judgment.

Madeleine let the curtain drop, her tears drying on her cheeks. A determined resolve flared brightly within her breast, and a bold plan took shape in her mind.

"Aye, something has to be done, Maddie Fraser, and ye're the one to do it," she vowed fiercely.

God help her, somehow she would see that the Frasers of Strathherrick would survive these awful times and live to prosper once again in the Highlands they loved so dearly!

Then come, thou fairest of the fair,
Those wonted smiles, O, let me share,
And by thy beauteous self I swear
  No love but thine my heart shall know!

Robert Burns

Chapter 1

Fort Augustus Inverness-shire
July 1746

Captain Garrett Marshall stirred on his narrow cot, awakened by slow, cautious footfalls across the planked floor. Instantly alert, he tensed. He reached for the knife beneath his thin mattress, then rolled over without making a sound.

A flickering light drew his attention to the entrance of the officers' bunkhouse, and he eased himself up on one elbow, his keen gaze piercing the darkness. He immediately recognized the intruder and relaxed. It was one of General Hawley's aides, a young corporal.

What could he want at this early hour? Garrett thought irritably, watching as the soldier quietly made his way down the long row of wooden cots, holding his sputtering candle high. The corporal stopped occasionally to lift the edge of a coarse blanket and peer into the face of a sleeping officer, then moved on. It was clear he was searching for someone.

Suddenly the soldier tripped over a pair of boots standing beside a cot, his whispered oath eliciting groans from several men. He froze, the candlelight bobbing as his hand shook, until the groans lapsed once again into loud snoring. Only then did he resume his search, moving gingerly down the narrow center aisle.

Garrett smiled grimly. Whatever the corporal's purpose, he obviously did not want to wake anyone needlessly and receive a sharp cuff on the ear for his trouble. Yet his method was most unwise. Perhaps Garrett should teach this lad a lesson that might one day save his life.

He lay back down and pulled the blanket well over his shoulder, shadowing his face. He waited, listening, until the corporal was standing over him. In one sudden movement, Garrett threw off the blanket and jumped up from the cot, seizing the unsuspecting soldier by the throat.

"It's dangerous to creep so among armed men, corporal," he said, his voice low and menacing. "Better to announce your presence, and wake us, than be mistaken for the enemy. We have been tricked before by a Highlander wearing the king's colors."

The soldier nodded vigorously, gulping at the deadly weight of a knife pressed against his belly. Sweat broke out on his brow as he stared up into vivid gray-green eyes. "Y-yes, sir, C-Captain Marshall!" he finally managed to stutter.

Satisfied, Garrett released him. He slipped the knife back beneath his mattress, then straightened and ran his hands through his dark blond hair. "What are you doing here?"

With a start the flustered soldier remembered his mission. "Wh-why, looking for you, sir," he blurted out, though not too loudly. "General Hawley has requested your presence at his quarters immediately. Your commander, Colonel Wolfe, was summoned earlier and awaits you there."

"Very well. Any idea what this is all about?" Garrett asked, pulling on his breeches and reaching for the white shirt which hung from a peg wedged into the stone wall. He glanced out the small window high above his cot and saw that it was still dark, perhaps an hour yet before dawn.

"No, sir, though a messenger and escort were admitted through the gates no more than a half hour past. An important dispatch, I'd guess, because he made straight for the general's quarters." The corporal shrugged. "I cannot say for sure if this dispatch concerns you, captain, or if it's some other matter."

Garrett quickly drew on his red waistcoat, fastened the buttons, and expertly tied his white cravat. He mulled over the corporal's words as he pulled on his black boots, buckled his sword belt about his lean waist, and donned the long red coat that reached just to his knees.

Why would General Hawley have summoned him so early in the morning? If he had been a higher ranking officer, it would have made sense. But he commanded a company of one hundred foot soldiers, nothing more, nothing less. It was hardly worth singling him out—

Garrett's jaw tensed, and his eyes narrowed. Perhaps he was being summoned to discuss some disciplinary action against one of his men. Dammit all, that was the last thing he needed for morale!

General Henry Hawley, a bastard son of George II and half brother to the duke of Cumberland, had not earned the nickname Hangman due to his generosity and friendly rapport with his troops. He ruled his forces with an iron hand, hanging any man who disobeyed him or displayed the least bit of cowardice in battle. Fort Augustus had recently been given over to his command, after the duke had returned to London last week. If one of Garrett's men had already earned the general's displeasure, Garrett could do little to save him.

After tying his hair back with a ribbon, Garrett lifted his black tricorn hat from another peg and set it atop his head. He followed the corporal from the bunkhouse, although he took the lead when they approached the imposing fieldstone building in the center of the fort. A mist hung in the cool air, and Garrett inhaled deeply, bracing himself for whatever might lie ahead.

The sentinels standing guard allowed them entrance, and the corporal followed him through a heavy oak door, down a dark corridor, and into a well-lit room. Garrett halted and stood at stiff attention at the first sight of General Hawley. He was seated at one end of a long table with Colonel Thomas Wolfe at his left.

"Thank you, corporal," Colonel Wolfe said, nodding a curt dismissal. "Come in, Captain Marshall."

Garrett stepped forward until he stood at the opposite end of the table, his gaze fixed on a distant point above the portly general's head. "Sir, Captain Garrett Marshall of Wolfe's Regiment, Fourth Company of Foot!" he said briskly.

"And, if I am not mistaken, the younger brother of the earl of Kemsley, court minister to King George?" General Hawley inquired, leaning forward.

Garrett dropped his gaze in surprise, meeting the general's shrewd and cunning eyes, which resembled those of his half brother. He shifted uncomfortably. "Yes, Lord Kemsley is my brother."

"Pray sit down, captain," Colonel Wolfe invited, motioning to a nearby chair.

Garrett swept off his hat and sat, perplexed by the direction of the conversation. He felt a sense of relief, however, that this meeting apparently had nothing to do with his men's behavior.

"Your family has a very interesting history," General Hawley continued. "Colonel Wolfe tells me you possess a bit of Scots blood, on your mother's side?"

Startled by this question, Garrett looked from the general to his commander, whose nod was barely perceptible, then back again. "My grandmother was born in Edinburgh, sir, though her family came from Sutherland in the north, a clan loyal to the Crown," he stressed pointedly. "She married John Ross, an English merchant, and afterward lived much of her life in London, as did my mother until she married my late father, Geoffrey Marshall, the sixth earl of Kemsley."

"Colonel Wolfe also tells me you are familiar with the Highlanders and their ways."

Garrett's brow lifted. One night over several tankards of strong ale, he had mentioned his Scots heri-

tage to the good colonel, who had become almost like
a father to him. He'd spoken in confidence, but obviously that confidence had been breached. "May I be
so bold, general, as to inquire why you ask this of me?"

"In due time, captain," Colonel Wolfe interrupted,
his voice tinged with caution. "Please answer."

Garrett leaned back in his chair and stared stonily at
the general. "When I was a child, my grandmother
told me stories of the Highlands, sir, stories of her clan
ancestors. I was born and bred in England, but if such
lore makes me more familiar with the Highlanders than
most Britons, then yes, I know something of their
ways."

"Good." General Hawley turned to Colonel Wolfe.
"I am satisfied, commander. You may proceed with
the plan we have already discussed. See that Captain
Marshall and a third of his men, the ones who prove
best in the saddle, leave the fort by noon tomorrow."
He rose from his chair, and the two officers followed
suit. "Now if you will excuse me, gentlemen, I intend
to catch another hour's rest before breakfast."

General Hawley strode toward the door, then
stopped and glanced at Colonel Wolfe, his expression
grim. "Commander, remember that if your humanitarian plan fails, I will send an entire regiment to sweep
through those blasted mountains. We'll find that bastard Black Jack if I have to burn every lice-ridden hovel
to the ground!"

The door slammed shut behind him, and a heavy
silence descended on the room. It didn't last long.

"What the devil—"

"Wait!" Colonel Wolfe hissed, squelching Garrett's
outburst with a wave of his hand until the sound of
the general's ponderous footsteps gradually faded.
Then he smiled wryly. "I don't know which one is
worse for ill temper, the duke or Hawley. They're both
cut from the same cloth, it seems." He laughed shortly,
walking over and taking the seat next to Garrett's.
"Which, of course, they are. One above the royal
sheets and the other below."

At any other time Garrett might have been amused by his commander's veiled reference to King George's mistresses, but he hadn't relished the general's personal questions. He was a private man who trusted few with details of his life. And the reference to his brother, Gordon, who at thirty-four was six years his senior, had rubbed salt in an open wound.

It was Gordon who had bought him the costly military commission Garrett had been honor-bound to fulfill. Garrett had no doubt his brother had hoped he would be killed in some foreign battle. Gordon would then inherit Rosemoor, the beautiful country estate their mother had left to Garrett.

It had been the countess's right to bequeath her own property to whomever she wished. She had chosen her favorite younger son, forever sealing Gordon's deep-seated resentment of Garrett and fueling his determination to claim Garrett's inheritance, using whatever means he could.

It wasn't enough that Gordon possessed all of their father's holdings, including the entailed family estate, Kemsley Grove, and the stately town house in London's most fashionable neighborhood. It wasn't enough that he had married the woman Garrett had long courted, Lady Celinda Gray. Gordon's greed to possess Rosemoor, the richest estate in Sussex, knew no bounds.

However, Garrett was equally determined to thwart him. Only their family honor had compelled him to fulfill his military commitment, not fear of his brother. Next time the matter would be settled in a duel, and honor be damned. He would suffer no more of Gordon's vengeful schemes or any further disruption of his life.

At least he was well over Celinda's slight by now, Garrett thought dryly. He wished he could say the same for his three-year commission.

He still had another year of service remaining before he could be free of this wretched army. After what he had seen during the past few months under the duke of Cumberland, beginning with the massacre at Culloden in which he had refused to play any part, and followed by the ruthless persecution of the Highlanders, he had more than his fill of butchery!

Colonel Wolfe's gravelly voice broke into Garrett's thoughts. "I know you're wondering what's afoot, Garrett, and I'll get right to the point. First I must apologize for betraying a confidence, but in this case I felt it necessary and justified."

Garrett merely nodded and sat down, tossing his hat upon the table.

"I received a dispatch less than an hour ago. Another of our supply wagons bound for the fort along General Wade's Road has been plundered, the third in two weeks," Colonel Wolfe continued. "Hawley's damn upset about it, especially since this load was carrying not only grain, but also some casks of wine he had ordered from London. The thought of this Black Jack fellow, a Jacobite sympathizer, swilling his vintage wine doesn't set well with him in the least."

"Who is Black Jack?" Garrett asked, his interest piqued by the unusual nickname.

Colonel Wolfe snorted derisively. "That's what the soldiers call the leader of the renegade band of thieves, because the scoundrel always appears in black clothing, with his face blackened to disguise his features. He hides well in the shadows while his men do the stealing, and he never says a word, although he always keeps two pistols cocked and ready. His men work swiftly, usually tying up the soldiers and throwing their weapons into Loch Ness or taking them along."

"Loch Ness? Have most of the raids been along Wade's Road?"

"Yes, those involving supply wagons. But ships docked along Inverness Firth have apparently also lost cargo to this thief, and cattle have been stolen up and down Glenmore as far south as Loch Lochy."

Garrett's expression grew thoughtful. "Have any soldiers been killed during these raids?"

"Surprisingly, no. A few men have been wounded,

but nothing serious. It seems Black Jack's only interest is theft. As soon as he's stolen what he wants, he and his men disappear into the night.''

''An interesting story, colonel, but what has this to do with me?'' Garrett asked.

Colonel Wolfe leaned his elbows on the table and lowered his voice. ''You and I are of like mind, Garrett. During the past three months we have seen a great deal of bloodshed, and much of it has been irrational, cruel, and against all sense of fair play. Culloden was proof of that, and now Cumberland's policy of harrying the glens . . .''

His voice trailed off, and he shook his head gravely. ''There has been enough slaughter of innocents. I simply cannot sit by and watch it begin anew. When Hawley got the dispatch this morning, his first impulse was to send my entire regiment to Strathherrick, beside Loch Ness, since all evidence points to that valley as Black Jack's main territory.''

''Where you would carry out his normal policy in matters concerning the Highlanders,'' Garrett said quietly. ''Torture, maim, rape, burn, and then ask questions.''

''Right. Instead I took a chance and suggested a more peaceful method of capturing this outlaw. Amazingly Hawley agreed to hear me out, probably due to the recent outrage expressed by clans loyal to King George about the atrocities committed against the defeated Highlanders.''

''It certainly wouldn't do to have those powerful clans join their Jacobite cousins against the excessive ravages of the English,'' Garrett commented.

''Indeed not. Now, it's my guess that Black Jack is carrying out these raids to provide food for that region,'' Colonel Wolfe rushed on. ''Opened sacks of the king's grain were found in a cave near the loch, and villagers have been found with good supplies of salted meat in their cellars.''

''Not likely for an area that lost its cattle and crops to Cumberland's more aggressive troops.''

"Exactly. I told Hawley if a large force of armed soldiers descended upon Strathherrick, Black Jack and his men would take to the mountains and never come down from hiding. We already know how well these people guard their secrets, despite the threat of death. Prince Charles has managed to remain on the run for three months, eluding thousands of our troops. It would be the same for Black Jack."

"So instead I'm supposed to take a third of my men and attempt to discover the whereabouts of the elusive Black Jack by living among the Highlanders of Strathherrick as an occupying yet peaceful force."

Colonel Wolfe nodded. "With your insight into Highland ways, the task may be easier than you think." He smiled broadly. "If I were a younger man, I'd relish the assignment. Your prowess with the ladies is renowned, Garrett. You're as much of a gentleman to the doxies who follow our troops as to the elegant damsels we've met in the cities. You've charmed them all. Perhaps you may find a willing Highland lass or two to aid you in your quest. Who knows what secrets might be betrayed at the height of passion."

Garrett laughed. He was not convinced that a pretty Highland wench would so willingly hop into bed with an English soldier, but the thought intrigued him nonetheless.

"I would suggest you and your men billet in a village, or perhaps in one of the few manor houses still left standing," Colonel Wolfe said. "I've heard of a place that might be large enough for all of you. Hmmm, what was the name of that village?"

He paused, rapping his knuckles absently on the table. "Ah, yes, now I remember. It's near Farraline, I believe. The owner may not take kindly to the inconvenience, but at least it's better than finding his home burned to the ground." He stood up. "Any more questions, captain?"

"One," Garrett replied. "How long do I have to find this Black Jack and bring him to the king's justice?"

Colonel Wolfe sobered, his features darkening.

"Hawley is an impatient man, Garrett. If our plan proves unsuccessful, he'll carry out his threat."

"Just as I thought," Garrett said, rising from his chair and following the colonel from the room.

Chapter 2

❦

❝**W**ill ye be ridin' out again this ev'ning, Maddie?❞ Glenis asked as she smoothed a clean cloth over the rough-hewn kitchen table. She glanced up when she received no answer. Her eyes, brown as dried berries, anxiously studied her young mistress. Madeleine was seated on a low stool by the window, poring over a worn and yellowed map balanced atop her knees.

Her brow creased in concentration, Madeleine traced her finger along the thin line of General Wade's Road, which stretched from Inverness to Fort Augustus. The road hugged Loch Ness for three-quarters of the way, then jutted out to the southeast around Beinn a Bhacaidh, a lesser mountain, and Loch Tarff. The narrow valley of Glen Doe lay just to the south of the tiny loch, and it was the site of tonight's raid.

❝ 'Tis a risky plan,❞ she whispered to herself, unaware of Glenis's scrutiny. There would doubtless be many soldiers so close to Fort Augustus, but that could not be helped.

According to her sources, a large herd of cattle was grazing in Glen Doe, cattle which until a few weeks ago had belonged to some hapless Highland villages. Well, she would simply ❝rescue❞ a few tonight, during the wee hours of darkness. Her people would have fresh meat for their suppers within two days.

A smile briefly touched Madeleine's lips, then faded as her thoughts turned once again to the impending

25

raid. She looked up from the map and gazed out across the apple orchard, the sun's bright rays warm on her face. The damp morning fog had long since burned away, leaving the sky overhead a pristine blue. The clear, sunny afternoon boded well for the weather later that night.

She and her five kinsmen would start out at dusk for the distant valley. They would ride the sturdy, dun-colored horses native to the Highlands and keep to the mountains they knew so well, away from Wade's Road and any unwelcome encounters with redcoats. On the rugged slopes above Glen Doe they would tether the horses and descend into the valley like silent ghosts to gather together a dozen cattle and drive them back into the mountains.

Moonlight would guide them along the footpaths of ancient drovers as they traveled as far as possible before daybreak, hiding in the forested brae beside the River Feohlin until nightfall. Then they would set out again. Once they reached Aberchalder Burn near Farraline, the cattle would be slaughtered and the meat distributed to the surrounding villages before dawn.

''Maddie, hinny. Dinna ye hear me?'' Glenis repeated. Again there was no reply. With an exasperated sigh the old woman walked to the window, stopping just behind the stool. She reached out and brushed an unruly chestnut lock away from Madeleine's temple. ''Maddie?''

Madeleine jumped up, the map sliding from her knees to the freshly swept floor. ''Och, Glenis, ye startled me!'' she exclaimed. ''I dinna know ye were standing there.''

''I'm sorry, lass,'' Glenis said as Madeleine bent to pick up the precious parchment, folding it into a neat square. ''But I feel as if I've been mutterin' to m'self in this kitchen like some mad hatter. Ye've not heard a word I've said to ye.''

Madeleine slipped the map into a side pocket of her gown and gave her servant a hug. Glenis Simpson had been with the Frasers of Farraline so long she was like a grandmother to Maddie. Serving as housekeeper and midwife, she had been present at the birth of Madeleine's father as well as Maddie's own, nineteen years ago.

Madeleine would never have lived to see her first day if not for Glenis, who had breathed air into her tiny lungs after she was born blue and silent, the cord wrapped around her neck. The determined Scotswoman didn't give up until the room echoed with Madeleine's lusty cries, and her grateful parents swore they had witnessed a miracle from heaven.

Now Glenis was frail, with stooped shoulders and gray hair like fine gauze. She had seen sixty-nine winters come and go. Yet she still ruled Mhor Manor with strict efficiency, the two remaining maidservants her obedient and respectful charges.

Madeleine was the only person Glenis could not control. She had tried over the years to tame Maddie's impetuous spirit and transform her into a "proper" young lady, especially after her mother had died when Madeleine was six years old. But Madeleine had always displayed a streak of feisty independence that could not be subdued, and Glenis's efforts had been largely unsuccessful. Maddie was a grown woman now, mistress of a sizable estate, yet Glenis still looked upon her as the wild child who used to roam the heather-strewn moors and rocky mountain slopes.

"What did ye ask me, Glenis dear?" Madeleine asked in a soothing tone, though she suspected she already knew the question. "Ye have my full attention."

Glenis grasped Madeleine's hands in her bony ones, her grip amazingly strong. " 'Tis worried I am, Maddie," she began, concern etching her wrinkled face. "Worried sick for ye!"

"Glenis—" Madeleine tried to interrupt.

"No, ye'll hear me out, lass," Glenis shushed her. "Ye've been about these raids almost ev'ry night now for two months, ever since those redcoats wrecked the house. Sometimes ye're gone for so long—two, three days and more—I canna sleep for the worry that plagues me."

She squeezed Madeleine's hands tightly as if to emphasize her words, making her wince. " 'Tis a noble thing ye're doin', Maddie, but how long do ye think 'twill be before the English set about to find ye in earnest? What if ye're captured? Do ye think they'll be merciful with ye, like they were to yer da and his clansmen at Culloden?"

"Yer fears are unfounded, Glenis. They'll not find me," Madeleine objected vehemently, her eyes flashing in defiance.

English bastards! The mere mention of her father's brutal fate made her all the more certain what she was doing was right, despite the constant danger she and her kinsmen faced. The raids they had committed against the redcoats gave purpose to her life and were a means of fighting back against the savage injustice her people had suffered. She could do no less, whatever the consequences. Her conscience, and her pride, would never allow it.

Glenis shook her gray head, unconvinced. "No, lass, if ye keep on, they'll surely find ye—"

"Enough, Glenis!" Madeleine demanded, cutting her off and pulling her hands free. Tears smarted her eyes, but she forced them back. "I'll not listen to any more of yer talk. I canna believe ye would ask me to cease the one thing that gives our people hope and puts food in their bellies!"

Madeleine leaned against the narrow window ledge and gazed beyond the orchard toward the village of Farraline, a cluster of small stone cottages nestled near Loch Mhor.

"Ye have walked in the village, Glenis. 'Tis a place come back from the edge of despair," she said, her voice impassioned. " 'Tis the same in Gorthlick and Aberchalder, and the other villages. The bairns no longer cry out from hunger, but scramble and play, and their mothers have milk again in their breasts for the wee ones. The men who are left have new hope for their families, and we can fill the sacks of the fugitives who come to our doors in the night with enough food to last them many days in the mountains.''

Madeleine swallowed hard, remembering the half dozen fugitive clansmen who had sought a few hours' refuge in the manor house only last week. They had brought her news that Dougald Fraser, her betrothed, had been taken prisoner only days after Culloden. He had been hanged as a traitor in the town square at Inverness while the clansmen watched from a tavern attic where they were hiding. Now she had two for whom to grieve, her father and Dougald.

Dougald Fraser had been big and strong, with a wide smile that dared to take on the world and hazel eyes that danced with a lust for life. Had she truly loved him, as a woman loves a man, or was her feeling merely the bond of friendship formed in childhood? Now she would never know.

She had accepted that she and Dougald would marry one day because it was the wish of her father, who had seen in his young kinsman a fine match for his strong-minded daughter. She had never thought to question his decision, for he was the only person whose word she had always obeyed.

Now she would never wed. She had sworn as much on the night she learned of Dougald's fate. The man who had earned her father's blessing was cold in his grave, and she would have no other. She would devote her life to her people, and when the time came to choose an heir for the estate she would find someone worthy to take her place from among her kinsmen.

How ironic, Madeleine thought bitterly. If her father had survived Culloden and been tried for treason, his estate and title would have been forfeited to the Crown upon his execution. It was only because he had died on the battlefield that the family estate still belonged to her. She was permitted to keep her land because as mistress of Farraline and a mere woman, she was considered harmless, no threat to the government. If they only knew . . .

"I said 'tis a noble thing ye do, Maddie," Glenis said, "and 'tis proud I am of ye." She bent her head and pressed her furrowed cheek against Madeleine's shoulder. "Yer da would be proud of ye, and yer dear mama. I'll not bother ye further with my fears, if only ye promise not to take any heedless chances." Her voice quivered and broke, while hot tears dampened Madeleine's sleeve. "If anything ever happened to ye, I'd have no one left."

"Please dinna worry," Madeleine said gently. "Nothing will happen to me, ye'll see. And if it will make ye happy, I promise I winna raid any redcoats unless I'm sure 'twill go as planned. Fair enough?"

Sniffling and nodding her head, Glenis fumbled in her apron pocket for a handkerchief.

"Besides, Glenis dear, only the five clansmen who ride with me know what we do. And ye, of course."

"I'll ne'er betray ye, lass!" Glenis exclaimed fiercely, wiping away her tears. "I'll take yer secret to my grave—"

"Shhh, Glenis," Madeleine calmed her. " 'Twas not my thought that ye'd betray me, and nor will the others. We're bound by a pledge of silence, sealed in blood. The people simply accept the food as God's blessing and ask no questions. They would never betray our cause. I believe that with all my heart."

"Och, very well, lass," Glenis said, loudly blowing her nose several times. "Ye'll hear no more from me. But if ye dinna mind, I'll keep ye doubly in my prayers, just for good measure."

Madeleine laughed, planting a kiss on Glenis's damp cheek. She glanced across the kitchen at the massive fireplace with its raised hearth, where a large black kettle hung above the peat fire. Steam rose from the bubbling contents, and a delicious aroma wafted through the room. "What's in the pot?" she asked, her stomach growling hungrily.

"Cock-a-leekie stew," Glenis replied, her brown

eyes twinkling again, her plucky spirit revived. "Yer favorite. I had a notion ye'd be ridin' out tonight, and I'll not have ye goin' on yer way without a good hot meal in yer belly. There's smoked herring, too, and fresh bannocks. I'll pack ye and yer men a hamper full for the journey. How long will ye be gone, lass?"

"Two days."

Glenis opened her mouth to protest, but she quickly shut it. "I hope ye'll have room for the apple pudding I baked ye," she said instead.

Madeleine sat down at the kitchen table. "Aye, Glenis, if ye think my figure winna be the worse for it," she replied playfully.

Glenis ladled a hearty portion of stew into a bowl and returned to the table. "Ye have nothing to fear on that score, lass. Ye're as sleek and slim as a colt." She set the bowl before Madeleine. "Now eat. I'll fetch ye some bannocks."

Madeleine savored the chunks of chicken and leeks in a thick broth laced with herbs, the warm oatcakes spread with golden butter, and the strong tea. Under Glenis's approving eye she finished every morsel, including a slice of pudding topped with brandy sauce. She knew it would be several days before she'd enjoy such a meal again.

But, God willing, if tonight's raid went as planned, she and the villagers would have a rich beef stew simmering in their kettles before the week was out.

Chapter 3

"'Tis time to wake, Maddie," Angus Ramsay whispered, shaking Madeleine's shoulder gently. "The moon is up."

Awakened so abruptly, Madeleine did not know where she was for a moment. Gradually the mists of sleep faded from her mind, and reality took its place. The pungent smell of pine, the soft lowing of cattle, and the rushing sound of a nearby river further heightened her awareness.

Remembering suddenly, she sat up and rubbed her eyes. They had made camp here this morning after their successful cattle raid. Now it was dark and time to move on toward Farraline.

Madeleine twisted around and groped along the woolen blanket. She found her black cap and set it atop her head, then stuffed her thick chestnut braid down the high collar of her jacket. Lastly she scooped a handful of peat ash from a pouch hanging at her belt and rubbed the soot on her face and forehead.

"Are the others awake, Angus?" she asked, accepting his hand as he helped her to her feet.

"Aye, we're ready to be off, lass," Angus replied, nodding to the four men who were already astride their horses. "I let ye sleep awhile longer," he added, almost apologetically. "Ye looked so tired when we stopped this morn."

Madeleine smiled. "That was kind of ye, Angus. I'm fine now." She swept up her blanket from the moss-

32

covered ground, ducking the fir branches that had served as a protective bower for her bed. She walked to her mount and crammed the blanket into the leather saddlebag.

She stifled a groan as she lifted her foot to the stirrup and threw a trousered leg over the horse. Her body was stiff and sore from the long journey, though she would never have admitted it to her kinsmen. No doubt they were just as uncomfortable. Driving cattle through the mountains was not an easy task.

Madeleine waited patiently while Angus mounted his horse, her eyes quickly growing accustomed to the darkness of the surrounding forest.

She noted the burly silhouettes of Kenneth and Allan Fraser, two russet-haired brothers who had fought at Culloden and had managed to escape with their lives. They were fugitives who now made their home in a remote cave on Beinn Bhuidhe, a mountain to the east of Farraline, but they had chosen to risk capture and accompany her on her raids against the English.

The Fraser brothers were a tough pair. They were much more inclined to shooting redcoats than stealing from them, yet they had obeyed her command that there would be no needless killing. She hoped she could continue to hold their thirst for revenge in check. Stealing was one thing, but cold-blooded murder was another.

Then there were Ewen Burke and his seventeen-year-old son, Duncan. They were true clansmen—as was Angus Ramsay—though they did not bear the Fraser surname. Clan Fraser was made up of many such men not related by blood, descendants of those who had sworn their allegiance to successive Lovat chieftains in exchange for a small parcel of rented farmland and the chief's protection.

Ewen, Angus, and Duncan had stayed behind last autumn—along with a small group of tenants from each village—to tend the cattle herds when the Frasers of Strathherrick had marched to war. Now these three men rode beside her, taking great pride in regaining a measure of what had been stolen from their clan.

Madeleine gathered up the reins, breathing a swift prayer of thanks for the five men who had so boldly taken up her cause. She could never have accomplished so much without them.

"Kenneth, ride ahead and keep watch," she directed, her voice low. "Until we reach Loch Mhor we'll be traveling a bit closer to Wade's Road than I'd like. But there's no help for it if we want to make Aberchalder Burn before dawn. Remember, if ye see anything suspicious, give us fair warning."

"Aye, Maddie," Kenneth replied, flicking the reins against his mount's neck. The spirited animal jerked forward, and horse and rider disappeared into the dense pine forest. Only the swaying branches marked their path.

"Allan, take the lead since ye know this land so well. Duncan, Angus, ye take the rear. Ewen and I will keep the cattle moving down the middle."

Without a word the men followed her orders explicitly. It made no difference to them that she was a woman, and barely nineteen. As it had been to her father, their loyalty to her was as natural to them as breathing, and if they had had any question at all about her ability to wage such a campaign against the redcoats, such doubts had long since vanished. She had proved time and again through her courage, daring, and sound judgment that she was born to lead.

The Highland cattle, with their shaggy, reddish-brown coats and long, curved horns, plodded along the narrow drover's path, tied to one another by a thick length of rope. Madeleine was still amazed by the smoothness of last night's raid, in which they hadn't encountered a single English soldier. The redcoats were most likely too comfortable lying next to their fires to guard the cattle, she thought scornfully as she recalled the distant orange glow of campfires at the mouth of Glen Doe near Wade's Road.

Tension gripped her body as a commotion at the

front of the line ground the procession to an abrupt halt. She dug her heels into the horse's sides and raced along the winding path, Ewen not far behind her.

"Allan, what's going on? Why have we stopped?" she hissed, suddenly spying Kenneth alongside him. Her heart leaped in her throat. If Kenneth had ridden back to them so soon, that could only mean trouble.

"There's redcoats up ahead, Maddie!" Kenneth blurted out in a loud whisper before his brother could answer. "They're camped just over the rise, less than a quarter mile from here."

"How many?" she asked tightly.

"Twenty-five, thirty. Most are bedded down near the fire, but a few are standing guard around the camp."

Madeleine sucked in her breath. A small troop of English soldiers right in their path. Damn! If there weren't so many of them, she might consider a skirmish. But thirty soldiers to her band of six did not make for good odds. Now they would have to cut farther east into the mountains, causing a full day's delay because they wouldn't make it to Aberchalder Burn before sunrise. A pox and the devil take them all!

"It looks as if we'll have to double back—" she began resignedly, only to be cut off by Kenneth's excited voice.

"Before we do that, Maddie, I think ye should know they have at least ten supply wagons loaded to the top with every manner of stuff. Sacks of grain, crates of chickens and pigs. Why, if we could only make off with two of those wagons we'd do well!"

"Did ye say ten, Kenneth?" she asked, her thoughts taking a decidedly different turn.

"Aye. What do ye think?"

By now Angus and Duncan had joined their little group, quickly learning the details. Madeleine carefully weighed the situation. Why would so few soldiers require such a quantity of supplies? she wondered. They were camped a good distance from Wade's Road on terrain that was easily traversed by wagons, yet they couldn't be a regular supply train. Supply trains never strayed from the road for fear of marauders like herself.

Perhaps they were raw recruits from Fort Augustus or Ruthven Barracks, sent out on some sort of training exercise to better acquaint themselves with the Highlands, she thought dryly. Spending a week or so away from an established military post could warrant the need for a good stock of supplies.

Well, whatever the reason, ten supply wagons was a strong temptation. Yet a raid on the camp was a highly dangerous proposition. She and her men were outnumbered by perhaps five to one.

Glenis's words of caution ripped through Madeleine's mind, along with her own promise not to take any heedless chances. In this instance it was best to seek the counsel of all involved, she decided.

"We have a choice to make," Madeleine said evenly, looking from one somber face to the next. "We can either make our way to Aberchalder Burn by another route, or we can take these cursed redcoats by surprise and add a few well-loaded supply wagons to our bounty. What do ye say?"

"I'm for raiding the bastards!" Allan spoke up first, with Kenneth not long behind him.

"Aye, and me, too!"

Madeleine had expected as much from the hotheaded Fraser brothers. They were always spoiling for a fight.

"What say ye, Angus?" she asked. Of all her kinsmen, she trusted Angus Ramsay's opinion the most. He was steady and cautious, and his thoughtful wisdom reminded her of her father.

"Given the number of soldiers, 'tis perilous at best, Maddie. But we've seen worse scraps before. I think if 'tis well planned, we have a good chance of capturing three wagons, but no more. With the cattle, 'twould be the most we could manage."

Madeleine nodded. "So ye'd support a raid then, Angus?"

"Aye."

"How about ye, Ewen?"

"If Angus believes 'tis possible, then I'm with ye."

"Duncan?"

"Aye, Maddie."

"Then it's decided," she said, smiling faintly. "After this raid we'll have so much food we'll have earned a week's rest." She leaned forward in her saddle, tense excitement bubbling within her. She loved a good challenge. "Now, Kenneth, if ye'll tell us the layout of the camp, we'll plan our next move."

Madeleine lay flat on her stomach with her elbows drawn up beneath her chest, scarcely breathing. She gazed intently at the English camp just ten yards away and down a slight decline, irritation gripping her.

Eyeing the blond officer seated by the fire with his broad back to her, she thought, if that bastard doesn't settle in soon, we'll have to abandon the raid.

A precious hour had passed since she and her kinsmen had tethered the cattle and crept up on the camp. They could have completed their business and been well on their way to Aberchalder Burn by now if not for that captain. He was the only man left awake in the camp, other than the three guards standing watch.

"Patience, lass," Angus whispered as if he sensed her thoughts.

Madeleine glanced over her shoulder at him, somewhat chagrined. He and Ewen Burke flanked her, their faces and hair also blackened with peat ash, caps pulled down well over their heads, and dark brown kerchiefs covering the lower halves of their faces.

They were waiting for her signal, as were Duncan and the Fraser brothers, who were hiding near the three guards positioned at cross angles about the camp. That signal could not come until that English officer settled in for the night.

A snapping branch startled her, and she turned back to the camp. The captain had risen to his feet and was walking around the perimeter of the clearing. He seemed to be searching the darkness beyond the glow of the fire, and they ducked their heads as he passed within ten feet of them.

Madeleine held her breath, the moist ground cold against her cheek. She waited, listening, until his footsteps moved away. When she looked up he was back by the fire and shaking out a blanket, his face to her.

Unwittingly she found herself thinking he was a very handsome man. He was tall and powerfully built, his hair a burnished gold in the firelight . . .

She bit her lip angrily. Fool! What was coming over her? How could she consider an English soldier handsome? He was a murderer, a beast. He might even be the man who had killed her father!

Madeleine kept that thought in her mind as she watched the officer lie down on the ground, wrap himself in the blanket, and roll onto his back. She decided grimly that it would become his death shroud if he made even the slightest motion to rise.

He did not. After another ten minutes, Madeleine decided the time had come. It was finally quiet in the clearing, and the only sounds were an occasional snore, the wind whooshing through the Caledonian pines and tall oaks, and the flames crackling and hissing. She took a deep breath and raised her arm above her head.

Her eyes widened as the three guards suddenly disappeared from their posts without even a struggle, attesting to the strength and skill of her kinsmen. She only hoped the Fraser brothers had knocked their opponents unconscious instead of slitting their throats.

She rose stealthily to her feet. The two men beside her followed her cue and fanned out among the trees, circling the camp in an effort to give the impression of far greater numbers.

When she was sure all pistols were drawn and flashing dirks were at the ready, she slowly nodded her head. Treading carefully and silently over clumps of moss, damp leaves, and pine needles, they advanced upon the camp until they were almost on top of the sleeping soldiers.

Waving the others on, Madeleine halted beside a

stout oak, hiding in the shadow of its lower branches.
She could not afford to be recognized as a woman.

Despite her efforts to disguise her sex, her black garb
could not completely hide her feminine curves. Luckily
she was tall for a woman and could be mistaken for a
man of slight build. Her blackened face and low-slung
cap hid the softness of her facial features well.

She leveled her pistols at the prone officer, noting
the steady rise and fall of his chest beneath the blanket.
Her expression was grim as she and her kinsmen
cocked their weapons. The staccato clicks echoed about
the clearing.

Barely asleep, Garrett awakened abruptly at the ominous sound. In one swift movement he rolled onto his
side and lunged for his sword, the hair rising on the
back of his neck as he heard orders barked in the King's
English with a thick Highland burr.

"Stay where ye are lads, or win a bullet between yer
eyes for yer efforts!"

Garrett froze, gritting his teeth. His hand was barely
on the hilt of his sword. He dared to lift his head a
fraction and look wildly across the clearing. Spying at
least four unrecognizable armed men in the dim light,
he quickly laid his head back down and clenched his
fists in frustration.

Damn! He should have known better than to camp
here for the night, becoming prey to any fugitive Highlanders. Despite the complaints of his men, they should
have marched on to Farraline. He had sensed something in the air, a palpable tension which had made it
difficult for him to sleep, but he had shrugged it off.
Why the devil hadn't he trusted his gut instincts?

"Now ye'll do us a favor and lie still whilst we gather
yer weapons," the menacing voice continued, cutting
into his thoughts. "Remember, lads, make nary a move
or ye'll be dead before ye draw yer next breath."

Garrett listened to the footfalls moving swiftly about
the camp and the chink of weapons being thrown into
a distant pile. Suddenly his blanket was wrenched from

beneath him, and a pistol was held six inches from his face as his own weapons were gathered up by a masked Highlander.

''Good ev'ning to ye, captain,'' said the gruff voice of an older man. '' 'Twas good of ye to finally lay yerself to sleep.'' He picked up Garrett's sword. ''I hope ye dinna mind if I take this. Ye'll not be needing it tonight.''

The Highlander's words confirmed Garrett's earlier intuition. They must have been in the woods all along, waiting for the right moment to spring their surprise attack. God, he hated feeling so helpless! There had to be something he could do.

''Now don't be issuing any orders ye might regret,'' the man added with a low laugh, sensing his discomfort. ''Just stay put along with yer soldiers, and ye'll live to see another day.''

Garrett made no reply as the man withdrew his pistol and moved on to the next soldier. He stared up into the inky blackness overhead, dotted with glittering stars, and wondered what these Highlanders might have in store for them. Revenge for Culloden, perhaps?

A heavy silence hung over the clearing after the last of the weapons was thrown onto the pile.

''All right, lads, ye can stand up now,'' the same voice commanded. ''Slowly does it. Keep yer hands out where we can see them.''

Garrett sat up and twisted around, attempting to take a more complete count of the enemy. As far as he could tell, there were five altogether, including the four he had seen earlier and one other, unless there were more Highlanders lurking in the woods . . .

A sudden movement a short distance from the clearing caught his attention. His eyes widened in amazement at the slight figure standing well back in the shadows, dressed from head to toe in black, the firelight glinting off two leveled pistols. The scene fit Colonel Wolfe's description exactly. Black Jack!

The irony of the situation hit Garrett hard. He had

been sent out expressly to capture this elusive outlaw, and now he and his soldiers had become the man's captives.

He glanced at the line of wagons winding back along the wide path they had taken from Wade's Road, with the horses tethered nearby. If what he had heard about Black Jack was true, these outlaws were more interested in the supply wagons than in revenge. If no one provoked them, that was. They had shot men before.

"On yer feet, captain," the nearest Highlander growled, aiming his pistol threateningly at Garrett's chest.

Garrett stood up, catching out of the corner of his eye the covert movement of the burly sergeant standing to his right. He whirled, but it was too late to stop him.

Pulling a knife from his boot, the sergeant flung it at the Highlander, who attempted to dodge the lethal missile. He wasn't quick enough. The blade sank into his upper arm, and he cursed loudly. At the same time a shot rang out in the clearing, and the sergeant sank heavily to the ground.

"I'm hit, captain!" the sergeant gasped as if he could not quite believe it. An ugly red stain widened around the singed hole just below his left shoulder, blood streaming through his splayed fingers.

Stunned, Garrett looked from the black-clad figure in the shadows who was holding a smoking pistol, to the soldier sprawled at his feet. He took a step toward the wounded man.

"Stop where ye are," the nearby Highlander grated. His pistol was still trained on Garrett though blood seeped from inside his sleeve and streaked his trembling hand. Without a sound, he pulled the knife from his flesh and hurled it to the ground.

Garrett's eyes narrowed angrily. "My sergeant needs help. Shoot me if you will, but I'm not going to stand here while he bleeds to death."

For a moment the Highlander simply stared at him as if defying him to make another move. Then he seemed to waver. He glanced at Black Jack in the shadows, who nodded curtly, and back to Garrett. "Go on with ye then," he muttered, rubbing his arm.

Garrett dropped to his knees beside the wounded man. He whipped his cravat from around his neck and used it to staunch the bleeding. "That was a foolhardy thing to do, sergeant," he said sternly, though he could not fault the man for trying.

"I'd do it again, Captain Marshall," the sergeant grunted, his face ashen. "The wily bastards!"

Garrett was silent. He, too, had a knife in his boot, as did many of the soldiers. Perhaps if their efforts were somehow coordinated, there still might be a chance—

The injured Highlander's voice boomed across the clearing, interrupting his thoughts. "While yer captain plays nursemaid, the rest of ye strip off yer boots and yer clothes and throw everything in one pile. Ye winna conceal any more weapons if we can help it. Then lie facedown on the ground. Move!"

Garrett swore softly. So much for that plan.

After a few minutes he lifted the soiled cravat from the wound, pleased to see that the bleeding had stopped. Yet the man would need medical attention to remove the bullet, which meant returning to Fort Augustus. He could well imagine Colonel Wolfe's face, not to mention General Hawley's, when they discovered what had happened. Dammit all! His mission had been thwarted before it had really begun, and he had no one to blame but himself.

"Up with ye, captain, now, and strip off yer fine uniform," the Highlander demanded. "It looks like yer sergeant will live, so he'll not be needing yer care for a while. And we've no more time to spend chatting with ye."

Garrett rose to his feet, his face darkening with fury as he yanked off his boots and began to undress. His soldiers were already stark naked and lying facedown in the dirt, while two of Black Jack's men tied their hands and feet together.

The Highlander gave a short laugh when he picked

up one of Garrett's boots and a knife fell to the ground with a thud. "It could have been ye with the ball in yer shoulder, eh, captain?"

Garrett didn't answer but merely shot a glance in Black Jack's direction. To his surprise, the outlaw was nowhere to be seen. He stepped out of his breeches, standing as God had made him in the center of the camp. The indignity of it was almost more than he could stomach.

"Lie down by yer men."

Garrett threw his clothes on the pile near the fire and grimly followed the Highlander's order. His hands were tied behind his back, then his feet were bound securely.

"That should hold ye for a while, lads," a different man said, his deep voice tinged with malice. "Perhaps when the brave sergeant regains consciousness, he'll see fit to let ye go. Hopefully for yer sakes 'twill be before any Highland wildcat roaming these hills picks up yer scent. Ye look to be a fine lot of trussed turkeys from this angle!"

Furious, Garrett longed to lash out and tell the man his raiding days were numbered, but he held his tongue. If he was given another chance to set out for Strathherrick after this fiasco, he did not want these outlaws to have any advance warning of what was in store for them.

A sudden whooshing sound startled him, and he began to cough when acrid gray smoke billowed through the camp. With a groan he realized the Highlanders had set fire to their boots and uniforms.

Just one more humiliation to endure, Garrett raged silently. One more score to settle with Black Jack.

His eyes stinging from the thick smoke, he turned his head and watched three of the Highlanders move toward the wagons, their arms loaded with confiscated weapons. They disappeared along the path, then he heard the anxious neighing of horses and wooden wheels creaking. They were hitching up the supply wagons.

Garrett mumbled a swift prayer that the wagon carrying extra clothing would be spared. If not, he doubted the few villages they had passed along Wade's Road could provide them with thirty pairs of boots and breeches. He and his men would become the laughingstock of the entire army if they were forced to retire to Fort Augustus barefoot and naked.

He blinked several times from the smoke, his watery eyes falling on Black Jack walking along the edge of the camp. The outlaw turned for a moment and looked back in their direction, then was gone, swallowed up by the dark woods.

"We'll meet again, Black Jack," Garrett vowed, gasping from the smoke. "And next time, I swear it will be to my advantage."

Chapter 4

Madeleine felt a warm satisfaction as she lifted the last basket from the cart and hooked it over her arm. "Will ye see to the mare, Neil, whilst I visit yer mama?" she said gently, smiling at the young boy who was hopping excitedly beside the cart.

"Oh, aye, Maddie!" he exclaimed, his ruddy cheeks aglow with health and vigor. His hazel eyes, wide as saucers, glanced at the basket. "Have ye anything for me?" he asked hopefully.

Madeleine feigned a stern expression though her eyes twinkled gaily. "Perhaps I do, Neil, but first ye must answer me this. Have ye been a good boy this week, and helped yer mama with yer two younger brothers now that the babe has come?"

Neil nodded his head vigorously, his reddish-blond hair glistening in the warm sunshine. "Mama says as the oldest, I make a fine man o' the house!"

Madeleine felt a rush of pity but gave no note of it in her voice. "And right she is, Neil Chrystie," she agreed heartily as she flipped aside the linen cloth and reached into the basket. She pulled out a white tissue-wrapped packet and handed it to the boy. " 'Tis fresh from Glenis's kitchen. Mind ye, remember to save some for yer brothers."

Neil hastily tore away the paper, his small face splitting into a wide grin as he revealed the sweet treasures. He bit eagerly into a thick square of tablet candy studded with sugared walnuts. Munching happily, he suddenly remembered his manners. "Thank ye, Maddie," he managed, his mouth full to bursting.

Thanks to the English is more the truth of it, Madeleine thought, walking toward the neat stone cottage. She had found the unexpected surprise of a large bag of walnuts in one of the supply wagons stolen earlier in the week.

Aye, it had been a most successful raid. Almost perfect, except for the shooting. She had never shot a man before. Yet she did not regret her action. She had done what was necessary to protect her kinsman, and she would gladly do it again if she had to.

Och, dinna think of the blasted redcoats, she scolded herself, or 'twill ruin yer outing for sure. She thought instead of what had transpired that day, and her sense of pleasure swiftly returned.

She had had a wonderful morning paying calls on the villagers in Farraline, especially the widows of Culloden and their children. The well-fed, contented faces that had greeted her at every turn were a reward more precious than gold. The stocked pantries and bubbling stew pots further gladdened her heart and heightened her belief that she had done the right thing.

Madeleine stopped and rapped several times at the stout wooden door of the cottage. "Flora? 'Tis Maddie." A lilting voice called out for her to enter. She had to duck her head as she stepped through the low doorway.

Her eyes quickly adjusted to the dim light in the one-room cottage, a stark contrast to the bright sunshine outside. The simple cottages of the clansmen were known as black houses because most of them could not afford glass for windows and used sacking instead. The peat fire in the middle of the room cast a welcome glow, its smoke curling through a hole in the thatched roof.

" 'Tis good of ye to visit, Maddie," Flora said. She began to rise from a chair set beside the cradle, but Madeleine waved her back down.

"Rest yerself, Flora. Ye dinna have to get up on my account," she said, placing the basket on a table. She walked quietly to the cradle and knelt in front of it, heedless of the dirt floor.

"Oh, she's a wee darlin'," Madeleine said admiringly, gazing at the cherubic face of the tiny infant who was barely one week old. A tuft of pale hair peeked from beneath a fleecy cap, and she couldn't resist reaching out and stroking the silken strands. Her hand brushed against the smooth magic stone placed beside the babe's pillow to ward off witches. It was a heathen custom in a Christian land, yet no Highland mother would do without it. "Have ye decided upon a name?" she asked.

"Mary Rose," Flora replied. "After my dead Neil's mother."

Madeleine glanced up at the young woman and met her sad eyes. " 'Tis a bonnie name for the lass, Flora," she said. "Neil would have been pleased by yer choice."

"Aye."

A silence borne of a common sorrow fell between them. Madeleine sighed as she looked down at the sleeping infant. She had always loved children. She marveled at the babe's tightly curled fists and her pink, pouting lips. A trail of milk was dried on her petal-soft cheek.

She noticed a slight movement in another corner of the room. Twin boys lay napping on a pallet in a tangle of plump limbs and tousled red hair. How fortunate Flora was, she thought, despite the loss of her husband. She had four beautiful children to sustain her, to care for, to give her strength.

"Would ye like to hold her, Maddie?" Flora asked. Without waiting for an answer, she leaned over and gently scooped the child from the cradle, placing her in Madeleine's open arms.

Madeleine felt a tightness in her breast as she held the infant against her. She would never know what it was to feel a babe grow within her, never experience the throes of childbirth, its agony and joy. Yet this knowledge brought her no great sadness, only a poignant understanding. She would never have a family of her own, but she would always have a larger family around her, consisting of her clan, her people. It was enough.

"Do ye have everything ye need, Flora?" Madeleine asked softly, her gaze sweeping the modest surroundings. Plain wooden furniture, earthenware pots, and a butter churn were the trappings of their simple life. A cast-iron pot hung above the fire, suspended from an oaken beam by a long hook. Steam was escaping beneath the lid, filling the room with the herbed fragrance of boiled beef.

"Aye, Maddie, ye mustn't worry for us. We've been well provided for, thanks to the brave soul who defies the English to lay food upon our doorstep. Between that and what ye kindly bring us with yer visits, we'll more than manage."

Madeleine smiled. "There's wild strawberry jam in the basket, herbs from Glenis's garden, some healing tea for ye, and a christening cake for the minister's visit tomorrow. Neil has no doubt eaten his fill of tablet candy by now, though I did ask him to save some for his brothers."

Flora laughed, her smile easing the premature lines in her pretty face. "I'm so pleased ye'll be standing up for Mary Rose before the minister, Maddie. It does me proud to think the mistress of Farraline will be my daughter's godmother."

"I'm honored ye asked," she replied sincerely. Suddenly the baby whimpered, her blue eyes fluttering open as she began to squirm in Madeleine's arms. "I think 'tis time for another feeding, eh, little one? Ye'll have to look to yer fine mother for that."

As if to confirm her words, the infant let out a lusty wail, her tiny hands grasping at the air. Madeleine handed the child over to Flora, who made soothing sounds to calm her. Neither heard the door swing open as young Neil rushed into the cottage.

"Maddie, come look! There's soldiers marching

through the village, with guns and wagons and everything!"

Startled, Madeleine was on her feet in a flash. "Neil, stay here with yer mother," she said, rushing to the window.

"But Maddie—"

"Hush, child," Flora silenced him sternly. "Go and sit with yer brothers." She lifted a corner of her thin chemise to suckle Mary Rose at her milk-laden breast.

Neil reluctantly did as he was told, though his eyes followed Madeleine. His brothers had been abruptly awakened by his shouting, and their confused crying added to the discord.

"Hush with ye now," he said importantly. "There's redcoats creeping about. Ye dinna want to bring them in here, do ye?" When his words showed little effect, he offered them some sticky tablet candy. The twins quieted immediately, their brown eyes wide and watchful as they sucked on the sugary squares.

Madeleine leaned on the stone ledge, her heart thumping hard against her chest. There were at least twenty redcoats marching alongside a long procession of ten wagons driven by more soldiers. God's wounds! What were they doing in Farraline?

She craned her head to get a better view. She couldn't get a close look at them because Flora's cottage was on a side street, but it was clear that they were merely passing through the village. Their pace did not slacken, and their commanding officer seemed to be waving them onward from atop a great bay horse. Most of the wagons had already turned onto the road leading to the next village, the same road that wound past her estate . . .

"Flora, 'tis best to keep the bairns inside 'til the soldiers have passed," she said urgently, facing her kinswoman. "I'm going to set out for Mhor Manor. Glenis is alone there, since the two girls have the day free. If she spies the soldiers on the road, she'll think the worst and panic for sure. I hope 'tis not another contingent sent to burn us out."

"Be careful, Maddie," Flora warned. Concern etched her pale features, and she hugged her infant daughter protectively.

Madeleine nodded. " 'Twill be faster if I leave the cart here and ride the mare back to the estate."

She smiled quickly at the three boys as she hurried from the cottage. She deftly unhitched the small cart and jumped on the mare's bare back, her skirt gathered between her legs.

"Off with ye!" she cried, clucking her tongue and kicking the mare with the heels of her sturdy leather brogues.

The startled animal lurched forward. They skirted the village along a familiar footpath, well out of view of the soldiers, then set off at a full gallop across the green valley toward Mhor Manor, Madeleine's hair flying behind her.

When he reached the outskirts of Farraline, Garrett pulled up on the reins. His massive bay gelding snorted and pawed restlessly at the heath. "Easy, Samson, easy," he murmured, untying his cravat and wiping the dust and sweat from his face.

He squinted against the midday sunlight, looking down the narrow road that wound ahead of them through the rugged Highland landscape.

Like the other roads they had traveled since abandoning the paved efficiency of Wade's highway, it was no more than two rutted, dirt tracks with a grassy strip in the center. He and his men had been forced to stop twice already and replace broken wagon wheels.

At least we're almost there, Garrett thought. In the near distance he could see whitewashed walls and a black slate roof framed by a backdrop of fir trees and jagged gray mountains. The large manor house Colonel Wolfe had suggested to him lay just ahead.

He twisted in his saddle and surveyed the rumbling line of supply wagons drawn by exhausted horses. Two soldiers marched between each wagon, their loaded muskets held crosswise in front of them. The wagon drivers had loaded weapons beneath their seats as an added security measure.

The rigorous strain of the long march showed in the soldiers' tired faces. Garrett had pushed them hard. They had not slept since leaving Fort Augustus and had paused only briefly for quick meals of salted beef, hard biscuits, and warm ale. They had followed a different route this time, staying well on Wade's Road until the last possible moment. He had taken every precaution to prevent another encounter with Black Jack.

He grimaced, recalling the reprimand he had received after his unexpected return to Fort Augustus, thankfully clothed. General Hawley's incensed ranting still rang in his ears. Only Colonel Wolfe's intervention had spared him twenty lashes with the cat-o'-nine-tails, and the colonel's persuasive arguments had convinced Hawley to grant him one more chance to capture the outlaw.

Yet such a lashing could not have intensified his burning commitment to bring Black Jack to justice. He had a personal score to settle for the humiliation he and his men had suffered, as well as for the injury inflicted on his former sergeant. They had barely reached Fort Augustus in time and the man had nearly died from his wound. Dammit, he would find the bastard!

"Sergeant Fletcher!" he shouted as he stuffed his soiled cravat in the side pocket of his coat.

A stout soldier stepped out from the line, slinging his musket over his shoulder. "Captain?"

"I'm going to ride ahead. See that the men keep moving. The manor house is just beyond that copse of trees."

"Very good, sir."

As Garrett dug his boots into the horse's sides and took off at a gallop, the sergeant's terse command cut through the air. "You heard the captain, lads. Keep up the pace. There'll be a swig of brandy awaiting each of you when we get to our new quarters."

Racing along the road, Garrett reveled in the great strength of the animal beneath him. It was exhilarating to allow the bay such freedom after holding him tightly in check for most of the journey. The landscape they passed blurred, melding into streaks of vibrant color: dark green heather, brown earth, blue sky. The white manor house with its two adjoining wings drew closer and closer . . .

Suddenly he veered sharply to the right as another horse appeared on the left racing onto the road from a narrow path hidden between two large trees, and bumped into his bay. Garrett swore loudly and firmly grasped the reins, his experience and the muscled power of his thighs enabling him to stay in the saddle.

The other rider was not so lucky. He heard a short high-pitched scream and the smaller horse whinnying in fright, then a crash as the rider, a slim young woman, pitched headlong into a row of unkempt box hedges at the foot of the drive leading to the manor house.

"Whoa, Samson, steady now!" he yelled, pulling the bay hard about. The startled animal reared and bucked, fighting him, but it gradually calmed enough to allow Garrett to jump to the ground. He ran over to the hedges, dreading what he might find. It would be a miracle if the wench survived such a fall.

Garrett spied a pair of leather shoes, snagged white stockings, and the torn hem of a plain brown skirt poking out from the dense thicket. He leaped over the hedges to the other side and knelt beside the woman. Her face was turned away from him. Relief poured through him when he saw her fingers move and heard a low moan breaking from her throat.

With great care he took her by the shoulders and pulled her slowly from the bushes, then rolled her onto her back. Her rich chestnut hair, glinting with strands of gold in the bright sunlight, fell across her face and obscured her features.

Garrett quickly felt her slender limbs for broken bones. There fortunately didn't seem to be any. Her breathing appeared normal, her chest rising and falling evenly. He leaned over her and gently moved her hair away from her face, his hand grazing her soft cheek. He felt a sudden catch in his throat.

If anyone had been blessed with the legendary Scots beauty he had heard so much about, it was this woman. She was stunning. This was not the porcelain perfection he had seen during a brief stay in Edinburgh, where the damsels mimicked Londoners in their use of rouge and lip stain. This woman possessed a beauty kissed by nature, breathtaking and unspoiled, like the wild Highlands about her.

Garrett could not resist tracing his finger along the high curve of her cheekbone. He marveled at the silken texture of her skin and its fresh hues of sun-warmed rose and cream. Her forehead was shapely, and slim brows arched above closed eyelids fringed with lush, dark lashes. Her nose was straight, almost patrician. Her lips were full, delicately curved, and as red as ripe berries above her soft and rounded chin.

He had a strong urge to press his mouth against hers and taste the inviting warmth of her lips, but he did not. Another soft moan forced his errant thoughts back to the matter at hand. The woman had not yet regained consciousness and needed care. She would do far better lying in a bed than on the hard ground.

Perhaps he should take her to the manor house, Garrett thought. She had been riding in that direction; she probably worked there as a maidservant. Her simple, frayed gown and her scuffed shoes certainly attested to such a post.

He bent down and scooped her into his arms, then rose easily to his feet. He stepped over the hedges and turned onto the dirt drive, striding toward the manor house. He could hear jingling harnesses and creaking wagon wheels, indicating his men were not far away. He walked faster. He was anxious to be done with this chore before they arrived. He was not in the mood for any coarse jests.

As he neared the front door, Garrett glanced once

more at the woman. His gaze traveled over her white throat, the enticing outline of her breasts straining against her bodice, and her narrow waist. Heat raced through his body.

What had Colonel Wolfe said to him the morning he first heard about Black Jack? Something about finding a lass to aid his quest, and secrets betrayed at the height of passion?

Garrett smiled thoughtfully. Perhaps this tempting wench might very well lead him to Black Jack.

If she worked as a maid in this house, he would see her often. Perhaps after a tender wooing—a few soft words, well-chosen compliments, and gentle caresses—she might prove willing and eager to warm his bed. Once he gained her trust, she might even share with him any knowledge she had about Black Jack. He was not one to wantonly mislead a woman's affections, but time was of the essence in this mission. It was worth a—

He exhaled sharply, grunting in pain as a stinging jab in the ribs caught him by surprise. The next thing he knew the woman pushed against him and wrenched free of his arms, kicking his shin and stamping on his toes as she found her footing. Her startling blue eyes blazed as she wheeled to face him.

"H-how dare ye!" she sputtered, confusion and rage reflected in her eyes. When she stepped back and began to stagger, Garrett feared she might fall. He reached out to steady her, but she darted away.

"Easy, lassie," he said softly. "I'm only trying to help you."

"Dinna lassie me, ye swine! Ye filthy redcoat!"

Garrett chuckled at her heated outburst. He walked slowly toward her, his eyes raking her from head to foot.

She was truly the comeliest woman he had ever seen, with a fiery spirit to match. Yet he still feared she might collapse. Her knees appeared wobbly, and she was massaging her left temple. He had better subdue her before she brought herself to more harm.

"Tell me your name," he insisted gently, moving closer. The woman shook her head fiercely. "Your horse ran into mine on the road. Do you remember? You took a hard fall, lass, and I think it's best you lie down for a while."

"Aye, I remember well enough, and I dinna need yer reminding," she spat, retreating another few steps. "Had ye not been riding where ye're not welcome, 'twould not have happened." A flicker of pain crossed her face, but she raised her chin stubbornly. "I'm fine now, as ye can see, though 'tis no business of yers. Now get off my la—"

"Oh, but it is my business, as is everything in this valley," Garrett interrupted, growing impatient. He looked beyond her shoulder at the first supply wagon turning into the drive. It gave him an idea. "My soldiers are arriving, lass. Come on now, I've no more time to argue with you."

At these words she whirled around, and Garrett seized his opportunity. In two steps he had her in his arms. She screamed, twisting and struggling, but he held her tightly. Tossing her over his shoulder, he gritted his teeth as her doubled fists rained blows upon his neck and broad back.

For a wench who had suffered a hard fall, she was certainly putting up a good fight, he thought wryly, holding her legs away so she couldn't kick him. Suddenly her body went limp, and she began to mumble incoherently. The strain of her recent injury had obviously proved too much for her, as he thought it might.

Garrett strode to the door and pounded on it. After a few moments he heard shuffling footsteps, then the door was opened by a frail-looking old woman. She gaped up at him, her hands flying to her throat. "Maddie!"

"So that's the spitfire's name," he said under his breath, walking into the dim hallway. He turned to face the woman. "And what is your name, dear lady?"

"Gl-Glenis," she stammered, her dark eyes wide with shock. "Glenis Simpson."

"Well, Glenis, this young woman had quite a nasty fall from her horse. She should be put to bed immediately, until she's feeling more like herself. Where are the servants' quarters?"

"Servants' quarters?"

"Yes. If you'll only show me the way, I'll explain what happened. And you might summon the master of the house—"

"Sir Hugh is dead, sir. He was killed at Culloden."

Garrett fell silent and felt awkward. He should have guessed as much. He softened his tone. "His wife, then, the Lady . . ."

"Fraser, sir," she finished for him. "Lady Jean died many years ago. There is only the young mistress now."

"Where is she?" Garrett asked, shifting the woman's weight on his shoulder. "We have much to discuss. And I wish to explain what happened to her maidservant here, Maddie."

Glenis's eyes lit with understanding. " 'Tis no maidservant ye're carryin', sir," she murmured gravely. " 'Tis the mistress of Farraline, Madeleine Fraser."

Now it was Garrett's turn to stare. He swallowed hard, his face flushing warmly. He had never felt so sheepish in his life. He didn't know quite what to do or say.

Glenis finally broke the uncomfortable silence. "If ye'll kindly follow me, sir—"

"Captain Garrett Marshall," he said.

"If ye'll follow me, Captain Marshall," Glenis said with great dignity, "I'll show ye to my mistress's chamber, where I might see to her needs."

Garrett simply nodded. As he climbed the stairs behind the aged Scotswoman, he could not help thinking that his mission had gotten off to another miserable start.

Chapter 5

Glenis closed the polished wardrobe door, clucking her tongue disapprovingly. "Ye've scarce given yerself time to rest, Maddie. 'Tis only been a few hours, and already ye're up and about. Ye took a bad fall accordin' to the captain. He told me all about it. He was quite sorry he'd caused ye harm. I think ye should climb back into bed and stay put until tomorrow morn."

"Since when do ye believe anything an Englishman tells ye?" Madeleine retorted. "I'm fine, Glenis." Her fingers worked furiously at the mother-of-pearl buttons on her bodice. Knowing what was going on downstairs, she could not dress fast enough. She winced at the sudden sharp ache in her head and bit her lower lip.

"There, ye see!" Glenis noted with exasperation, wagging a bony finger. "I should have forced more of my nettle tea into ye, whether ye liked the taste or no. At least ye'd still be asleep and ye wouldna be feelin' so poorly."

Glenis moved to the bed and flung back the flowered coverlet. She patted the mattress firmly. "Back to bed with ye, Madeleine Fraser. Ye can speak to the captain in the morning. From the looks of it, those soldiers plan to be stayin' at Mhor Manor for quite a while."

"They winna if I can help it," Madeleine fumed, ignoring Glenis's suggestion. Redcoats under her own roof! She could hardly believe it. She bent down to

57

fasten the brass buckles on her brogues, then straightened, smoothing the skirt of her clean linen gown. "What did ye say was that captain's name?"

Clearly frustrated, Glenis sighed heavily and sank down on the bed. She gave Madeleine a look she had known all her life, reproaching her for her stubbornness. "Captain Marshall. Garrett's his Christian name."

"I dinna care one whit about his Christian name," Madeleine muttered under her breath. Without another word she flounced from the room.

How dare they invade my home, she thought furiously as she rushed down the hallway to the main staircase. While she had slept the afternoon away, thirty-odd redcoats had taken over the entire right wing of Mhor Manor. Glenis had told her they were building bunks in the dancing room and the spare guest rooms. Bunks!

Madeleine felt another sharp pang, and she paused, leaning against the wall, until it subsided. Her thoughts were still fuzzy, her memory of the accident earlier that day only fragmented pictures in her mind. She distinctly remembered the wild ride from Farraline, but what followed was no more than a streaking blur of events. Everything had happened so fast.

There had been a violent jolt as her mare struck the other horse, then she had flown through the air. After that she recalled only blackness until she opened her eyes to find herself in the arms of an English soldier. It had been like a terrible nightmare.

She remembered a struggle to free herself and the sound of his deep and steady voice, but not his words. Nor could she recall her own words, only her feelings of anger as he seemed to stalk her, drawing closer and closer. She had had the strangest sensation she had seen him somewhere before . . .

Then she had been in his arms again, fighting and cursing, the breath knocked from her body as he had thrown her over his shoulder. The next thing she knew, she was lying in her bed, Glenis spoonfeeding her that bitter tea. She had fallen asleep, only to wake a short while ago to find Glenis nodding off in the rocking chair by the window.

Madeleine pushed away from the wall and walked to the top of the staircase. She looked down into the main hallway. Her eyes narrowed as a young soldier entered through the front door, his arms full of bedding.

Indignation seized her. The scene reminded her of the last time redcoats had violated her home. She had been powerless to do anything on that occasion. This time she was not. She practically flew down the stairs and gave the soldier a good shove. He fell back, grunting in surprise, blankets and linen sheets tumbling to the floor.

"What do ye think ye're doing?" she cried, throwing herself between him and the hall leading to the adjoining right wing. "Get out of my house, ye freckled weasel! Now! And take yer bedclothes with ye!"

The startled soldier mumbled something unintelligible, his face a bright shade of red that nearly matched his uniform. He began to step backward, keeping one eye on her while he glanced over his shoulder for the door.

"Stop right where you are, soldier," a deep voice commanded him from directly behind Madeleine.

The young man froze. "Yes, sir," he said miserably.

Madeleine spun around to meet this new adversary, a stinging retort on her lips. It died when she came face to face with the handsome, blond officer who loomed in the archway, the powerful breadth of his shoulders blocking out everything behind him. His eyes, a compelling shade of gray flecked with green, studied her quizzically.

It was he. The man who had accosted her, she thought angrily. A familiar sensation gripped her. She could swear she had seen him before today, but where?

Suddenly her memory cleared, like sunlight piercing through a mist. Her last raid! He had been the commanding officer, forced to strip with his men . . . She felt a blush scorch her skin, and she bowed her head so he wouldn't see her discomfort. Her mind raced.

Easy, lass. Stay calm, she assured herself. She and her kinsmen had nothing to fear. They had been well disguised during that raid. 'Twas only a strange coincidence, nothing more.

"That's hardly a way to treat your new guests, Mistress Fraser," the officer began, interrupting her thoughts. "Allow me to introduce—"

"There's no need for introductions," Madeleine snapped, quickly recovering herself. She looked him full in the face. "I know who ye are, Captain Marshall."

"Garrett."

"Whatever. Glenis has told me all about ye."

"Ah, then. I hope it was complimentary."

Garrett smiled as his gaze wandered over her. He took in every aspect of her comely appearance, from her glossy curls to the trim fit of her lavender gown. Its buttoned bodice, demurely edged with lace, revealed a full swell of creamy bosom. She was definitely not a maidservant, he thought appreciatively. How could he have so misjudged her?

He was also pleased to observe that she looked none the worse for her accident. Her cheeks were flushed with a healthy rose color, her eyes were lively and sparkling. He took a step toward her. "How are you feeling?"

"What are ye and yer sorry lot of soldiers doing in my house?" she demanded, disregarding his soft-spoken question. His frank appraisal was unsettling, and she shivered, acutely aware of his striking good looks. She placed her hands on her hips and eyed him belligerently, forcing her mind from this baffling attraction.

"Perhaps we could sit in the drawing room while we discuss a few matters, rather than stand here in the hall. Or we could stroll outside. The sun is about to set and it's a lovely summer evening."

"I'll not sit down nor walk in any garden with the

likes of ye," Madeleine said evenly, raising her chin. "Ye'll kindly answer my question, Captain Marshall. Why are ye turning my home into a . . . a bunkhouse?"

"Very well." Garrett gestured to the soldier, who was still standing stiffly to one side. The man quickly gathered up the bedding and hurried past them. Only when he disappeared down the hallway did Garrett speak again. His expression sobered.

"I'll be brief, Mistress Fraser. Your manor house will be serving as headquarters and billeting for myself and my men for an indefinite period of time."

"Billeting?"

"Yes. We've been ordered by our chief commander, General Henry Hawley, to occupy Strathherrick."

Madeleine started. She had heard of Butcher Cumberland's bastard brother. His cruelty had far surpassed the duke's at Culloden. If this man was one of his officers, surely he was cut from the same maggot-infested cloth. "For what purpose, captain, if I might ask?"

Garrett did not readily reply. He could not tell her the truth because it might jeopardize his mission.

If she knew anything about Black Jack, she could possibly warn the outlaw of their intent to capture him. No doubt the bastard would flee into the mountains at the first whiff of trouble. Then all would be lost, for himself and the people of Strathherrick. Perhaps if he could ever trust her, it might be different, but for now . . .

"Our purpose is simple," he lied. "We've been stationed in this valley to keep the peace."

She stared at him incredulously. "Keep the peace? Surely 'tis a jest, Captain Marshall," she scoffed. "Since when have ye redcoats been interested in anything more than cruel slaughter, the rape of innocent women and young girls, and the burning of homes and the stealing of cattle?"

Garrett's jaw tightened. He could not contradict her, even if he had wanted to. There was truth in her words, demonstrated time and again these past months. Yet he hated being lumped with the rest of his overzealous, and often unscrupulous, compatriots.

Obviously he and his men would have to prove that they meant no harm to the Highlanders of Strathherrick. This would be a peaceful occupation, just as he had discussed with Colonel Wolfe. Better to establish such a tone from the start.

"No, it is not a jest," he replied quietly. "We're here to ensure the welfare of those Highlanders who abide by the new laws. The English laws. But I agree with you wholeheartedly, Mistress Fraser. Too many innocents have been punished unjustly for the sake of a few troublemakers."

Madeleine was taken aback. Such words from an Englishman? If she did not know better, she might have considered his statement to be some sort of an apology. Yet smooth words only made her more suspicious of him.

"What troublemakers do ye mean, captain?" she asked tightly, a vision of her father flashing before her. "Do ye refer to the brave clansmen who fought and died for the rightful heir to the throne of Great Britain, King James? Or perhaps ye mean the ones who've escaped the noose and yer filthy gaols, only to be hunted mercilessly in their own homeland by the lot of ye bloodthirsty cowards."

Garrett felt a quickening of anger, but quelled it. He knew she was baiting him. He would not give her the satisfaction of justifying her preconceptions about all English officers. He decided a half truth was better than none.

"I admire bravery in any man, friend or foe," he said. "I'll not speak ill of those who fight for their beliefs. The troublemakers are the thieves and outlaws who now prey on the Englishmen and Scotsmen loyal to King George. Whether they commit their crimes for profit or revenge, the outcome is the same. It is the innocent people who will suffer and bear the blame if these outlaws are not stopped."

Madeleine had to force herself to breathe steadily. His cryptic words fell together like pieces of a puzzle in her mind.

God's wounds! This officer and his men had been sent to look for her! That had to be it. They must have been traveling to Farraline when she and her kinsmen raided their camp. Yet it was clear he didn't suspect her, or she would have surely been arrested already.

"So what ye're saying, Captain Marshall, is that some of these . . . troublemakers are in Strathherrick?" she asked innocently, belying her inner turmoil.

Garrett perceived he had given more information than he had intended. It seemed his hostess was very inquisitive.

"As I said, Mistress Fraser, we've been stationed here to keep the peace. You and your people have nothing to fear from us." He quickly changed the subject. "Perhaps you might accompany me through the house," he ventured. "I'd like to show you that my men have taken great care not to damage your property." He paused, then added dryly, "Unlike the soldiers who have been here before us."

"Aye, yer brothers in arms already did a fine job of it," she muttered under her breath. She was frustrated that he hadn't answered her question. Yet she sensed her intuition was correct. She would have to speak with Angus and Ewen at once, that very night, and warn them of this new danger.

Garrett held out his arm to her. "Shall we go, then, Mistress Maddie?"

Madeleine shot him a look of pure venom. "Only my kinsmen call me by that name, Captain Marshall," she said hotly. "Ye may have taken over my house, but ye dinna have the right to consider yerself part of the family. Ye and yer men are unwelcome here, and not a day shall pass that I dinna tell ye so. Now, if ye'll kindly step out of my way."

He did so, and she brushed past him into the narrow hall. "And I dinna need yer invitation to survey my own home," she flung over her shoulder. "I'll see to yer men's clever handiwork m'self!"

Garrett stared after her, surprised by the ungentlemanly direction of his thoughts and the quickening of his desire. God, but she was lovely!

He admired the provocative sway of her skirt—the lustrous fabric skimming her slender hips and the teasing hint of lace petticoat peeking from beneath the hem. It pleased him that she wore no hoops, a ridiculous fashion which had obviously not made it to the Highlands. Her simple gown stirred his imagination, conjuring a tantalizing vision of her hidden charms.

An amused grin lit his face. He had never been so intrigued by a woman before, and the devil knew he'd had his share. Everything about her fascinated him— the way she moved, the timbre of her voice, and her flashing blue eyes. Her every gesture and her every word bespoke passion and spirit.

She was so different from the passive beauties he had known in England, with their carefully schooled smiles, empty heads, and conniving mothers who were eager to wed their daughters to a fortune. Even his memory of Celinda paled in comparison. This woman spoke her mind, and with a vengeance. Damn, it was refreshing!

A curious thought struck him. Other than the obvious act of leaving her home, what would he have to do to bring a smile to the beauteous Mistress Fraser's lips? he wondered wryly. Could kindness, gallantry, gentle wooing, and a healthy dose of patience win her favor? Perhaps his earlier plan when he had thought her a maidservant was not so far off the mark after all.

If he could gain her trust, even her slightest affection, she might be able to help him. As the mistress of Farraline, she probably knew a great deal of what went on in Strathherrick. Perhaps she even knew where to find Black Jack . . .

Garrett strode after her, eager to put his new plan into action. From what he had seen of her so far, he had no doubt Mistress Madeleine Fraser would fight him every step of the way. Yet the thought did not daunt him.

His Scots grandmother had told him once there was no woman more stubborn and headstrong than a Highland wench. Yet when her favor was won, however hard fought, there was never a woman more true.

Such a woman's trust was more than worth the challenge . . . if it might lead him to Black Jack.

Chapter 6

An hour later Madeleine stormed into the kitchen and slammed the door behind her. She startled Glenis, who was draping a fresh tea towel over a pan of hot scones.

"What is it, lass?" Glenis asked, whirling to face her disgruntled mistress. "Though I must tell ye, I canna stand too many more surprises in one day."

"Have ye seen the dancing room lately?" Madeleine blurted out angrily. She plopped into one of the wooden chairs placed around the table, her gown cascading in rippling folds to the floor. Without waiting for a reply she rushed on, determined to vent her spleen.

"Ye'd never know 'twas once reserved for our Highland reels and dances and the playing of the pipes. It looks to be a barracks, with twenty bunks lining the walls and men sitting upon them, cleaning their weapons, polishing their boots, laughing and joking and carrying on as if 'twas a common thing to intrude upon another's home!"

She drew a deep breath, pushing her hair behind her ear. "The guest rooms have fared no better. Mama would surely be having a fit if she'd lived to see redcoats lying upon her fine needleworked coverlets and satin pillows."

"Dinna speak so of your mother, Maddie," Glenis chided, her voice shrill and cracking. " 'Tis bad luck, and well ye know it. Leave her spirit to rest in peace.

66

We dinna need any ghosts summoned forth to add to our troubles."

"I'm sorry, Glenis," Madeleine said distractedly. She rubbed her temples; the dull pain was still plaguing her. She was certain it would have been gone by now if not for that infuriating Captain Marshall. He'd given her twice the headache in the span of one short hour!

First he had followed her into the dancing room like a second shadow after she told him she could manage alone. Then he had insisted on introducing her to each of his men, as if she cared to know them: Sergeant Lowell Fletcher, Corporal Denny Sims, the hapless soldier she had shoved in the hall, and so many others whose names had simply flown by her.

To her surprise, the men had been quite respectful and courteous, though a few rough-looking soldiers had eyed her with more than passing interest. At those times Captain Marshall had acted in the most peculiar manner. His expression had darkened, his tone had grown brusque, and he had quickly steered her to the next man.

She would have balked at the possessive pressure of his hand on her elbow if she hadn't been surrounded by so many soldiers. But his attention gave her an odd sense of security, and she realized grudgingly he was the only buffer between herself and his men. If he appeared protective, so much the better. At least she wouldn't have to fear any unwelcome advances from them.

That thought reminded Madeleine of a decision she'd made while making her excuses to Captain Marshall and finally fleeing the dancing room. She jumped up from the chair and hurried over to Glenis, who was expertly turning another batch of scones on a buttered griddle set atop the hearth. She kept her voice low in case any soldiers were walking outside near the kitchen windows.

"Glenis, I have something important to discuss with ye."

"Hold on for a moment, lass, whilst I finish these scones," Glenis said. She turned the last one, then set down her wooden spatula and wiped her hands on her apron. "All right, what is it ye wish to tell me?"

Madeleine held her finger to her lips, indicating they should speak softly. "In the morning I want ye to tell Meg Blair and Kitty Dods not to come to the house anymore. 'Tis for their own good whilst the soldiers are here."

"Who'll help me with the cleaning and washing then, Maddie?" Glenis protested, raising her voice. At Madeleine's stern look her tone fell to an agitated whisper. "With my old bones, 'tis a wonder I can still move about the house at all!"

"I'll help ye," Madeleine said. "I'm no stranger to housework, if ye remember." She smiled faintly. "I can wield a broom and dustcloth just as surely as a pistol, Glenis, though I may not like it as well."

"Och, but that's just it, lass. Ye've got yer other duties to think about. Ye've no time to be helpin' me. And knowin' ye to be as stubborn as yer da, I dinna expect ye'll be ridin' out any less than before, soldiers or no!"

Madeleine fell silent. To be truthful, she wasn't quite sure what she and her men were going to do now that the English soldiers had come to Strathherrick. Their situation had become much more precarious. Yet she wouldn't make any final decision until she spoke with her band later that evening.

That is, if she managed to sneak out without being detected. She had no idea how many guards Captain Marshall was planning to station around the manor house, or where. Their positions would certainly be a crucial factor in any future raids.

"Glenis, there's something else ye must know," she began. She quickly relayed the details of her encounter with Captain Marshall in the main hallway, and of the last raid. Glenis's eyes widened as she listened, her forehead furrowing with concern when Madeleine reported her suspicion about the purpose of Captain Marshall's mission.

"I told ye they'd come lookin' for ye one day!" Glenis hissed, wringing her hands. "Ye wouldna listen! Och, 'tis a woeful day, Maddie. What are ye goin' to do?"

Madeleine shook her head. "I winna know until I speak with Angus Ramsay and the Burkes tonight, in Farraline. They'll send word to the Fraser brothers. Together we'll decide if we press on or lay low until the soldiers leave."

"Dear God, what a choice ye have to make, lass!"

"Aye. Either way, 'tis risky. If we go on with our raids, we may be found out. If we stop, the villagers will run out of food. We have enough stores hidden in the caves of Beinn Dubhcharaidh to last awhile, but it could be gone before Captain Marshall and his men depart Strathherrick. I, for one, dinna wish to see children starving again. I'll say as much to Ewen and Angus tonight."

Glenis grew pensive, then her eyes widened in apprehension. "Are ye mad, lass?" she blurted, as if she had just realized what Madeleine had said. "Ye canna walk out the front door tonight, just as ye please, without the soldiers or Captain Marshall wantin' to know where ye're goin' at such a late hour!"

"Shhh, Glenis," Madeleine warned, looking fearfully at the window. "Someone will surely hear ye." She bent her head close to her servant's ear. "Ye've forgotten about great-grandfather's tunnel."

Glenis sighed heavily, her shoulders appearing even more stooped than before. "Aye, so I have . . ." She glanced sternly at Madeleine. "If I wasna already an old woman, ye'd be turnin' my hair gray, Madeleine Elisabeth Fraser. I told ye before I wouldna burden ye with my fears, and I winna now. I'll pray for ye, though, good and hard, so ye'll be certain to journey safely to Farraline and back again, and make the right decision."

She sniffed suddenly, her nose wrinkling. "Och, the

scones, lass, they're burnin'!'' She turned back to the hearth and grabbed the spatula, deftly flipping the scones one by one from the griddle. "Just in time," she said. "I made yer favorite, cinnamon, nutmeg, and treacle. I thought 'twould cheer ye after the day ye've had . . . you'll be needing them now more than ever."

She took a white china plate from the cupboard, placed two golden-brown scones on it, then handed the plate to Madeleine. "I understand yer worries for Meg and Kitty. Yet I dinna think ye should be botherin' yerself with house chores. If I know ye as well as I think I do, ye'll be out on a raid before another week is past."

Before Madeleine could reply, Glenis gestured to the table. "Go on, lass. I'll fetch the tea."

Madeleine obliged her and sat down while Glenis followed with a delicate china teapot. She set it on the embroidered runner and leaned against the table.

"Let Meg stay on, Maddie. She's a good head on her shoulders and she works hard. Kitty's impetuous and far too pretty for her own good." Glenis paused, her gnarled hand smoothing the runner. She sighed sadly. "There's few young men left in the valley to court her now, and she might easily be swayed by smooth words, even from a redcoat. The girls know nothing of yer raids, to be sure, but I'd trust Meg over Kitty to keep quiet if she saw anything she shouldna."

Madeleine was silent for several moments, mulling over the request. Glenis was right, she decided. The girls were both sixteen, but Meg was far more mature. She could be trusted. And Glenis could certainly use the help.

"Very well, ye win," she said at last. "Meg may stay on. But if I see the soldiers giving her a rough time of it, she'll have to go. Agreed?"

"Aye, ye know best," Glenis replied. She sat down across from Madeleine and poured them both a cup of hot, strong tea. "I've made barley soup for supper, if ye've a mind to taste it," she offered.

"The scones will be enough for me," Madeleine said,

breaking one apart. Steam drifted up from the crumbly surface, melting the sweet butter she had slathered on it. She took a bite, enjoying the melded flavors of spices and molasses.

A companionable silence fell over the kitchen. Madeleine ate quickly while Glenis sipped her tea. She was anxious to retire to her bedchamber.

It was her plan to wait until the house grew quiet, then creep down the side stairs and into the drawing room. If she could make it that far without being detected by any guards, she could surely make it to Farraline. The trap door leading to the secret tunnel was hidden in the drawing room closet.

When her great-grandfather had built Mhor Manor a hundred years ago, he had dug a tunnel beneath it in case the family should ever need an escape route in time of war. It ran from the closet, the trap door concealed in the intricate floor planking, to a copse of ancient fir trees some forty yards beyond the house. As far as Madeleine knew, the tunnel had only been used once for its intended purpose.

Madeleine finished the last of her tea and set the cup down with a clatter. "Ye make the best scones, Glenis," she said, rising from her chair and planting a kiss on her forehead.

"Are ye sure 'tis enough to hold ye, lass?"

"Aye, 'tis plenty. Sleep well tonight, and dinna worry for me." She opened the kitchen door. "Och, I almost forgot. If Captain Marshall should come looking for me, tell him I've retired early. He mentioned some nonsense about one of his soldiers being a fair cook and asked that I join him for supper. Can ye imagine? I told him the food would grow cold and rot before I'd ever sup with him."

She began to close the door, then glanced back over her shoulder, smiling wickedly. "Better still, I know what ye can say, Glenis. Tell him I'm a delicate lass. The excitement of the day was simply too much for me."

"A delicate lass indeed," she heard Glenis mutter as

she shut the door. "As daring as any man, she is, and
with enough spirit to prove it!"

Madeleine walked through the dining room and up
the stairs. The hall was nearly pitch dark, but she could
see well enough. She strolled toward her room, hum-
ming a lilting Scottish air.

She stopped suddenly, her blood pounding loudly
in her ears. She stared wide-eyed at the faint sliver of
light shining from beneath the door to her father's bedchamber. Visions of phantoms and ghosts leaped in
her mind. Could it be that her father's restless spirit
had come to haunt Mhor Manor?

She quickly dispelled the thought, scolding herself
for her fears. It was obvious she had been listening far
too much to Glenis's superstitious rambling. There was
a logical explanation for the light. There had to be.
Glenis or one of the girls had left a lamp burning while
cleaning the room, or someone else was in there . . .

She tested the latch. The door was unlocked. She
leaned against it, tripping inside the dimly lit room as
the door was abruptly pulled open from the inside.

"Oh!" Madeleine exclaimed, knocking into something broad and hard. A strong arm circled her waist
and prevented her from falling. Crisp curls brushed
her cheek. She began to scream, but she was silenced
by a large hand pressed over her mouth. Panic rose in
her throat, and she twisted frantically, trying to free
herself.

"Easy, Mistress Fraser, easy. I'd rather you not bring
my entire corps to your rescue, so if you'll kindly re-
frain from screaming, I'll remove my hand."

Captain Marshall! Madeleine tensed at the familiar
voice, but she was grateful her captor wasn't one of
those rough-looking soldiers. She looked up, meeting
his eyes, and nodded.

She inhaled sharply as he dropped his hand, but instead of releasing her, he drew her closer. Her breasts
were pressed tightly against him, and the warmth of
his skin seemed to burn through her gown. His warm,
male scent swamped her racing senses, and a soft, star-

tled gasp broke from her throat as his fingers gently caressed the small of her back.

A bewildering current of excitement shot through her, and she flushed with embarrassment as she felt her nipples grow taut and rigid, thrusting against her bodice. Her eyes fell to his rugged chest, sprinkled with dark blond curls, and with a start she realized he was naked from the waist up. Anger bubbled within her at his bold presumption, rescuing her from the traitorous sensations flooding her body.

"Release me at once, ye filthy—"

"Redcoat, swine, bastard?" Garrett finished for her, painfully aware of the hardness swelling under his breeches. He regretfully willed away his growing ardor, smiling as Madeleine clamped her mouth shut and glared at him. "You seem to have a limited vocabulary when it comes to English soldiers, Mistress Fraser. Perhaps you might try calling me by my Christian name."

"I'll do nothing of the kind," she snapped. She braced her hands against his bare chest and pushed, but her efforts were futile. He held her too tightly, his arms as powerfully muscled as his chest . . . a fact which strangely excited her once more. Infuriated by her errant feelings, she threw her head back, her eyes crackling with fire. "Let me go!"

"Garrett."

Madeleine could see she had no choice in this verbal tug-of-war. "Garrett," she muttered through clenched teeth.

Suddenly he released her, and she felt strangely bereft, but only for an instant. She stepped back, her temper flaring anew as her gaze swept the large room. Garrett's personal belongings were everywhere, his scarlet coat draped over the chair by the mahogany desk, his waistcoat and white shirt lying on the tartan bedspread, a massive, brass-bound trunk at the foot of the canopied bed . . .

"What do ye think ye're doing in my father's room?" she demanded, her fists clenched.

Garrett sobered, the smile fading from his lips. Her

late father's room. He had guessed as much, from the
masculine decor and heavy furnishings. He had also
anticipated her response to this new intrusion, but
there was no help for it. He needed the space and the
privacy.

"I have decided to use this room during my stay,"
he explained. "We've run short of space for an extra
bunk in the dancing room, and the guest rooms are
full."

"Ye should have tried the stable first," Madeleine
said bitterly. "Ye'd fit in nicely. There's plenty of room,
now that most of the stalls are empty. Yer countrymen
stole our finest horses, as well as our cattle and sheep."

Garrett was cut by her insult, though he did not
show it. He knew there was great pain fueling her
words, a sorrow that only time would heal.

Until trust grew between them, if it did at all, she
would likely continue to hurl such insults at him. He
would simply have to deflect them and keep his temper firmly in check. It would not further his plan to
lash out at her, or to demand her compliance as one of
the conquered.

If he stayed his course, perhaps he could crack her
defiant exterior and expose the passionate woman beneath, a woman who might be willing to help him . . .
and thereby help her people. These past few moments
had already granted him a fleeting glimpse of desire
burning in those incredible blue eyes. It seemed his
effect on her was much the same as hers on him—a
most intriguing discovery.

"I'm sure you can understand the stable would not
be suitable," Garrett said, smiling faintly. "If there was
another acceptable chamber on this floor, I would certainly—"

"There is, just down the hall," Madeleine interjected. "It's next to mine . . ." Her voice trailed off,
and she flushed warmly, which only unnerved her further. She had never blushed so much before this man
had entered her life.

She didn't want him to think she was suggesting

anything, she thought, chagrined. She only wanted
him to leave this room for another.

"What I meant to say," she began, groping for
words, "is that there's a room . . . on the same side of
the hall as my own."

"I know what you meant, and I already considered
it," Garrett said gently, touched by her obvious embarrassment. "Unfortunately, that room faces the
mountains," he continued. "Though it is a magnificent view, I prefer to stay here. These windows face
the road and Farraline. As a commander, I must consider the safety of my men and our position. I'm sure
you understand."

"Aye, I understand," Madeleine said hotly, "and
I'll have ye understand this, Captain Marshall. Yer be-
ing in this room is an affront to my father's memory.
Ye disgrace it with yer presence."

Garrett remained unperturbed. "I'm sorry you feel
that way," he said. "I consider it an honor. Your father must have been a very brave and good man to
earn such loyalty from his daughter." His voice fell. "I
envy you. My late father and I were never very close."

Sudden tears glistened in Madeleine's eyes. "Aye,
my da was a fine man," she barely managed, her throat
tightening, "and I'd rather ye not speak of him. 'Tis
an insult as well. He might still be alive if not for the
treachery of yer kind."

Her words stung, and Garrett flinched impercepti-
bly. How he longed to take her in his arms again, to
smooth back her hair and stroke her cheek and tell her
that he deeply regretted the massacre at Culloden . . .
that he had had no part in it.

The senseless slaughter was an act of inhumanity he
would relive until his dying day. He carried a deep
sense of shame within him, not only for the men who
had committed the atrocities, but because he and a few
other officers who felt the same had been powerless to
stop it.

He took a step toward her, then restrained himself.
No, this was not the time. She would spit the words

back in his face and call him a liar. How could he blame her? She had never seen English soldiers behave in any manner other than abhorrently, like maddened beasts.

Have patience, man, he warned himself. You might have a chance with her, but only if you're patient. He turned and walked over to the washstand, where he picked up a thick bar of soap.

"I was just about to wash up for dinner," he said, changing the painful subject. "My cook, Jeremy Witt, has concocted a decent chicken stew in the kitchen tent he set up behind the house. He has also baked some of his famous pan bread. I'd be honored if you would reconsider my earlier offer and join me. Perhaps we could eat in the dining room. My men won't bother us there. They seem to prefer eating under the stars, swapping stories in front of a blazing fire."

Madeleine stared at him as if he were insane. She blinked back her tears, her ire surging once more. "I dinna care about yer cook's chicken stew, nor his pan bread, and I hope yer men choke on their food! I told ye before, I'll never sup with the likes of ye."

Garrett smiled as he dipped the rough cloth into the basin of sudsy water. "You don't have to eat, then. Just sit with me," he said, scrubbing his face. "My Scots grandmother told me many stories about the Highlands, and I'm curious to hear more."

Madeleine gaped at him. If he'd suddenly grown horns and a forked tail, she couldn't have been more stunned. "Yer grandmother was a Highlander?" she asked, her voice almost a whisper. "Ye've Scots blood in ye?"

"Aye, that I do," Garrett said playfully, attempting a Scottish burr. He toweled himself dry. "She grew up in Edinburgh, but her people were one of the clans in the north."

Now you've done it, he thought, watching her expression cloud and darken. It was obvious his rash tongue had only made things worse.

"What clan might that be?" Madeleine asked, though she already sensed his answer. Many of the clans in the northern Highlands had fought under King George's banners at Culloden, traitors against their own people.

Garrett threw the towel on the stand. He sighed heavily. "Clan Sutherland."

Madeleine's tone was scathing. "So, now I not only have a horde of redcoats under my roof, but their fine commander's Scots blood is traitorous to boot. To think ye'll be sleeping in my father's bed. I hope he comes back to haunt Mhor Manor, and I hope he runs his sword right through yer black traitor's heart!"

"Madeleine . . ."

"Dinna Madeleine me. Ye've no right, same as ye've no right to be staying in this room and no right to be here in my house!"

She turned and fled down the hallway, ignoring his calls for her to stop. Once in her room, she slammed the door shut behind her and locked it. She heard his footsteps approaching and her breath caught in her throat.

"Ye better not think to enter my room by force, ye devil," Madeleine mumbled, her back to the door. She pulled up her skirt and reached for the dirk she always wore strapped to her right thigh, ever since the day the soldiers had plundered her home.

It was the last gift her father had given her, smaller than most such weapons, with a silver hilt especially made to fit her hand. She held the razor-sharp blade against her breast and waited in the darkness of her room, listening.

She exhaled as his footsteps stopped abruptly and retreated back down the hallway. She waited a short while longer, then sheathed the dirk. She walked over to the bedside table, struck a flint, and lit a thick, tallow candle. As golden light filled the room, she noticed her fingers were shaking.

Bastard! she fumed, moving to her wardrobe. She changed quickly into a dark gray gown of coarse wool, suitable for her furtive outing. Then she sat on the bed and deftly braided her hair, securing it with a black ribbon. She flung the braid over her shoulder and fell back on the mattress, pounding it in annoyance.

If only she could leave for Farraline now! She couldn't wait to talk to her kinsmen, and she knew exactly what she was going to say. No more indecision wracked her.

She would do everything in her power to persuade them to continue the raids, whatever the danger. She was not going to allow this English dog, this . . . this Captain Garrett Marshall, to deter her from aiding her people.

Madeleine sat up and blew out the candle, then settled herself on the mattress again. She reached over and pulled a soft pillow under her head, closing her eyes.

A vision of Garrett appeared unbidden before her, just as she had seen him only moments before: his long, lean form bent over the washstand, his strong profile etched in the lamplight, water dripping from his tanned face and down his broad chest, over glistening blond curls. She saw his flashing smile, his startling gray-green eyes studying her, unnerving her, as if he could guess what she was thinking and feeling . . .

Madeleine punched her pillow angrily, forcing the disturbing image from her mind. It was not so easy to dispel the memory of his powerful embrace. Wholly frustrated, she grabbed the tartan blanket folded neatly at the end of the bed and covered herself, then rolled over onto her side.

Aye, she would go on with her raids right under his nose, she thought defiantly, tucking her legs beneath her. And she would relish every minute of it!

She yawned, growing drowsy. After a short nap she would set out through that secret tunnel, her mission clearly before her. Her decision had been made. There would be no turning back.

Chapter 7

ᴃright sunlight streamed in through the windows, blinding Madeleine as she opened her eyes. She pulled the blanket over her face and yawned. She could hear birds chirping outside and squirrels busily chattering along with the gently rustling leaves and creaking branches stirred by a soft breeze. They were such lovely sounds, she thought drowsily. She loved summer mornings . . .

Summer mornings! Suddenly Madeleine threw back the blanket and sat up, squinting against the brightness.

"God's wounds, girl, ye've slept the whole night away," she said to herself, exasperated. Obviously yesterday's excitement had proved too much for her. She cast the blanket aside in disgust and rose from the bed.

She was stiff and sore from sleeping at such an awkward angle, crosswise, with her legs curled up beneath her, and she winced painfully. She stood on tiptoe and stretched her arms high above her head, then dropped them to her sides. She took a few steps, almost tripping because her skirt and her linen petticoat were tangled about her legs.

She shook the material out vigorously. Her gaze darted to the porcelain clock on the mantelpiece, one of her few belongings that had escaped the soldiers. It was quarter past eleven.

Madeleine sighed heavily, furious with herself. So

much for giving her kinsmen advance warning and alerting them to their new danger, she thought bitterly. By now they would have heard from someone else that English soldiers were billeted at Mhor Manor. News traveled fast in Strathherrick, especially when it had anything to do with redcoats.

Well, there was nothing to be done about it now. She would have to wait until later that afternoon to tell them her decision. She had a christening to attend first. She had promised Flora she would be there, and she never broke a promise.

She opened her wardrobe, her hand drifting across the small collection of better gowns hanging to the left side of her everyday wear. Her fingers lovingly caressed the three gowns she had inherited from her mother, gowns of silk, point lace, and satin, with quilted brocade underskirts.

Lady Jean Fraser had worn them long ago, during trips with her husband to Edinburgh and Glasgow. She had been a well-educated woman, fond of the theater and opera, and Sir Hugh had lovingly indulged her cultured tastes and love of finery. She had just begun to instill such interests in Madeleine when she died so tragically, bitten by a venomous adder while picking brambles in the woods.

Sir Hugh never went to the theater again, and he traveled very little. When Madeleine asked him once if they could journey to Edinburgh to see a Shakespearean play, he had quietly refused her. Even as a young girl, she sensed such diversions were simply too painful for him, evoking memories of happier days. She had never asked again.

Madeleine absently smoothed a satin flounce. The gowns were still considered fashionable thirteen years later, at least in the Highlands, though she didn't care one whit about fashion. It merely pleased her that they fit her so well and had belonged to her mother. Occasionally she would try them on in secret and whirl in front of the oval full-length mirror, the shimmering fabrics bringing hazy recollections of the beautiful, chestnut-haired woman who had once worn them.

Her hand skimmed over her other gowns. Simpler in design and fabric, they had been made especially for her by an accomplished seamstress in the village and were reserved for special occasions. She smiled. Today was such an occasion.

Madeleine chose a gown of printed linen, admiring the delicate pattern as she lifted it from the wardrobe. It was very pretty, with lilac stripes on a cream background and sprigs of rose, lemon-yellow, and green. She laid it out carefully on the bed so as not to wrinkle it, then began to strip off her drab gray dress.

A sharp knock on the door startled her, and she immediately thought of Garrett. Her heart began to pound. If he had come to ask her to have luncheon with him . . .

"Who's there?" she called, rushing to the wardrobe. She grabbed a white cambric robe and whirled it around her shoulders.

"Glenis, lass," her servant called through the door. "Ye've slept so late I thought I should wake ye. I dinna want ye to miss the christening."

Madeleine unlocked the door and pulled it open. She was relieved, yet she felt an odd twinge of disappointment. She shrugged it off. "Ye're just in time to help me into this gown, Glenis. I fear 'tis one time I'll not be able to get by without those blasted stays."

Glenis's furrowed face broke into a smile, and she chuckled as she set a tall pitcher filled with warm water on the washstand. She turned to the armoire and pulled out the top drawer. "So ye'll be dressin' like the true lady ye are, eh, Maddie?" she teased, filling her arms with linen underclothes and a starched petticoat. She plopped them on the bed. "Well, let's be at it."

After Madeleine quickly bathed, she drew on the lace-edged chemise and drawers, then held firmly to the bedpost as Glenis laced her stays with an astounding vigor that belied her advancing age. "Ye'll strangle me for sure if ye pull any tighter," she protested. "I can hardly breathe."

" 'Tis the proper way," Glenis replied, smiling her approval as she tied the starched petticoat around Madeleine's narrow waist. "No wider than a man's two hands may span it."

Madeleine rolled her eyes at that statement but said nothing. She would not spoil Glenis's enjoyment. She slipped into the gown, adjusted the square-cut bodice which was a bit low for her taste, then finally drew on her best pair of brogues. She quickly undid her braid, brushing her hair until it shone, and secured it with two silver combs.

"Ye look lovely, Maddie!" Glenis exclaimed. "I wish I could see ye like this more often. Ye're as pretty as a picture."

" 'Tis not practical, and ye well know it," Madeleine objected mildly. "Not with what I'm about."

Glenis's smile faded. Her voice fell to a whisper. "How did it go last night, lass? What have ye and yer men decided?"

"I dinna make it to Farraline," she said dryly. "I fell asleep, and only awoke a short while ago." She ignored Glenis's pleased expression. "I'll be seeing the men later."

" 'Tis just as well, lass," Glenis said. "Ye needed the rest. And there was a fierce storm last night, with the wildest thunder and lightning."

"I dinna hear it," Madeleine said. It seemed the house could have come down about her ears and she wouldn't have known it, she thought with annoyance.

"Och, 'twas bad. I couldna sleep for the racket. 'Tis glad I am ye were safe in yer bed, though I wished I'd known it at the time. I wouldna have prayed so hard!"

Madeleine could not help laughing. "Come on, Glenis, let's go downstairs. I'll have to grab a wee bite of something, then be on my way if I'm to make it to the church by one o'clock. I left the cart at Flora's, and I canna ride in this dress, so I'll have to walk."

She stopped midway to the door and glanced at

Glenis. "Are the soldiers about this morning?" she
asked. She had no wish to run into Garrett. If he was
somewhere in the house, she would attempt to avoid
him altogether.

"Only a few," Glenis replied, frowning. "The rest
set out for God knows where just after dawn. One of
the sly foxes must have stolen the scones I baked. They
were gone from the table when I went into my
kitchen."

Madeleine cursed under her breath, but not for the
missing scones. She had a strong suspicion Garrett and
his men had set out to survey the valley, perhaps
searching for any clues as to the whereabouts of the
outlaw he was seeking.

It was just as well, she decided. If he was snooping
about the valley, then he wouldn't be minding what
she was doing. That was fine with her!

The sun was blazing high in the sky when Madeleine
stepped from the small stone church, cradling the
sleeping infant in her arms. She held up her hand,
shielding the tiny, pink face from the warm sunshine
while Flora put a frilly lace cap over her daughter's
head.

"Well, Mary Rose Chrystie, ye're baptized fine and
proper now," Madeleine said and tenderly kissed the
babe's cheek.

"Aye, she did well," Flora said with a smile. "Not
a peep out of her, not even a burp to startle the minister."

Madeleine smiled as she gently handed the child to
Flora. She looked down the narrow street to where
Flora's three boys were playing with several other children. Their shrieks of laughter and boisterous shouting
rent the air.

"Mary Rose winna sleep for long with that din," she
said, chuckling, "but I wouldna think of quieting them.
'Tis like music to hear them laugh so."

Flora nodded, rocking the baby in her arms. "Would

ye join us for luncheon, Maddie? I've made a fine
roast.''

Madeleine shook her head, her expression apolo-
getic. ''I canna, Flora, but thank ye for asking. I must
see to some business with Angus Ramsay. With those
redcoats stationed at Mhor Manor, the men in the village must know what I've been able to glean from the
captain.''

''I understand,'' Flora said softly. ''Ye dinna have to
explain.'' She looked at Madeleine with concern. ''I'm
afraid for ye, Maddie. I talked to Kitty this morning,
and she's grateful ye thought of her welfare. But I have
the same fears for ye. All those soldiers sleeping under
yer roof. I've heard such terrible stories about what's
happened to so many women . . .'' She shuddered.

''Dinna worry, Flora,'' Madeleine tried to soothe her.
''Captain Marshall seems to be an honorable man,
more so than any other redcoat I've seen. He'll keep
his soldiers in line.''

She nearly bit her tongue in surprise. She'd never
said a kind word about any English soldier before. It
felt strange, but it was the truth. At least from what
she had seen of Garrett's manners so far. He had been
quite the gentleman since his arrival at Mhor Manor,
except for the incident in her father's room.

She flushed hotly, remembering the exciting feel of
his arms around her. She could not blame him entirely
for what had happened between them. It was her own
foolish curiosity that had brought her into the room in
the first place . . . stumbling into his arms as she did.

Flora looked startled, her cheeks spotting with vivid
color. Her tone grew harsh. ''I dinna know there was
such a thing as an honorable redcoat, Maddie. If so,
where were they at Culloden when my Neil fell
wounded?''

Embarrassed, Madeleine was unable to answer. She
had not meant to give the impression she was com-
mending Garrett.

''Forgive me,'' Flora said, seeing her discomfort. Her
voice softened, and she clasped Madeleine's arm.

"Sometimes the bitterness in me grows so strong, I canna fight it down."

" 'Tis no matter," Madeleine said quietly. "Come. I'll walk with ye to yer house."

She and Flora strolled down the main street, avoiding the puddles still remaining from last night's storm. Their conversation was purposely light; they chatted and laughed about the boys' latest antics. No more was said about English soldiers. Finally they reached Flora's front door.

"Into the house with ye, lads. 'Tis time for dinner," Flora called, laughing as her hungry brood brushed past her. She smiled warmly. "Thank ye for standing up for Mary Rose, Maddie. Having ye for her godmother means a great deal to me." She stepped over the threshold, then added gently, "I hope ye're right about the captain. If 'twas me, I wouldna trust him as far as I could see."

"Ye need have no fear of that," Madeleine replied. "It'll never be said in Strathherrick that I trust an Englishman."

She waved goodbye and walked briskly down the side street, holding her skirt high above the mud. In a few moments she was standing in front of Angus Ramsay's cottage, which sat at the north end of the village back near the church. She rapped firmly on the door.

" 'Tis Maddie," she said as the door swung open. To her surprise Angus took her arm and roughly yanked her inside.

"What are ye doing?" she cried, rubbing her elbow.

Angus merely pointed out the window, his thick graying brows knit anxiously. She followed his gaze to a large group of redcoats on horseback, just now turning onto the main street.

Her eyes widened as she spied Garrett at the lead on his massive bay. He looked so at ease and sure of himself in the saddle. She felt an inexplicable rush in her stomach, but quickly attributed it to hunger pains.

"Och, lass, I'm sorry if I hurt ye," Angus apologized. "I dinna think 'twould be a good idea for ye to be seen by them, that's all."

Madeleine almost laughed out loud. "Angus, they're living in my house! 'Tis why I've come to talk to ye. Dinna ye suppose they already know who I am?"

"I meant yer coming in here, Maddie. Captain Marshall—"

"How do ye know his name?" Madeleine asked, sobering.

"That's what I'm trying to tell ye. He was in the village earlier this morning and stopped to wish me a good day, of all things! I recognized him from the raid last week. He said I had a fine Scottish burr . . . the devil take him! I think he recognized my voice!"

Madeleine paled, though she tried to think rationally. "No, 'tis not possible, Angus. Ye're jumping to conclusions. Ye hardly spoke a word that night, except for a few short commands. 'Twas Kenneth who did most of the talking, as always. Besides, I'm the mistress of Farraline, and well Captain Marshall knows it. 'Tis my right to visit anyone I please."

Angus seemed not to have heard her. He moved from window to window, not taking his eyes from the soldiers until they had ridden through the village. When they were gone, he turned to her at last, his usually ruddy face ashen and his features drawn.

"I dinna like the looks of this, Maddie," he said, sinking into a chair.

Madeleine sat down beside him. "If ye dinna like the looks of the soldiers, ye winna like what I have to tell ye, either."

Angus shot her a puzzled glance. "What do ye mean?"

She shook her head firmly. "Ewen and Duncan must be here, too. This is a decision we must make together." She felt a rush of pity. She had never seen the stoic widower so shaken. "Perhaps ye'd feel better after a dram of whiskey, Angus."

"Aye, now there's a good idea," he agreed, brightening somewhat, his normal color gradually returning.

"A wee dram of the water of life to help an old Scotsman think more clearly." He reached behind him and took a tall glass decanter from the rough-hewn cupboard. "Would ye like a half?"

"Aye."

Angus poured them both a small glass of the clear, amber liquid, then set the decanter down in front of him. "To our Bonnie Prince Charlie!" he toasted, raising his glass.

"Prince Charlie!" Madeleine echoed. She followed Angus's suit and drained her glass in one swallow. It would have curled her toes if she had not been brought up on the stuff since childhood. The liquid still burned her throat like wildfire.

"Better?" she said, trying not to gasp.

"Aye." Angus poured himself another, downed it, then rose to his feet. "I'll fetch Ewen and Duncan." He put on his cap, then strode through the door, slamming it behind him.

The silence in the large, shadowed room was overwhelming. Madeleine fingered her glass while she waited, turning it around and around, rehearsing her words in her mind. She would have to be doubly persuasive because of what Angus had told her. She hoped her kinsmen would agree to continue their raids, whether Garrett had recognized Angus's voice or not.

Either that, she considered grimly, or she would have to go it alone. And she would, too! No one would recognize her voice. She had never said a word on any of their raids. She had nothing to fear.

Chapter 8

"So we're decided?" Madeleine asked, looking around the small table. "We'll continue the raids, soldiers or no?" Ewen and Duncan quickly nodded their assent while Angus stared thoughtfully at his folded hands.

"Angus?"

He glanced at her, his brow creased, his deep-set eyes mirroring his turmoil. "Aye, Maddie, I'll go along," he said reluctantly. "Though I think I'm more trouble to yer cause than I'm worth."

"Nonsense," she objected. "We need ye, Angus. I need ye. And Captain Marshall couldna know yer voice from a few simple ayes and mutterings about the weather." She rose from her chair. "Duncan, will ye see that Kenneth and Allan know what we've discussed today?"

"Aye."

"Good. I have no doubt they'll choose to ride with us. Ye might also ask after Kenneth's arm, Duncan. If he needs more healing salve, ye must let me know." She sighed. "I guess 'tis a good thing the Fraser brothers are hiding in the mountains. If Captain Marshall ever saw the scar from that knife wound, it would give Kenneth away for sure."

She walked to the door, then turned around, her somber gaze sweeping the little party. "If we're careful and dinna make any wrong moves, there'll be no trouble. Just be about yer business as before. In no time

those soldiers will leave Strathherrick, none the wiser."
She smiled faintly. "Until tomorrow, then. I'll meet
you at the old yew tree at midnight."

Madeleine closed the door on the low buzz of male
voices. She knew her kinsmen would probably share a
few drams of whiskey and no doubt discuss their next
planned raid on Wade's Road before they dispersed.
As for herself, two halves were quite enough. She felt
a bit dizzy. She set off through the village and then
down the winding road leading to Mhor Manor.

She was not surprised that the puddles dotting the
road earlier that afternoon had vanished altogether,
leaving the surface hard-packed and dry. The day was
unusually warm for the Highlands, and the hot sun
was relentless.

As she walked Madeleine could feel the sweat trick-
ling down her back and between her breasts. The heat
was so oppressive her breathing was becoming labored, and she cursed the constricting stays she wore.
She thought longingly of a cool sip of water and suddenly had an idea.

It had been well over a week since she'd gone swimming in Loch Conagleann at the foot of Beinn Bhuidhe.
The tiny loch was one of her favorite places, secluded,
peaceful, with a mountain-fed waterfall refreshing its
pristine depths. Aye, that was it. A swim was just what
she needed.

Madeleine quickened her pace, eager to be rid of her
thirst and her sweat-soaked clothing. She left the dusty
road behind her, opting for a footpath she had used
since childhood. It was the quickest way she knew to
the loch.

She almost shouted for joy when she finally reached
it. The clear aquamarine water seemed to beckon to
her. The calm surface stretched out before her like a
shimmering silver mirror in the bright sunlight, disturbed only by a plummeting waterfall at the northern-
most end. The tall fir trees rimming the shoreline
rustled with the barest breeze, fanning her flushed face.

She immediately kicked off her brogues and rolled

down her stockings, holding everything in one hand
as she tramped along the gently sloping banks looking
for a choice, shaded spot. The grass tickled her toes,
and she paused to pick a handful of bluebells and sweet
yellow primroses. She inhaled deeply, the delicate fragrance bringing a wide smile to her lips.

How odd, she thought. It felt as if she had not truly
smiled in years. She marveled that the simplest things
could bring such quiet joy, such serenity.

She strolled on. The stark eastern slopes of Beinn
Bhuidhe towered above her in stunning contrast to the
lush greenery surrounding the loch. The Fraser brothers were up there somewhere, in their remote mountain cave. That thought brought with it a rush of
sadness for their plight, though she knew they were
luckier than many. At least they still lived.

She breathed in the perfumed scent of her bouquet
once more, willing such melancholy thoughts from her
mind. She wanted to forget and enjoy herself, even if
it were only for a short time. She wanted no painful
memories, no responsibilities, no decisions to be made.
Just sparkling water, sunlight playing upon her skin,
and fresh mountain air.

At last she stopped beneath a spreading sycamore
tree, the low branches providing some mottled shade.
She dropped her shoes and stockings and set her wildflowers almost reverently atop a boulder that had tumbled from the mountain in an ancient landslide. Then
she turned her back to the loch and hastily began to
slip out of her gown.

She was standing in her chemise and linen drawers,
her fingers furiously working at the laces of her stays,
when a loud splash sounded from the north end of the
small loch near the waterfall. She gasped and whirled
around but saw nothing, only a ripple growing in ever
widening circles and gentle waves marring the mirror-
like surface.

What could it have been? she wondered. There were
fish in the loch, but hardly big enough to create such

a splash. Perhaps a rock had rolled down the steep hill
and into the water . . .

Suddenly a bronzed man shot up from the depths in
a glittering spray of sunlit droplets only twenty feet
away from her. Madeleine jumped back in surprise and
darted behind the large boulder. She cautiously peeked
out at the unwelcome intruder who was now standing
in waist-deep water.

The man's back was to her, powerful bands of muscle knotting across his broad shoulders as he raised his
arms and ran his hands through his wet blond hair.
Then he turned, and she glimpsed his face just before
he arched his body and dove cleanly beneath the surface. It was Garrett!

Madeleine sank to her knees, pounding her curled
fist on the craggy rock. So much for a quiet afternoon
of peaceful solitude. She should have guessed it
wouldn't take long for him to find her favorite place!
But why now, when she so wanted to be alone? At
least she could be thankful he hadn't seen her.

She rose to her feet once again and peered over the
top of the boulder. Garrett was swimming with forceful strokes toward the surging waterfall, his long legs
kicking vigorously. She watched as he disappeared beneath the thundering white cascade, and she felt a moment's fear.

Those rocks beneath the falls were sharp and jagged,
the currents unpredictable, the waters churning and
deep—a treacherous snare for even an accomplished
swimmer. Stories abounded of those who had lost their
lives in such waterfalls. Children were warned away
from them by the tale of a phantom water beast, the
uruisg, who was said to live in waterfalls and waited
hungrily for unwary swimmers.

So she had been warned as a child. Glenis had told
her the strange tale and she had never forgotten it,
though she no longer believed it. She had been thirteen when she had finally dared to swim beneath this
very waterfall, and she remembered the swirling cur-

rents trying to drag her down into the depths like cold, grasping fingers.

Madeleine held her breath, her heart pounding. Seconds passed, and still there was no sign of Garrett. What should she do? What could she do? Perhaps it was already too late . . .

Relief poured through her when she saw him hoist himself up onto a flat, overhanging rock near the base of the waterfall. She was stunned by her emotion.

He was an Englishman. A soldier. Why should she care if he lived or died? Was it because he was a quarter Scots? Or was it simply compassion for another human being . . . ?

He stood up tall and straight on the rock, and she drew her breath in sharply. Her confused thoughts fled her mind. He was naked . . . dripping wet and naked. His lean, tanned body was so beautiful, glistening and golden in the sun, that she could not tear her eyes away.

She watched in reluctant fascination, knowing she should not be staring, feeling like a naughty child caught at some prank. Her skin was tingling, a strangeness she had never felt before. She was breathless, her breasts heaving beneath her tightly laced stays.

She had seen near naked men before at many a Highland game when the contestants threw off their kilts in the heat of exertion and wrestled or tossed the caber in a meager loincloth. She had seen Dougald Fraser at such a game, his massive body muscled and strong, his powerful thighs the size of her waist. She had felt embarrassed, aye, and thrilled . . . but never like this.

Why had she not felt this before, during the raid? she wondered. She had seen Garrett and his men unclothed, tied up and lying defenseless on the ground. But it had been different then. They had been forced to strip. Was it because she had sensed their deep humiliation, their vulnerability before their enemies? Was that why she had walked into the dark woods, unable to watch?

Madeleine shivered. It was the whiskey, she thought dazedly. The whiskey and the hot sun had addled her brain. It seemed she had no sense of anything but the physical beauty of the man standing almost beneath the tumbling waterfall.

Her eyes roamed at will over his body, across his sculpted chest and the rugged span of his shoulders, down his flat stomach, tightly corded with muscle, to his slim hips and the dark triangle of curls below . . . God's wounds! Had she no shame?

He turned suddenly, poised to dive off the side of the rock. His long, sinewed legs braced, and his thighs and calves flexed creating a muscled indentation where his hips met his buttocks. Then he was gone, scarcely a ripple cutting the water where he disappeared.

Madeleine felt herself slowly sinking to the ground, and she rested her forehead on her hands. Why did she feel so faint all of a sudden? It had to be the whiskey, the heat, and her stays. Glenis had laced them far too tightly. She fumbled at her back trying to loosen the laces, but it seemed her fingers were so many thumbs. Her hands fell to her sides, and she slumped against the boulder.

Madeleine had no sense of how long she had lain there when she felt a sharp tug and heard a jagged tearing sound. All she knew was that one moment she could scarcely breathe, then the next she was free.

She gulped in great gasps of air, crying out as she was lifted by strong arms. She tilted her head back, her stunned gaze meeting a pair of smiling gray-green eyes.

"It has always been my belief that those garments should be considered instruments of torture and banned from public use," Garrett said easily, though his tone belied his concern.

He could not have been more surprised to find Madeleine crumpled behind the boulder. How long had she been there? He had thought he was alone at this jeweled loch. He had just finished dressing and was walking along the shore when he saw her lying there unconscious. He was relieved to see her color return swiftly, her skin blushing a becoming rose shade.

"I'm sorry about your stays, but I think you're better off without them. Especially on such a blistering hot day as this." He held her close against his chest as he carried her to the shoreline. "Would you like a sip of water?"

At Madeleine's quick nod he bent down on one knee and set her beside him on the grass, supporting her with his arm. He cupped his hands and dipped them into the water, then brought them to her lips. She drank thirstily, unaware that most of the water was running down her chin and throat, soaking her filmy white chemise.

Once more he brought cool water to her mouth until she pushed away from him and bent over the loch. She splashed her face and throat, then cupped her hand again and again until her thirst was sated. At last she sat back on her heels, a half smile on her lips as she swept back her damp hair.

"I thank ye," Madeleine murmured hesitantly and shrugged. "I dinna know what happened. I think 'twas the heat . . ." Her voice trailed off, and she looked out over the shimmering loch, embarrassed.

Garrett swallowed hard. His eyes were not on the loch. He stared at her full breasts . . . high and rounded, perfect. The pink nipples pushed tautly against her drenched chemise, the fabric like transparent gauze upon her skin.

A streak of fire shot through his body, a streak of blazing hunger. How he longed to reach out and cradle a tempting mound, to circle a teasing nub with his thumb, ever so slowly, to feel its hardness and taste its sweetness . . . She was so close to him, he could feel the heat of her body, could smell the heady scent of her skin, her hair, warmed by the sun.

It happened before he realized what he was doing. He rose to his knees, trancelike, and reached out for her. He crushed her to him, his mouth capturing hers. He heard a roaring in his ears as the blood pumped wildly through his veins, and his fingers caressed a firm breast that seemed to leap into his hand.

Madeleine's heart jumped to her throat. Suddenly she was dizzy all over again, her body trembling and quaking, held captive by his overwhelming embrace. She did not think of fighting him. Sweet, aching sensation drove all thought of escape from her mind.

Fragmented pictures flashed through her awareness: Garrett standing in the middle of the camp, his hair like spun gold in the firelight; Garrett bending over the wash basin, sleek and muscular; Garrett beneath the waterfall, his powerful golden-bronze body wet and gleaming.

The pictures quivered and faded, as all her feelings, and all her perception centered on the wonder of his kiss. His lips were both rough and gentle as his tongue demanded entrance and filled her mouth, relentlessly searching. She felt as if she were drowning, the world falling away beneath her. She wanted more, she wanted . . .

"Madeleine," Garrett whispered huskily, his loins throbbing with desire. He pulled away and kissed her flushed cheeks, her eyelids, and her lustrous sable lashes. His fingers were twined in her hair. "Sweet, beautiful Maddie, lie down with me . . . now, here."

At the sound of her name, Madeleine's eyes snapped open as if a knife had stabbed her flesh. The sunlight blinded her, forcing into full consciousness.

God in heaven, what was she doing? Had she gone mad? He was an Englishman, a redcoat! She shoved him so hard he lost his balance and fell sideways, right into the loch. The cold water splashed her in the face, like a chilling slap. She reached down and grabbed for her dirk, but the leather sheath strapped to her thigh was empty.

"I believe this is what you're looking for," Garrett said wryly, sprawled in the shallow water. He pulled the dirk halfway from his boot, the silver hilt flashing in the sun. "Before I removed your corset, I thought it best to confiscate your weapon." He laughed shortly.

"Just in case you might object to my offer of assistance."

"Ye son of a whore!" Madeleine hissed, her eyes narrowed. "Give it to me."

He merely shook his head in answer. He looked at her steadily, his lips drawn into a tight line.

She wiped her mouth, then spat upon the ground. "That's what I think of ye and yer kind assistance. Dinna come near me again, Captain Marshall, or I swear ye'll regret it!"

She wheeled around, nearly stumbling, and hurried over to the boulder, where she quickly donned her petticoat and gown. All the while she kept her eyes on Garrett, who hadn't moved an inch. Finally she grabbed her shoes and stockings, shoving them under one arm, and swept her tattered stays from the ground.

"And I'll tell ye something else, Captain Marshall," she said hotly, stamping a bare foot. "If ye pride yerself on yer kisses, ye might know this: I've had better!"

She held up her skirt and set off running along the shore. Although she did not once look back, she could feel him watching her.

She had lied. Dougald had kissed her before, but it had never been like this. Never. Her skin was still ablaze from his caresses, and her lips were on fire. His heat remained . . . a burning ache, a hint of rapture.

She ran as fast as her legs would carry her back to the manor house, as if she could escape the haunting memory.

Madeleine did not see Garrett the rest of the day. When she went to bed that night, she found a bedraggled posy of bluebells and primroses on her pillow, along with a folded note and her dirk.

What manner of man was he? she wondered. She sat on her bed for a long time before she read the note. Her fingers were shaking as she opened it, and her eyes quickly scanned the bold, masculine script:

"Mistress Madeleine Fraser, please accept my humble apologies for my ungentlemanly behavior this afternoon. Respectfully, Garrett.''

At the bottom of the crisp paper, a hastily scrawled line was added: ''I have never known a kiss such as yours.''

Madeleine unconsciously ran her fingertip over the line while she reread it. *I have never known a kiss such as yours . . .*

Shivering, she crumpled the note and threw it at the wall, climbed into bed, and blew out the candle.

Chapter 9

$\sim$ ◯◯◯ $\sim$

It was early in the morning and still Garrett could
not sleep. Angry at himself, he had been staring at
the ceiling for hours, watching the shadows dance on
the plaster and listening to the howling wind.

What had come over him at the loch? What had become of his resolve to be patient? The questions echoed
over and over in his mind, like a taunt, even as he
knew their answers.

He had wanted Madeleine Fraser more than he had
ever wanted any woman. He wanted her even now,
and he was astounded by the strength of his feelings.
How had this woman so bewitched him in so short a
time? It seemed that whenever he thought of her, or
was near her, he lost all control.

Garrett felt like laughing out loud at the absurdity
and the sheer hopelessness of his rampant desire. She
would never have anything to do with him, not after
what he had done. She would probably never trust
him. He could only hope his short note and the return
of her dirk had soothed her temper.

He didn't exactly like the idea that she carried such
a weapon, and it violated English law. But when he
saw the fine engraving on the hilt, he knew he had to
give it back to her. It was a gift from her father. She
had lost enough already. He would just have to watch
his step in case she chose to reward his generosity by
a stab in the back!

Garrett rolled onto his side and tucked the pillow

98

under his head. He wondered what she had thought
of the last line of his note, or if she had even read it.
He had debated whether to write it, but then had
thrown caution to the wind. It was true. He had never
known such a kiss . . . It was all sweetness and fire,
proving an inner passion as wild and tempestuous as
her spirit.

He felt a sudden pang of jealousy. Were her words
true as well? He would be a fool to think such a beauty
had never been kissed before. Perhaps she already
loved a man, had lain with a man . . .

Enough! Garrett thought silently, closing his eyes in
frustration. He had to get some sleep! In only a few
hours he and his men would resume their search of
the valley for any signs of Black Jack.

If they were as unsuccessful as they had been yesterday, he would have to begin questioning the villagers, but without giving away his mission. He held no
illusions that the wary Highlanders would offer much
information, but perhaps a mistaken word or an expression might give him a clue, something to scent the
trail.

Colonel Wolfe had made it clear to him that he didn't
have a lot of time before General Hawley would take
matters into his own hands. He certainly couldn't afford to wait and risk his entire mission because of one
woman. After what had happened at the loch, he
doubted Madeleine would give him the time of day, let
alone come to his bed and regale him with secrets. He
must have been crazy to think it was ever a possibility.

Garrett sighed heavily and tossed onto his other side.
It seemed that sleep was determined to elude him tonight. All he could think of was Madeleine. Her lips
were so red, so warm, and her breasts were so soft.
Her lithe body had felt so good pressed against his
own. God, he would surely go mad!

He forced the provocative image from his mind and
willed himself to think calmly, rationally. Obviously he
wasn't ready to give up on his original plan, no matter
how farfetched.

He would proceed with his search of the valley, yet he would also continue to try to win Madeleine's trust. He was certain she might be able to help him. She was mistress of Farraline and a leader to the people of Strathherrick. Surely she knew something that might lead him to Black Jack.

Garrett threw one arm over his head and shut his eyes once more. An unsettling question nagged at him. Did he want to win Madeleine's trust purely for the sake of his mission, or was there another, more selfish reason?

If he knew the answer, he wasn't admitting it even to himself. Not yet.

Garrett awoke three hours later to the sun slashing through the windows and across the bed. He groaned, flinging his arm over his eyes. He felt as if he hadn't slept at all.

A firm knock on the door rattled his senses still further.

"Who is it?" he shouted irritably.

"Sergeant Fletcher. The men are up and ready to ride, sir," a brisk voice intoned through the door.

"Very good, Fletcher. I'll be right down." Garrett threw back the covers resignedly and rose from the bed.

He rubbed his shoulder, which he had bruised on a jagged rock beneath the waterfall. He should have known better. He dressed quickly, ignoring the persistent ache, his mind already on the day ahead. He left his chamber and walked out into the silent hallway.

His gaze instinctively flew to Madeleine's closed door, but he turned the other way and headed downstairs. He stopped abruptly at the landing when he heard a woman's voice just outside the front door. It sounded like Meg, the young maidservant Glenis had introduced him to yesterday. Surprisingly she was the only other help in this huge house.

"Please let me go, sir. I've told ye, I dinna need yer help with my basket. 'Tis empty, see for yerself. Now I must be on my way. Glenis is expecting me."

"What's your hurry, chit?" a deep male voice groused unpleasantly. "That old goose can wait. Walk with me into the orchard, like I've asked you, nice and proper. We'll pick some apples, eh, what do you think about that? Then we'll spread your apron on the ground and sample a few."

Garrett bristled as he recognizing the soldier's voice. Damn that Rob Tyler! If there was any man in his company born to make trouble, it was that one. He'd been a thief before buying a commission in the army to save his neck from the hangman's noose. Garrett had only brought him along because Tyler was an expert marksman. He strode to the door.

"I winna ask ye again, sir . . . Och, what do ye think ye're doing?" There were sounds of a scuffle, a frightened gasp as something ripped, then a resounding slap.

"Don't think to cuff me again, wench, or I'll—"

"You'll what, soldier?" Garrett exploded, wrenching the door open so fiercely it slammed against the wall and nearly fell from its hinges.

"Captain Marshall!" Rob blurted out. He jumped away from a sobbing Meg, who was clutching her torn bodice.

The plump blond maidservant tried to skitter through the door, but Garrett gently caught her arm. She looked up at him in complete terror, tears staining her reddened face.

"I heard everything, Meg," Garrett said quietly, hurt by her expression. "You needn't worry. The man will be punished, and he won't bother you again. You have my word."

She looked startled, then nodded gratefully and disappeared through the door.

"Wh-what do you mean, captain?" Rob stammered, backing up a few steps. He was large man, nearly as tall as Garrett, but his stance revealed his apprehension. "I didn't do anything." He shoved his hand into his scarlet coat and pulled out a tarnished pocket watch. "See this? She tried to steal it from me. Had it in her basket. When I tried to grab it from her, the basket caught on her dress—"

"Shut up," Garrett cut him off, his voice barely above a whisper. "Do you think I'm blind, man? Or stupid?" He scarcely turned his head as Sergeant Fletcher rushed up beside him.

"Is anything amiss, captain?"

"See that this man is given ten lashes, sergeant, then set him on his horse. When we return this evening, shackle him and put him under guard. Is that clear?"

"Yes, sir."

"And warn the other men as well. If any of them so much as looks cross-eyed at the women of this house, or any women in this valley for that matter, they'll suffer the same fate and worse."

"But—but Captain Marshall, they're only stinkin', whorin' Highlanders," Rob pleaded, sweat running down his unshaven face.

"Get this scum out of my sight," Garrett said, his fists clenching. One more word out of the lying bastard, he thought furiously, and he'd strike him down. He should have done so already.

Sergeant Fletcher obeyed him at once. He pulled out his pistol and aimed it at the offender's chest. "Move, soldier. Now."

Rob shot a surly glance at Garrett and began to saunter down the flagged path with Sergeant Fletcher at his heels. He walked faster when the sergeant roughly stuck the butt of the pistol in his back.

Garrett's face was grim as he stepped back into the house and headed directly for the kitchen. He found Meg sitting at the table, still sobbing while Glenis patted her shoulder.

If they heard him come in, they did not turn around. He stood there uncomfortably. Women's tears had always confounded him. He cleared his throat and stepped forward, feeling awkward. Both women were staring at him now.

"I want to apologize, Meg, for my soldier's behavior," he said, glancing out the window as a man's loud scream sounded from somewhere near the cooking tent.

He heard the zinging of the lash, followed by another cry, a wail of pain that reminded him of a wounded animal. He raised his voice. "You needn't fear it will happen again. I've seen to that."

Meg flinched in her chair as another scream rang through the air. Her face was ashen. "Th—thank ye, sir," she barely managed, covering her ears.

Glenis moved toward him. "Aye, thank ye, Captain Marshall. I'm well past my prime, as ye can plainly see, and I need Meg's help here. I dinna want to worry for her every time my back is turned, what with yer soldiers about the house."

Garrett nodded. For Meg's sake, he was thankful that the screams had finally stopped. It was a wretched thing to hear such misery, however well deserved. "Meg will be safe, Glenis. I promise."

"I believe ye, captain," Glenis said, then asked, "May I call ye Garrett?"

He smiled at her request and the unexpected warmth in her dark eyes. "Of course. I'd like that."

"Good. Well now, Garrett. I've baked some scones. Would ye like one or two for yer breakfast?" She rushed on before Garrett could reply. "Och, that reminds me. Did ye happen to sample some yesterday morn by chance?"

"Yes, now that I think of it. Rob Tyler . . . the man who's just been punished," he said dryly, "had a dozen or so and gave one to me. He said my cook had baked them special. They were quite good, actually, the best I've ever tasted. Cinnamon and—"

"Treacle," she finished for him matter-of-factly. "Aye, that's the ones. Then ye've tasted my cookin', Garrett. Yer soldier helped himself to my kitchen before ye rode out. Stole every last one of them, he did. Shall we agree one of the lashes was for the scones?"

Garrett wanted to throw back his head and laugh, but instead he shook his head solemnly. "Yes, I think that's fair. And I'd love to try a few more."

The old servant smiled faintly and moved to the hearth. "Meg, will ye pour the captain a cup of tea?"

"No, thank you, Glenis," Garrett said with regret. "I'll have to eat my breakfast in the saddle. Perhaps another morning."

She wrapped two fat scones in a white linen napkin. "Will ye be goin' far? I could pack ye a few extra."

Garrett wasn't fooled by her seemingly innocent question, a clever way of asking after his plans. It didn't bother him. His Scots grandmother had told him the Highlanders were a curious people by nature.

In fact, Glenis reminded him of his grandmother. Maybe that's why he felt such a fondness for this spry old woman, as if he had known her far longer than a few days.

"No, Glenis, not far," he replied. "Though I can't say when we'll be back." He smiled as he took the linen packet from her outstretched hand. "Could I ask a favor of you?"

Her expression became guarded, but her eyes remained kind. "Aye."

"Would you ask Madeleine—Mistress Fraser—if she might care to go for a ride with me tomorrow? I'd ask her myself, but as I said, I don't know when I'll be back today, and it might be late. There are some places I'd like to ask her about. She knows the valley so well, and its lore and history. Perhaps she might consider . . ." He stopped, feeling awkward again, almost like a schoolboy.

"Aye, I'll ask her for ye," Glenis said simply.

If she sensed his discomfort, she gave no notice of it. Meg was studying him strangely, though, and he decided it was time to take his leave.

"Thank you for the scones, Glenis," he said. He left through the kitchen door and walked to the front of the manor house, where his men were waiting for him. He mounted his bay gelding and glanced over at Rob Tyler.

The soldier was glaring at him, with his back hunched over and his coat thrown carefully over his shoulders. He lowered his head at Garrett's grim expression.

"Ride," Garrett ordered tersely. He and his men set out, leaving only a few soldiers behind to guard their supplies. Their horses' hooves kicked up a thick cloud of dust as they galloped down the drive and onto the road to Farraline.

Madeleine watched from the kitchen window until they had disappeared. She straightened and looked directly at Glenis.

"Since when have ye taken such a liking to the captain?" she asked. She had heard their exchange from the dining room where she had hidden, waiting for Garrett to leave. She had heard everything from the moment the front door had slammed against the wall, rudely waking her from her sleep. The entire scene between Garrett and his soldier had been played out as she stood at the top of the stairs, still wearing her nightdress.

" 'Tis not a liking, hinny," Glenis objected quietly. "A kindness, that was all. The captain stood up for Meg here. I'm grateful to him, and so ye should be."

"Aye, if he hadn't come along, Maddie," Meg agreed, her voice quivering, "I dinna like to think what might have happened to me." She shuddered visibly.

Madeleine fell silent and looked out the window. Aye, 'twas true, she thought. He had had one of his own men beaten for accosting Meg.

She had witnessed the punishment from her room, counting each stroke, wishing she were the one wielding the biting lash. She hadn't even blinked when the soldier was cut down from the post, his back striped and bleeding.

"Maddie, did ye hear what Garrett asked of me?" Glenis asked softly.

She did not turn from the window. "Aye."

Her reply did little to satisfy Glenis. "Well, will ye ride with him tomorrow or not? He seems to be a fair man, but I dinna like the thought of ye out alone with him.''

Madeleine did not answer but only shrugged, a faraway expression in her eyes.

Garrett Marshall was a most unusual man, for a redcoat. She didn't understand him in the least. Nor did she trust him.

Perhaps she should go riding with this Englishman and learn more about him, she decided. He was searching for her, wasn't he? Her gut instincts had told her as much.

If she knew more about him, perhaps she could use such knowledge to her advantage. He might think it strange that she would so readily accept, but he had apologized after all.

''Maddie?''

She smiled thoughtfully at her servant. ''We'll see, Glenis. We'll see.''

Chapter 10

It had been dark for several hours when Madeleine crept silently across her chamber to peer at the mantel clock. The porcelain face was just visible by the faint light of the moon shining through her windows.

It was quarter to eleven. Time to set out through the secret tunnel if she was to meet her kinsmen at the yew tree near the village of Errogie by midnight.

Dressed in her gray cotton gown and already wearing her sturdy black boots, she wrapped a tartan shawl around her head and shoulders, clutching it with one hand. Under her arm she carried the black clothes she wore during her raids in a tight roll. When she was sure she was ready, she tiptoed to the door and lifted the latch.

She grimaced as the door creaked ever so slightly. Holding her breath, she peered into the dark hallway and listened. She heard nothing. Garrett and his men had returned to Mhor Manor only two hours ago, but fortunately they had all retired at once.

At least she thought they had. Now that she was standing in the hallway, she could see a faint light shining under Garrett's door.

Wasn't it like him to still be awake, no doubt plotting his next move to capture his infamous outlaw. She turned and crossed the hallway, thankful for the carpeting which masked her movement, and stepped gingerly down the side stairs.

At the bottom she paused as her eyes adjusted to the

blackness. A dim light burned in the main hallway, and she heard snores from the guard stationed there. What would Garrett think if he knew his soldier was sleeping at his duty station? she wondered. Well, she didn't care. She had one less guard to worry about.

She walked cautiously into the drawing room and headed directly to the closet, dodging the small side tables placed near the brocade armchairs. She lifted the latch quietly and stepped inside the narrow enclosure, found the round peg, and pulled the door shut behind her.

Madeleine drew a deep breath, her heartbeat drumming loudly in her ears. She shivered with nervous excitement. She hadn't been in the tunnel since she was fourteen, when her father had showed it to her for the first time, though she had heard about it since childhood. She dropped to her hands and knees near the back wall and groped along the intricately planked floor.

Where was that notch? Her fingers ran along the cracks, searching, until she found one that was slightly wider than the others, just large enough for her fingertips. She pushed against the wood, which was springy to the touch.

Suddenly a thick wedge of planking popped up, leaving a space wide enough for her hands. She gritted her teeth and lifted the trap door until the iron hinges would go no further.

A wave of dank, musty air assaulted her nostrils, and she barely stopped herself from sneezing. Still in pitch darkness, she crouched and lowered one foot into the gaping hole.

Her foot caught immediately on a wooden ladder off to one side. She climbed down carefully, her hand grasping the wooden handle on the trap door while she descended into the tunnel. As the trap door settled back into place, years of dirt and dust rained down upon her. She sneezed loudly, once, twice, praying that no one could hear her down there.

The air was quite chilly, and Madeleine was glad she

had worn her shawl. She heard the sound of dripping water and tentatively reached out and touched one earthen wall. It was damp and spongy. She wrinkled her nose in distaste. Mold.

She drew out a candle stub and a small pewter tinderbox from her pocket. Kneeling, she deftly struck the flint and lit the candle. Instantly she was surrounded by soft yellow light, the wick sputtering and hissing. She gasped when she looked up.

The tunnel loomed ahead of her, melting into a black abyss beyond the flickering light of her candle. The wooden beams supporting the ceiling were draped with spiderwebs, reminding her of a crypt. She stood and wrapped her shawl more tightly around her, glancing up one last time to make sure the trap door was securely sealed.

Madeleine began to walk, slowly at first, but then faster. She had no wish to tarry in this spooky underground passage. She tried to imagine her ancestors rushing through the tunnel, but the countless spiderwebs distracted her. As soon as she swept one aside, another was tangled in her clothes, in her braided hair, even in her mouth.

She spat distastefully. God's wounds! She couldn't wait until she was free of this place. She began to run, her panting breaths echoing in front of her and behind her. She remembered enjoying this far more at fourteen, but her father had been with her then, holding her hand, talking reassuringly to her, and making her laugh so she wouldn't be frightened.

Madeleine thought she might scream by the time she reached the end of the tunnel. Disgustedly she swatted a fat brown spider from her shoulder. If it weren't for Garrett and his blasted redcoats, she thought, she would be going about her raids as before without having to resort to such drastic and repulsive measures.

At the end there was another trap door which was much heavier to lift than the other. She knew it was covered by six inches of sod above ground. She extinguished her candle, plunging the tunnel into darkness, and set it with the tinderbox in one corner. Then she scrambled up the ladder and heaved her shoulder against the trap door with every ounce of her strength.

Finally the trap door gave way and fell back against a tree trunk. She climbed out, ducking the low branches and swallowing great lungfuls of fresh, night air. She was grateful for the thick cover of fir trees, which hid her from view.

She glanced behind her at the manor house some forty yards away, glowing a pale white in the moonlight, then back to the yawning trap door. What an ordeal that had been, but she would have to repeat it again and again until the English soldiers left Strathherrick.

Och, if it benefited her people, then so be it, she consoled herself. That was worth every hardship. She closed the trap door, smoothed the grass-laden sod, and set off at a brisk walk toward Errogie, which was just over two miles away.

She could have asked her kinsmen to wait for her closer to Mhor Manor, but that would have been far too dangerous with the soldiers billeted there. It was better for her to meet them at the ancient yew tree where her clan had cut their badges for hundreds of years. Such a meeting place would surely bring them good luck.

Halfway there Madeleine changed clothes, which allowed her to quicken her pace. It was much easier to tramp upon the peaty, heather-strewn moors in trousers than in an unwieldy gown. The nights were cool in the Highlands, no matter how hot the day, and her heavy woolen jacket gave her extra warmth.

She ran the last distance because she didn't want to be late. She had instructed her kinsmen to wait no longer than fifteen minutes after midnight. If she didn't arrive by then, it meant the raid should be abandoned.

Night sounds surrounded her as she ran, adding a haunting quality to the starlit night. There wasn't even a hint of the fog which was so common in the Highlands.

She started as a hind barked nearby, alerting other red deer to her presence. Small animals—pine marten, voles, rabbits, and field mice—rustled and squeaked in the darkness. A peregrine falcon, startled from its perch, shrieked from a high treetop. She loved these wild sounds, the cries of the night.

She rounded the northern tip of Loch Mhor, stopping for the briefest moment to gaze breathlessly at the long stretch of water. A ribbon of moonlight streamed across the placid surface, melting into the inky black depths. It was so beautiful, and she found herself wishing she had someone to share such a bewitching sight with her. Unwittingly, she thought of Garrett . . .

She shivered, banishing him from her mind. What was coming over her? Her kinsmen were waiting for her and were no doubt wondering what was taking her so long. She set out once again, determined to think of nothing but the impending raid.

Madeleine raced over the last hill, holding on to her black cap. She spied the towering yew tree, but there was no sign of her kinsmen. Her heart knocked against her breast. She knew she wasn't late. Had something happened? She slowed to a furtive walk as she looked around.

"Maddie, over here!"

Relief poured through her at the sound of Ewen's voice. She looked to her right and smiled broadly as five familiar shapes materialized out of the blackness. Six horses followed behind them, the animals nickering softly.

"Ye had me worried for a moment," she whispered once she was in their midst. "Why dinna ye wait for me by the yew tree?"

"A small group of soldiers passed by here a half hour ago," Angus said, his gruff voice low and anxious. "Probably a few of the devil's lot searching for our prince. It seemed they were on their way north to Inverness, but we decided not to take any chances. We hid well back in those trees there, just over the rise."

He sighed heavily. " 'Tis a good thing ye came no sooner, Maddie.''

"Dinna fret over it," she said. "The danger is past. See, our yew has already brought us luck once this evening.''

"Aye, so it has," Angus agreed as the others nodded their heads. "Here are yer pistols, lass, all primed and ready.''

"Thank ye," she said, taking the two pistols from him and slipping them into her belt, which also held her dirk. She was glad Angus had convinced her to allow him to care for her weapons, especially now that redcoats were quartered in her house. These pistols were the last thing she wanted found in her possession.

Madeleine sensed her kinsmen's eagerness as they gathered close around her, waiting for her command. It matched her own.

"We'll ride to Wade's Road, as we planned, and settle in at the pine grove near Inverfarigaig," she said quietly. "Ye'll wait for my signal. If 'tis safe, we'll take the first supply train that comes along. Any questions?''

There were none.

"All right, then. We've had a week's rest and a few unwelcome surprises"—she paused, deciding not to mention Garrett's name—"since last we rode together. But we'll not think of that now. We'll think only of the villagers who need fresh meat for their cooking pots.''

They quickly mounted their horses and broke into a gallop along the narrow road to Inverfarigaig. As they passed the ancient yew tree, Madeleine veered her mount toward it. She reached up and yanked off a fresh sprig, sticking it into the pocket of her jacket.

Aye, now she was well protected. She caught up with her kinsmen and passed them, swiftly taking the lead.

* * *

Garrett lay staring at the ceiling, his head resting in his hands. It was the second night in a row he couldn't sleep.

He exhaled slowly. If this kept up, he'd be sleeping during the day when he was supposed to be about his mission, which might not even matter. After the miserable day he'd had, he was no closer to discovering anything about Black Jack than if he and his men hadn't gone out at all. The Highlanders of Strathherrick were as tight-lipped as they come when they were protecting one of their own.

He rolled over and reached for the gold pocket watch lying atop the bedside table. He held it up and squinted at it in the faint moonlight.

Damn! It was half past three already. He'd finished writing in his military journal and had gone to bed near midnight. He had spent almost four useless hours tossing and turning, all the while wondering how he was going to accomplish his mission and if he would ever hold Madeleine in his arms again.

Garrett threw the watch onto the table in disgust and leaned on his elbow. Well, he had a few choices. He could either remain here in bed and chase sleep for another hour, or he could perhaps get something to eat from Glenis's kitchen. He hoped she wouldn't mind his intrusion too much.

Or maybe he could take a walk outside, he thought. Some fresh air and exercise might help clear his mind and perhaps even make him drowsy.

He made a quick decision and flung back the covers. It took him only a moment to dress, then he was out the door and walking quietly down the dark hallway.

Suddenly he stopped and turned around slowly. Good God, what was possessing him? He walked back past his room and toward the other end of the hallway . . . toward Madeleine's room.

His hand touched the latch. He told himself he merely wanted to see that she was well. Yet he knew it was more than that.

He had the strongest desire to gaze on her beauty while she slept. He hadn't seen her since the afternoon at the loch, and he felt as if he were starving for a glimpse of her.

Garrett stepped into her room, leaving the door slightly ajar. It had flashed through his mind that she might awaken and take unkindly to his presence in her bedchamber. And she was armed, he thought dryly. He had seen to that. Better to leave the door open, in case he needed to exit quickly to escape her dirk.

He moved stealthily toward the bed as his eyes adjusted to the darkness. He could see a slender form outlined beneath the coverlet. He forced himself to breathe slowly and steadily, although his heart was pounding. He reached out and touched his fingers lightly on the folded edge of the coverlet.

A strong gust of wind suddenly blew into the room from the open window, billowing the long gauze curtains. They flapped and twisted in the breeze, and Garrett backed away, fearing she would wake and find him there. He glanced at the bed regretfully and quickly left the room, closing the door softly behind him. He did not notice that he had failed to secure the latch, and the door slipped open again.

Somewhat shaken, he strode down the hallway to the main staircase. Obviously he would have to wait until tomorrow to see her again, which was probably just as well. If she had found him in her room her curses would no doubt have awakened the entire household. Her language seemed to become inspired whenever she saw him.

Garrett hurried down the steps, his eyes narrowing angrily. Heaven help him, were his men becoming as careless and undisciplined as they seemed? The guard was sleeping so soundly, with his chair tilted against the wall and his mouth gaping open, that he didn't even hear Garrett's approach.

Garrett kicked one of the chair legs as he walked by, and the chair fell forward. The soldier sprawled onto the floor, groaning and mumbling incoherently.

"Is this how you hold your position, man?" Garrett asked, his expression hard. He slid the knife from his belt, bent over the gaping soldier and grabbed him by the hair. He rested the sharp blade under the man's right ear.

"Don't you realize a Highlander could sneak in without a moment's warning and slit your sorry throat?" He traced the cold tip along the soldier's neck from ear to ear to drive home his message. The man was so terrified he couldn't speak. He only nodded, swallowing furiously.

"Get up," Garrett said sternly, withdrawing his knife and sheathing it. The soldier jumped to his feet, swaying slightly. It was obvious his knees were shaking. "I'm going out for a walk. See that you're awake when I get back."

"Y-yes, sir. Yes, sir!"

Garrett opened the door and strode outside. The three soldiers patrolling the drive stopped and snapped to attention. He was glad to see at least they had not deserted their posts.

"Good evening, Captain Marshall . . . er . . . I mean good morning," one of the soldiers offered.

Garrett acknowledged the greeting with a short nod. "I take it everything has been quiet tonight."

"Yes, captain."

"Good. Carry on." He walked away from them, aware that they were wondering what he was doing up so early in the morning. He shrugged it off. It was good to keep them on their toes.

He hiked down the drive and onto the road to Farraline for a good distance, then doubled back the other way. He knew he'd made the right choice. The cool night air was working like a tonic on his senses, drawing everything into sharp focus and clearing his mind.

Garrett stopped and stared up at the black sky, sprinkled with thousands of winking stars. The moon hung like a pale white crescent just over the mountains.

His gaze fell on the great, hulking shadows soaring directly in front of him. Somewhere in those craggy

hills and hollows dwelled the man he was seeking, he
was sure of it.

"Where are you, Black Jack?" Garrett said softly, his
words lost on the sighing breeze. "Dammit, where are
you?"

He turned and began to walk in a wide arc around
the manor house, his boots sinking into the spongy
moor. The fir trees were thick here, tall, ancient trees
that had withstood many a Highland winter. He ram-
bled on, content to be outside amid such rugged
beauty. He drew in great breaths of the bracing air,
slapping his arms vigorously. Perhaps he should have
worn his coat—

"What the devil?" he exclaimed suddenly, crouching on his haunches. Had he just imagined it . . . or
was someone creeping across the moor?

Garrett held himself completely still with his senses
alert and his body poised for action. He watched and
listened.

Yes, there it was again! His keen eyes followed a
lone figure who was stealing like a silent cat across a
stretch of barren moor. Then the shadowy form disappeared into a copse of fir trees, the branches swallowing him up and covering his flight.

Garrett could not believe it. A black-clad figure in the
dark night. Could it possibly be . . .

He didn't dare to hope. There was no time for
thought, only action. He sprinted toward the trees, his
heart racing, his eyes searching for any sign of movement.

Garrett fell to the ground as the figure darted out
again only thirty feet away from him. His fingers
groped for his knife, and he pulled it out, clutching it
in one hand. He jumped up and bolted after the fleeing
form.

Garrett cursed under his breath as the figure dashed
into another copse of trees just ahead of him, no more
than ten feet away. He did not slow down. He was so
close, and he had to catch the bastard!

His lungs were on fire and his thighs were pumping

hard, but his footfalls made little sound. He headed straight for the trees, knocking the branches out of the way as he plunged into the wooded grove. The figure was only an arm's length away now.

Garrett reached out and lunged, catching a handful of thick fabric. He yanked hard, and the figure fell in front of him, tripping him.

Garrett lurched forward, the momentum of his body toppling him over and over as he rolled on the ground. He hit the tree trunk so hard it knocked the breath from his body. He lay there on his stomach, stunned, his mouth full of dirt.

Then he felt a heavy branch striking him on the side of the head. He yelled out in pain, saw blinding streaks of light bursting in front of his eyes, then nothing . . .

Madeleine dropped the branch and stepped back, her chest heaving furiously. She massaged her aching shoulder, which she had bruised in her fall.

Damn, just when everything had gone so smoothly, this had to happen. The soldier's cry still rang in her ears, still echoed about the fir grove. She had to get out of there fast, in case any guards had also heard his cry.

She didn't bother to turn the soldier over to see if he was still breathing. There was no time, and she would discover soon enough if he lived or died.

She found the bundle of clothing she had dropped when she was tackled and ran swiftly toward the center of the grove where the tallest fir tree stood. She stooped under the low-lying branches, sifting her hands through the tall grasses for the loose square of sod. She found the concealed trap door and lifted it. Taking one last deep breath of fresh air, she clambered down the ladder, pulling the door down over her.

Again she was showered by dirt and debris. She coughed and wheezed, fumbling in the dark for the candle and tinderbox. She hurriedly lit the candle, her fear easing as golden light flooded her end of the tunnel. She dripped some wax on one of the rungs and twisted the candle into it.

Madeleine shook out the bundle of her gown and shawl and quickly changed out of her black garb.

At least she would be wearing proper clothes if she were caught in the drawing room. She could easily explain that she had been awakened by the cry in the woods and had dashed down the stairs to find out what had happened. If they found her near the closet, or even inside it, she could say she was looking for lamp oil. The closet was stocked with oil, candles, and many other household items.

She wrapped the shawl around her shoulders, broke off the candle, and hurried through the tunnel. The shadowed passage didn't bother her as much this time. Her mind was too preoccupied, and her thoughts were spinning.

She had never had such a close call before. That soldier, whoever he was, had almost caught her. She had only heard him running up behind her at the last moment, right before he grabbed her jacket. Thankfully he had stumbled over her and rolled away, instead of coming down on top of her. Otherwise she might never have escaped.

Madeleine fingered the sprig of yew tucked in the bodice of her gown. Once again it had granted her good fortune. She swore that from that moment on she would never go out on a raid without her clan badge.

She reached the other end of the tunnel and doused the light, threw her black clothes in a corner, then climbed the ladder and fumbled for the wooden handle. The trap door practically flew open on its hinges. She crawled out, heaving a great sigh of relief. From what she could hear inside the closet, the house was quiet.

Madeleine rose to her feet and shut the trap door firmly. Until next time, she thought, straightening her gown and smoothing the top of her hair. She pushed open the closet door and stepped into the drawing room, holding her breath. The soldier in the hallway was awake. She could hear him pacing. She was tiptoeing toward the side stairs when the front door suddenly crashed open and a soldier yelled, "It's Captain Marshall. He's been hurt!"

Madeleine gasped. Garrett—hurt? Dear God, he had been the one who had grabbed her in the fir grove!

There was instant commotion in the hallway; men's voices, raised and shouting, a chair scraping out of the way, and then from the right wing of the house, the sounds of running feet and more shouts.

Madeleine flew up the stairs, heading straight for her room. She stared wide-eyed at her door, stunned that it was open. She thought back uneasily. She had left the door closed, hadn't she? Yes, she had, she could swear it. Someone must have been in her room while she was gone.

She felt sick, her stomach lurching. She closed the door and bolted it from the inside. As she quickly lit the candle on the table by her bed, her gaze swept the room. Everything was the same as she had left it. She looked at her bed. The coverlet was still pulled over the two pillows she had heaped beneath the sheets, and it lay undisturbed.

A sudden breeze blew in the window, stirring the curtains. Maybe it had been the wind, she reasoned, watching the embroidered gauze billow and curl. The breeze could have been strong enough to force open the door if she hadn't latched it properly.

Madeleine started as footsteps and anxious voices sounded down the hall, Sergeant Fletcher's voice booming above the rest.

"Easy now, lads, that's it. Let's get him into the room and lay him down on the bed. Watch it, you fool! Good, now hold his shoulders fast while we get him through the door . . ." His voice trailed off as the men moved into her father's room.

Exhausted and spent, Madeleine sank down on the edge of the bed, twisting her hands nervously.

It was so dark in those woods, it had been virtually impossible to make out the identity of the soldier who had attacked her. And even if she had known it was

Garrett she doubted she would have done anything differently. Her survival had been at stake. Hers and the people she served. If she had been caught, everything would have been lost.

Yet even as she reasoned with herself, she felt a poignant pain, a tumble of mixed emotions that both confused and angered her.

How badly was he hurt? She hadn't hit him that hard, or had she? What if he should die?

She felt another stab of pain. What was the matter with her? She didn't care in the least if he lived or died. He meant nothing to her, absolutely nothing. He was a murdering and lying redcoat.

Yet she knew that was not the truth. Garrett Marshall was a redcoat on the surface, but he was altogether different from what she had imagined an Englishman to be like. He had shown himself to be a man of honor and integrity, not at all coarse or crude, a man of humor, a fair man . . . a man who could send her senses reeling with his slightest touch.

Madeleine put her trembling fingers to her temples. Her head felt as if it were about to explode. She almost screamed at the sudden loud banging on her door.

"Who's there?" she said, forcing her voice to remain calm and steady.

"Sergeant Fletcher, Mistress Fraser. I must speak with you at once."

"Just a moment." Madeleine crossed to her wardrobe and whisked off her gown and boots, replacing it with her white bedgown and cambric robe. She quickly unbraided her hair and ran a brush through the tangles to remove bits of grass and twigs. Then she rushed to open the door.

"Forgive me, Mistress Fraser," the sergeant began, his eyes moving over her appraisingly. He cleared his throat when he saw her sudden frown, and rushed on. "Captain Marshall has been injured in a mysterious accident. Would your housekeeper . . . uh . . ."

"Glenis."

"Yes, Glenis. Would she have any medicine? We're

looking for our medical supplies, but they've been misplaced somewhere. It's urgent, I'm afraid. We've stopped the bleeding, but he's weak—"

"Of course, Sergeant Fletcher," Madeleine said, frightened at this news. "If ye'll follow me, we'll fetch Glenis. She is well versed in treating many ills."

Aye, Glenis would help Garrett, she thought, walking swiftly down the stairs with the sergeant close behind her. Unwittingly, she said a silent prayer for the injured man who lay in her father's bed.

Glenis would know what to do.

Chapter 11

Glenis dipped the linen cloth into the basin and wrung it out. She laid it across Garrett's forehead, carefully covering the bruised, swollen knot above his right temple. She touched his stubbly cheek and found that his skin was cool. He was sleeping peacefully. After four long days and nights, his fever had finally broken.

She smoothed the blanket and tucked it beneath his wide shoulders. Then she rose wearily from the chair and turned around.

"He's seen the worst of it, Sergeant Fletcher," she said quietly. "The fever's gone, ye'll be glad to know. As soon as we can get some nourishment into him, he'll be as good as new."

The stocky soldier nodded gratefully, a look of admiration for the stooped old woman showing on his face. "We can't thank you enough, ma'am. You've saved his life . . . you and Mistress Fraser."

Glenis smiled faintly. She picked up the basin and moved to the door. "I've some beef broth simmering in the kitchen, and good hot tea in the kettle. Ye must let me know when he wakes, and I'll bring up a tray. He'll be thirsty, but dinna let him drink too much water. He needs the broth first, for strength."

"Yes, of course," Sergeant Fletcher agreed. "Whatever you think is best." He sat down by the bed as Glenis left the room.

She walked stiffly down the hall, stopping at Madeleine's door. She peeked in and shook her head in exasperation.

Madeleine was curled up on her bed with the tartan blanket thrown carelessly over her. Rain was pouring in through the open windows, the drenched curtains hanging like sodden rags from the wooden rods.

"Och, that child," Glenis muttered. She set down the basin and crossed to each window in turn, closing them firmly. The last one slipped and crashed down with a loud thud.

Madeleine stirred beneath the blanket. "Glenis?"

"Aye, Maddie. 'Tis me. Go back to sleep."

She sat up, rubbing her eyes. "No, no. I've slept enough. How is he, Glenis?"

Glenis sighed and sat down on the bed beside her mistress. "The fever's broken, thanks to yer fine care during the night, Maddie. Ye know, I could have stayed up with him—"

"'Twas no matter," Madeleine interrupted her gently. She yawned widely and stretched. "I dinna mind, and ye needed yer sleep. We canna have ye taking sick, Glenis. The household would be a shambles without ye."

She swung her legs to the floor and patted her servant's thin shoulder. "Ye've a kind heart, Glenis Simpson. Ye cared for the captain like he was yer own kin, redcoat or no." She glanced at the clock and saw the hands just touching noon. "Ye've been with him all morning. Now it's my turn. And it's time for ye to have another rest."

"Aye, I do feel a bit tired."

"Then it's settled. Come on, I'll walk with ye to yer room."

Madeleine took her servant's arm and helped her to her feet. While they walked downstairs and into the kitchen Glenis told her what she had advised the sergeant.

"Not too much broth, mind ye," Glenis instructed, stopping by the hearth to give the pot's bubbling contents a quick stir. "Give him a wee taste and see if it

stays in his stomach. Then give him a bit more. And
see that he drinks a full cup of my special tea."

"Aye, Glenis, dinna worry," Madeleine said. She
pushed open the door to Glenis's room, just off the
kitchen. "Go on with ye. And dinna mind about supper. I can see to myself."

"Ye're a good lass, Maddie Fraser."

Madeleine smiled and closed the door quietly. She
turned around just as the sergeant strode into the
kitchen.

"Oh . . . Mistress Fraser," he said. "I was looking for your housekeeper, Glenis. The captain is
awake—"

"She's resting, sergeant. I'll see to the tray for Captain Marshall."

Madeleine quickly ladled some steaming meat broth
into a bowl and poured a cup of tea. When the tray
was ready, she followed the sergeant back up the stairs.
Her mind was racing as she walked slowly down the
dim hallway, careful lest she spill anything.

Garrett was awake at last. She could hardly believe
it. He was going to live . . .

When she had first seen him lying on her father's
bed so ashen and still, with a bloodied gash in his forehead, she had thought he would die for certain. She
had tried not to blame herself, knowing in her heart
she had done what she needed to survive, yet she had
felt responsible nonetheless.

Perhaps that was why she had worked side by side
with Glenis and Sergeant Fletcher, fighting to save
Garrett's life. If not for the loss of blood, he might have
been up on his feet the next day. But a burning fever
had set in. Never before had she seen such agony and
such thrashing as his body was wracked by chills and
then fiery heat.

The nights she had sat by his bed were a blur of
changing sweaty sheets, cooling his face and feverish
body with wet cloths, administering Glenis's healing
potions, and enjoying occasional respites when he slept

fitfully. During the days she napped and took turns at his bedside with Glenis or Sergeant Fletcher.

The second night had been the worst. Garrett's tormented cries had chilled her to the bone. He had shouted out names—Celinda, Gordon—accompanied by wild oaths. Who were these people, and why would he curse them so?

His strong body had shaken with tremors at one point, and he had become delirious. She could not forget his words, which had driven into her heart like piercing arrows.

"No, stop them. We've got to stop them! They're wounded men . . . my God, stop the killing! Damn Cumberland! Damn Cumberland to hell! Here . . . drink this . . . it will help the pain . . . No, don't shoot, he's dying, can't you see . . . No, I won't stand away . . . Don't shoot him . . . No! God help us, have they all gone mad?"

She shuddered as she remembered his face twisting in grief and the tears staining his cheeks. She had felt tears sting her own eyes, and she had been unable to swallow. Could he be speaking of Culloden? Surely he had been there. Had he witnessed the slaughter? Had he tried to stop the senseless killing?

He had slept then, exhausted, his face pale and deathlike, only to awaken an hour later, calling her name. She had been alone with him because Glenis had gone to fetch some fresh water. He had tried to sit up and she had forced him back down, stroking his hair and soothing him while he whispered her name again and again.

Another name had come to his lips, an odd name, a nickname. Black Jack. He said it several times, murmuring to himself. *I will find you. I will find you, Black Jack.*

She had sensed at once who he meant. Black Jack. That must be the name the English soldiers had given her. It fit perfectly. She dressed in black and raided only at night.

His vehement words finally confirmed her suspicions and gut intuition. Captain Garrett Marshall had been sent to look for an outlaw, and she was that outlaw. She was Black Jack.

While sitting beside him, watching him drift into another restless sleep, Madeleine had suddenly remembered something else he had said to her the first day they met.

It is the innocent people who will suffer and bear the blame if these outlaws are not stopped.

An ominous chill had gripped her. What had he meant? Was it a threat, a hint of violence to come if his search for her proved unsuccessful?

"Would you like me to carry the tray, Mistress Fraser?" Sergeant Fletcher asked, his voice jarring her back to reality.

He was staring at her, a puzzled expression on his face, and with a start Madeleine realized that she had stopped in the middle of the hallway. Her hands were trembling slightly, rattling the china teacup in its saucer.

"No. I'm fine, sergeant," she said, her calm tone masking her agitation. She could swear her heart was thumping loudly enough to be heard in Farraline!

She held the tray firmly and walked toward the master bedchamber. The sergeant opened the door for her, and she stepped inside the candlelit room. Her gaze flew to the wide, canopied bed. The green velvet bed curtains were drawn back and tied with a fringed cord, revealing Garrett propped up against three plump pillows, his head back and his eyes closed.

He was such a handsome man, Madeleine found herself thinking, despite the gauntness of his face. She had come to know his features intimately during the past few days, and now it seemed she always carried a vivid picture of him in her mind.

His dark blond hair reminded her of autumn grain rippling in the sun. His brows were a darker color, straight and thick over deep-set eyes, and his forehead was strong, marred only by the nasty gash she had given him.

His nose was straight, his mouth sensuous and pleasing, and his jaw square-cut and shadowed with dark whiskers. The rugged planes beneath his cheekbones were hollow, but that was to be expected after what he had suffered. He had not eaten in days.

She was glad to see his color was better. He was wearing a clean white bedshirt that buttoned down the front, and silken blond curls showed at the neckline. She looked away as a blush crept across her skin, and then walked to the bedside table where she set down the tray.

She stirred a spoonful of heather honey into the tea along with a bit of cream and then poured in a dram of whiskey. She was unaware that Garrett had opened his eyes and was watching her until she heard his deep voice.

"You're doing this for me, Mistress Fraser?"

She jumped, dropping the spoon with a clatter. She met his gaze. His eyes were as warm and smiling as she remembered, and their vivid gray-green depths seemed to hold her captive. He was studying her face intently, as if he were seeing her for the first time. She felt a flush of heat at his admiring perusal.

"Mistress Fraser and her housekeeper, Glenis, have been caring for you from the start, captain," Sergeant Fletcher revealed before she could reply. "They've been here night and day—along with myself, of course."

"Is this true?" he asked quietly.

"Aye," Madeleine said simply, trying to ignore the shivers racing along her spine. If only he would stop looking at her so!

"I wonder what I've done to deserve such fine treatment," Garrett said with a thin smile. "I only wish I had done it sooner."

Madeleine couldn't tell if he was jesting or not, and she certainly wasn't about to tell him the truth behind her presence in his room. She chose to ignore his statement and glanced over at the sergeant.

"Could ye kindly push that chair closer to the bed?"

Sergeant Fletcher nodded and quickly did as she asked. She sat down and cradled the bowl of broth in her hands.

"That's enough talk for now, captain—"

"Please," he cut her off, his expression sobering, his eyes serious. "Garrett. And I'd be honored if you would allow me to call you Madeleine."

Madeleine stared at him and then shrugged. 'Twas no harm in it, she decided. She would humor him, for now.

"Very well, Garrett. Glenis's orders were for ye to eat this broth, but only a little at a time." Ignoring his unsettling gaze, she concentrated on holding the spoon to his mouth and tilting it. He swallowed weakly and smiled again.

"That's good. More, please . . . Madeleine."

She almost laughed out loud in spite of herself. "I told ye, Glenis said slowly."

His hunger was a good sign, she thought as she fed him more. She blushed anew when she spilled some broth on his upper chest, the liquid disappearing beneath his bedshirt.

"I-I'm sorry," she said uncomfortably, setting down the bowl. " 'Twas so clumsy of me." She undid the buttons and wiped his chest and tautly muscled abdomen with a linen napkin, not daring to look at his face. Her fingers shook as she refastened his shirt, and she fumbled with the last few buttons.

"It's no matter, Madeleine," Garrett said softly, bringing his hands up to cover her own. She started, meeting his eyes, and for an instant she was lost, aware of nothing but his touch and the heated expression in his gaze.

Sergeant Fletcher's embarrassed cough finally broke the spell between them. Madeleine's heart thundered as she slid her hands from beneath Garrett's and reached for the cup of tea. "Glenis said ye're to drink this down. It's her special remedy."

"What's in it?" Garrett asked with a smile. He

sniffed the dark, clouded liquid and eyed her skepti-
cally.

"Never ye mind. Now drink. 'Tis no longer hot, so
it winna burn yer throat."

He took a sip and grimaced. "I'd say there's a bit of
Scots whiskey in this tea." He wheezed, his eyes
smarting. He took a longer draft. "I'd swear to it." He
lifted the cup and gamely finished it off, presenting it
to her with a small flourish. "You must tell Glenis I
enjoyed the broth and the tea very much. And I especially enjoyed your kind assistance, Madeleine."

Flustered by the quiet intensity in his voice, Madeleine rose to her feet. "Ye must rest, Garrett. Could ye
ease up a bit so I might fix yer pillows?"

Garrett leaned on one elbow as she plumped the pillows. Suddenly he winced in pain, his hand flying to
the knot on his head. He touched it gingerly.

"That's where the bloke hit you, captain, whoever
he was," Sergeant Fletcher said, looking at his commanding officer with concern. "We searched the entire
area around the house, but there was no trace of him,
not even footprints. It's like he was swallowed up by
the moor."

Madeleine's eyes widened. If the sergeant only knew
how close he was to the truth. She bent over Garrett
and tucked the tartan bedspread around his lean waist,
very much aware that he was watching her. She felt a
shiver and stepped away from the bed. "There now,
Garrett. Ye can lie back."

He did so, exhaling sharply, and it was clear to Madeleine that his small movement had taxed him greatly.
He would no doubt remain bedridden for several days,
which was fine with her. While Garrett was recuper-
ating she could resume her raids without fear of his
personal intervention.

Now that he was feeling better, her conscience was
soothed. Well, only somewhat, she admitted to herself. Yet Glenis and Sergeant Fletcher would have to
see to Garrett without her now. She had to plan her
raids. Just last night Ewen had sent word to her

through Duncan, who had passed himself off as a blacksmith looking for work, asking when they would ride again. She would no longer make her kinsmen wait.

She picked up the tray and turned to leave but stopped when Garrett gently touched her arm.

"Would you sit here with me awhile, Madeleine?" he asked quietly, staring into her eyes. "Please. I'd appreciate your company. Fletcher will take the tray back to the kitchen, won't you, sergeant?"

Before Madeleine could refuse, the sergeant walked over and took the tray from her. "It will give me a chance to fetch some lunch for myself, if you don't mind, Mistress Fraser," he said. He moved briskly to the door. "I'll be back shortly." Then he was gone, leaving Madeleine standing awkwardly beside the bed.

"Please . . . sit down," Garrett bade her.

Madeleine sighed softly, then sat, deciding there was no harm in lingering for a little while. She stared at her folded hands, not knowing quite what to say. She hadn't expected this at all.

"Sergeant Fletcher told me I've been out for four days," he said, breaking the silence. "I can hardly believe it. That must have been some bump on the head."

Madeleine winced. She coughed slightly and raised her head. "Aye, ye gave us quite a scare . . ." She faltered, her cheeks suddenly very warm. "I mean yer men, they've been worried sick for ye, and Sergeant Fletcher—well, Glenis and I thought for sure he'd fall ill himself when ye became delirious. He was so upset that we had to send him outside for fresh air."

He chuckled, and she smiled. His face looked so boyishly handsome when he laughed, so honest and open. If not for the fact that he was a redcoat, she might have liked this man.

Madeleine looked away, disturbed by her thoughts.

"I suppose I filled your ears with a lot of nonsense," Garrett said, startling her. "I've seen people with fevers before. My father had one just before he died, as did my grandmother. It's like listening to someone's nightmare.''

She stared at him, wondering if he was well enough for her to ask him about Culloden. She quickly decided against it when he grimaced and his hand strayed to his bruised forehead. His memories were obviously painful, perhaps too painful to discuss right now. In a few days she would ask him, when he was more fully recovered.

"Ye did mumble a bit," Madeleine allowed. "Well, it was more swearing, really."

"Swearing?"

"Aye. Ye dinna have kind words to say for Gordon, or Celinda."

Garrett seemed stunned for a moment then laughed softly, but Madeleine sensed there was no humor in it.

"Gordon, the earl of Kemsley, is my older brother," he replied, his tone edged with bitterness. "It's because of him I'm in the military. He bought a commission for me as a token of his high esteem and affection," he added sarcastically.

"Ye were forced?" Madeleine asked, confused.

Garrett smiled wryly. "In a way. I could have turned it down, but our family honor demanded I accept. I've one year left, then I'm a free man."

Madeleine's mind raced. So Garrett was an aristocrat. That explained his gentlemanly ways and refined speech. She knew the English army was a common refuge for younger sons of the nobility, who usually possessed no estate of their own.

Perhaps the earl had been thinking of Garrett's welfare and provided him with a profession, at least for a few years. Yet it was clear Garrett resented what had happened to him. Had he been forced to leave a woman behind, a mistress, a betrothed? Celinda?

Garrett's fingers lightly touched her arm, dispelling her thoughts but not the twinge of jealousy that pricked her.

"Now I believe I should thank Gordon," he said,

staring at her intently. "This is the most pleasant assignment I've ever had, because I met you."

Madeleine's eyes stared into his, and her skin tingled from his featherlight touch. Perplexed, she shifted uncomfortably in her chair and drew her arm away.

"And who is Celinda?" she asked, trying to keep her voice nonchalant. As Garrett looked at her curiously, she had the strangest feeling he could sense how furiously her heart was pounding.

"Celinda is Gordon's wife," he replied. "We courted for a time, but she opted for my brother's title."

"I'm—I'm sorry," Madeleine stammered, surmising she had touched a raw nerve. No wonder he had cursed Celinda's name. To be so slighted, and for his own brother! How terrible. Garrett must have truly loved Celinda to express such emotion in his delirium.

Discomforted by that thought, she rose from the chair. "Forgive me for prying, Garrett. Ye really should rest now." She gasped as he caught her hand.

"Celinda was a youthful fancy, nothing more, Madeleine," he said, stroking her trembling fingers with his thumb.

"Ye dinna have to explain—"

"There's no one else," he insisted, leaning up on his elbow.

Why was he telling her this? she wondered wildly, her pulse racing. She didn't care, or did she?

"What of you, Maddie Fraser?" Garrett asked suddenly, causing her heart to skip a beat. "An enchanting woman like yourself—"

"Humph! Ah, excuse me, captain," Sergeant Fletcher said loudly, clearing his throat as he pushed open the door. "I've brought you some more hot tea."

Madeleine snatched her hand away as she felt her cheeks firing bright pink. She glanced from the grizzled soldier to Garrett. His eyes clearly showed his disappointment at the sudden interruption.

"Lie back with ye now," she said briskly, attempting to mask her rampant emotions. She smoothed the tartan spread and stepped away from the bed, threading her fingers together nervously. "Ye must see that he gets some rest, Sergeant Fletcher," she advised, passing by him as she walked quickly to the door. "If ye need anything, ye've only to ask."

"Madeleine," Garrett called out to her.

She leaned for an instant on the door frame and drew a steadying breath before she turned around. "Aye?"

"I owe you and Glenis my life. I'm grateful to you."

She felt a dizzy rush of warmth as his eyes bored into hers, and her knees grew weak. Embarrassed by his sincerity, she flashed him a small smile, then fled the room.

Madeleine leaned against the wall just outside the room and closed her eyes. She could not deny that his words had pleased her.

Whatever was the matter with her? She had never felt so breathless and giddy in her life! It was almost as if Garrett wielded some mysterious power over her whenever she was near him, eliciting a strange yearning within her she could not comprehend. A yearning such as she had felt at the loch, shattering her reason and her will. A yearning that frightened her—

"If you're up to it, captain, maybe you could tell me what happened the other night."

Madeleine froze as she overheard Sergeant Fletcher's words, her eyes snapping open. Her jumbled emotions receded into the background. She listened carefully, scarcely breathing.

"I think it was Black Jack," Garrett began, describing his pursuit of a black-clad figure across the moor until the moment he was struck on the head. "I could swear it was he. I believe we've been searching too far afield, Fletcher. Perhaps this outlaw resides nearby, maybe in the mountains directly to the east, maybe even in Farraline. I want you to double the guards at night, and we'll also begin patrolling the village."

Madeleine swore softly. She should have been more careful, but she hadn't expected anyone to be out on the moor at that time of night. Now her task would be harder than ever.

"I've some important news for you, Captain Marshall, especially in light of what you just told me. It came by special courier yesterday from Colonel Wolfe. Perhaps we should discuss it later, if you're feeling tired."

"I'm fine, except for this blasted ache in my head. What is the news?"

"Black Jack and his men raided another supply train, just north of Inverfarigaig, on the night you were injured. It could very well have been he out on the moor, on his way back from the raid."

"Damn!"

"It seems our presence hasn't daunted the bastard in the least, captain."

"Was there anything else in the message?"

"Yes. I've got it right here."

Madeleine heard the crisp rustling of paper, then another vehement outburst from Garrett.

"Three weeks? He's given us only three weeks to capture the outlaw? The colonel must be mad, or, more likely General Hawley had something to do with it. He probably lost more of his precious wine in that supply train."

Madeleine gulped. There had been several casks of wine in one of the front wagons. Since wine was useless to them, Kenneth and Allan had dumped the casks into Loch Ness, to make more room in the wagon for foodstuffs.

They had lowered their voices, and she couldn't hear them. Frustrated, she crept closer to the door. What she heard then filled her with apprehension.

"I think it's time I tell Madeleine about our mission."

"Why, captain? She's just a slip of a girl. What could she possibly know about Black Jack?"

"She's the mistress of Farraline, Fletcher. The Frasers of Strathherrick are her people. She must know something about what's going on in this valley. If I bring our mission out into the open, she might be willing to help us. Especially if she knows the danger her people face if Black Jack isn't captured soon.''

"You would trust her with this information, captain? A Highland wench? Say she does know Black Jack's whereabouts. What if she warns him and we never find him?''

"We'll have to take that risk. I have no choice but to trust her. Three weeks is not a long time, Fletcher, and you know Hawley. Madeleine may be our best chance to end this peacefully. I only hope she'll trust me enough to believe what I tell her.''

"Would you like me to talk to her, sir? You should rest, at least for another day or so. You look tired, and I've burdened you enough already.''

"No, I'll take care of it. I'm sure I'll soon feel more like myself.''

"I hope so, captain. You gave me the devil of a scare. I'll leave you now so you can get some sleep.''

Madeleine blanched and backed quickly away from the door. She held her breath as she hurried along the hallway and down the stairs. She didn't stop until she had reached the kitchen, where she slumped into a chair.

So Garrett was planning to take her into his confidence and to ask her questions about Black Jack. Well, she had some questions of her own. She rested her forehead in her hands, her mind reeling.

What was this danger he had mentioned? Did it have something to do with what he had said last week about innocent people suffering and bearing the blame? How did that fat swine, General Hawley, fit into all this?

Exasperated, she slammed her small fist on the table. She didn't have time to sort it all out now. Her kinsmen were waiting for her in the village, waiting to plan their next raid. She'd sent a message to Ewen saying she would meet them that afternoon at Angus's cottage if she could get away.

With so many people to feed in Strathherrick, the food they'd stolen a few nights ago would not last much longer, and the stores hidden in the cave on

Beinn Dubhcharaidh were being depleted with each passing day. She did not have time to waste wondering what the redcoats were up to. Besides, if Garrett was true to his word she would know the answers to her troubling questions soon enough.

Madeleine grabbed a thick woolen shawl from a peg by the kitchen door and wrapped it securely around her, covering her head. She opened the door and stepped out into the drizzling rain, ignoring the guards' curious stares as she sloshed along the puddled drive.

If she had her way, they would set out on another raid that night. It would be the very distraction she needed to free her mind from what she had just overheard and the strange foreboding that still gripped her.

Chapter 12

Garrett groaned as he drew on his shirt, waving away Sergeant Fletcher, who was standing nearby. He had never known his muscles to feel so tight and sore. His trembling fingers worked at the buttons one by one while he stood somewhat shakily in the middle of the room. Finally he was done. He reached for his coat, staggering ever so slightly. The sergeant rushed to his side and caught his arm.

"Captain, are you sure you want to do this? Another day won't matter so much. Perhaps you should stay in bed—"

"I'm fine, Fletcher," Garrett insisted sharply, for what seemed like the hundredth time. He shrugged on his coat. "You're worse than a nagging nursemaid."

When he saw his sergeant's wounded look, he chided himself for his thoughtlessness. The man had had much to do with his recovery. He softened his tone. "Don't worry, Fletcher. It's time I got up on my feet. Lying in bed another day won't make it any easier for me to regain my strength. I've got to start moving around again, go walking, riding. I need some fresh air—it's the best cure I can think of."

"Very well, captain," Sergeant Fletcher said, though he did not look completely convinced.

"I know what you're thinking," Garrett said wryly. "But it won't happen again. I feel better already, just standing here."

He remembered all too clearly his first attempt to rise

from the bed yesterday, not long after Sergeant Fletcher had left the room to let him sleep. His legs had buckled beneath him, and he had crumpled to the floor. The sergeant had rushed in to find him on his knees clutching the bedspread, vainly trying to stand.

He would have tried again if it hadn't been for Sergeant Fletcher's strong insistence that he resign himself to one more day of bed rest. Glenis had vehemently seconded the opinion later, when she heard about his futile effort. He smiled as he recalled her heated words.

"How dare ye get out of bed when ye're just over the fever," she had scolded him. "I dinna nurse ye these past four days to see ye take sick agin, Captain Garrett Marshall. Ye'll do just as the good sergeant has asked ye, and as I'm tellin' ye!"

She reminded him of his grandmother at that moment, with her hands on her narrow hips and her dark eyes flaring. He had no intention of crossing her. He had obediently remained in bed, and she had rewarded him with the best beef stew he had ever tasted, and more of that fiery Scots tea. He slept more soundly after that meal than he had in days.

Garrett's stomach suddenly rumbled. It was so loud that Sergeant Fletcher laughed.

"If you're that hungry, captain, then you must be feeling better, just as you say."

"Come on, let's go downstairs," Garrett said, walking stiffly to the door. "Maybe Jeremy has baked some of his pan bread for breakfast."

In the hallway he glanced over his shoulder at Madeleine's room. He was not surprised to see her door wide open. It was late, almost ten o'clock, and no doubt she had already been up for hours.

She probably wasn't even at home, he thought, holding on to the sturdy banister and taking the steps carefully.

Sergeant Fletcher had told him she had spent much of the previous day and well into the evening in Farraline. He found himself wondering what, or who, had caused her to return so late to Mhor Manor. A lover, perhaps, whom she hadn't seen for several days because she was nursing him? Probably so. She certainly had gaped at him when he brought up the topic yesterday.

Garrett felt a familiar sting of jealousy, but swiftly quelled it. Madeleine had every right to visit the village and her people as often as she wished. If she was meeting her lover, well, that was not his concern.

He walked outside, his gaze narrowing at the distant thatched heather and turf roofs of Farraline. He heaved a sigh as a tightness welled up inside him.

He was lying to himself if he thought he didn't care whether she had a lover. He cared deeply. He hadn't realized how much until he had opened his eyes to find her standing beside his bed. It had been like a sweet dream becoming reality.

Beautiful Madeleine was talking with him, feeding him, caring for him, her hand lightly grazing his shoulder as she plumped his pillows. His pulse had surged at her touch, stoking the fire raging deep within him.

Frustrated, Garrett turned away and followed his sergeant to the back of the manor house, where the cooking tent was set up. He smelled bacon frying, the fresh-baked aroma of pan bread and brewed coffee, but he seemed to have lost his appetite. He halfheartedly took the full plate Jeremy Witt offered him.

"It's good to see you up and about, Captain Marshall," the bantam-size cook said cheerfully. "Here you go, sergeant. The rest of the men have already eaten."

Garrett sat on a rough-hewn bench while the sergeant settled himself on the grass. Fletcher dug heartily into his plate, gulping down huge mouthfuls of food with hot coffee.

"Is something wrong, captain?" Sergeant Fletcher asked mid-swallow, surveying Garrett's untouched plate.

"No," Garrett replied tightly. Knowing he needed the nourishment, he forced himself to eat. The food was good, and after a few bites he felt his appetite gradually returning. He finished everything on his plate and even enjoyed another serving of pan bread.

He was on his second mug of coffee when he spied a slight figure walking briskly toward the manor house from the direction of the tiny loch. His cup stopped midway to his mouth as he realized it was Madeleine. He set his plate and mug on the bench and rose to his feet, watching her intently.

She was so lovely.

He drank in the fetching vision she made, feeling as if he could stare at her forever. Her blue skirt skimmed her curved hips, its hem swaying as she walked. Her chestnut hair shone glossily in the sun and curled about her face in damp tendrils. She had a towel in her hand, and she was swinging it jauntily.

So she hadn't gone into Farraline this morning, he thought, feeling a surge of pleasure mixed with relief. She must have been bathing in the loch. He could tell she hadn't seen him yet, and he enjoyed the sensation of catching a brief glimpse into her private world. She was smiling faintly, and he wondered what was she thinking.

The moment was over too soon. Suddenly she spied him, and he watched the smile fade from her lips. She looked surprised, then her expression became guarded. He sobered as well, feeling a twinge of resignation as he recalled yesterday's discussion with Sergeant Fletcher.

Three weeks. That's all he had left. He had hoped to have enough time to win her trust, to develop some understanding between them, perhaps even to . . .

Thunderous desire ripped through him, his senses reliving the fleeting instant at the loch when he had held Madeleine in his arms. He could feel once again her firm breasts pressed against him, her lips, warm and exciting, opened to him like the ruby-red petals of a flower to the sun, moist and eager for his kiss. With supreme effort he forced his mind back to the urgent matter at hand, though his body was not so easily swayed.

Think of your mission! he berated himself. Your
duty! When so many innocent lives were at stake, this
was not a time to think of his own selfish needs, his
burgeoning desire—

Garrett started. For the first time he realized that was
exactly what he had been doing. He had been thinking
only of himself. He stared at Madeleine, who was
drawing ever closer, though she had slowed her pace.

Well, no more, he thought grimly. The sooner he
spoke with her about Black Jack, the better. Either she
would believe him and agree to help him, telling him
anything she knew about the outlaw, or she would not.
Of course, there was always the chance she knew
nothing.

Garrett turned away, frowning. He didn't even want
to consider that possibility! He addressed his sergeant,
keeping his voice low so it would not carry.

"Fletcher, see that the men go about their assigned
duties today," he ordered quietly. "Double the guard
as we discussed, and send a patrol of four men on
horseback to Farraline. Have them check in every two
hours, then on the sixth hour change the patrol. Any
questions?"

"No, sir," Sergeant Fletcher said, hauling his bulky
frame to his feet. He glanced beyond Garrett's shoulder to Madeleine, who was strolling through the dense
fir trees bordering the disheveled lawn. His expression
was anxious as he sought his commander's face once
again. "Are you sure you want to tell her, captain?"

Without a word, Garrett nodded firmly. He turned
and strode across the lawn, ignoring his stiff, aching
muscles. He easily narrowed the distance between
himself and Madeleine.

"Good morning," he said pleasantly, noting the
wariness in her stunning blue eyes. It hurt him that
there was little welcome shining in those amazing
depths, yet his amiable tone did not betray his feelings.
"I see you've been for a swim."

Madeleine stopped, gripping her towel in both

hands. Garrett's deep voice thrilled her, though she tried hard not to show it. She swiftly appraised him.

She almost had not believed her eyes when she saw him standing near the cooking tent. She had expected him to remain in bed for at least another day or so. Now here he was, looking none the worse for his illness.

"Good day to ye, Captain Mar—," she paused, then quickly decided it made no difference. "Garrett." She avoided the unnerving subject of the loch altogether, an intimate moment she would rather forget. "Ye're looking well."

"Yes, I feel much better," he said, smiling. "I wanted to thank you again for what you did for me. It was so . . . unexpected."

" 'Twas no matter," she mumbled, pretending interest in a colorful patch of wildflowers.

Better to squelch any ideas he might have about why she had nursed him, she thought nervously. She didn't want him to imagine that she cared.

She glanced back at him and said nonchalantly, "Glenis couldna tend ye all on her own, Garrett. She needed my help. I canna have her working herself to the bone for every crisis besetting my house. We seem to have quite an abundance these days."

Madeleine saw that her words had the desired effect. His face darkened, but only for a moment. In the next instant he was studying her curiously, as if he was trying to discern her thoughts. She lowered her eyes, suddenly flustered.

"Would you like to go for a ride, Madeleine?" he asked, ignoring her breezy statement. "I would relish the exercise and it would give us a chance to talk privately. I have a matter of some importance to discuss with you."

Madeleine fought to breathe steadily and to keep her voice calm. "Glenis said ye asked about going for a ride the other day."

"Yes, I did," he said with a short laugh. "That was before . . ." He indicated the healing gash on his forehead with a wave of his hand. "It was postponed a few days, that's all. Perhaps we could ride along Loch Ness, on Wade's Road? I enjoy that route, and Foyer's Falls is breathtaking."

"Aye, 'tis a beautiful place. One of my favorites," she agreed, her calm response belying her tumbling thoughts.

At last she would have answers to her plaguing questions! Neither the previous night's raid nor her morning swim had distracted her as she had hoped they would. She nodded. "I'll ride with ye, Garrett."

"Good. Shall we meet within the half hour in front of the house? I'll have your mare saddled for you."

"Aye, very well. If ye'll excuse me, I'll go and change." She rushed past him in a flurry of blue skirts, petticoats, and tousled chestnut curls.

Confused, Garrett watched her disappear around the house. He had not expected her to accept his invitation so readily, at least not without some explanation of why he wanted to speak with her. She had spurned him soundly on every other occasion when he had asked her to accompany him so they might talk.

Except for yesterday, he thought. Perhaps the short time they had spent together had softened her opinion of him after all.

Chapter 13

❧

"**I**'ll lead the way, if ye dinna mind, Garrett,"
Madeleine said when they set out from Mhor
Manor twenty minutes later. A curious smile tugged at
Garrett's mouth, and she thought he might protest,
but instead he inclined his head in deference to her
wishes.

"Lead on, Mistress Fraser," he said gallantly.

She smiled briefly in return and kicked her dun-
colored mare into a gallop. She purposely veered them
away from Farraline and the much-traveled roads con-
necting the villages in Strathherrick, opting instead for
a lesser known route across the valley.

She had no intention of passing through any villages
in the company of a redcoat. It was bad enough that
word had already been spread that she and Glenis had
nursed Garrett back to health. Meg was less trustwor-
thy than Madeleine had thought, it seemed.

Her kinsmen had questioned her about the rumor
when she met them to plan last night's raid, but fortunately they had accepted her explanation that Glenis
had taken pity on Garrett and required her help. An
old woman's lapse was easily forgiven. She, on the
other hand, had to be more careful.

She could not afford to fan the flames of gossip any
further by riding brazenly at Garrett's side for all to
see. Her people trusted and respected her, and she
wanted it to remain that way. If this route took them

longer, so be it. At least her credibility would be preserved.

They rode in uncomfortable silence for the first half hour, skirting Loch Mhor and the village of Errogie, then headed northwest, where they forded the River Farigaig.

The lathered horses seemed to enjoy the crossing. The day was very warm, and the sun was brilliant in the blue sky scattered with clouds. The river's shimmering depths and shady banks offered a cool respite from the midday heat.

Madeleine was halfway across the rushing stream when her mare paused for a long drink. If the river had not been so swollen from recent rains she would not have cared, but she feared the strong currents might topple them. She tugged at the reins, but to no avail. The mare would not lift her head.

"Ye stubborn beast," she said with exasperation as Garrett drew up alongside her. "On with ye now."

"Problems?" he asked.

" 'Tis plain to see, Garrett. She winna budge!"

With a hearty laugh he took the reins from her and gave the recalcitrant mare a good yank. Madeleine nearly lost her seat as the mare bounded forward after his massive bay, and the horses splashed across the river. When she and Garrett made it to the shoreline, they were soaked and laughing uproariously.

She smiled at him through the water droplets clinging to her lashes. "Will ye look at us," she exclaimed breathlessly. "We might as well have fallen into the river!"

"We'll be dry soon from this heat," Garrett said with a grin. He reached out and gently wiped a damp tendril from her flushed cheek. "The water felt good, though, didn't it?"

"Aye," Madeleine replied, sobering at his touch. She felt a flutter deep inside her breast as he handed her the reins. It was all she could do to murmur her thanks.

They resumed their journey, but the strained tension between them had been lifted. Madeleine began to point out sights of interest here and there, especially when they reached Wade's Road. Loch Ness stretched to the north and south as far as the eye could see, a great expanse of smooth, blue-gray water flanked by sweeping green hills and steep rock walls dropping into its depths.

There was a decidedly gloomy air about the loch, despite the bright sunshine. Perhaps it was because the waters were so vast and so deep. Or perhaps it was the eerie stories that leaped to mind whenever one beheld the mysterious loch. Madeleine shuddered, and her skin tingled with goosebumps.

"Is it true that the Scots believe a monster roams these waters?" Garrett asked, pulling up beside her. "When I was a boy my grandmother told me such a tale, and I had nightmares for days."

She glanced at him in surprise, wondering how he had read her thoughts. "Aye, 'tis true," she replied, staring back out across the dark water. " 'Tis said to be a great black beast with humps, a long neck, and wee horns on its head. I've never seen it, but my parents swore they did once."

"Really? When was that?"

"Long ago, when my mother was carrying me. They were sitting over there." She pointed to a green plateau high atop a rocky cliff, aware that Garrett was watching her with a curious mix of wonderment and skepticism. His interest spurred her on. She enjoyed telling this story immensely.

" 'Twas a cloudy, late autumn day and the wind was strong, ruffling the surface of the loch. Suddenly the water began to bubble and churn. The beast rose up from the depths and cut through the water with great curved paddles, like black wings. It left a huge wake, then 'twas gone." She chuckled, a faraway look in her eyes. "Da thought for sure my mother would birth me there on the cliff, she was so frightened."

"And you believe this story?"

Madeleine stared into his eyes. "Aye, I believe it, if my father and mother said 'twas so." She said nothing for a long moment, then gave another little laugh and looked away. "I used to complain whenever we journeyed by the loch, because I was never gifted with a sight of the beast." She grew thoughtful, her voice soft and quiet. "My da always said 'twas a good lesson. 'Maddie,' he would tell me, 'it teaches ye to believe in something ye canna see.' "

She sighed, touched by a wave of sadness. To think of her parents together and happy, her father alive and whole. She felt close to tears but choked them back.

"Your mother must have been very beautiful," Garrett said sincerely, startling her. "Why is there no portrait of her at Mhor Manor?"

"All the family portraits were slashed to ribbons by the redcoats who came before ye," she replied, watching his eyes darken.

"I'm truly sorry, Madeleine. If I'd been there, I would have done what I could to prevent—"

" 'Tis over with, Garrett," she said with a small shrug, cutting off his unexpected apology. "I'd rather not speak of it."

He fell silent, looking out across the loch, and she wondered what he was thinking. She felt surprisingly little resentment toward him. She could hardly blame him for what had happened to her home, nor could she imagine him ever participating in such madness. She sensed a decency in him that reminded her of her father.

Madeleine bit her lip, stunned by her comparison. Dougald had never elicited such thoughts from her, nor had he ever looked at her quite the way Garrett did, making her flesh tingle and her heart hammer, fanning the heat building within her.

No! Dinna forget Garrett is yer enemy! she chided herself fiercely. Ye canna compare him to yer da or to Dougald. 'Tisn't right!

Oddly enough, her self-reproach rang hollow within her. Things didn't seem so clear anymore, at least not when she was around Garrett. He seemed to have the uncanny ability to soften her hatred. He was becoming less of a redcoat in her eyes and more of a man, a most intriguing man.

With great effort she forced the whole confusing matter from her mind. "Ye were right about my mother," she began anew. "She was said to be the prettiest lass in Strathherrick—lively, sharp-witted, and a bit stubborn when 'twas needed."

"She sounds just like you, Madeleine," Garrett said softly.

His compliment caused her to shift uncomfortably in the saddle. "Do ye see that faraway bluff on the northern shore?" she asked, abruptly changing the subject. She flushed under his amused scrutiny and was more than relieved when he looked to where she was pointing. " 'Tis the ruins of Castle Urquhart. 'Twas a fine castle once, belonging to the Grants. There's little left now but crumbling walls and a dungeon."

"A dungeon? I suppose it's haunted by ghosts, as many of Scotland's castles are rumored to be."

"No, I havna heard any stories of ghosts at Castle Urquhart," Madeleine replied. "But there are two vaults in the dungeon, left unopened for hundreds of years. One's rumored to have treasure in it, and the other the plague."

"That's a choice I would not wish to make," Garrett said with a deep, rumbling laugh. He glanced back at her, his expression growing serious. "I've enjoyed these stories, Madeleine, but I think we should move on to Foyer's Falls. Perhaps we can find a nice spot overlooking the waterfall where we can rest and talk further. Jeremy was good enough to pack a lunch for us."

Madeleine nodded. She suddenly felt foolish and a little hurt. Here she was carrying on about water beasts, ghosts, and castle ruins, when all along Garrett had nothing on his mind but Black Jack.

"I dinna mean to bore ye, Garrett," she said defensively. "Nor waste yer precious time." She jerked on the reins and kicked her mare, urging the animal into a fast trot.

Garrett was caught unaware by her swift action. She left him behind, but he quickly overtook her, his bay's powerful strides far surpassing those of her mare. Again the silence lay oppressively between them, both keeping to their own thoughts as they rode side by side along Wade's Road.

Madeleine ignored the groups of English soldiers they passed, her eyes fixed straight ahead as she and Garrett dodged in and out of the bustling highway traffic.

She was grateful that the paved, steeply graded road was heavily traveled during the day. The crowded highway prevented many of the supply trains from traveling between Inverness and Fort William in the daytime. If supplies were to get through at all, the redcoats had little choice but to use the road at night, despite the threat of raids. There was no other route across the mountainous Highlands.

Madeleine was pleased to see the vast number of rickety carts and lumbering wagons vying for space with pedestrians carrying bundles and baskets. A sleek black carriage drawn by four elegantly matched horses clattered by, the liveried driver paying little heed to the common folk scurrying out of harm's way. Madeleine caught a glimpse of the carriage's rich, well-dressed occupants, and her mood darkened considerably.

Probably some of fat King Geordie's loyal Scotsmen—the vile traitors, she thought bitterly. She vehemently hoped the carriage would lose a wheel while crossing the humpbacked bridge up ahead and tumble straight into the loch.

It didn't. The carriage proceeded safely, much to her disappointment. It followed Wade's Road to the left while she and Garrett reined their horses into a walk along a narrow dirt road. Foyer's Falls were straight ahead, only a short distance away.

Madeleine's resentment was tempered by a rush of excitement, and she forgot the carriage. She could hear the majestic roar of the falls growing louder and louder. She inhaled the damp air, laden with moisture; it was

becoming cooler as they neared the steep, rocky gorge.
Then suddenly they were upon it, one of the most
magnificent sights imaginable. It took her breath away.

One spectacular waterfall thundered into another
and another, forming tiers of foaming white water. Mist
soared high into the air, a rainbow arcing within the
infinite sparkling droplets. The falls merged and
melded; the water cascading into the turbulent River
Foyers at the bottom of the gorge.

Madeleine stroked the mare's smooth neck, attempting to calm her. The horse was snorting and stamping
her hooves on the ground, clearly terrified by the deafening roar. Madeleine turned to Garrett, who was intently watching the falls. She had to shout to be heard.

"Would ye mind if we rode down closer to the river?
Otherwise I might find myself taking a dive into the
falls!"

He nodded, noting the tight grip she had on the
reins, and quickly took the lead. As they moved away
from the precipitous gorge overlooking Loch Ness, the
mare quieted considerably. Several hundred feet farther and the falls were a dull thunder in the distance,
though still visible. Garrett halted his bay and twisted
in the saddle to face her.

"We could stop here if you'd like," he offered, indicating a gentle hill that sloped gradually into the
River Foyers. A thick beech wood ran the length of the
green hillside, promising welcome shade.

"Aye, 'tis a fine spot," she agreed tersely and dismounted. She saw Garrett grimace as he eased himself
from the saddle, and she guessed he was still suffering
from his illness. A pang of guilt tweaked her conscience, but she shrugged it off. He was feeling better,
wasn't he? He was certainly well enough to renew his
single-minded search for Black Jack!

Almost angrily she strode down the hill and tethered
her mare to a tree. She plopped on the grass, watching
as Garrett did the same. She made no effort to help
him as he spread out a woolen blanket beside her.

He knelt and dumped out the contents of his saddlebag: a loaf of thick-crusted bread, a small wheel of cheese, and some rosy apples. It was simple fare, but Madeleine's mouth watered. She'd had no breakfast, and the long ride had fueled her appetite.

She immediately tore off a chunk of bread, ignoring his chuckle at her haste. She split the cheese in thirds, offering him two pieces and keeping one wedge for herself. She took a bite, savoring the aged cheddar flavor. It was an English cheese, but she had to admit it was quite good.

"Here. You must be thirsty," Garrett said as he poured a cup of red wine from a wineskin and handed it to her.

"Thank ye," she said. She took a long draft, her eyes widening in surprise.

The smooth wine was hardly what she had expected. It was a French vintage which she had no trouble stomaching; the French hated the English almost as much as the Highlanders. Yet how had Garrett come by such a wine? French imports were prohibited in England, since the two countries were forever at war, or taxed so highly they were well out of reach to all but the rich.

"Do you like it?" Garrett asked, noting her stunned reaction.

She lowered her cup, licking her lips self-consciously. "Aye, 'tis very good. I've always liked French wines."

"Ah, so you're familiar with foreign vintages."

His casual comment pricked her temper. "We're not savages here as ye might have supposed, Garrett, though yer kind treat us as such," she spouted hotly. "My da taught me a great deal about fine wines, and dancing, and proper table manners. He saw to it I was well educated, just as my mother had been. Ye might be interested to know I can read and write as well as any of yer aristocratic lady friends!"

"Better, I'd warrant," he said under his breath, a wry smile tugging at the corners of his mouth. When she looked at him quizzically, he sobered. "I did not mean what I said as an insult, Madeleine. Forgive me if it seemed so. And it has not escaped my attention

that you possess many exquisite qualities.'' His voice
became husky, his eyes blazing into hers with a strange
but compelling fire. ''A man would easily become the
envy of any court with a woman such as you by his
side.''

Madeleine stared at him, surprised by his candor,
her heart thumping wildly. She thought to take a sip
of wine, but her hands were trembling so badly she
dared not attempt it. She did not want him to see how
much his words had affected her.

''Did yer brother, Gordon, give ye the wine as a
parting gift?'' she asked with feigned flippancy, desperately hoping to veer their conversation from its unsettling course.

''It's my own private stock,'' he replied tightly, a
scowl appearing on his handsome face. ''I brought a
cask with me from England. My life as a soldier would
truly be desolate without such small pleasures, and
fortunately I've the means to provide myself with some
comforts, Gordon be damned.''

Madeleine sensed his anger and said no more. Obviously there was a deep rift between the two brothers,
a rift she did not wish to explore. It was also clear Garrett had some wealth of his own to afford such wine,
making him one of the luckier younger sons of the nobility. She hastily decided it was none of her business
to pry any further into his personal affairs.

She looked on silently as Garrett lifted his cup and
drank deeply, wiping his mouth with the back of his
hand. He gazed out over the rumbling river for a very
long moment, as if composing his thoughts, then back
at her. His eyes caught and held hers.

''Tell me, Madeleine. Do you recall our discussion
the day my soldiers and I commandeered Mhor Manor?
About troublemakers and outlaws?''

Madeleine fought the swell of apprehension rising in
her heart. ''Aye,'' she said, gripping the cup tightly.
''I asked ye if there were outlaws in Strathherrick.''
She shrugged her slender shoulders. ''Ye wouldna answer.''

Garrett sighed, his gaze never leaving her face. His expression was hard and grim. It frightened her.

"You must listen carefully to me, Madeleine. I must ask you to trust me, as I'm about to trust you."

Madeleine stared at him, incredulous. "I trust no Englishmen," she declared emphatically, setting down her half-empty cup. "Ye're mad to even think—"

"In this case you must," he said, cutting her off impatiently. "Please hear me out, Madeleine. That's all I ask."

She said nothing, eyeing him sullenly. He interpreted her silence as an assent and rushed on.

"I was sent to Strathherrick to search for an outlaw. We call him Black Jack."

She flinched inwardly. "Black Jack? 'Tis a clever name."

"Yes. A clever name for a very dangerous man. He's been raiding English supply trains for about three months now, from Inverness Firth to Loch Lochy. Several English soldiers have been shot either by him or by his men. One almost died."

There, he'd said it, she thought with relief. A very dangerous man. He had no idea his notorious Black Jack was sitting right across from him. She wondered fleetingly if he referred to the man she had shot.

"I must find Black Jack within three weeks, Madeleine. I thought you might be able to help me. Do you know anything at all about this outlaw? Anything."

She could not believe her ears. Did he truly think she would help him? He must, or he wouldn't be looking at her so expectantly. How utterly absurd. Little did he know that if she helped him, she'd be settling a hangman's noose about her own neck! She shuddered at the dreadful thought, her anger piqued once again by his presumption.

"I know nothing of yer outlaw, Garrett, and ye're a fool if ye think I'd ever help ye, even if I did."

Suddenly his hands gripped her arms cruelly, and he pulled her against him, his face within inches of her own. She tried to wrench free, but he held her fast.

His breath was warm on her skin and fragrant with wine; his eyes had darkened to the color of slate.

"Would you say the same thing, Mistress Madeleine Fraser," he asked, his voice low and intense, "if you knew that within three weeks the Highlanders of Strathherrick would suffer more deeply than ever before?"

Madeleine gasped, her throat tightening painfully. "What do ye mean?" she whispered hoarsely.

"I believe I mentioned my chief commander's name to you, General Henry Hawley, the duke of Cumberland's half brother. The general has a remarkable talent for brutality. I have no doubt you've heard of some of his recent exploits."

She bobbed her head. "Aye."

"If I cannot find Black Jack within three weeks, General Hawley has sworn to descend on your valley like the angel of death himself. He'll start by burning every house in Strathherrick, even your own. Only then will he ask questions about Black Jack, and believe me, Hawley won't rest until he has that outlaw in chains. His methods are not pretty, Madeleine, but if you want, I can describe them for you—"

"No!" she cried, her fingers desperately prying at his hands. "Ye're hurting me!"

"He'll hurt you, too, Maddie, only far worse." He released her so suddenly that she toppled back onto the blanket. She scrambled to her feet, rubbing her arms. Her flesh stung where he'd gripped her. Tears smarted her eyes and rolled unchecked down her pale cheeks.

At the sight of her tears Garrett rose beside her, heaving a ragged sigh. His expression was no longer hard. His eyes desperately searched her own.

"I'm sorry, Madeleine," he apologized. "Forgive me. I only want you to understand the seriousness of General Hawley's threat." He reached out to her, but she darted away. "I don't want to see anything happen to you—"

"Liar!" Madeleine spat, her wet eyes flashing. She

panted, straining hard to catch her breath. Was this the danger Garrett had spoken of to Sergeant Fletcher? she wondered crazily. Surely it wasn't true! The picture he painted was so brutal, so horrible that she could not think rationally.

"What have they promised ye for telling these lies, for threatening me with the lives of my kinsmen, innocent women and children?" she asked challengingly.

"Not lies, Madeleine. It's the truth, I swear it. You must believe me."

She glared at him, clenching her fists. "I can see what ye've been doing, Captain Garrett Marshall, with yer gentlemanly ways and fine compliments! Ply the Scots wench with wine, give her a kiss or two, and if ye're lucky, maybe she'll believe yer flattery and maybe," she hissed, "the Highland lass will fall into yer arms, perhaps even yer bed, and tell ye anything ye need to know. If that doesna work, threaten the stubborn wench with lies. She'll surely come 'round, either way, and ye'll have yer outlaw in a flash!"

She advanced on him, the pent-up fury of the past months overwhelming her completely. "What's yer reward for such lies and deceit?" she shrieked. "The rank of major? A pot of gold?"

The next thing Madeleine knew she was striking him with her fists, pounding his broad chest as hard as she could. He stood there a moment and allowed her to beat on him, until at last he grabbed her wrists with one hand and yanked her arms behind her back.

She struggled and kicked, but he held her so tightly she could hardly move. Finally she went limp in his arms, exhausted, her tears coming in a fresh flood.

Garrett held her as she wept miserably, her head against his chest, her slim body wracked by a storm of emotion. He tenderly stroked her hair until her sobs quieted. When he spoke, his voice was barely above a whisper.

"My reward is simple, Madeleine. I cannot bear to see Strathherrick become another Culloden. I'll never forget that day as long as I live, and it is the same for my commander, Colonel Wolfe. It was his idea to send me here, to use peaceful means to find Black Jack. You may find it hard to believe, but there are those of us who abhor what has been done to the Highlands."

Stunned, she looked up at him through dimmed eyes. "So ye were there, at Culloden."

"Yes," he answered quietly, a shadow passing across his face. "All of us aren't butchers, Maddie, despite what you may think. After the battle some of us tried to stop the slaughter—"

"Ye said so during yer fever," she interrupted, using her palm to smudge away her tears. "Ye cried out such terrible things. 'Twas my plan to ask ye about it once ye were on yer feet again."

He swallowed hard, his voice catching. "Yes, it was terrible, like living through hell on earth. A madness seized our soldiers; it was a bloody frenzy. Cumberland told us he had intercepted a letter from the Jacobites saying they'd offer no quarter to the wounded if they won the battle, so our troops were ordered to do the same."

" 'Twas a lie! My father would never have done such a thing, nor would my kinsmen!"

"I know, Madeleine. I know. But the damage was done. Once the massacre was started, there was no stopping it. There was nothing I could do."

She felt his body tremble as he held her, his face etched with pain.

"Just as the battle ended, a Highlander not far from me fell with a gaping stomach wound," he said tonelessly. "When I heard Cumberland's order to take no prisoners, I ran to the man, hoping to drag him safely from the field. I wasn't fast enough. I had barely given him a sip of brandy to ease his pain when another officer shoved me aside and shot the Highlander through the heart." His voice fell to a hoarse whisper. "My uniform, my hands, were soaked in his blood. Dammit, the man was already dying!"

Madeleine blinked, startled to see unshed tears glistening in Garrett's eyes. She felt her throat tighten painfully, and she looked away, overwhelmed by his emotion.

She would never have thought to hear such a story from a redcoat. It shook her long-held belief that all Englishmen were murderers and the devil's spawn. Garrett seemed all too human, with feelings and a deep sense of right and wrong. Perhaps that was even harder for her to bear.

Such knowledge battered the defenses she had built up within herself, the hatred and distrust that had already been weakened by the intimate moments they had shared. Despite her accusations, she could not deny the stirring power Garrett held over her.

"Madeleine."

She glanced up, meeting his eyes. His gaze was somber, piercing into her own.

"As mistress of Farraline, you can help me," he said, his voice throbbing with intensity. "I would like nothing more than for the Frasers of Strathherrick to live in peace . . . for you to live in peace, among your people. I ask only that you consider what I've said. Please. Please weigh everything carefully. It's been a terrible shock for you, but it is God's truth. Just remember, I've only got three weeks."

Madeleine dropped her gaze as he finally released her. Her mind was spinning and her thoughts and emotions were raging a furious battle. She sensed he was telling the truth, yet she could not bring herself to believe it. She needed time to think.

"I want to go home," she said, turning away. She heard him sigh heavily. His voice was weary, resigned.

"Very well."

While Garrett gathered up the refuse from their meal, she walked to her mare and mounted. She did not wait for him. She flicked the reins, and the mare galloped up the hill.

She avoided Wade's Road altogether and set off at a hard pace northward across the valley. She barely noticed the vibrant purple patches of heather, just beginning to bloom, a sign of the approaching autumn.

It did not take long for Garrett to catch up with her. When he reined in his bay beside her mare, she did not acknowledge his presence. Nor did she answer when he said her name.

Garrett did not speak again. Theirs was a long, silent ride back to Mhor Manor, accompanied only by pounding hooves and the whistling wind around them.

Chapter 14

❧❧

"What's wrong, lass?" Glenis asked as she cleared the supper dishes from the kitchen table. "Ye've hardly said a word today"—she picked up Madeleine's plate, shaking her head in disapproval—"and ye've not eaten but a mouthful of food. 'Tis been the same for two days. Tell yer Glenis what's on yer mind this minute, or I'll harp at ye 'til ye do!"

Madeleine stopped gazing out at the black night and turned from the window, her eyes meeting Glenis's. "How is it ye always know when something's amiss, Glenis?"

"Humph, lass, ye've made no effort to hide yer troubles from me. When ye winna eat my fine cooking, when ye winna talk but to answer aye or nay I know! Now I've had enough of yer brooding. Are ye not feelin' well? Was it yer raid last night?"

"No, 'tis not the raid, and I feel fine," Madeleine said, toying with her spoon. She winced inwardly. She was hardly fine.

How could she tell Glenis about the terrifying decision she had made? It was difficult enough to admit to herself she was frightened, let alone reveal her fear to someone else, even if that person was Glenis.

"Maddie—"

Madeleine heaved a sigh. "Och, Glenis, ye've a right to know," she admitted aloud. " 'Twill affect yer life as well as mine."

"What are ye talkin' about, Maddie?" Glenis asked,

159

clearly confused. She set down the plate and pulled out a chair.

"Aye, 'tis a good idea to sit down," Madeleine said cryptically. "Ye'll not like what I have to tell ye, any more than I like saying it."

Glenis leaned forward in her chair, her dark eyes searching Madeleine's. "Dinna leave me wondering, lass. Out with it now!"

Madeleine exhaled sharply. "When Garrett and I went for a ride together to Foyer's Falls a few days ago—"

"What happened?" Glenis gasped, clasping Madeleine's hands tightly. "He dinna touch ye, did he?"

"No, Glenis, no. Just hear me out." She kept her voice low as she recounted what Garrett had said to her about General Hawley, his plea for her to help him and lastly, her decision. Glenis's hands began to tremble, and Madeleine's heart went out to her old servant, who listened so quietly to her grim news.

When Madeleine finished, a heavy silence fell over the kitchen. It was finally broken when Glenis rose from her chair and picked up some dishes, her movements slow and wooden as she walked to the wash table. She methodically scraped the plates and dumped them into a large pan of steaming water, but instead of scrubbing them, she just stood there, staring at the wall.

"Glenis—" When Madeleine received no response she jumped up and rushed over to Glenis's side. There were tears streaking her servant's lined face.

Madeleine threw her arms around Glenis's shaking shoulders, assailed by guilt. She shouldn't have been so abrupt, she should have prepared her somehow. Worst of all, she didn't know what she could say to comfort her.

"So ye're going to give yerself up," Glenis said softly, turning her head to look at Madeleine. "I always knew 'twould come to this one day. From the first moment ye told me ye were plannin' to raid the English, I knew."

" 'Tis the only thing I can do," Madeleine replied, swamped by a sense of desperation. "Surely ye can see that, Glenis. I canna risk the lives of our kin on the slim hope that Garrett is lying, or even exaggerating the danger. I'd be a fool to take such a chance. I have to believe the danger is very real. Tell me ye understand!"

"Aye, I understand," Glenis said softly, wiping her damp eyes with her apron. "Though it doesna make it any easier for me. Have ye said anything to him yet about helpin' him to find his Black Jack?"

"No, and I winna, not for another week or so."

"Surely he'll demand an answer from ye, lass. The captain does not appear to be a man to be trifled with, even though he's shown himself to be fairer than most. Ye said he had less than three weeks left."

"I already gave him my answer yesterday morning. I told him I couldna help him."

Glenis looked at her sharply. "Ye speak in riddles, lass, and ye're playin' with my poor heart. Which is it to be?"

"I only told him I knew nothing of his outlaw because I needed to buy m'self more time, Glenis. I'll not help him 'til I've provided enough food for our kin to last the winter. 'Twill take another half dozen good raids to fill the cave on Beinn Dubhcharaidh. Then," she emphasized, "I'll give m'self up, with enough time to spare before that devil Hawley sets foot from Fort Augustus, if he's indeed planning such a move."

"Do Angus and the rest of yer kinsmen know of yer decision, lass?" Glenis asked quietly.

"No, not yet," Madeleine replied, a brittle edge to her voice. "First I must think of a way to spare them whatever fate the English have in store for me. I'll not have them suffer for following my cause. And if they wonder why we're raiding so much during the next few days I'll tell them the truth, that we must fill the cave for the winter."

Glenis sighed raggedly. "Och, lass, 'twill be hard goin' on as before, knowin' what I do now. I'm fearin' for ye, lass." She faltered, fresh tears coursing down her hollow cheeks.

"Ye must, Glenis," Madeleine insisted softly. "If ye're strong, 'twill help me to be strong. We canna show our fear, especially when I may need ye to cover for me in the days ahead. Ye must keep yer wits about ye more than ever. Are we agreed?"

"Aye." Glenis grabbed Madeleine's arm, a plea shining in her dark brown eyes. "Ye must let me know when ye tell the captain, Maddie. I dinna want to wake up some morning and find the redcoats have taken ye away . . ."

"Dinna fear," Madeleine soothed her, a hard lump in her throat. "And we'll work something out for ye when I do, for I'll not have ye bearing any of the blame." She gave Glenis a fierce hug, then released her. She glanced over her shoulder at the half-cleared table. "Let me help ye with the dishes, Glenis," she offered.

"No, hinny, I'll manage," Glenis objected with a weak smile. "I think I'd like to be alone for a while . . . if ye dinna mind."

Madeleine nodded and quickly left the kitchen, unable to bear the pain she saw etched in Glenis's eyes. All she could think of was seeking the solace of her bedchamber.

She had wrestled with confiding in Glenis since she returned from Foyer's Falls, and now that she had, her emotions were spent. She ignored the soldier standing guard in the dimly lit hall and reached for the banister.

"Damn!"

She started at the softly uttered curse, recognizing Garrett's voice. It had come from the drawing room. She immediately thought to run up the stairs and avoid him once again, as she had done so well since their encounter yesterday.

It had been a brief but unpleasant scene. Garrett had said little when she told him she couldn't help him; only his eyes had registered his shock and dismay. There was also a trace of suspicion, as if he did not quite believe her. His frustration was evident when he abruptly left her and joined his men, who were waiting for him in front of the manor house. She had never seen him lash his bay so harshly as when they rode out to spend another long day searching the valley.

Madeleine hesitated at the landing, unsure what she should do. If she continued to purposefully avoid him, he might suspect her all the more. Perhaps it was better to seek out his company and act as if she had nothing to hide. Her heart began to pound at the thought, and she walked nervously toward the drawing room.

She paused in the archway, her eyes widening at the comfortable scene. Garrett was seated before the hearth, his legs stretched out in front of him, an opened book in his lap. He appeared so at home, except for the fact that he was not reading but instead was staring into the leaping flames with a troubled look on his handsome face. She could well imagine what he was thinking and quickly determined she would leave at once if he pressed her further about Black Jack.

"Good evening to ye, Garrett."

Garrett rose suddenly from the chair, the book falling to the floor with a thud.

"Madeleine," he said, stunned by her unexpected appearance. Her unadorned beauty never failed to astound him. She could be dressed in rags and covered with filth but still she would outshine any woman he had ever known. "I thought you had long since retired for the evening."

"Glenis and I just finished a late supper," she replied. Her gaze moved to the armchair across from his. "May I join ye? The fire looks so welcome."

"Yes, of course," Garrett said. "You don't have to ask me if you might sit in your own drawing room, Madeleine."

She made no comment as she stepped into the room. He caught a whiff of her scent as she walked past him.

It was sweet and clean, like sunshine, fresh air, and heather. To him it was a fragrance more heady than the most expensive perfume. It aroused his senses, making him all the more aware of the startling effect she had on him.

Drawing a deep breath, he picked up the book and sat down, watching quietly as she settled herself. He could not help but wonder why she was joining him when she had gone out of her way to avoid him these past few days.

Except for yesterday, he thought dryly. He found his mood darkening once more, despite Madeleine's stirring presence. Should he ask her again? Her adamant denial had not totally convinced him she knew nothing about Black Jack. And after today's fruitless search for leads, he was still no closer—

"What are ye reading?" she asked, her soft, melodic voice lulling his anxious thoughts.

Garrett held up the small, leather-bound book. "*As You Like It*, by William Shakespeare." He glanced over at the narrow bookcase, lined with well-dusted volumes. "You have quite a nice collection of his works. I'm glad they survived the soldiers who came here in May."

"Aye," she said simply, quickly skipping over the disagreeable topic. "My mother was very fond of Shakespeare. She and my father would travel as far away as Edinburgh to see one of his plays, though I've not seen any yet." She smiled wistfully. "I would love to see *As You Like It* performed on the stage. 'Tis my favorite comedy."

"Mine also," Garrett said with a wry note in his voice. "That's why I picked it out. I thought a comedy might ease my mind."

As the smile faded from Madeleine's lips, he felt like kicking himself. It was a wondrous thing when she smiled, and talking to her like this was a rare gift. He decided it was worth it to avoid any mention of Black Jack, just to see her smile again.

He would just have to find the cursed outlaw on his

own, he thought resolutely. Right now, he just wanted to concentrate on Madeleine, to sit with her and savor her enjoyable company.

"Tell me what you like best about the play," he asked, encouraged when he saw her expression brighten.

"Och, so many things, really," she began, " 'Tis a love story. She hesitated, her pretty blush eliciting a surge of warmth in Garrett. "But most of all, I like the character of Rosalind. She knows her own mind, and she's not afraid to speak it."

Garrett chuckled as he thumbed through the book, looking for a certain passage. He found it and began to read, his voice soft and resonant: " 'From the east to western Ind, No jewel is like Rosalind. Her worth, being mounted on the wind, Through all the world bears Rosalind. All the pictures fairest lin'd Are but black to Rosalind. Let no face be kept in mind, But the fair of Madeleine."

"Ye mean Rosalind," Madeleine corrected, smiling self-consciously.

"Ah, so I do," Garrett said softly, studying her intently. "Rosalind." When she turned and gazed into the fire, he quickly found another page, sensing he had embarrassed her. "Here's a line of fair Rosalind's wit. I've always pitied poor Orlando when he swears he will die of love if he cannot have her, and she tartly answers: 'Men have died from time to time, and worms have eaten them, but not for love.' " He feigned a woeful sigh. "Such feminine cruelty."

" 'Tisn't cruelty," she responded with a small laugh, glancing back at him, "but sheer common sense. Orlando is so besotted he's become absurd in his praise. Rosalind is merely saying if he canna have her, he would find another reason to live."

"I don't know, Madeleine," Garrett countered, staring at her thoughtfully. "If I loved as deeply as Orlando, I would find it difficult to agree with your argument."

Distracted by the intensity of his gaze, Madeleine

shifted in her seat, then suddenly stood up. "The fire is very warm," she muttered, proceeding to shove the armchair away from the hearth.

"Let me help you," Garrett offered. He rose and lifted the chair easily, setting it back a few feet. "How's that?"

"That's fine, thank ye," she said, sitting down. She watched him as he pushed his chair a bit closer to hers, thinking how beautiful his hair was in the firelight. Not fully blond nor brown, but a golden shade in between. She wondered what its texture might feel like if she were to run her fingers through it . . .

"I'll tell you what I like about this comedy," he said, his voice breaking into her errant thoughts. "Rosalind disguising herself as a man." He laughed, a rich, rumbling sound. "What an intriguing double identity. She can make fun of love and yet be a lover."

Madeleine nearly choked. Was he baiting her? she wondered, looking at him sharply. His open smile revealed no trickery, but it did not still her thundering heart. She quickly sought to change the disturbing subject.

"Do you have other favorites among Shakespeare's plays?" she asked lightly.

"*A Midsummer Night's Dream* and *The Tempest*," he replied. "And you?"

"Aye, *The Tempest* is a fine play," Madeleine agreed in a rush, "but I've always liked *Romeo and Juliet* the best." The minute she said it, she wished she hadn't. The way he was looking at her made her feel quite dizzy.

"Then you are a true romantic at heart," Garrett said softly. "Not a pragmatist, like Rosalind." He leaned forward in his chair. "Tell me more about yourself, Maddie."

Garrett's use of her nickname did not unnerve her as much as his unexpected request. She had the feeling she'd revealed quite enough about herself for one night. She rose abruptly, her gaze shifting from him to the yawning archway, her means of escape, and back again.

"Ye must be tired, Garrett," she began somewhat lamely.

"Not at all."

"I mean it's been a very long day. Perhaps we can talk again—"

"Tomorrow night, then," he replied easily. "I'm looking forward to it already." He stood and gallantly took her arm, smiling at her. "Allow me to escort you."

Before she could think to refuse him, they were walking together from the drawing room and up the main stairs. She caught a glimpse of the guard staring after them, and she flushed to her toes. Between his bemused expression and the tingling pressure of Garrett's hand on her arm, she felt as if she were in a daze. Before she knew it they had reached her door, and Garrett had opened it for her.

"Your charming company has been most appreciated," he said huskily, standing so close to her that she could sense the heat emanating from his powerful body. "Good night, sweet Madeleine." He bent and lightly kissed her cheek, then he turned and strode down the hall to his room, disappearing inside.

Madeleine stood there a long moment, not quite sure what had just transpired between them, or how she felt about it. Bewildered, she closed the door and leaned on it, caressing her cheek. Her skin seemed to burn where he had kissed her.

"Good night, Garrett," she whispered in the dark.

One evening a week later, Madeleine sat on the edge of her bed, staring out the window as the mountains towering behind Mhor Manor became stark silhouettes in the gathering dusk.

"So much for taking a nap," she muttered resignedly. She could have used it. Tonight she planned another raid, her fifth since Garrett had told her about Hawley. Only a few more and the cave would be full.

She struck a flint and lit the thick candles on her bedside table. Once again, her restless thoughts had not allowed her to sleep. Never would she have imagined the perplexing double life she had come to lead. It was like an intricate web spun with the finest gossamer, easily torn by one misplaced emotion.

The past week had flown by in a blur. During the day she had seen little of Garrett as they went their separate ways, he and his men to search the valley and question villagers, while she either rested after a raid or planned the next one with her kinsmen. Those were the times when it was easy to keep her emotions firmly in check and her mission clearly before her.

It was in the evenings that her emotions ran rampant, making her forget all else but the pleasure she found in Garrett's company. She did not know at what point her conscious decision to seek him out had transformed itself into an inexplicable desire to be with him, but it had happened.

She was drawn to him despite herself, and despite the nagging voice which forever warned her she was acting like a fool. Knowing the dark days which lay ahead of her, perhaps she craved some happiness, and she found it with Garrett.

The light conversations they shared—discussing music, art, and literature, funny childhood stories, even hunting—somehow lessened the chilling fear she always carried with her. Thankfully he had made no mention of Black Jack, or of Hawley's threat; she surmised he needed some respite, too, from the troubles which weighed heavily on his mind. The delight she had found in his wit and intelligence, his humor, and his warm laughter made it easy to forget she would soon become his prisoner, destined to be executed for high treason.

"Och, dinna think of what's to come or ye'll surely go mad," Madeleine whispered under her breath, shuddering as she forced the bleak picture from her mind. She walked to the window and drew aside the curtain, her breath fogging the cool glass. She traced a name upon the pane. Garrett.

She sighed with longing. He was waiting for her in the drawing room. She could sense it. She had agreed to meet him downstairs by seven o'clock and have supper with him. She glanced at the clock on the mantel. It was a quarter past. Perhaps he had already realized she wasn't coming. She would simply have to tell him tomorrow she had changed her mind.

She could not go to him. She wanted to, badly, but she could no longer allow herself to share his company. Not tonight, and not tomorrow night, if she hoped to fight the forbidden desire growing ever stronger within her.

Aye, she knew now that the strange yearning that had plagued her was a desire which would surely make her a traitor to her people if she gave it free rein.

When she was around Garrett, nothing made sense anymore. It was so easy to forget that she was an outlaw and to forget why she had become one, to forget the raids and her waiting kinsmen. She forgot Garrett was an Englishman, a redcoat, and therefore her sworn enemy. And that she could not afford to do. She needed a clear mind to continue her raids and to face what lay ahead.

"No more, Maddie," she murmured to her reflection in the glass. "Ye canna fail yer people. They need yer full attention, now more than ever before."

Tonight there would be no lighthearted discourse with Garrett, no shared laughter, and no conflicting emotions as he walked her upstairs. She would stay in her room until it was time to sneak out through the tunnel. By then, she hoped, he would have retired for the night. She would simply have to find some other way to pass the time.

Madeleine's gaze swept her chamber, awash in soft candlelight, and settled on her open wardrobe. She caught an enticing glimmer of sapphire-blue satin and knew exactly how she would while away the hours. She would try on her mother's gowns for one last time.

It was a girlish fancy, perhaps, but she did not know when, or if, she might have another chance.

She crossed to the wardrobe and pulled out the blue satin gown with its silver brocade bodice and under-skirt, then ran to her bed. She was overcome with nostalgia as she changed, her troubled emotions forgotten for the moment. The fabric glided like cool water over her skin and pooled at her bare feet.

It had been such a long time since she had tried on this beautiful gown. Her fingers trembled as she pinned the bodice to her chemise, knowing it would not look quite right without stays but not caring. She hadn't worn a corset since that afternoon at the loch.

The memory of Garrett's kiss came flooding back to her as if it had happened that very day, and her wretched torment began anew. She tentatively touched her lips, feeling again the blazing heat of his mouth upon hers.

She had found herself thinking of that moment many times over this past week, especially in Garrett's presence. He seemed to elicit the wildest imaginings in her—

"No more," she warned herself unconvincingly, crossing to the full-length mirror. As she stared at her shimmering reflection, she tried to shrug off the vivid memory, but the unsettling sensations stayed with her, taunting her.

Would Garrett find her lovely in this gown? she wondered, shivering with excitement. She trailed a finger along the low-cut bodice and up the lush curve of her breast, sighing softly.

She turned, her satin skirt rustling and swaying, and stood in profile. Her hands strayed to her white throat. She lifted up her hair, envisioning a more sophisticated style, then she let it tumble down her back in a riot of tangled chestnut curls.

She closed her eyes, her hand sliding slowly down her body from her neck to her curved hip. An image of Garrett leaped into her mind, and she sighed again.

He was dripping wet, naked and his strong hands were caressing her own wet skin . . .

"I far prefer your hair down, Madeleine, wild and unfettered. Like you."

Madeleine's eyes flew open and she whirled on her intruder, mortified that he had seen her . . . God's wounds, she had never felt so embarrassed!

"Garrett! How—how long have ye been standing there?"

"Not long," he said quietly, stepping inside the room. "Forgive me for startling you, Madeleine. When you didn't meet me in the drawing room, I decided to come and find you. I knocked, hearing your footsteps, and opened the door slightly." He paused, his eyes raking her from head to foot. "I see you've dressed for dinner."

Madeleine moved away from the mirror, flustered by the way his gaze was fixed upon her, as if he would devour her whole. She shivered at the thought, struggling to maintain what little was left of her composure.

"Garrett, ye really must leave. I canna sup with ye tonight."

"No?" he asked, drawing closer to her. "Then why the gown? It is a most becoming one, I might add."

" 'Twas my mother's," Madeleine blurted, becoming increasingly unnerved by his presence. "I wanted to try it on, that's all."

"It fits you perfectly, Madeleine," he said appreciatively. His gaze wandered to her breasts, which thrust against the daring neckline. "Perfectly." He met her eyes, his expression growing serious. "Why won't you dine with me?"

She retreated a step, her heart pounding furiously as she took another desperate stab at dismissing him. "I'm feeling a bit out of sorts, Garrett," she said, smiling weakly. "Perhaps another night."

He did not reply but studied her closely. Odd tremors shot through her, and she had to fight to calm her breathing.

Her gaze moved over him, and her pulse fluttered as she noted the simple elegance of his clothes. He wore tight-fitting black breeches which accentuated his slim hips and sinewed thighs, and a full, white shirt which heightened the golden cast of his skin, the open collar revealing a nest of dark blond curls. His hair shone like burnished flame in the flickering candlelight, while his striking features were half cloaked in shadow. Oh, why did he have to be so handsome?

"I've been feeling a bit out of sorts as well," he said at last, his voice laden with a deep intensity she had not heard before. "Perhaps we suffer the same malady, you and I."

"M-malady?" she stammered.

Garrett nodded, his eyes searing into hers. "A fever, a fire burning in the blood, an ache that has but one cure. That's how I feel whenever I'm around you, Madeleine." He reached out and smoothed a silken tress. "Who were you thinking of when you stood before the mirror? A lover, perhaps?"

Madeleine gasped, her cheeks firing hotly. She gave no answer but frantically attempted to brush past him. Her foot caught in her skirt, tripping her, and she cried out as she began to fall. The next thing she knew she was staring into Garrett's eyes, his arms tightening like a vise around her trembling body.

"Who were you thinking of, Maddie?" he whispered huskily, his warm breath fanning her cheeks.

She shook her head, unable to speak. Unbridled sensations rippled through her body. Then his mouth found hers, and she knew nothing but the passionate power of his kiss. His lips ravaged hers, his tongue flicking at her teeth, and she opened her mouth to him. She moaned as he held her to his chest, his fingers twined in her hair.

"Tell me who you desire," he demanded hoarsely, forcing her head back and covering her throat with biting kisses.

Madeleine nearly screamed aloud as his mouth found the hollow between her heaving breasts, his lips like hot brands upon her flesh. In a passion-dimmed daze, she felt his hand cup her, his fingers dragging away her bodice and chemise. His tongue circled a sensitive nipple in a ring of moist, molten fire. It was hot, insistent, provoking the forbidden hunger already raging within her. If she did not deny him now, she would be lost.

"No," she murmured, bracing her hands against his chest even as every part of her cried out to meld with him, to feel the wonder of his skin against her body. "No, Garrett, please. I want ye to stop . . . Stop!"

Her wrenching cry echoed about the room, and tears sprang to her eyes as Garrett pulled abruptly away from her. His expression was unreadable, though his eyes were gray and storm-tossed, his breathing jagged.

"It seems I was wrong once again," he said cryptically, running his hand through his hair.

Madeleine straightened her bodice, fighting against the tears that would course down her flushed cheeks. "Please, go," she managed to say, glancing away from him.

"My apologies, Mistress Fraser," he said stiffly. "I promise you it won't happen again." He strode across the room and was gone, his determined footsteps resounding in the hallway.

Madeleine stumbled to the door, scarcely able to see through the tears swimming in her eyes. She shut it and drew the bolt, then leaned her forehead against the polished wood.

How she wanted to fling wide the door and run after him, to tell him that he was the man she desired! But she would not be a traitor to everything she loved, everything for which she had fought so dearly.

"Ye're the mistress of Farraline," she whispered fiercely, walking back toward the bed. "Dinna forget it! Yer people are depending upon yer care and good judgment."

Strangely the words gave her no comfort. She threw herself on the mattress, the full burden of her responsibility pressing down on her like a terrible weight.

For the first time she cursed the task her father had given her. She buried her face in a pillow and began to weep bitterly, overwhelmed by fear, intense longing, and regret for all that she would never know.

Chapter 15

Garrett angrily paced the drawing room, a crinkled piece of paper in his hand. He stopped near the window and pushed aside the curtain, holding the paper up to the fading light.

He read the terse message again, for probably the tenth time. It was written in Colonel Wolfe's distinctive scrawl, punctuated by numerous ink blotches. The words seemed to jump off the page and burn into his brain.

Black Jack had struck again, this time just west of Inverness. General Hawley was furious and threatened immediate action. It was the seventh successful raid in two weeks, not counting the thirty cattle mysteriously stolen in Glen Tarff, a few miles south of Fort Augustus. Seven blasted raids in two weeks, spread out all over the county . . .

"Damn Black Jack to hell!" Garrett cursed aloud, turning away from the window. He balled up the paper and stuffed it into his coat pocket. He hated to admit it, but this message was further proof that his peaceful mission was a dismal failure. Despite everything he had done—endlessly searching the valley, interrogating villagers, and recently staking out roads at night—it appeared the elusive outlaw was unstoppable.

He sat down heavily in the armchair, pounding his fist on the padded brocade. Time was slipping away from him. General Hawley would no doubt be there within days, maybe sooner from the scathing tone of the message.

Was his mission really going to end as he feared, in flaming cottages and the helpless screams of men, women, and children? Soon it would be nightfall. Would Black Jack ride again, while he and his men chased shadows across the valley?

A flash of forest-green skirt, bright tartan shawl, and tousled chestnut hair caught his attention. He moved once more to the window and watched as Madeleine walked toward the house. She gave no notice to the soldiers standing guard. Her eyes were straight ahead, her step brisk and determined.

So she's finally returning from Farraline, he thought bitterly. From visiting her people, and her lover. While there were so many lives at stake she busied herself with God-only-knew-what, as if there was nothing amiss, no danger looming on the horizon. Her lack of concern was incredible! Could it be she hadn't believed him about Hawley after all?

Garrett frowned, at a total loss. He had looked for her earlier, determined to ask her one last time for her help, especially now that he had received this message. He still could not bring himself to believe that she knew absolutely nothing about Black Jack, despite her claim of ignorance. It just didn't make sense, considering her respected position in the valley.

Glenis had told him merely that Madeleine had gone to the village and would say nothing more. It seemed even the old woman had turned against him, avoiding him at every opportunity. Madeleine had certainly evaded him ever since the night he had gone to her room and fairly forced himself on her, thinking she might feel as he did.

His jaw tightened, a wave of frustration possessing him. Fool! Once again he had allowed his personal desires and misguided emotions to get in the way of his mission. He should have pressed her further, as he had intended. Instead he had been bewitched by her company, her smiles, and his own fantasies of how things might be between them when Black Jack was captured.

Garrett flinched as the front door slammed and Madeleine's light footsteps sounded in the hall. He strode from the drawing room, almost bumping into her. She jumped back, startled, and clutched her basket tightly. It was plain to see that he had unnerved her.

"I was wondering when you might return from the village," he said, gesturing for the guard to disappear. The man obeyed him quickly, ducking into the hall leading to the soldiers' sleeping quarters. "We have to talk, Madeleine."

Madeleine stared at him wide-eyed, aware of the nervous flutter in her stomach and the heat flooding her body. She had scarcely seen him since—

She forced the potent memory from her mind, not trusting herself to remain here with him any longer. "I-I'm sorry, Garrett," she said, conjuring a convincing half lie. "I'm very tired. A kinswoman in Farraline is near childbirth. I may be called back during the night to bring more of Glenis's herb medicine. Perhaps we can talk in the morning." She brushed past him and moved toward the staircase.

Aye, she really was tired, she thought wearily. That much was true. She'd spent much of the afternoon planning tonight's raid with her kinsmen. It would be their last one together, though they didn't know it yet. Now she needed nothing more than a long nap. Midnight would come soon enough, and she had to be well rested and alert—

She started when Garrett suddenly grabbed her arm. "No, Madeleine," he said firmly, turning her about to face him. "This can't wait until tomorrow."

His gaze was so insistent she knew she would not escape him. "Very well," she relented, her heart racing. Was he going to ask her about the other night? she wondered anxiously. Surely he wasn't going to drill her about—

"Two weeks ago you claimed you knew nothing about Black Jack," he began, confirming her suspicion.

His grip tightened around her arm. "I've just received word that there have been seven raids since that day. I'll ask you once more, Madeleine. Do you know anything at all about this outlaw?"

Anger erupted within her at his rough treatment, mixed with a sense of desperation. She couldn't tell him yet! She had one last raid to complete, then there would be more than enough food in the cave to last the winter. She would tell him in the morning, but not now. She had planned everything so carefully. By tomorrow night, Garrett would have his Black Jack.

"Ye're hurting me!" she exclaimed hotly. She tried to wrench free, but he held her fast. "I told ye! I know nothing of yer outlaw. Now let me go!"

Garrett sighed heavily as he reluctantly released her. She did not wait to see if he had anything further to say but dashed up the stairs, feeling his eyes bore into her back. Once she was in her room, she bolted the door against him. She knew he was still thinking of her, wondering why she would not help him. If he only knew how afraid she truly was.

Ye've put him off, lass, 'tis all that matters, Madeleine assured herself shakily, setting down her basket and throwing off her shawl. She kicked off her brogues and lay down on the bed, hugging her arms to her chest.

How she wished at that moment that she was a little girl again, with no more worries than how she would elude Glenis's stern and watchful eye, or which of her favorite ponies she should ride across the moor. Life had been so simple and carefree then.

"Ye canna escape yer troubles by wishing them away," she whispered fiercely. "Ye're a grown woman now, Maddie Fraser, and ye must face what life has brought to ye."

She closed her eyes, willing her body to relax even while her thoughts continued to tumble and whirl.

She was astounded by how smoothly the raids had gone so far, despite Garrett's placing extra patrols in Farraline and on some of the roads surrounding the village. The supply trains had also been more heavily guarded, but the element of surprise had not failed her and her kinsman yet.

With Glenis's help she had even feigned a slight illness when she and her kinsmen had journeyed overnight to Glen Tarff to steal another herd of cattle. While she was gone, Glenis had virtually camped outside her door for two days, allowing no one in her room, not even Meg.

'' 'Tis a woman's ailment,'' was all her faithful servant offered as explanation. It soon would pass, but until then, Madeleine needed complete rest and solitude. Thankfully, Garrett had been deceived.

Aye, that ruse had been risky, as had all her raids, but it was well worth it. The cave at Beinn Dubhcharaidh was nearly stocked from floor to ceiling with barrels, crates, and sacks containing every manner of foodstuff, from salted beef to turnips. If anything happened to her, she could be assured her people would have enough food to survive the winter.

If anything happened to her . . .

Madeleine shivered, suddenly ice-cold. She rose abruptly from her bed, her hand clutching her throat.

How could she possibly rest when she imagined the noose tightening around her neck with each passing moment? Dear God, where would she ever find the courage to face what was ahead?

She walked swiftly to the door despite the wooden feeling in her legs.

She would speak with Glenis. Glenis never lacked for words of wisdom and strength in trying times; it was her comfort that had seen Madeleine past her father's death. It would be hard for them to discuss what lay ahead, but it was better than suffering alone. And it was time Glenis knew of her plans.

Madeleine hurried downstairs, grateful there was no sign of Garrett. She ignored the guard who had returned to his post and rushed into the kitchen.

She was disappointed to see that Glenis was not there. She checked her room, but it was empty. She was about to double back and search the rest of the house when she heard a soft knock on the kitchen door.

Her brow knit anxiously. It was dark out already. Who would be about at this supper hour? She thought of her kinsmen and hurried to the door.

She cracked it open, peering outside. She could barely make out an old woman's stooped figure in the thin sliver of candlelight cast from the kitchen. A large fringed bonnet covered the woman's bowed head, shadowing her features.

"Forgive me, lassie, for this intrusion," the woman wheezed in a gruff voice. "Could ye spare a cup of hot tea and a slice of bread for a weary traveler?"

Madeleine hesitated only an instant. She drew open the door, studying her unexpected visitor in the flood of light. "Aye, of course," she said graciously. "Come in."

From what little Madeleine could see of the woman's face, she had never seen her before, and she doubted her visitor was from the valley. If she was a fugitive, Maddie had never seen a more unlikely one. Yet she could not deny this woman her hospitality. It was an unwritten code among the Highlanders that strangers were always made welcome. Except for redcoats, she amended dryly.

"Thank ye," the woman said, glancing furtively over her shoulder before entering the kitchen. As Madeleine closed the door behind her, she shuffled to the table and immediately sat down, heaving a loud groan of relief. The chair creaked ominously under the woman's weight.

Madeleine stifled her reaction, but she could not help noticing her visitor was amazingly stout, her hunched shoulders broad and rounded beneath a threadbare shawl. The woman was wearing a gray fustian gown that seemed to lack a clear waistline, appearing almost sacklike in its loose proportion. From beneath the ragged hem peeked dusty black boots, the largest pair

Madeleine had ever seen on anyone, let alone a
woman.

Madeleine chided herself for staring and quickly
fetched a steaming mug of tea. She cut a thick slice of
fresh-baked bread and slathered it with butter, then set
the plate in front of the old woman.

"Is there anything else ye'd like?" she asked. She
nodded toward the black kettle hanging above the
hearth. "My cook, Glenis, always has a good pot of
stew at the ready."

"Aye, 'twould be lovely," the woman said between
slurps of tea, without lifting her head.

Madeleine brought a brimming bowl to the table
along with more bread. She refilled the woman's mug,
not surprised to see her hungrily devour the stew,
soaking up every last drop with the breadcrusts. Madeleine was beginning to believe this woman was indeed a fugitive. It was clear she hadn't eaten a good
meal in days.

After three bowls of stew, a pot of tea, and nearly a
loaf of bread, the woman's ravenous appetite was
sated. She pushed back from the table and raised her
head ever so slightly.

"Sit with me, lass, for a wee bit," she croaked in a
husky tone that was more a command than a request.

Madeleine sat down across the table, eyeing the old
woman's broad features in the candlelight. A bulbous
nose, massive jowls, a fat double chin. She had the
strangest feeling she had seen her somewhere before.

"Ye recognize me, dinna ye, Maddie Fraser?"

Madeleine gasped at the decidedly male voice, her
eyes widening in surprise. "God's wounds, could it
be?"

Low, rumbling laughter erupted from her visitor at
her astonished statement, a distinctive chuckle Madeleine had not heard in more than a year. Not since the
red grouse hunt early last summer. Her father had
hosted the event for his tacksmen and his guest of
honor, Lord Lovat, the chief of Clan Fraser.

She leaned forward in her chair, staring incredu-

lously at the grinning old man. It was Simon Fraser
himself, a hunted fugitive since Culloden, disguised as
a woman. And the place was swarming with redcoats!

What could Lord Lovat be thinking? Didn't he realize his danger? Hadn't he seen the guards posted along
the drive? Hadn't he seen the soldiers through the
windows, bunked in the dancing room and the guest
rooms? She tried to speak, but her throat was constricted so tightly no words came.

"Calm yerself, lassie," Simon Fraser said softly, sobering at her obvious distress. "I've seen the redcoats,
if that's what ye're wondering. And they dinna see
me. If they had, they wouldna care two whits about an
old woman calling at the house. I'm not worried, nor
should ye be. Believe me, there's fewer redcoats in
Mhor Manor than out on the roads tonight scouring
the mountains. 'Tis safer by far."

When she continued to gape at him, he sighed and
patted her hand. " 'Tis why I'm here, Maddie. I long
for nothing more than a good night's rest in a warm
bed. Ye've already seen to the fine meal. My old bones
grow weary from this chase. 'Tis mad I suppose, but
the lights in yer house looked so inviting from Beinn
Bhuidhe, despite yer English guests. I couldna help
m'self."

"Ye've been hiding on Beinn Bhuidhe?" Madeleine
asked, finding her voice at last.

"Aye, for a week now. I was in Badenoch for quite
a while, staying here and there, and before that Glen
Cannich to the north . . ." His voice trailed off, his
shoulders slumping with exhaustion. "Och, Maddie,
'tis a long story, and I've no heart for it tonight. 'Tis
my plan to set out for the west Highlands before dawn.
Loch Morar. I've friends there who'll help me. 'Tis my
hope to find a ship to France."

"France?"

"Aye. 'Tis the safest plan. My lands are lost to me,
my castle burned to the ground. I canna hide there.
And my kinsmen risk much to shelter me, even disguised as I am." He forced a weak smile. "I know 'tis

a dangerous thing to ask ye, Maddie, but if I could stay here only one night, I'll be off before the sun rises in the morn—''

''Of course ye must stay!'' Madeleine whispered vehemently. ''Dinna think to ask me again, m'lord. I'd be insulted if ye did. The chief of Clan Fraser is always welcome in my home, redcoats or no. I'm honored ye chose to entrust me with yer care.''

''Ye're a brave lass, Maddie, and I thank ye. Ye do the memory of yer father proud, God rest him.''

Madeleine felt a sudden lump in her throat, but she forced herself to think of the task at hand. She rose and swiftly cleared the table. The sooner Lord Lovat was settled somewhere in the house, away from prying eyes, the better. But where?

He couldn't sleep in Glenis's room, she decided, dumping the dishes into the washpan. It wasn't safe enough. There was no lock on the door, and Garrett and his soldiers were forever passing through the kitchen, sometimes even waking Glenis to ask for this or that. It would not do if they found Lord Lovat instead, despite his disguise.

Nor could he sleep upstairs, she thought, walking back to the table. If Garrett heard any noise coming from the two empty guest rooms across the hall from his own chamber, he would surely become suspicious. Lord Lovat's masquerade was well played, but it might not hold up under close scrutiny or a barrage of questions. No, she would have to think of something else.

She was struck by an idea, farfetched, yet she sensed it might work. Perhaps Lord Lovat could sleep upstairs in her room. No one would bother him there, especially if the door was bolted. Garrett believed she had already gone to bed for the night. Meanwhile, she could hide quietly in one of the guest rooms and wait for the dawn . . .

She was so lost in her thoughts that she jumped when Glenis walked abruptly into the kitchen, while Simon gasped at the footsteps behind him. He ducked his head so the bonnet hid his face, and he clutched his shawl tightly.

Madeleine rushed over to her stunned servant's side, her finger to her lips, her eyes flashing caution. " 'Tis all right, m'lord," she said reassuringly over her shoulder. " 'Tis only Glenis."

"M'lord?" Glenis said, her dark eyes widening at the stout female figure hunched in the chair. She glanced questioningly at Madeleine. "M'lord?"

"Aye. Ye mustna breathe a word of this to anyone, Glenis. 'Tis Simon Fraser, our Lord Lovat."

At Madeleine's words, Simon twisted around and gave Glenis a wink. " 'Tis good to see ye again, Glenis darlin'."

"God protect us!" Glenis blurted, blanching white as a sheet. She rolled her eyes heavenward, looking as if she might faint. Madeleine grabbed her arm and gave her a good shake.

"Shhh, Glenis, keep yer wits about ye," she demanded. "We dinna have time for any hysterics. I need yer help. We've got to get Lord Lovat upstairs and into my room without anyone seeing him. He'll be staying at Mhor Manor tonight."

"Yer room?" Glenis asked, totally confused.

"Aye. I'll explain later. Listen to me, Glenis. Go into the drawing room and break something. Anything. That should lure the guard away from his post. We'll need only an instant to sneak up the stairs. Now go!"

With a last wide-eyed glance at Simon, Glenis bobbed her head and fled the kitchen as fast as her stiff legs would carry her. A few moments later there was a crash of breaking china.

Madeleine wasted no time. She looped her arm through Simon's, and together they hurried into the main hallway. The guard was on his knees in the drawing room, his back to them while he helped Glenis retrieve shards of a shattered plate.

Madeleine assisted Simon up the stairs, hoping Garrett had not heard the clamor. She had a story brewing in her mind just in case. Her great-aunt Morag had come for supper and was suddenly taken ill . . .

Fortunately it appeared she wouldn't have to use her story. The hallway was dark and silent, no light shone from beneath Garrett's door. Madeleine quietly led the way with Simon close behind her until they reached her room. She fairly pushed him inside and bid him a hasty good night.

"I'll wake ye in the morning, m'lord, before dawn," she whispered. "Bolt the door, mind ye, and dinna open it 'til ye hear four short knocks. We'll have to trick the guard again, but 'tis no matter. These redcoats are a dim-witted lot. Ye'll be safely on yer way before dawn."

"I thank ye, Maddie," he said. "Sleep well."

The door closed with a small click, and she heard the bolt slide into place. Satisfied, she turned and made her way back down the hallway.

Sleep well, she thought wryly. She wouldn't sleep a wink tonight. While the chieftain of Clan Fraser was under her roof, she was charged with his protection.

Suddenly she stopped in her tracks. The raid! She sighed resignedly. Och, there was nothing to be done about it now.

It seemed she had raided her last supply train. The foodstuffs they had gathered in the cave would have to be enough. There was no time to carry out any more raids after tonight, other than what she had planned for the following evening. But then she would be alone.

At least her kinsmen would know to abandon the raid when she failed to meet them at the yew tree, she thought as she continued down the hallway. She had no doubt they would understand. It was her duty to guard Lord Lovat with her life, as would any Fraser. She would do whatever was necessary to ensure his safety.

Madeleine's hand was on the door latch to the guest chamber when a loud thud sounded from her room, followed by a blustered oath. She grimaced, scurrying back to her door.

''Lord Lovat, are ye all right?'' she called softly.

''Aye, lass. Just a bit clumsy is all. Dinna worry.''

Relieved, she leaned her head against the doorjamb. It was going to be a long night. She pushed away from the door, stiffening as a hand suddenly touched her shoulder, and her heart sank into her shoes.

Chapter 16

"Madeleine, what's going on?" Garrett asked, his deep voice tinged with concern. "I was just coming up the stairs, and I heard someone fall. Are you all right?"

Madeleine whirled around, gaping at the familiar silhouette looming in the darkness. A quick lie jumped to her lips.

" 'Twas nothing, Garrett. I merely tripped on a pair of brogues when I was leaving my room. 'Twas stupid of me, dropping them in the middle of the floor like that." She bent down and rubbed her knee convincingly, moaning a little. "Och, it hurts a bit, but I think I'll be fine."

"Come with me," he said firmly. "We should take a look at it in the light."

Before she could protest, he swept her into his arms and strode down the hallway to his room. He leaned into the door, shoving it open, and made straight for the bed, where he set her down gently.

Madeleine listened as he fumbled about the bedside table for the flint and steel. At least he hadn't tried to carry her back into her own room, she thought gratefully. She heard him strike the flint, and she blinked as warm candlelight flooded the large room.

Garrett knelt in front of her, his eyes meeting her startled gaze. "Could you lift your skirt for me, Madeleine?"

She nodded, her heart thumping fiercely against her

187

breast. As she raised her skirt slowly, a fiery blush burned her cheeks. She draped the hem over the top of her legs and held it down modestly.

"Which knee is it?"

Madeleine gasped at the light pressure of his hand on her ankle. "The—the left one," she stammered.

"Do you mind if I pull down your stocking?" he asked gently.

She shook her head, mesmerized by the sight of his hands slipping beneath the hem of her gown. She felt a sharp intake of breath as his fingers barely grazed her thigh. He deftly slid the thin white stocking down her leg.

"Here?" he inquired, tenderly touching her knee. His smooth fingertips pushed and explored, around and around, tickling her, though she tried hard not to show it. She feigned a wince of pain.

"Oooh, 'tis there," she said, pursing her lips. She lifted her head to find him studying her, his attention no longer on her knee. His penetrating gaze seemed to devour her, though his expression was inscrutable.

She shivered, unable to tear her eyes away. He was looking at her just as he had the other night!

The taunting memory of his lips at her breast leaped into her mind. She flushed hotly and forced it away, shifting on the bed. Her movement broke the spell, for Garrett looked down, caressing her left knee with his thumbs.

"There's no swelling," he said quietly. "I think it is only bruised." He began to pull up her stocking.

"I can manage, thank ye," Madeleine said, embarrassed. As he rose to his feet, she drew the stocking over her knee and quickly shook out her skirt.

"From the sound of your fall, I'm surprised it was no worse," he said.

"Aye, 'tis a lucky thing," she agreed. She stood up slowly, testing her weight on her "injured" knee. " 'Tisn't hurting so badly now. Thank ye for yer trouble, Garrett." She affected a slight limp as she padded toward the door in her stockinged feet.

"I'll see you to your room, Madeleine," he offered, taking the pewter candlestick from the bedside table.

Madeleine stopped abruptly, her breath catching in her throat. "No, that winna be necessary," she objected lightly. She glanced at him over her shoulder. "I can see my way well enough."

"I insist," Garrett said, his features set with determination. He was at her side in two strides and wound his arm through hers. "I'll not have you injuring yourself further by tripping about in the dark."

Madeleine's mind raced frantically. If Garrett accompanied her to her room only to discover the door bolted, he would surely demand to know why. She could not risk Lord Lovat being found out. What could she possibly say to dissuade him? She walked slowly, stalling for time.

"I thought you'd gone to bed an hour ago, Madeleine," Garrett said, matching her pace. "I was surprised to see you were still up."

His soft-spoken statement jolted her, reminding her of why she had left her room in the first place. It gave her a chilling idea.

Perhaps if she talked to him now about Black Jack, it would divert his attention, she thought wildly. There was no longer any reason to wait until morning.

Once Garrett knew she was going to help him find his outlaw tomorrow evening, she hoped he would forget all about escorting her and rush out to inform Sergeant Fletcher. When he returned, she would be gone to bed, or so he would think. Aye, that's what she would do. She had no other choice.

A flicker of fear coursed through her body, and she found she was trembling. She had the oddest sensation she was about to leap from the edge of a precipice into a pitch-black chasm. Once she offered her help, there would be no turning back, no second thoughts, and no hope of rescue.

Courage, lass, she bolstered herself. 'Tis for the well-being of yer people. Yers is only one life to their many. 'Tis as good a time as any to seal yer fate.

Madeleine turned to face him, hoping he would not sense the depth of her fear. "I did go to bed, but I couldna sleep. I've been thinking about what ye said about Black Jack, and about General Hawley. I was coming to find ye, Garrett. I thought we might talk."

Garrett was so stunned he wasn't sure he had heard her correctly. After she heatedly refused his last plea, he had resigned himself to the conclusion that she would never help him. Now here she was, in his room, saying she wanted to talk about Black Jack!

Don't get your hopes up, man, he thought, forcing himself to remain calm. Hear her out first. She might yet disappoint you.

He felt her tremble and sensed she was nervous. "Sit down, Madeleine," he said gently, leading her to an armchair. He set the candlestick on the small, three-legged table behind her. "Would you like a glass of wine before we talk?"

"Aye."

He filled two goblets from the cask set atop the desk, then returned quickly to her side. He offered her one, noting how her hand was shaking as she lifted the goblet to her mouth and drank deeply. He took a sip, barely tasting the wine. His eyes never left her face.

Her large blue eyes were luminous in the candlelight and tinged with a hint of resignation that he had never seen there before. She looked so vulnerable, so unlike the defiant young woman he knew. He pulled up another armchair and sat down beside her.

"What about Black Jack, Madeleine?" he asked, hoping he was not rushing her. She took another long draft of wine before she answered, then held the goblet in her lap.

"I've decided to help ye find him," she said evenly, staring into his eyes. "I believe ye've told me the truth about Hawley. Tomorrow night, I'll deliver Black Jack into yer hands, and then ye and yer kind can leave Strathherrick in peace."

Garrett sharply drew in his breath. So his instincts had been right after all! Madeleine not only knew of Black Jack, she was going to lead him to the outlaw. This was more than he had ever hoped.

"But why have you waited until now to tell me this?" he asked with a twinge of irritation, thinking of the raids he could have prevented. "You've told me twice you knew nothing."

"Ye've asked me to do a hard thing, Garrett," she responded, her voice almost a whisper. "I needed time to think, to weigh . . ." she shrugged slightly, falling silent.

Yes, he did understand, he thought. It could not have been an easy decision. He quickly changed the subject.

"What of the five men who ride with Black Jack?" he asked, realizing she had made no mention of them.

She shook her head stubbornly. "I canna help ye there. I dinna know who they are, nor where to find them."

Garrett leaned forward in his chair, his expression grim. "I must have them all, Madeleine."

She looked at him sharply. "And ye must trust me in this, Garrett, as ye asked for my trust two weeks past. Once Black Jack is captured, ye winna have to worry about the others. They winna ride again, not without their leader."

Garrett sat back in his chair, pondering her statement. He was tempted to ask her how she could say this with such certainty, but he decided against it.

First and foremost, he wanted Black Jack. If she claimed the others would cease their raiding, it must be true. She knew what was at stake if they did not.

He nodded. "Very well. I only hope I can convince General Hawley. He's no doubt set his mind on hanging the whole thieving lot, then posting their heads on spikes as a warning to other Highlanders who might choose such a path. Black Jack's head will have to satisfy him."

He saw her flinch, her face growing deathly pale. He

immediately regretted his callous and gruesome statement. "I'm sorry, Madeleine—"

"Ye're sorry?" she blurted suddenly. Her laugh was harsh; her eyes flashed brightly. "I'll have ye know this, Captain Garrett Marshall. If not for Black Jack, there would be far more fresh graves dotting Strathherrick, full of women and children who starved because yer fine countrymen saw fit to steal the bread from their tables. Fortunately we've food enough now to last the winter and seed to plant come spring. I'm giving ye Black Jack only to save my people more suffering and pain. The kind yer General Hawley would inflict upon them! The kind they'd not survive even with food in their bellies. Dinna forget it!"

She tossed down the last of her wine and set the goblet shakily on the table. "I've had my say. We can discuss the details in the morning. I dinna want to keep ye from sharing yer wondrous news with Sergeant Fletcher. I'm sure ye've much to gloat over together, plans to make. Good night to ye, Garrett."

She stood up abruptly, but he caught her hand in a steely grip.

"Do you really think I would gloat, Madeleine?" he said softly. "Sergeant Fletcher will hear of this soon enough."

He set aside his goblet and rose from his chair, so close to her the brass buttons on his coat snagged her bodice. She jumped back as if stung, but he held her fast.

"Don't you think I understand something of what your decision has cost you, Madeleine?" he demanded, his eyes searing into her own. "Don't you think I sense your pain? To betray a kinsman, even for the sake of so many—"

"Ye'll never know the half of how I feel!" Madeleine exclaimed, her voice throbbing with anguish.

She twisted free of his grasp and hurried to the open door, scarcely remembering to limp. She heard his footsteps behind her and she knew she would not escape him. He seemed determined to follow her.

She didn't stop to think. In one swift movement she slammed the door, bolted it, and whirled around to face him.

Her eyes locked with his as he drew closer. She did not know in that moment if she was staying to protect Lord Lovat, or surrendering at last to the inexorable yearning that had taken over her senses, her body, and her will from the first time Garrett had held her in his arms.

All she knew was that soon she would face her death, by the hangman's noose if she was brought to trial, or even more unnerving, by a brace of loaded pistols tomorrow night. She could almost feel the searing bullets ripping into her flesh, and she closed her eyes tightly, crossing her arms protectively over her breasts.

It wasn't fair, it just wasn't fair! her mind screamed. Hopeless tears squeezed beneath her eyelids. She had barely lived, had barely loved . . .

"Madeleine, what's wrong?" Garrett's voice called to her, his arms pulling her toward him. They enveloped her, and she sensed a seductive comfort like nothing she had ever known. She pressed against his broad chest, as if she could melt against him and be safe.

She opened her tear-filled eyes. His face was so close to hers, and his breath was warm against her skin.

"Why are you crying, Maddie?" he asked softly and gently. His finger traced a tear down her cheek. "Tell me, sweeting, tell me."

She heard the words escape her lips with a voice she did not know. It was tremulous and frightened . . . so horribly frightened.

"Is it true what ye said at the falls, Garrett? That ye dinna want anything to happen to me?"

"Yes, it's true," he said, hugging her fiercely. "I've been so worried. But now you'll be safe. You've given me what I need to protect you, Madeleine. You needn't be afraid. Nothing will ever happen to you. Not if I can prevent it."

She pulled away slightly and looked into his eyes, her slim hands reaching up to cradle his face. "Ye care, then, Garrett Marshall? Truly care about me?"

He nodded wordlessly and held her tighter, so tight she thought he might be able to drive the terrible fear from her heart. She wanted so much to forget the horror that was to come, if only for a little while.

"Love me, Garrett," she pleaded. "Show me ye care, as a man cares for a woman. I must know . . . must know . . ."

"Maddie, do you realize what you're saying?" Garrett asked huskily, cupping her chin. He searched her face and her eyes. "You've fought me all along. I thought I would always be something you hate and despise. And now you ask me to—"

Her kiss silenced him as she stood on her toes and found his lips. It was a kiss so desperate and so passionate that he groaned against her mouth and crushed her to his chest. She felt him lift her in his arms, felt the rugged strength of his body through his long strides, then fell back against softness and knew she was lying with him on the bed.

Garrett stretched his hard length atop her and pinned her arms above her head with one strong hand. His dark blond hair, loosed from its band, fell to frame his face like a sheaf of gold in the candlelight. His gray-green eyes were alight with a ravenous hunger held too long in check.

"I've wanted you from the first moment I saw you, Maddie Fraser," he whispered, his breath on her cheeks, her lips, like a sweet caress. "Wanted you so badly I could not sleep from the ache of it. I wanted you so badly that when I finally slept I dreamed of nothing but you."

He seized her lips, kissing her until she was breathless. "Tell me what you want, Maddie," he demanded brokenly, his panting breaths merging with her own. "If you truly want me, you must say it. I must be sure."

"I want ye, Garrett Marshall," she whispered urgently. "Ye must show me what it is to love—and be loved."

Her words pierced the turbulent cloud of desire raging within Garrett's mind. Stark realization gripped him, together with a flood of bittersweet exultation. He released her wrists and brought himself up on his elbows, his fingers buried in her tangled chestnut curls.

"Am I the first?" he asked gently, yet with a hint of desperation. He sensed her answer, yet he needed to hear it from her own lips. He could not fathom why it mattered so much to him, but it did. If there was no lover, perhaps he could dare to hope her heart was yet free.

"Aye," Madeleine breathed. "Ye're the first." She reached up and trailed her finger down his clean-shaven cheek to his lips. She traced the sensuous curves of his mouth, her eyes brimming with wonder and passion. She smiled ever so faintly. "And I've never known a kiss such as yers, Garrett."

A ragged sigh escaped his throat, wrenched from the depths of his soul. He captured her in his arms and kissed her deeply, knowing that he had been given a most precious gift. A gift to be savored, treasured, and awakened slowly. He reluctantly pulled away from her lips and rose from the bed.

"Dinna leave me," Madeleine moaned, her eyelids fluttering open. Her whole body ached, her reeling senses acutely aware of his absence. She felt cold, missing the warmth of his weight upon her, until a flush of heat raked her from head to foot.

What a glorious sight to behold! Entranced, she leaned up on her elbow, watching in bold fascination as Garrett undressed swiftly before her.

A thrill of anticipation shot through her as his powerful body was bared before her, revealing the masculine perfection she remembered so vividly from the loch. Her eyes raced over him, drinking in his male beauty, the hard ridges and angles, the knotted muscles, as his every lithe movement was illuminated in candlelight and shadow.

"Come to me, beautiful Maddie Fraser," he bade her suddenly, his voice a husky whisper that rocked her to the very depths of her being.

Shivering uncontrollably, she bounded from the bed and flew into his arms. His warmth enveloped her, his bronzed skin both rough and smooth beneath her frantic touch. Their lips fused and parted as his tongue stroked hers, searching, delving into the velvet recesses of her mouth even as his hands expertly divested her of her gown and petticoat.

"Fairest Madeleine, you are my Rosalind," he murmured as he turned her around, one arm hugging her slender waist. "I want to see every beauty you possess, to know it, taste it, touch it." He trailed fiery kisses across her shoulder while he deftly pulled her chemise over her head, then buried his face in her hair, inhaling its fragrance.

She let out a small gasp of pleasure as his hands disappeared beneath her drawers and slowly crept up her body, grazing her hips, his fingers caressing her belly and the narrow curve of her waist. Then he cupped her full breasts and squeezed, ever so gently.

Madeleine jumped in breathless surprise, moaning when his thumbnails grazed her taut nipples. He teased them until she was light-headed and giddy, certain that her knees would buckle beneath her. She felt a hardness straining against her backside; his arousal was most evident. She blushed furiously, thrilled by her wanton imaginings.

Suddenly Garrett knelt behind her, his hot breath fanning along her spine. He slowly slid her linen drawers over her hips and down her legs, then followed with her stockings. He lifted first one slender foot and then the other, kissing and caressing each in turn, his breath tickling her toes.

"You won't be needing this, I trust," he whispered, running his hands lightly between her thighs as he untied the strap holding her dirk and tossed both weapon and sheath onto a chair.

She gasped sharply as he nipped her bare bottom,

then he twirled her around, his palms plying and stroking the silky length of her. She threw her head back and reveled in his sweeping touch, feeling as if he would caress every inch of her body. His voice came to her as if in a dream, his whispered words from a text she knew nearly by heart, *Romeo and Juliet.*

" 'O, she doth teach the torches to burn bright! Did my heart love till now? Forswear it, sight! For I ne'er saw true beauty till this night.' "

Tremors of breathless excitement rippled through her limbs as Garrett kissed her navel and his fingers strayed ever so briefly into the soft chestnut mound at the juncture of her thighs, then he rose to his feet and caught her in his powerful embrace.

"Sweet Maddie," he murmured thickly, smothering her slim throat, her shoulders, and her breasts with kisses. He sought her lips, and she was lost in oblivion, scarcely aware he had lifted her onto the bed.

She was drunk with his touch and powerless against the dizzying sensations wracking her body. Her flesh burned from his countless kisses. Her blood sizzled and surged through her veins, filling her completely with liquid heat.

So this was the magic! This was the mystery between men and women, this was the caring, the wanting, the loving that she so urgently sought, so desperately needed.

Madeleine opened her eyes dazedly to find Garrett bent over her, his muscled thighs straddling her hips. He lingered at her aching breasts, savoring first one then the other, his tongue torturing the swollen tips, his fingertips lightly stroking the pink aureoles until she thought she might scream. Then he was above her, his eyes blazing into hers with potent heat, inflamed from wanting her.

" 'O blessed, blessed night!' " he murmured huskily, sweeping a chestnut tendril from her face. " 'I am afeard, Being in night, all this is but a dream . . .' "

Madeleine reached up and drew him down to her, his verse the sweetest seduction. She kissed him deeply, with all the passion she possessed, then whispered against his lips, "Aye, 'tis the night, Garrett, but 'tis not a dream. Love me, please love me."

She watched, spellbound, as he lowered his head once more, his mouth blazing a molten path across her fluttering belly to her navel. A madness seized her as his tongue speared into the sensitive hollow at the same moment his fingers found the moist silken cleft between her thighs.

She cried out and arched wildly against his hand, her frenzy mounting when his darting tongue began to stroke and tease where his fingers had been only moments before. Her hips tilted instinctively as she opened herself for him, her jagged breaths a rising cadence to the sweet agony he inflicted.

"Garrett . . . no . . . oh, please," she whimpered, quivering and shaking. A swell of intense pleasure was rising deep within her, with streaks of rippling sensation radiating from the secret point of his relentless onslaught. She ran her fingers through his hair, moaning and imploring until she felt him rise abruptly and cover her writhing body with his powerful weight.

"Maddie, my love, it will hurt only for an instant, I promise," she heard him whisper, his lips capturing hers.

She sensed a hard, fervent nudging and innately arched against it, every fiber of her being striving for the unknown fulfillment she craved so dearly. She gasped as his pulsating strength plunged into her softness, a lightning stab of pain overwhelming her pleasure.

"Shhh, sweeting," Garrett murmured hoarsely against her mouth, shunting his hips gently to and fro. "It will soon pass. Shhh . . ."

Calmed by his soothing whispers and tender caresses, she marveled at how swiftly the pain receded and disappeared. Her body seemed to have a will of its own as she matched his movements, slowly at first, then more urgently, her senses rocked once more by intoxicating waves of pleasure.

She trembled anew, a fiery heat engulfing her. Unwittingly she pulled Garrett to her, winding her arms about his muscled back, her slim legs tightly encircling his waist as if she would never let him go. She met his heightened thrusts with savage abandon, demanding everything he had to give and more.

Her panting breaths were one with his as they clung to each other, their bodies buffeted and tossed by a storm of passion. She heard him groan and hoarsely cry out her name as he exploded deep within her, a great, shattering release that catapulted her to unbelievable heights of shimmering revelation.

"Hold me, Garrett! Hold me!" she cried, certain she would die from the sheer wonder and infinite splendor of it. She drove hard against him, tears of rapture streaking her face as wave after cascading wave of tumultuous ecstasy finally revealed the mystery of love.

A shuddering sigh escaped Madeleine's lips, and she suddenly went limp beneath Garrett's weight, her limbs slipping from his body. Stunned, he realized she had fainted. He rolled over onto his side, bringing her with him, and cradled her in his arms. He kissed her tenderly, tasting the salt of her tears.

Long moments passed. Gradually Garrett's labored breathing eased, returning to some semblance of normal.

He could not help smiling. He was sure he had never before loved anyone so completely. He knew he had never felt such an overwhelming sense of contentment. It settled over him like a soothing cloud, merging with his utter exhaustion.

He yawned, and his gaze drifted to the candle across the room. It sputtered and hissed, the yellow flame flaring in the cool night breeze wafting from the cracked window.

Better to let it burn itself out, he decided, hugging Madeleine closer to his chest. He did not want to wake her.

He grasped the tartan bedspread and pulled it over them. The thick wool would keep them snug during the night. He rested his chin gently atop her head, stroking her silken hair and reveling in the warmth of her lithe body. Her breathing had slowed, and its soft, measured rhythm was a sign that all was well.

"Mistress Madeleine Fraser," he murmured quietly, closing his eyes. "Lady Madeleine Marshall, mistress of Farraline, lady wife of Rosemoor."

Garrett smiled faintly. He was not surprised by the direction his thoughts had taken, or by the strength of his emotion. He was in love. He had never been more certain of anything in his life.

He was in love with a fiery Scotswoman who took his breath away every time he gazed into her flashing eyes. A beautiful, stubborn, and passionate Highlander. Some might insist she was his enemy, yet he knew he could not live without her.

Never until this night had he dared to hope such a love was possible. Now it seemed she truly cared, and in time she might consent to become his wife. Yes, he could hope. He could dream.

Garrett hugged her protectively, sleep stealing over him. "We've a new beginning, you and I," he whispered softly against her hair. "After tomorrow, the worst will be over. The danger will be past. We'll start afresh, Maddie Fraser."

Chapter 17

Madeleine snuggled deeper into the warm mattress, rubbing her cheek contentedly against the soft feather pillow. Her eyelids fluttered open ever so slightly.

"Hmmm . . ." she murmured sleepily, closing them once again. It was pitch dark in the room and hours yet before dawn. Plenty of time until she had to wake Lord Lovat.

She swiped languidly at her tousled hair, pushing it away from her face. Her hand dropped back down and dangled limply over the edge of the mattress. Her fingers brushed against smooth velvet, and she toyed with it absently, waiting for sleep to lull her once more.

Funny that the bed curtains should be drawn shut, she thought sluggishly. The evenings weren't that cool yet—

Realization suddenly flooded her.

"Och, surely ye havna overslept again," she moaned, her eyes snapping open. It was so dark she couldn't see a thing. She sat up, her hands groping at the heavy drapery. She found the fringed hem and flung the curtain aside, gasping as a blinding shaft of sunlight cut across the wide bed.

"Damn!" Madeleine fumed under her breath. Her gaze swept the illuminated interior, surrounded by opaque draperies on every side and the sloping canopy overhead. It reminded her of a silent green-velvet tomb. No wonder she had thought it was still night.

Her heart leaped to her throat. Oh, no! She had promised to wake Lord Lovat before dawn.

She fumbled frantically for the gold pocket watch on the bedside table, squinting from the room's brightness as she peered at its face. It was almost half past ten. Dear God, how would she ever get him out of the house and on his way without anyone seeing him now?

She threw off the bedspread, her gaze falling on the barren spot next to her. She touched the rumpled sheet. Garrett must have already been up for hours.

Her cheeks flamed, wanton images of the night before streaming through her mind. Her hand strayed to his pillow, still indented in the center. She could almost sense his warmth, his stirring touch. Her skin puckered with goosebumps, and she shivered, remembering . . .

"Dash it, Maddie, ye've no time to think of that now," she whispered vehemently, forcing away the seductive memories. She climbed out of the bed.

"No time to think of what?" Garrett asked, rising from the chair behind the mahogany desk. His openly admiring gaze swept over her. "I thought I heard some rustlings behind those curtains. Good morning, Madeleine."

Madeleine started and fell back against the mattress. She grasped the bed curtain and yanked it in front of her to cover her nakedness. "G-Garrett. I dinna know ye were still here," she barely managed, her eyes wide with shock. She swallowed hard, determined to avoid his question.

"I only came back in a short while ago," he replied lightly. "I've been writing in my military journal, one of my more mundane duties as an officer." He closed the large leather-bound volume and looked up at her once more. He smiled warmly. "When I got up this morning, you were sleeping so soundly I didn't want to wake you. I drew the bed curtains so you would have some quiet. I hope that was all right."

" 'Tis no matter," she said distractedly. How was she ever going to get to Lord Lovat now? she wondered. Her gaze fell on her clothes, draped neatly over an armchair. Her dirk lay upon the brocade seat, its silver hilt gleaming brightly. She glanced from the chair to Garrett.

He was leaning on the desk, his arms folded, staring at her as if he could see right through the velvet drapery. She felt a flush race from her scalp to her toes and she shifted self-consciously. She held the curtain more snugly across her breasts.

"Garrett, if ye dinna mind, I'd like to get dressed," she said, attempting a firm tone. "I'll catch a chill standing here. Could ye kindly leave the room?"

He looked nonplussed, almost hurt, and it seemed he might protest. Then he sighed. "If that is what you wish," he agreed, his reluctance evident in his voice. He strode to the door, where he turned and glanced back at her. "If you'd like, I'll bring you some breakfast. I haven't eaten yet myself. I was waiting for you. I was hoping we might talk and perhaps discuss those particulars you mentioned last night."

She nodded quickly, stung by his words. Obviously he was already thinking about Black Jack. "Aye, 'twould be fine, Garrett," she said quietly, deciding it was just as well.

Her reply seemed to brighten his spirits. He smiled again. "Good. I'll be back shortly."

As he closed the door behind him, Madeleine rushed to the armchair and grabbed her clothes. She dressed quickly, her mind spinning.

She hoped that while Garrett was in the kitchen, she'd have enough time to see to Lord Lovat. He must still be safe or the house would surely have been in an uproar. Garrett would certainly have made some mention of it to her if he had found an unexplained houseguest in their midst. His demeanor had suggested nothing out of the ordinary, other than the unsettling current of intimacy between them now.

Once again she had to banish the vibrant memories which leaped to her mind. She lifted her skirt and pulled on her stockings, wondering how she was going to explain to Lord Lovat her failure to wake him at the appointed hour.

How was she going to explain it to Glenis, for that matter? Her servant no doubt wondered where she had disappeared to for the entire evening.

Madeleine strapped on her dirk and ran over to the large wall mirror. She quickly surveyed her reflection.

It was strange that she appeared no different after last night, she mused. She certainly felt different. The only disparity she could see was the expression in her eyes. It was one of calm acceptance, almost serenity, so unlike the simmering fear she had seen there for the past two weeks. Perhaps after voicing her fateful decision, she was finally ready to face whatever was to come.

Enough! Ye're wasting time, she chided herself. She raked her fingers through her hair, but the knots and tangles were impossible. She would have to brush it out later. With a final tug at her bodice, she hurried from the room.

She nearly fainted when she saw her chamber door was half-open, golden sunlight splashing across the carpeted hallway. She dashed the short distance and burst into the room. It was empty but for Glenis, who was calmly making the bed.

"Good morning to ye, Maddie," Glenis said nonchalantly, glancing over her narrow shoulder. "Ye might shut the door, lass, before ye say a word. Ye look like ye've seen a ghost.'Tis only yer Glenis."

Madeleine could not seem to move her limbs. She only stared, her feet rooted to the floor. "Glenis, where's—"

"Dinna say it, lass. Wait," Glenis shushed her, scurrying over and closing the door herself. She walked to Madeleine's side and gave her a fierce hug. "All's well, Maddie, ye dinna have to worry. Sit down on the bed."

Stunned, Madeleine obeyed her. She slumped on the mattress, and Glenis sat down next to her. "What do ye mean, Glenis?" she said. "Where's Lord Lovat?"

"Here. Read this," Glenis replied, reaching into her

pocket and drawing out a single sheet of paper. She pushed it into Madeleine's limp hand. "I found it under the pillow. 'Twill explain everything."

As Madeleine read the hastily scrawled letter aloud, her voice a mere whisper, a surge of incredible relief washed over her.

My thanks for your kind hospitality, Maddie darling. When you did not come to wake me, I was sure the excitement of my unexpected arrival proved too much for you. I'll not blame you for that, and 'tis almost better this way.

I've taken it upon myself to bid farewell by way of your great-grandfather's tunnel. Aye, I've known about it for years. Your father showed the tunnel to me when he was a lad, so proud of it he was. We chieftains know of a great many such secrets. 'Tis how we live so long and so well.

One final word to you, Maddie. You're a brave lass and 'tis proud I am of what you've been about these past months. Aye, I know of your cause. When I heard rumors of a fearless outlaw in Strathherrick, I knew 'twas you.

You've your father's courage and loyalty to Clan Fraser, God rest him forever, and your own caring heart. With your mother's fine beauty, you're quite the lassie indeed. I only ask you to be wary around these redcoats. Never before has such a hateful scourge set upon our beloved Highlands. God be with you, Maddie.

Simon Fraser

Madeleine's hands dropped into her lap. "Great-grandfather's tunnel!" she said incredulously.

"Aye, he must have gotten clean away, otherwise we'd surely have heard the ruckus," Glenis stated matter-of-factly. "I wonder how he managed to elude the guard downstairs, 'tis all." She shrugged, her wrinkled face breaking into a grin. "Och, they call him Simon the Fox with good reason," she said, chuckling.

Madeleine would have joined in her laughter if she hadn't been so astonished. She ripped the letter into small pieces after a final perusal and handed the bits to Glenis. "Will ye see that this is burned in the kitchen hearth? We dinna want to risk it falling into the wrong hands."

"Aye, lass," Glenis agreed, sobering.

Madeleine heaved a small sigh as she rose from the bed. "It seems there's nothing more for me to do here. All's well, Glenis, just as ye said."

"Is it, Maddie?"

She looked down at Glenis, noting the anxious lines etched deeply into the old woman's face. "Aye, as far as our Lord Lovat is concerned," she answered gravely.

"I wasna referrin' to Simon Fraser," Glenis said softly. She met Madeleine's eyes, but there was no judgment reflected in her perceptive gaze. "Was the captain gentle with ye, hinny?"

Startled, Madeleine felt a sudden rush of shame. She thought to deny it, but decided it made no difference, not now. "How did ye know?"

"I've raised ye since ye were a wee bairn, Maddie. There's not much that escapes yer Glenis Simpson." She stood up stiffly and cupped Madeleine's chin. "Ye havna given him more than yer maidenhead, have ye? Yer heart, mayhap? I'd think 'twould only make it harder for ye, caring for the man who'll see ye to prison."

"No! I dinna care for him! How could ye say such a thing, Glenis?" Madeleine exclaimed defensively. "I only went to his bed to protect Lord Lovat." She bit her tongue, knowing that was half a lie, but she could not bear for Glenis to know the selfish truth.

"Have ye told him yet about Black Jack?"

"Aye, last night."

Glenis sharply drew in her breath but said nothing, her dark eyes full of pain.

"He knows I will help him find the outlaw, that's all," Madeleine continued carefully. "He doesna know 'tis me, not yet. He'll only discover that tonight, out on the moor.''

''But how—''

''Glenis, I dinna have the time to tell ye all the details right now,'' she cut her off gently, clasping Glenis's worn hands. ''Later we'll talk. Garrett is expecting to find me in his room, expecting to hear how I'm going to lead him to Black Jack. I must go.'' She kissed her on the cheek, then abruptly turned and left the room.

Now ye must think only of what lies ahead, Madeleine told herself firmly, choking back the hard lump in her throat. She squared her slender shoulders as she walked determinedly down the hall.

First she had to explain to Garrett where he and his soldiers would find Black Jack, then she had to visit her kinsmen in Farraline. They had to know why they would not be riding with her tonight, why they would never ride for her cause again. And if Garrett asked her where she was going, she would simply tell him she had to take more of Glenis's herbal medicine to the kinswoman who was in childbed.

She heard the clatter of china teacups on a tray and knew Garrett was already back in his room. She felt strangely calm, considering that she was about to sign her own death warrant.

Once Garrett knew where to find Black Jack, her fate was all but sealed.

Chapter 18

❦

"**N**o, Maddie! Ye winna ride by yerself!'' Angus exclaimed heatedly, stamping about his large cottage. He halted abruptly and slammed his fist into the rough-hewn cupboard, rattling every cup and dish on the open shelves. "Damn those redcoats!'' he shouted, striking it again. "Damn Hawley, Cumberland, Captain Garrett Marshall, the whole blasted lot of them to hell's fire!''

Ewen reached out just in time to save the whiskey decanter, which was rocking precariously. "Will ye go easy, Angus?'' he said with a heavy sigh. "Ye've already smashed one chair. We feel the same as ye do. Ye dinna have to wreck yer house to prove yer anger.''

Angus stared at his longtime friend with clenched fists, his heavy brows knit together, his feet planted in a defiant stance. His normally ruddy face was beet-red.

"Do ye truly feel the same as I, Ewen? Do ye believe Maddie shouldna ride alone?'' he asked suspiciously. "Ye've the most to gain by staying home. Ye've yer family still under yer roof, yer fine son, Duncan, yer bonnie wife. I've only m'self now, my two sons dead at Culloden, my wife gone these past five years, my daughter moved to Duhallow with her husband. I've nothing to lose save my pride if I dinna ride with Maddie tonight!''

"Ye dare to question my loyalty to Maddie?'' Ewen

said darkly, rising from his chair. Though he was shorter by a head, his thick build more than made up for his slighter stature. He faced his kinsman squarely. "Aye, my family is dear to me, but not so dear I'd let Hugh Fraser's daughter take the full blame and punishment for what we've done together."

Duncan jumped up beside his father, his deep blue eyes flaring. "Are ye saying I'd cower at home, Angus, whilst Maddie faced the English?" He spat upon the floor. "I'd rather die by the hangman's rope than let it be said in Strathherrick that Duncan Burke chose to hide from the redcoats rather than fight them."

Madeleine leaped to her feet, her knuckles white from gripping the table. "I'll not have ye arguing and fighting amongst yerselves! Stop it, I tell ye. Stop it!" She drew a deep breath, eyeing one sullenly silent man after the other. The tension was so thick it hung over the room like a smothering fog. "Sit down, all of ye."

"Aye, 'tis not the time to be quarreling," Ewen agreed gruffly, taking his seat. Duncan soon followed, but Angus held his ground.

"I'll not sit 'til this matter is decided," he insisted. He leaned against a whitewashed wall and crossed his arms over his burly chest.

"Very well, then, Angus. Stand if ye wish," Madeleine said. She sat and looked around the gloomy party. "I appreciate yer loyalty and yer willingness to ride with me tonight, no matter the consequences," she said evenly. "But I canna allow ye to do that. 'Twould be riding to yer deaths, and ye well know it. I'll not have that upon my conscience. 'Tis bad enough I've involved ye this deeply."

"Ye canna be sure 'twould lead to our deaths, Maddie," Angus retorted. "How do ye know they winna simply throw us in prison? All we've done is steal a bit of food for our starving kinsmen. Surely the court would show some pity . . . perhaps sentence us to a few years' time in an Edinburgh gaol—"

"Have ye forgotten that we've shot English soldiers, Angus?" Madeleine cut in sharply. "The court winna

look kindly upon that indiscretion, ye can be sure.''
She winced, recalling what Garrett had said about sev-
ered heads and spikes, but she could not bring herself
to mention it. ''Captain Marshall has given me reason
to believe General Hawley wishes to make an example
of Black Jack,'' she said instead.

''Black Jack indeed,'' Angus sputtered under his
breath. He pushed away from the wall and began to
pace the dirt-packed floor. ''Ye seem to have set great
store by what Captain Marshall has told ye, Maddie.
What if he lies? Perhaps he has concocted this threat
about Hawley to trick ye into giving him what he
wants, easy and without a fight.'' He walked to the
table suddenly and leaned over it, looking at her almost accusingly. ''I·canna believe ye would so readily
trust a redcoat, lass.''

Madeleine stared back at him, anger gripping her.
''Aye, I trust him, Angus,'' she said tersely. ''In this
instance I trust him completely.'' Her words struck a
deep chord within her, and she fleetingly remembered
her vow to Flora that she would never trust an Englishman. How dangerously far she had come in such a
short time!

''And if he lies?'' Angus queried harshly, hardly
convinced.

''I've considered that possibility, and I've decided I
winna take such a chance with our people's lives.
Enough said on the matter, Angus. I've made up my
mind.'' She stood up, her voice adopting a forceful
tone she had heard her father use time and again. ''I
will ride alone tonight. If I'm wrong, then 'twill only
be my neck that is forfeit. I demand ye swear to me ye
winna interfere.''

There was a heavy, brooding silence in the room as
the men glanced at one another, then back at her.

''Swear to me ye winna interfere,'' she repeated
shrilly. ''Captain Marshall believes I know nothing of
yer whereabouts or even who ye are. And when they
catch me, I'll carry yer names to my grave, I swear it!

Ye're safe, dammit. Safe! Dinna ye hear me? Now swear it!''

Angus was the first to slowly shake his head, followed by his two kinsmen. '' 'Tis no disrespect to ye, Maddie, but I canna swear such an oath,'' he said quietly. His grim expression mirrored his words. ''Ye've not considered one important thing.''

''And what might that be?'' she snapped, then immediately regretted her shrewish tone. Her kinsmen cared deeply about her, that much was plain.

''Do ye truly think Captain Marshall will believe ye're Black Jack, especially when he finds ye alone?'' he said, painting the scene for her. ''To him, ye're the mistress of Farraline. He'll think ye've only disguised yerself as Black Jack to protect the outlaw and yer people. He'll laugh in yer face, Maddie, and think ye're playing him for a fool.''

Madeleine stared blankly at Angus, his somber words hitting her with full force. She sank slowly into her chair.

'Twas possible, she thought dazedly. She had never considered Garrett would not believe she was Black Jack.

Once she was captured, she had planned to supply him with information about her raids, especially when she and her kinsmen looted his camp. But would he believe her? Maybe he would claim she had heard the stories from the outlaws themselves. Either that or he would say it was gossip and hearsay, secondhand knowledge she had collected from villagers who knew the identity of the outlaw or his men.

Madeleine felt like laughing and crying from the sheer absurdity of it all. She was Black Jack, yet Garrett thought the outlaw was a man. He had no reason to believe otherwise.

Garrett could continue his fruitless search until General Hawley came to ravage the valley, and even then they wouldn't find the man they were seeking. That man didn't exist! Garrett would never believe she was Black Jack unless—

"Ye must ride with me," she said, giving voice to her numbing realization. Her eyes held each man's in turn. "All of ye.'Tis the only way."

"Aye," Angus affirmed, nodding gravely. "We must ride together."

"I'll not say a word against it," Ewen agreed. "Duncan?"

"Ye may count me in, Maddie," he blurted excitedly, as if his life were not soon to be in danger. "As soon as we're finished here, I'll set out for Beinn Bhuidhe and tell Kenneth and Allan. Ye know they'll ride with us. 'Twill give them a chance to settle a few scores when the redcoats come upon us."

"What do ye mean?" Madeleine asked, startled.

"Ye canna think we would allow them to lead us away by the nose like meek cattle," Angus said with a short laugh. " 'Tis not the Highlander's way, and ye know it well, Maddie Fraser. If we surrender easily, Captain Marshall might think ye rounded up some of yer villagers for a midnight masquerade ball, the whole lot of us passing ourselves off as Black Jack and his men."

"Aye, 'tis true," Ewen interjected. "He'd no more believe we were his dangerous outlaws than if he'd found ye alone."

Angus came around the table and put his work-callused hand on Madeleine's shoulder. "We must fight, Maddie," he continued. "As we would fight if an entire company of redcoats surprised us during any of our raids. As we would fight if our very lives depended on it. Only then will Captain Marshall believe he has found his Black Jack."

Madeleine shivered, a cold chill cutting through her body. She knew if such a skirmish took place, there would be casualties on both sides. Maybe herself, maybe Garrett, maybe several of his soldiers. Doubtless one or more of her kinsmen would be wounded or killed before they were overpowered by sheer strength of numbers and taken captive.

She looked up at Angus, meeting his eyes. He was

usually the most cautious of all her kinsmen. Now here he was, anxious to fight and die if need be.

She glanced at Ewen, a man she'd known and trusted all her life, her father's friend. And Duncan, so young, only seventeen. She thought of Kenneth and Allan Fraser, living in a rude cave for months, yet riding by her side whenever she needed them.

Such brave men they were, and so dear to her heart. They had risked everything to take up her cause. She could not deny them their final stand together. Maybe 'twas best this way after all.

"Very well," she agreed quietly. "We'll fight."

Angus squeezed her shoulder approvingly. "Ye said ye already told Captain Marshall where he might find Black Jack?"

Madeleine nodded. "I told him this morning that Black Jack ventured out only at night from his secret hideout on Beinn Dubhcharaidh," she recounted. "I mentioned a certain mountain path he usually traveled which skirts Loch Conagleann, and I urged Captain Marshall to ambush the outlaw there, rather than wait until he met his men for a raid."

"A clever plan, lass," Ewen broke in with a low chuckle, "if 'twas how ye meant to have Black Jack captured alone."

"Aye," she said, smiling thinly. "I told Captain Marshall if Black Jack sensed he was being followed, he would melt into the night and they would never find him. Better to nab him quickly than let him get away."

"That plan winna work for us now, Maddie," Angus said. "What will ye say to him since we're riding with ye?"

Madeleine's expression grew pensive, then she shrugged. "I'll tell him I've changed my mind, that's all. I'll say I've thought about it and decided 'tis better if he captures every last one of the outlaws, just in case General Hawley winna be satisfied with only Black Jack. 'Tis more than plausible."

"So where will we meet?" Duncan asked eagerly, leaning forward in his chair.

"At the yew tree at midnight," she replied, "then we'll set out for Wade's Road. I'll explain to Captain Marshall the route Black Jack and his men would most likely take if they were planning a raid for tonight. He and his soldiers will no doubt hide somewhere along the way." She fell silent, then continued softly. " 'Twill be as much a surprise for them as for us when we finally come upon each other in the dark."

" 'Tis a sound plan, Maddie," Angus said simply. "So be it."

He walked over to the cupboard and grabbed the whiskey decanter and four glasses, setting them on the table. He filled the glasses and passed them around, then raised his own high above his head.

"A toast," he stated reverently. "To our chief, Lord Lovat, God keep him safe to France. To our raid tonight, God grant us strength and courage to face our enemy. And to Mistress Madeleine Fraser, the bravest lass ever to walk the heather!"

Exuberant ayes echoed about the cottage as they drank the fiery liquor. One by one the empty glasses slammed onto the table.

What a stubborn hardheaded lot, Madeleine thought warmly, accepting their tribute with a tremulous smile. She should have known that once her kinsmen cast their lot for her cause they would never desert her.

Tears smarted her eyes as she whisked on her shawl and bid hasty goodbyes. She practically fled from the cottage. She knew she would break down completely if she heard another such toast, and she had decided long ago never to let her kinsmen see her cry.

She set out at a brisk pace along the road to Mhor Manor, wiping away the tears with her palms. She inhaled deeply and filled her lungs with heather-scented air.

It had grown cooler since she had walked to Farraine earlier that afternoon. The whistling wind caught at her hair, flipping it behind her shoulders, and dragged at her skirt. The fresh air steadied her racing emotions, and she looked around, reveling in the wild Highland beauty.

The sun was hidden behind a bank of ponderous gray-white clouds, and its rays bathed their ragged borders in gold fire. Occasionally a bright shaft of light illuminated the barren mountain slopes, then just as quickly faded, plunging the world into muted color and shadow.

Madeleine threw out her arms and twirled along the road, her face turned up to the darkening sky. She loved it when a thunderstorm was brewing. As a child she would rush outside into the rain to dance about and stomp in the mud puddles. Poor Glenis would run out with a blanket, sputtering and scolding, and try to catch her until she was soaked to the skin as well.

Madeleine's arms dropped suddenly to her sides, and she stopped, overcome by dizziness.

Glenis. She had talked to everyone today but Glenis. She had been in such a rush to get to Farraline and see her kinsmen that her faithful servant still did not know what was to happen that night. And now the plans had changed, becoming even more deadly.

She quickened her pace, oblivious to the rugged scenery she had delighted in only moments ago. Her mind sped with everything she had yet to say and do.

Glenis would have to leave Mhor Manor as soon as Garrett and his soldiers rode out in their pursuit of Black Jack, she decided grimly.

She would give Glenis what little gold coin she had to help provide for her future needs, and a sturdy horse and cart for traveling. Glenis could stay the night at Meg Blair's, then set out in the early morning for her widowed sister's cottage in Tullich. Glenis would be safe there, far away from the horrors of whatever was happening at Mhor Manor.

Madeleine turned into the drive, spying Garrett almost immediately where he stood conversing with his

guards. He looked over and began to walk toward
her.

Her heart thudded painfully at the sight of him. She
met his eyes for an instant and then forced herself to
turn away. She headed quickly for the kitchen door,
but he followed right behind her.

"Madeleine," he called out, his long strides no
match for her own. He caught her arm gently, and she
stopped. "I've been wondering when you'd get back,"
he said.

His gaze raked over her and settled on her wind-
burned cheeks and tangled hair. He swept a stray lock
behind her ear, his fingers grazing her earlobe. She
shivered, marveling that his simple touch could arouse
her so.

"Has the babe come yet?" he inquired lightly.

"Babe?" Madeleine replied, confused. She gasped,
suddenly remembering her excuse of a kinswoman near
childbirth. She nodded vigorously. "Aye, 'tis a fine
strapping boy, born just an hour past," she blurted
out, noting he was eyeing her quizzically.

"Mother and child are doing well?" he asked, a
curious smile playing about his lips.

She laughed nervously. "Och, they couldna be better, though 'twas a good thing I brought more of Glenis's herbs. 'Twas a long, difficult birth." She glanced
pointedly at the kitchen door. "Glenis is waiting for a
full accounting, Garrett," she rushed on. "She's a keen
interest in birthing bairns, ye know. Even though she's
too old for midwifery now, she likes to keep up on
such things." She paused, catching a breath. "If ye'll
kindly excuse me."

"By all means," Garrett allowed gallantly, caressing
her arm before he released her. "Perhaps after you've
spoken with Glenis, we could share supper tonight.
Say, in an hour? We won't be able to linger very long,
but I'd be honored by your company, even for a short
while."

Madeleine stopped midway through the door, her

pulse racing as she considered his unexpected invitation.

She didn't like the thought of being alone with him again, recalling the mixed torrent of emotions she had experienced at breakfast, but there didn't seem to be any way to avoid it. Supper would probably be her only opportunity to talk with him privately before he rode out, and he had to know her change of heart concerning Black Jack's compatriots.

Besides, an hour would give her just enough time to see to everything Glenis might need and counter any of her protests about leaving Mhor Manor.

Madeleine peeked at him over her shoulder. "Aye, I'll sup with ye, Garrett," she said. Then she disappeared into the kitchen and closed the door.

Garrett stood there a moment, a familiar sense of bewilderment washing over him. He had experienced it during his every encounter with Madeleine since . . .

He had first felt it that morning when she had asked him abruptly to leave the room, hiding herself from him as if he hadn't so recently delighted in the wondrous perfection of her body. Her subdued greeting had hardly been the welcome he had expected after the wildly passionate night they had shared.

Then at breakfast, she had been thoroughly preoccupied despite the seriousness of their conversation. Even when their talk changed to more lighthearted topics and he had reached his fingers out to touch hers, she had pulled her hand away. She had seemed agitated and had finally excused herself, saying she had to change clothes and then journey into Farraline to see after her kinswoman.

He sighed heavily, staring at the door in consternation.

Her behavior had been peculiar at best, and highly disconcerting. He could not help wondering if there really had been a new birth in Farraline. He could swear she had no idea what he was talking about when he first asked her about the babe. Yet why would she have made up such a story?

Garrett shrugged, at a complete loss. He walked back toward his men, shaking his head.

Maybe it was he. Maybe he was so distracted with the thought of finally capturing Black Jack that he was imagining difficulties where none existed.

He couldn't wait until the bastard was clapped in chains and the whole unpleasant matter settled once and for all. Then he could devote his entire attention to Mistress Madeleine Fraser!

Chapter 19

Madeleine peered out the kitchen window, taking care to hide well behind the curtain. She watched until the last of Garrett's soldiers disappeared down the drive, their shapes swallowed up by the deepening dusk.

A jagged streak of lightning suddenly cut across the sky, briefly illuminating the dark world outside. She glimpsed them once more before she turned from the window. Garrett was in the lead on his huge bay, followed by twenty-four mounted soldiers riding in pairs.

Madeleine leaned against the windowsill. She still couldn't get over the frenzied activity of the past half hour. One moment she and Garrett had been eating supper in the dining room and engaging in light conversation, then she had abruptly mentioned Black Jack and everything had changed.

Garrett had almost dropped his fork when she said she had changed her mind about Black Jack's men. His eyes had bored into hers, his mouth tightening as she told him she believed he might find the entire band of outlaws on the narrow road between Errogie and Inverfarigaig.

That had been the end of supper. Garrett had excused himself immediately, saying that he and his men were setting out at once to position themselves along the road. It might be hours before Black Jack rode by, but at least they would be well hidden and ready.

Within minutes Garrett and his soldiers had assembled in front of the house, Sergeant Fletcher's sharp commands mingling with the excited buzz of men's voices and neighing horses. A heavy drizzle had done little to dampen the soldiers' enthusiasm.

There had been an air of nervous excitement among them that had chilled Madeleine to the marrow. To her, it had seemed like a macabre carnival. She knew within hours many of them would be dead.

Madeleine heaved a ragged sigh and pushed away from the windowsill. She could not think of that right now. She crossed the kitchen and knocked on Glenis's door.

"Glenis, are ye packed and ready?" she called softly, careful lest she be heard. Garrett had left six soldiers behind to patrol the manor house. She could hear Corporal Sims chatting with several guards stationed just outside the front door. Their jovial laughter carried into the kitchen.

"Glenis!" she hissed, more loudly this time. The soldiers' high spirits were beginning to grate on her nerves, which were already stretched taut. Did they have to be so brazenly overconfident? Those six men were fortunate they had not ridden out with the others!

The grating sound of the latch lifting interrupted her grim thoughts. She stepped back as Glenis drew open the door.

Madeleine could not help thinking how fragile her servant appeared, how frail and stooped. The furrows in her face were deeper and more pronounced. It looked as if Glenis had aged another ten years since Madeleine had told her tonight would be the final raid. Yet Glenis's dark brown eyes were glittering brightly, reflecting her plucky temper. Madeleine found solace in that, believing Glenis realized it was best that she leave Mhor Manor.

"Aye, lass, I'm ready," Glenis muttered, blowing out the solitary candle resting in a wall sconce. She walked slowly into the kitchen, carrying a large basket over each arm.

"Here, let me help ye," Madeleine offered, but Glenis shook her gray head.

"I can manage these two," she insisted firmly. "There's a sack on the floor ye can carry for me."

Madeleine picked up the bulky sack and hoisted it over her shoulder. "The cart's just outside the kitchen door, Glenis," she said. "The redcoats were so busy they dinna notice what I was about."

Glenis merely nodded and shuffled to the door. She set down one of the baskets for a moment and drew the hood of her thick woolen cloak over her head. She took a last sweeping look at the dimly lit kitchen, then picked up her basket and opened the door.

They stepped outside into a light rain, thunder roaring dully in the distance. The storm that had threatened earlier seemed to have bypassed the valley, though occasional streaks of lightning still flashed across the sky.

Madeleine lifted the sack into the cart, then the baskets, and covered everything with a heavy blanket to protect the meager belongings from the rain.

"There, Glenis," she said, turning to her servant. "The blanket should hold fine 'til ye get to Meg's. 'Tisn't raining so hard ye need to worry about yer things."

"I dinna care if they float away," Glenis sputtered vehemently, her face suddenly etched with sorrow. "They mean nothing to me, Maddie Fraser. Nothing. Ye're the only thing on God's earth I care about. And to think there's nothing I can do to stop what's to happen to ye . . ." Her voice faltered, sobs shaking her hunched shoulders. Her trembling hand gently caressed Madeleine's wet cheek. She struggled to say something, but no words came.

"Hush with ye now," Madeleine whispered, folding her beloved servant into her arms. It pained her heart terribly that she had no solace to offer. She hugged Glenis fiercely, the old woman shuddering in her arms, until at last she drew away. "Ye must go, darlin' Glenis."

"Aye," Glenis sighed, wiping the tears from her eyes. Her quavering voice was tinged with sudden resolve. "I must go." She turned and grasped the edge of the cart. "Help me into the seat, lass."

Madeleine obliged her, handing her the reins when Glenis was settled, her cloak drawn tightly around her slight frame. "Godspeed," she said simply. Without waiting for a reply, she slapped the horse's rump. The animal jerked forward, the wheels creaking and churning in the mud.

"Hold on, there!" a male voice shouted.

Madeleine spun around just as Corporal Sims rushed up and grabbed the harness, staying the startled animal's course.

"Where do you think you're off to?" he blurted, looking from Glenis to Madeleine. "What's going on here?"

Madeleine's eyes flashed a quick warning to Glenis, urging her to be silent, then she turned back to the corporal. "Dinna Captain Marshall tell ye Glenis was traveling into Farraline this ev'ning, Corporal Sims?" she asked innocently, smiling at him. "On a special mission."

"Why, no . . . uh . . . he didn't," the young soldier stated, clearly distracted by her winsome smile.

"Och, with all the rushing about, he most likely forgot," she said lightly. She leaned forward, speaking to him in conspiratorial tones. "Can I trust ye to keep a secret, corporal?"

He glanced over his shoulder at the other guards standing by the front door, then looked back at her. He stepped closer, inclining his head. "What secret?"

"Captain Marshall asked Glenis if she wouldna mind fetching a cask of Scots whiskey for him from her cousin in Farraline," she whispered into his ear. "Her cousin's one of the finest distillers in Strathherrick."

"Whiskey?"

"Aye. Captain Marshall wants it for the celebration after, well, ye know. 'Tis a surprise for ye and the rest

of the soldiers. To thank ye for all yer fine efforts, I
suppose."

"Oh," Corporal Sims breathed, licking his lips.

"I'd go m'self," Madeleine continued, "and spare
Glenis the trouble, but she'd like to visit with her
cousin. He's been sickly of late, and she has some herb
medicine for him." She paused, smiling at him apologetically. "I hope ye dinna mind me spoiling the surprise for ye, corporal, but ye did ask."

"No, no, I don't mind," the soldier stammered. His
expression clouded. "It's a dangerous night to be out,
though, Mistress Fraser, for you or your housekeeper.
Perhaps I should accompany her—"

"That winna be necessary, Corporal Sims," Madeleine objected firmly, "but I do thank ye for yer kind
offer just the same. I'm sure Captain Marshall would
find yer efforts better spent in guarding Mhor Manor."
Her voice fell to a insistent whisper. "Glenis should
really be on her way, ye know. I dinna want to think
of the captain's displeasure when he returns to find his
whiskey has been delayed."

Corporal Sims's eyes widened, and he sharply
sucked in his breath. "I've held you up too long already," he said, waving on the cart.

When Glenis clucked her tongue to the horse and
flicked the reins, the cart squeaked into motion, and
Madeleine caught the corporal's sleeve. "Ye winna say
a word to the others, will ye, Corporal Sims?"

He glanced down at her hand on his arm and swallowed hard. If it hadn't been so dark she would have
seen he was blushing to the roots of his scalp. He met
her searching gaze. "Not a word," he declared emphatically. "I'm in command . . . uh . . . while Captain
Marshall and Sergeant Fletcher are gone, of course. If
I say it's none of their business, they won't ask me
again."

"Thank ye, Denny," Madeleine said warmly. "I'll
be sure to mention yer kind cooperation to the captain."

He seemed stunned that she'd used his first name,

or even remembered it. "My—my pleasure, Mistress Fraser," he stuttered, smiling sheepishly. He turned around so abruptly that he stubbed his boot on a flagstone and almost tripped. He straightened his shoulders, however, and kept on walking as if nothing had happened.

At any other time, Madeleine might have laughed. On this occasion she felt only relief that another unforeseen obstacle had been overcome. She waited until the corporal had rejoined the other guards, then she caught up with the cart as it rumbled down the drive. She held on to the seat, running alongside. Her other hand clutched her muddied skirt to keep it from tangling in the wooden spokes.

"Who taught ye to tell such stories, Maddie Fraser?" Glenis scolded, feigning a reproachful tone. She glanced tenderly at Madeleine, her eyes awash with tears, then her gaze skipped back to the curved drive.

Madeleine felt hot tears streak her face, mingling with the cool rain. Her lips were quivering as she attempted a smile. "Ye did, Glenis Simpson," she panted. "Every time . . . ye caught me in some scrape . . . ye told me I better have a good story . . . or else."

Her hand fell away from the seat as the cart picked up speed at the bottom of the drive, the horse veering onto the road to Farraline. "I-I love ye, Glenis," she gasped, not knowing if her old servant had heard her or not. But it didn't matter. Glenis knew.

Madeleine stood there for a long time in the gentle rain, her eyes fixed on the distant lighted windows of Farraline. At last she turned back to the house and trudged up the drive. She was aware she must look a sight with her hair plastered to her head and her sodden gown dragging in the mud, but she didn't care.

She ignored the guards' curious stares and walked right through their midst, heading determinedly for the front door. She stepped inside, trailing rivulets of water as she climbed the stairs. Her brogues made squishing noises as she hurried to her room.

She quickly stripped out of her wet clothes and

changed into the black garb she always wore for her raids, the guise that had earned her the name Black Jack. There was no need to use extra caution at this point and wait to change later, as she usually did. When it was time to go, she would simply wrap her brown linen dressing gown around herself until she was safely in the drawing room closet, then she would discard it in the tunnel.

She peered at the clock on the mantelpiece. The porcelain face was almost impossible to read in the darkness, but she didn't want to light a candle. She looked closer, barely making out the time. It was just past nine o'clock. Two hours yet before she would leave the manor to join her kinsmen at the yew tree.

She dragged the rocking chair from the far corner of the room and set it in front of the window nearest her bed. She opened the window, the cool breeze catching the curtains and filling the room with sweet, rain-scented air.

Madeleine sat and began to braid her wet hair. The chair's gentle rocking motion and the sound of rain droplets plunking on the leaves outside soothed her frayed emotions, and gradually she felt some of the tension easing from her body.

She was weary, but she would not allow herself to rest or even close her eyes. She laid her head back and stared out the window, envisioning the wild tumble of gray mountains soaring beyond the estate. It was a view she had known all her life, a cherished view which she doubted she would ever see again.

Fleeting memories of happier times crowded her mind. She smiled, remembering when Mhor Manor had resounded with her father's exuberant laughter and the lively voices of his tacksmen and tenants, gathered for a twice-yearly ceilidh around a roaring peat fire on the back lawn.

Even as a child she had been allowed to join them, listening raptly while the bards spun their fantastic stories and poems of legendary deeds and epic valor. She could almost taste the heady heather ale passed around the fire; she could almost hear the stirring melodies of harp, pipes, and fiddle.

She fondly recalled the one occasion when her father had allowed her a tiny swallow of ''stop-the-breath'' whiskey, a dangerously potent brew. It was the only time she had ever heard Glenis reprimand her father in public, her servant's anxious scolding rising shrilly above Madeleine's red-faced coughing and teary gasps for breath.

Madeleine chuckled to herself and hugged her arms to her chest. She would never forget the plaintive songs sung round the blazing ceilidh fire, laments for heroes long dead, and the rousing recitations of clan battles hard fought and won.

She shivered suddenly, remembering the poignant songs of love; love's bitter betrayal, love denied and unrequited, love tragically lost.

How many times had she seen tears glisten in her father's eyes when he listened to the mournful verses? Her throat had always tightened, a sense of helplessness welling up inside her as she longed to comfort him, yet she knew she could not. All she could do was wish for the melancholy songs to end, hoping a smile touched her father's face once more.

Madeleine sighed. She had never ceased to wonder why no one ever sang of love's joy and devotion, the glorious rapture surrounding two people in love.

She vividly recalled seeing such happiness when her mother was alive. Her parents had found delight in each other's company and their life together, enjoying joyous embraces and fervent kisses which had made her giggle when she was a child. Love could not possibly be all heartbreak and sorrow.

Madeleine ceased her gentle rocking, sitting still and silent in the chair.

She had known such rapture last night with Garrett.

Aye, she could admit it to herself now. There was no need any longer to repress her emotions or pretend her burgeoning feelings for him did not exist. The truth could no longer be denied, especially in light of her mortal danger. Her love for Garrett burned within her mind like a beacon, pure and blindingly radiant.

She had never known such joy as she felt in his arms, never known such happiness, such searing fulfillment. If that was what it felt like to love, then she loved Garrett as surely as she lived and breathed.

She had made love to him completely, without question, bestowing upon him everything she had to give, even as he met her with a passionate force that far surpassed anything she had ever dreamed possible.

Madeleine gripped the chair, an impassioned yearning bursting forth from the depths of her soul.

How she wished things were different! How she wished she could know such love forever!

If only she and Garrett had met in another place, another time, when they were not enemies, were not fettered by generations of hatred, mistrust, and cruel bloodshed. A place and time where they could have loved forever.

Madeleine's shoulders slumped, her hands falling limply into her lap. A solitary tear rolled down her cheek, a tear for everything that might have been.

"Och, Maddie, ye're a fool," she murmured brokenly, wiping the tear from her face. With great effort, she forced herself to concentrate on what lay ahead.

She was certain of one thing. When they came upon Garrett and his soldiers, she would fire her pistols harmlessly into the air. It would not be her bullets that found him, even if fate decreed he fall wounded, or die.

Chapter 20

Garrett glanced up at the moon, a white, luminescent disc hanging like a shining medallion in the night sky. He breathed a silent prayer of thanks that the rain had stopped over an hour ago, the thick clouds giving way to long swaths of misty vapor that did little to obscure the moon's brightness.

He and his men now had a better view of their surroundings, even though a swirling fog shrouded the ground. It lent an eerie quality to the night, sharpening their already finely honed nerves and heightening their senses.

They had been waiting by this slight turn in the road for several hours, a site Garrett had carefully chosen because of the wide stream just behind them. The rushing water would mask their movements, a crucial consideration if they were to maintain their element of surprise.

He was especially grateful for it now. The dozen soldiers still mounted were shifting constantly in their saddles to ease cramped muscles while their horses snorted beneath them and pawed the damp earth. The other twelve men were leaning on trees or pacing, their mounts tethered nearby. The long wait was growing more interminable with each passing moment, and there was still no sign of Black Jack.

Garrett drew out his gold pocket watch and pushed the tiny spring releasing the ornate lid. Eleven o'clock. He slipped the watch back into his pocket, his expression tightening. God only knew how much longer they would have to remain hidden behind these fir trees—

A sudden movement farther up the road caught his attention, the hair prickling on the back of his neck. He motioned to Sergeant Fletcher.

"Aim your weapons, men, and hold fast!" the sergeant hissed. "Don't dare move a whisker until I tell you!"

The soldiers obeyed instantly. Those standing shouldered their muskets and took cover behind the trees. The mounted soldiers sat rigidly in their saddles, one hand gripping the reins while the other held a cocked pistol. They waited tensely for the sergeant's signal.

Garrett stared intently between the branches, scarcely breathing as a dark shape moved closer and closer. He could make out a horse, its head bobbing as it plodded along, and what appeared to be some sort of small wagon with a lone, huddled figure upon the seat.

Not even a wagon at that, he amended, but a cart. It was hardly the mode of transportation he would have expected from Black Jack, but perhaps several of his men were hiding beneath that blanket, and the others were following on horseback.

"Easy," Garrett whispered, the cart almost in front of him. "Easy. Now, Fletcher!"

"Halt where you are!" Sergeant Fletcher roared, his pistol firing into the sky. The deafening report echoed above them as Garrett and his mounted soldiers swooped onto the road and surrounded the wagon. A woman's piercing scream ripped through the air.

"Please dinna shoot, Captain Marshall . . . Dear God, dinna shoot me!" a quavering voice wailed. " 'Tis me, Glenis! Glenis Simpson!"

"What the devil?" Garrett cried, wheeling his bay around sharply. He rode up alongside the wagon and yanked the hood off the cowering figure. His eyes widened. "Down with your weapons, men!" he commanded, holstering his pistol and jumping to the ground. He lifted the sobbing woman from the seat and cradled her in his arms. "Glenis, what are you doing here?" he said in stunned disbelief.

"Och, it's taken me so long to find ye, Garrett," she choked through her tears, shuddering against his chest. She pointed accusingly at the cart. "That blasted animal wouldna go faster than a slug." Suddenly she clutched his coat, her wet eyes wide with terror. "'Tis not midnight yet?"

"No, Glenis, not even quarter past eleven," Garrett soothed her, though he had no idea why she would ask him such a question.

"There's still time, then," she replied, her sobs quieting. "Still time . . ." Her voice cracked and faded as she drew a labored breath.

Garrett knelt on one knee and set her upon the ground, supporting her in the crook of his arm. "Still time for what, Glenis?" he asked impatiently. "Tell me why you've come this far—"

"'Tis Madeleine, Garrett!" Glenis blurted. "Ye must help her. Ye must!"

"What has happened?" he demanded, an icy chill running down his spine. "Has she been hurt?"

"No, not hurt. Ye must listen to me, Garrett," Glenis pleaded, twisting to face him. Her dark eyes glistened in the moonlight, burning with a strange fire. "Ye care for my Maddie, dinna ye? I know ye took her to yer bed last night."

Garrett flushed warmly beneath her intense scrutiny. He heard an embarrassed cough and glanced up to find his men had dismounted and were gathered in a loose circle around him, listening intently. "Go on with you!" he shouted angrily. "Fletcher, get the men back to their positions. Now!"

"Yes, sir!" Sergeant Fletcher snapped briskly. "You heard the captain. Back on your horses. Move!"

Garrett waited until they had swiftly dispersed, then he met Glenis's searching gaze.

"This is madness, Glenis," he said with exasperation. "Surely Madeleine told you what was afoot this evening—"

"Aye, she did," Glenis retorted heatedly, "and I'll not say anything further 'til ye answer me."

Garrett sighed in frustration. "Of course I care for her, Glenis," he stated in a rush. "I love her." He snapped his mouth shut, realizing what he had just said. He had never voiced those words aloud to anyone before, and he felt naked, as if he had revealed a part of his soul.

Glenis's eyes seemed to drill into him all the more. "So ye love her, then," she said under her breath. "'Tis more than I could have hoped."

"Glenis, you must tell me what this is all about," Garrett demanded, glancing beyond the cart and back again. "Yes, I love Maddie. But what has that got to do with your being here, at this time of night, and especially since you're aware of the danger?"

"Ye're the one in danger, Garrett," Glenis shot back, her dark eyes ablaze. "Ye and yer men. Black Jack knows ye're waiting here! They're going to fight ye, Garrett. Fight ye to the death, unless ye stop them in time."

Garrett stared at her, his mind racing. Had Madeleine betrayed him to Black Jack? Had she deliberately set up some sort of trap? No, it couldn't be, not after . . .

"Glenis, what the hell is going on?" he yelled, shocking himself at the loudness of his voice.

She struggled to her feet, her narrow chest heaving with exertion. "I'll tell ye what's goin' on, Garrett Marshall. Black Jack knows ye're here—because my Maddie is Black Jack!"

Garrett gaped at her, certain she had gone mad. He stood up suddenly, towering above her. "What did you say?" he asked harshly, as if daring her to repeat herself.

"Madeleine Fraser, the mistress of Farraline, is yer outlaw, Garrett," Glenis said steadily, undaunted by his thunderous look. "She's yer Black Jack. She's been raidin' ye English since a month after her father was killed at Culloden—raidin' to put food in her people's bellies.''

Garrett shook his head in disbelief. ''While my soldiers and I have been stationed at Mhor Manor? That's not possible, Glenis.''

''Aye, 'tis more than possible,'' she objected. ''There's a tunnel beneath the house runnin' some forty yards beyond its walls. Ye'll find it in the drawing room closet. 'Tis the perfect way to sneak in and out without anyone takin' any notice at all.'' She stepped toward him and lowered her voice. '' 'Twas how ye got that nasty knot on yer head, Garrett. Ye surprised her coming home from a raid. Ye nearly caught her that night.''

Astounded, Garrett rubbed his forehead. ''That was Madeleine?''

''Aye,'' Glenis said, nodding. She fluttered her hand impatiently. ''Och, Garrett, I could tell ye so much more, but there's no time for it. Maddie's kin have convinced her 'tis best to fight ye, otherwise ye wouldna believe she was Black Jack if she surrendered to ye easily.'' She drew a ragged breath and rushed on. ''There'll be a terrible spillin' of blood, maybe Maddie's, maybe yer own, unless ye stop it. I'd rather see my Maddie in prison than dead on the ground. If ye truly love her, Garrett, as ye say ye do, ye'll capture her and her kin before a single shot is fired!''

Glenis's impassioned words drove into Garrett's mind with resounding force. Madeleine was Black Jack. It was so farfetched he was inclined to believe it. The woman he loved was an outlaw, a thief!

Good God, she was the bloodthirsty bastard who had shot his sergeant. His sweet, tempestuous Madeleine!

He gripped Glenis's spindly arms. ''I believe you, Glenis,'' he said grimly. ''Tell me what I must do to avoid this fight.'' He felt her knees buckle beneath her, and he quickly grabbed her by the waist.

''God love ye, Garrett. Thank ye,'' she said gratefully, her eyes flooding with fresh tears, her rasping voice quivering with emotion. "Thank ye—"

"Glenis!" Garrett interrupted urgently. "You can thank me later if you wish. Tell me what I must do!"

"Aye, ye're right." Glenis hiccoughed. She drew herself up, standing steadily on her feet though she was visibly trembling. "There's an ancient yew tree just north of Errogie on the left side of the road, but before ye round the north tip of Loch Mhor. Ye winna miss it, Garrett. 'Tis the tallest tree ye'll see, with a huge, twisted trunk. The leaves will appear dark to ye, like black velvet—"

"I've seen that tree before," Garrett interjected. "I remember noting it because the yew sprig is the Fraser badge."

"Aye, that's the one," Glenis confirmed. "Maddie will meet her kinsmen there at midnight, then they'll set out for Inverfarigaig knowin' ye're waitin' somewhere along the way. Ye must ride like the wind, Garrett, and surprise them at the yew tree. They winna expect ye there. I only hope ye've enough time to make it now."

Garrett pulled out his watch, his breath escaping in a rush of relief. "We've more than a half hour, Glenis. Plenty of time to get there and hide, unless Maddie's kinsmen are already there waiting for her." He grimaced. He didn't even want to consider that bleak possibility or its consequences.

His commanding voice roared above the sound of the rushing stream. "Mount up, men, and secure your weapons. Prepare to ride like you've never ridden before. You'll never call yourselves foot soldiers again if we manage this stunt."

He turned back to Glenis. "I'll have two of my men escort you back to Mhor Manor."

"No, Garrett, I'll not be returnin'," she said resignedly. " 'Tis a traitor I am now to Maddie and her kinsmen. I've betrayed her trust. She'll not want the likes of me around her home." She glanced at the cart. "I'll be goin' on to my sister's in Tullich."

Garrett wanted to argue with her, but there was no time. "My men will escort you safely to Tullich, then." He bent and kissed her damp cheek. "You're no traitor in my eyes, Glenis. I only hope one day I may thank you for what you've done." He walked her to the cart and lifted her onto the seat.

"Take care of my Maddie," Glenis said, clasping his hand tightly. "Dinna let anything happen to her."

If God wills it, he thought grimly, and the English courts. What the next hour would bring was uncertain at best, the future a yawning black hollow he did not want to contemplate.

"I'll do everything in my power to help her," Garrett said with quiet intensity. "That I promise you, Glenis." He squeezed her hand, then stepped away from the cart. "Sergeant Fletcher, I need two men to accompany Glenis Simpson to Tullich."

"Very good, captain."

Within minutes the cart was creaking down the road toward Inverfarigaig, a well-armed soldier flanking each side. Garrett knew it was a circuitous route to Tullich, but better that than steer Glenis back toward Errogie and the skirmish that would shortly ensue.

He mounted his powerful bay, the animal snorting restlessly beneath him.

"What's our destination, captain?" Sergeant Fletcher asked, reining in his horse beside Garrett's.

"The ancient yew of Clan Fraser," Garrett replied cryptically. At the sergeant's confused expression, his tone grew even darker. "I'll explain along the way, Fletcher."

Garrett dug his heels into the bay, leaning into the saddle as the horse lunged forward in a spray of wet dirt. Sergeant Fletcher quickly followed suit, catching up with him as their horses galloped neck-and-neck along the road, the soldiers thundering not far behind them.

Chapter 21

❧❧❧

Madeleine slowed her fast sprint, stopping abruptly when she reached the bottom of the hill. Breathless, she bent over and rested her hands on her knees, her lungs burning as she inhaled great gasps of air.

She always ran this last distance to the yew tree as hard as she could. It never failed to exhilarate her and clear her mind. She needed that more than ever tonight.

She stood up, adjusting her black cap and checking to see that her thick braid was stuffed into her jacket. As she smeared powdery peat ash on her face, her gaze instinctively darted in the direction of the yew tree.

The swirling fog had gathered so thickly here she could see only a few feet in front of her. Even the full moon was almost obscured from view, no more than a pale orb through the incandescent vapor. She wondered if the road to Inverfarigaig was buried in mist and fleetingly prayed it was not.

Madeleine began to walk in what she believed was the right direction, allowing her instincts to guide her. She sensed it was near midnight. She had left Mhor Manor as she usually did, at quarter to eleven. Fortunately she hadn't encountered any obstacles that would have slowed her progress.

She had easily slipped into the drawing room closet while the guard in the main hallway was idly chatting with one of his compatriots. The tunnel had offered no

235

difficulty, other than the disgusting spiders clinging to the dank walls. The trap door at the far end had been harder to lift because of the water-soaked sod, but that had only taken her a few extra moments. So far, this night had been like any other.

"'Tisn't like any other," she whispered vehemently. She stopped for a moment to get her bearings.

Why did she have the sensation that she was walking in the wrong direction? she thought irritably. Damn this fog! The yew tree couldn't be more than twenty feet away, yet at this rate she wouldn't find it unless she stumbled headlong into its gnarled trunk.

A sudden noise startled her, and she whirled around, unable to see through the dense fog. Her heart knocked against her chest and her skin tingled with goosebumps.

She could have sworn it sounded like a groan, but it had ended so abruptly she couldn't be sure. She turned in a slow circle, listening, her eyes straining for any hulking shapes that might be her kinsmen.

A sharp whinny cut through the air. Madeleine nearly jumped out of her muddy boots.

"Och, what's come over ye, Maddie?" she chided herself nervously. It was only one of her kinsmen's horses. She took a few steps in the direction she thought she had heard the whinny, then hesitated.

Should she call out to them? she wondered anxiously. She was wasting precious time blundering about like this in the fog. If she didn't meet up with them soon, they would abandon the plan, thinking perhaps she had decided against it for tonight.

Madeleine frowned, repelled by the thought. She had no intention of agonizing and waiting through another entire day. She quickly made up her mind.

"Angus, 'tis Maddie!" she hissed, cupping her hand to her mouth. "Where are ye?"

A long silence followed, then she heard a faint rustling somewhere off to her right. She tensed, holding her breath, then tried again. "Ewen? Duncan? Answer me!"

"Aye, Maddie. Over here," a gruff male voice responded this time, again to her right.

Relief poured through Madeleine's body, her legs feeling strangely weak. She hurried in the direction from which the voice had come, her boots making squishing noises in the soggy turf. She discerned the faint outline of a tree looming overhead—the ancient yew!

Madeleine began to run, unaware of stealthy shapes moving in behind her, following her. She was almost to the tree when she heard a crackling sound, like a branch snapping in two, in back of her. She wheeled around but found only twisting fog and shadow. She did not see the dark forms pressed to the ground only five feet away from her, melding into the tufted peat.

"A-Angus?" she stammered, stepping backward. She had a creeping sensation that something was terribly wrong. Surely her kinsmen would have been gathered by the tree, along with their horses. Where could they possibly be—?

"Och!" she gasped, bumping into something hard. She felt strong hands suddenly grip her shoulders, then spin her around so roughly her head snapped back.

"An odd time of night for a stroll, Madeleine," her captor said, "or should I say—Black Jack."

Madeleine's eyes widened, her scream dying in her throat. "Garrett!" she exclaimed hoarsely, her mind reeling.

He had called her Black Jack! she thought wildly. Garrett knew she was Black Jack. He had said it with such certainty, such grim conviction. But how?

"Aye, 'tis Garrett," he acknowledged, imitating a gruff Scottish burr. "Not yer Angus, or Ewen, or Duncan, as ye might have supposed, nor even yer two flame-haired Fraser kinsmen who put up quite a fight, I can tell ye."

Madeleine drew a ragged breath as cold realization seized her. So it had been Garrett who answered her a few moments ago! He knew the names of her kins-

men. God's wounds, then the groan she heard must
have been . . .

"What have ye done with my kinsmen?" she
blurted, wincing as his fingers bit cruelly into her arms.
"Where are they?"

"They live, Madeleine, which is more than I could
have said if you'd ridden out to meet us on the road
to Inverfarigaig as you had planned," Garrett answered bitterly. "That's the Highland way, isn't it,
Maddie? Go out fighting, taking as many of the filthy
redcoats with you as you possibly can? How glorious!"
he spat furiously. "A bloody death befitting Strathherrick's brave outlaws, to be sung about for years to come
around the ceilidh fire."

Madeleine was stunned by his scathing words.
Someone must have told him she and her kinsmen
were meeting at the yew tree, perhaps the same person
who had told him she was Black Jack. Who would have
so betrayed her, even if it had spared her life, and the
lives of her kinsmen, for a time? It had to be someone
Garrett trusted, otherwise he would surely have never
believed she was his outlaw.

"Would you have taken me down as well?" Garrett
inquired, his low-spoken question splintering her
thoughts. His voice throbbed with undisguised anguish. "You're a hard lass to figure out, Maddie Fraser. You lie in a man's arms one night, then you plan
to shoot him dead the next—"

"No!" Madeleine cried, struggling against his vise-
like grip. "I'd never have shot ye!" She would have
admitted more, but she was suddenly aware of someone standing directly behind her. She clamped her
mouth shut and hung her head, overwhelmed by the
spinning events.

"What is it, Fletcher?" Garrett barked.

"The captive, sir, the one who was shot—"

"Who's been shot?" Madeleine rasped, twisting to
peer at the sergeant.

"Kenneth Fraser," Garrett answered for him. "At
least that's the name Angus gave us. Angus Ramsay

kindly provided us with all of your kinsmen's names, after a bit of reasonable persuasion."

"What happened to Kenneth?" she demanded, not wanting to consider what that persuasion might have entailed. "Ye said my kinsmen were unharmed."

"Not unharmed," Garrett responded grimly. "Alive." At Madeleine's horrified expression he softened his tone, but not by much. "Your kinsmen were roughed up a bit, Maddie, which is to be expected considering they did not wish to surrender easily."

"That's putting it mildly, captain," Sergeant Fletcher growled under his breath. "It's a good thing the blokes didn't have time to draw their pistols." He grunted and fell silent at Garrett's dark look.

"Kenneth was the only man shot," Garrett continued. "He had the good fortune to tackle with Rob Tyler, who didn't take kindly to being kicked in the groin or having his arm sliced open. If it had been one of my other soldiers, your Kenneth might very well be dead. Tyler's an excellent shot, even in a thick fog like this. He winged Kenneth in the leg to put him down." He glanced at Sergeant Fletcher. "What's the matter with the prisoner?"

Madeleine started. Prisoner. Aye, that's what she and her kinsmen were now. Prisoners of Captain Garrett Marshall. No doubt to be handed over to General Hawley as soon as possible and their heads to be proudly displayed upon tall spikes within the week. Her stomach lurched queasily at the thought.

"It's his wound, sir," Sergeant Fletcher replied, breaking into her morbid reverie. "The bleeding's stopped, but it needs attention we can't give him here. The same goes for Tyler's arm."

"Very well, Fletcher," Garrett said. "Have the men mount up." He paused, his gaze sweeping Madeleine from head to foot, as if he could not quite believe what he was seeing. "Now that we've caught our Black Jack, there's no reason to linger."

"Yes, sir." Fletcher turned around and appeared to address the mist. "Up with you, men, and onto your horses. Captain Marshall has the prisoner well in hand."

Madeleine gasped as ten soldiers materialized out of the fog just behind her, some springing up from the uneven ground where they had crouched, hiding.

"In case you had run the other way, instead of backing into me," Garrett said, reading her mind. "We couldn't risk losing you in this fog." He sighed raggedly. "Let's go, Madeleine."

He walked with her to a beech grove where his bay was tethered, a short distance from the towering yew. The air was alive with sounds now, as all around them soldiers were mounting their horses, their voices raised and animated.

Garrett said nothing as he drew a thick piece of rope from his saddlebag and tied it securely around her wrists.

"I winna try to escape," she said dully.

"I know," he replied. "It's for appearances. My men already suspect . . ." His voice trailed off, realizing he had said more than he wanted to right now.

There would be time to talk later, when they were alone. He could well imagine the questions tumbling in her mind. How had he known to find her at the Fraser yew? How had he discovered she was Black Jack? All this and more he would answer for her, but not now.

To Garrett's relief, Madeleine seemed to ignore what he had said. He lifted her onto the horse tethered to the same tree, then mounted his bay. He grabbed both sets of reins and nudged his horse with his boot. "Get on with you, Samson."

He and Madeleine fell in line with the rest of the soldiers, though the fog was still so dense he could see no farther than the horse in front of him. That soon changed when they rode up the hill and left the swirling mist behind them. The moonlit sky reappeared, scattered with myriad twinkling stars. It felt as if they had left a place of shadow and danger for a world of tranquil order.

Garrett studied Madeleine in the moonlight as she rode so silently beside him. He had to admit she looked exactly like the outlaw who had raided his camp, with her black jacket, trousers, and boots and her smudged face.

Garrett's gaze swept the double line ahead of him, then he twisted in his saddle and assessed the small group behind him, checking to see that all was well. The subdued prisoners were flanked by soldiers. Their hands were trussed behind their backs, and thick ropes secured them to their saddles.

The last had been an extra precaution and probably unnecessary, he conceded. He doubted the Highlanders would attempt an escape. Their fierce loyalty to Madeleine was too ingrained. They would go with her wherever she was taken, sharing whatever fate would be hers.

Garrett gritted his teeth as a gut-wrenching sense of despair overwhelmed him. He glanced at Madeleine, but she was staring straight ahead of her. If she was aware he was looking at her, she gave him no indication.

Her soiled face was haunting in its calm repose, her eyes glistening in the moonlight. She was so beautiful, this defiant, courageous, and passionate woman who had so captured his heart. And she was his notorious Black Jack. But no matter who she was or what she had done, his love for her had not changed. Yet an aching desperation gnawed at him, tearing his secret dream into tattered shreds.

How was he possibly going to save her? Garrett raged silently. Apprehending her—and ambushing her hot-tempered kinsmen, for that matter—had been nothing compared to the dangers that loomed ahead. The biggest danger was General Hangman Hawley, the one brutal man who held the power of life and death over every Highlander. If he had his way, Madeleine would become the gallows' bride instead of Garrett's. Hawley had shown little mercy to Highland women before. Why should he now?

Garrett's tortured thoughts were interrupted by a shocked gasp from Madeleine. For a moment he imagined she was looking at Loch Mhor as they skirted its northern bank, perhaps admiring its shimmering beauty in the moonlight. It was indeed a bewitching sight, the placid black water mirroring the night sky.

"Och, no, please, it canna be," Madeleine breathed, her frantic whisper rising to a cry of terrible pain. "No, no!" She was gazing in horror toward Farraline, great sobs wracking her shoulders.

"What is it, Maddie—" Then he saw it, his voice strangling in his throat. His eyes widened in disbelief as furious anger seized him.

A bright orange glow rose above Farraline, lighting the sky like an aura of destruction. Towering flames shot up from thatched roofs while distant screams pierced the evening stillness.

"Liar!" Madeleine screamed at him, hitting him with her clenched hands. "Ye lied to me. Ye said if I gave m'self up, this wouldna happen!" She hit him again, this time with every ounce of her strength. "I hate ye! Ye lied, ye blackhearted bastard! Ye lied!"

Suddenly she violently kicked the sides of her horse. "On with ye! Go!" she yelled. The startled animal lurched forward, the reins snapping out of Garrett's hands.

Madeleine grabbed the pommel and held on tightly, leaning low in the saddle. Her thighs gripped the horse's heaving sides, the pressure of her knees keeping the terrified animal on course. In an instant she had flown past the astonished soldiers, the horse galloping at a breakneck pace along the dirt road to Farraline.

She did not hear Garrett's massive steed thundering behind her. She did not hear his desperate shouts for her to stop.

All she heard was the blood roaring in her ears, the anguished cries tearing from her throat, and the terrible litany pounding in her brain, rising to a manic pitch.

She should never have trusted a redcoat! She should never have trusted a redcoat!

Chapter 22

Madeleine raced into Farraline, her sweat-lathered horse almost crashing into a large group of English soldiers standing in formation near the intersection of the road and the village's main street. She frantically dodged the outstretched hands attempting to yank her from the saddle and kicked her horse onward.

They careened along the main street, surrounded on every side by chaotic confusion. Everywhere Madeleine looked people were running. Soldiers waved lighted torches above their heads, and men, women, and children bolted from their smoke-filled cottages. Terrified screams, shrieks, and raucous laughter rent the air.

Finally Madeleine's horse would go no further, rearing in fright and wildly flailing its hooves despite Madeleine's frenzied urging. She clutched at the horse's coarse mane until she could slide off the saddle, then began to run dazedly through the village.

She coughed and wheezed, her lungs burning from the acrid smoke, her chest heaving painfully. Her eyes stung and tears spilled down her cheeks. She stumbled and fell heavily to her knees but dragged herself back up and ran on, her stricken mind barely comprehending the devastation before her.

The cottages at the south end of Farraline were completely engulfed, rolling orange flames pouring from every blackened window and yawning door. Several dozen English soldiers were methodically setting fire to the thatched roofs of another row of cottages while officers on horseback guided their progress.

Once again screams filled the air as villagers abandoned their homes at the last possible moment, forced out by the soldiers' warning shouts and the thick, billowing smoke. Madeleine spied Flora Chrystie, her tiny daughter in her arms, and her three boys fleeing to the safety of the moor with their neighbors.

"Stop it, I tell ye!" Madeleine yelled hoarsely, overcome by blind rage. "Stop!" She dashed toward the nearest mounted redcoat, catching him from behind. Before the startled officer knew what had hit him, she had grabbed his wide belt and pulled him with all her might from his horse. She bent over and wrenched his pistol from his belt, clutching it with her tied hands.

"Ye devil!" she cried, pointing the muzzle shakily at his ashen face. Her finger grazed the trigger, and she closed her eyes.

"Madeleine, you can't stop it this way!"

Garrett's anxious voice seared into her consciousness, and she whirled around just as he dismounted from his heaving horse a few feet away from her. His eyes were the color of slate, boring into hers as if demanding she acknowledge the desperate plea written there.

"Put down the pistol, Madeleine," he said urgently. "I'll never be able to help you if you shoot someone."

"No," Madeleine said numbly, shaking her head. She took a step toward him. "Ye lied, Garrett. I believed ye, trusted ye—"

"You can still trust me, Maddie," he interjected, holding out his hands. "Everything I told you was the truth. I knew nothing of this. You must believe me."

"No," she breathed fiercely, aiming the muzzle at his chest. "I thought ye were different, Garrett, but ye're the same as the rest of yer kind—"

Suddenly she felt a sharp, sickening blow to the back of her head, and her words died on her lips. She staggered, blackness washing over her. The last thing she saw before crumpling to the ground was Garrett rushing toward her.

"That'll teach the bastard," the young lieutenant grunted, patting the polished butt of his musket. He prodded Madeleine's prone body with his toe. "He's lucky I didn't put a ball right between his shoulder blades instead. He surely deserved it, pointing a gun in my face—"

"Get away from her!" Garrett snarled, falling to his knees. He pushed off her black cap and cradled her head gently, relieved to see there was no swelling or bleeding. Her breathing was shallow but even, another good sign. At worst when she woke up she'd have a terrible headache.

Garrett gathered Madeleine into his arms and stood up quickly, his eyes ablaze. "I'm Captain Marshall, assigned to this valley by General Henry Hawley. Who's in command here? Who gave you the order to burn this village?"

"Why, General Hawley," the officer blurted, stunned. "He's personally leading our regiment." He peered at Madeleine's face, streaked with tears and soot. "If I'd known she was a woman, captain, I wouldn't have hit her so hard."

Garrett ignored the man's curious stare, his jaw tightening. He recalled the terse message he had received the day before from Colonel Wolfe and cursed his own carelessness in not taking the warning more seriously.

It was clear General Hawley had made good on his threat to take immediate action, far sooner than Garrett would ever have expected. Colonel Wolfe must have told Hawley that he suspected Black Jack's activities were centered around Farraline. Garrett had told his colonel as much in a message he had sent to Fort Augustus several weeks ago.

"Where's the general?" Garrett asked gruffly.

"Right over there, captain, near that stone church," the lieutenant replied, pointing toward the north end of Farraline.

Garrett grimaced. He must have ridden right past Hawley in his haste to overtake Madeleine. He would have caught up with her sooner if not for Hawley's blasted soldiers blocking the road. At least it would have spared her the cruel blow to her head.

He glanced down at Madeleine's face, so pale beneath what little black soot remained. Once again she had thought nothing for her own safety, trying in vain to stop what was happening to Farraline. Garrett had to get to General Hawley at once if he was to save the rest of the village from the torch. He looked steadily at the lieutenant.

"Tell your men, and those of the other officers as well, to stay their torches until further orders are received from General Hawley," he commanded.

"I can't do that, Captain Marshall," the lieutenant objected. "Our orders are to keep going until there's nothing left standing—"

"I said stay your torches," Garrett said ominously. "I've news for the general that will undoubtedly reverse his orders. If one more cottage is burned, lieutenant, I'll hold you personally responsible."

The young officer swallowed hard, clearly daunted by Garrett's murderous expression. He nodded.

"Good. Get on with it." Garrett watched as the lieutenant hurried over to the other mounted officers, who each in turn glanced guardedly at him. They began to call off their men.

Garrett waited no longer. He turned and strode toward the church, hugging Madeleine to his chest.

Each step was excruciating as his mind waged a final battle with his raging emotions, his soul demanding that he find a way to hold on to his dream. How he longed at that moment simply to ride out of Farraline with Madeleine safe in his arms, leaving this horrible dilemma far behind them.

Yet Garrett knew he could not. If there was one thing he understood about Mistress Madeleine Fraser, however painful for him, it was that she would sacrifice everything, even her life, for her kinsmen.

By turning Madeleine over to General Hawley as
Black Jack, Garrett would be helping her people. To do
otherwise would only earn him her hatred. It was bad
enough she already believed he had lied to her. Her
screams still echoed in his ears, her words twisted cruelly into his heart . . . *I hate ye . . . I hate ye . . .*

God, he could not think of it! He had to believe there
was another way he could save Madeleine from Hawley's wrath. He had to believe he had not lost his dream
forever—

"Welcome, Captain Marshall," a loud voice rang out,
shattering his tormented thoughts. "So now I see how
you've been wasting your time. A wench in trousers,
no less."

Garrett's eyes narrowed at his supreme commander,
who was sitting astride a gleaming white stallion that
seemed dwarfed by the man's ponderous weight. Illuminated by the towering flames, Hawley's massive
bulk cast a grotesque shadow on the church's stone
walls.

"General Hawley," Garrett said curtly, stopping in
front of the general and his plumed retinue of high-
ranking officers.

A quick glance told him his only ally, Colonel Wolfe,
was not among them. He would have to fight this out
alone. He drew a deep breath and was about to speak
when Sergeant Fletcher suddenly rode up to the
church, followed by the rest of his soldiers and their
sullen prisoners.

Sergeant Fletcher dismounted and rushed over to his
side. "You caught her, captain," he blurted with relief.

"Caught whom?" General Hawley inquired, his
shrewd, heavy-lidded eyes swiftly assessing the scene
before him.

"Black Jack," Garrett stated clearly. He nodded toward the trussed Highlanders flanked by his soldiers.
"And the five men who've been riding with her."

General Hawley quickly masked his astonishment
and adopted a look of studied amusement. "Surely,
you jest, Captain Marshall." He pointed to Madeleine

with the feathered end of his horsewhip. "Are you telling me that this woman is the outlaw who's been attacking my supply trains?"

"Yes, I am, general," Garrett replied evenly. "We captured Black Jack and her kinsmen an hour ago, after discovering the location of their meeting place. They would have been in your custody by tomorrow night." He paused, glancing pointedly over his shoulder. "This matter could have been resolved peacefully, as we had planned."

"Do I detect a hint of criticism in your tone, captain?" General Hawley asked sharply, anger shaking his voice. "If so, you'd do well to keep it to yourself. Am I understood?"

"Yes, sir," Garrett said.

General Hawley snorted with derision. "Your humanitarian effort has cost the Crown a great deal of money replacing the food supplies continually stolen by this blackguard." He waved his horsewhip toward the burning cottages. "If I'd done this a month ago as I had planned—before Colonel Wolfe interfered, Black Jack and her men"—he spat—"would have hanged by now and saved us quite a bit of trouble." He leaned forward in his saddle. "Not to mention the soldiers who've been shot by these six bastards. I should have swept through this valley with fire and bayonet until these Highlanders served up Black Jack on a silver platter!"

Garrett had no response to this long tirade, which seemed to irritate General Hawley all the more.

"Does this woman . . . this Black Jack, have a name?" he asked, staring at Madeleine with evident distaste.

"Madeleine Fraser, mistress of Farraline," he answered. "Her father was a baronet, Sir Hugh Fraser, who died at Culloden."

"How fascinating," General Hawley said. "A baronet's daughter. Then she must have lands, an estate nearby? They will be forfeited to the Crown, of course, for her vicious acts of treason. That should put some gold coin back into the king's coffers."

Garrett bit his tongue. It enraged him to hear General Hawley accuse Madeleine of vicious acts! "Yes," he replied. "She has an estate, Mhor Manor, where my men and I have been billeting since our arrival in Strathherrick."

There was an ominous silence, broken only by the crackling flames in the distance. When General Hawley finally spoke, his fleshy face was bright red with anger.

"Do you mean to say, Captain Marshall, that while you were quartered under her roof, Mistress Fraser continued to carry out her raids with no interference from you or your men?"

Garrett stared back at him stonily. "Certainly we would have captured her sooner, general, if we had detected her activities." He chose his next words with care, aware that Madeleine's kinsmen were within earshot. Madeleine would learn of Glenis's assistance from his lips alone. "I have discovered there is a secret tunnel beneath Mhor Manor. That was how Mistress Fraser was able to pass unnoticed from the house and continue her raids despite our presence."

"A secret tunnel!" General Hawley snorted. "These Highlanders are the craftiest lot." He flicked his horsewhip impatiently. "I would see this Mhor Manor," he stated. "I assume it will adequately accommodate my commanding officers and myself? Most of the manor houses still standing in the Highlands are hollow shells, not fit for beasts."

Garrett felt bile rising in his throat. To think that Hawley might sleep in the bed where only last night he and Madeleine had slept. "The house is well appointed," he heard himself answer woodenly.

"Good. I assume there is a stable where the prisoners may be housed?"

Garrett stared at him incredulously. He glanced at Madeleine, still unconscious in his arms, and back to the general. "Mistress Fraser has been injured," he said. "She needs care, as does one of her kinsmen, who was shot during the ambush. The stable is drafty and it leaks, hardly the place—"

"Captain Marshall!" General Hawley roared, cutting him off. "If I did not know better, I might accuse you of harboring some affection for these Jacobite dogs. Surely you don't expect me to sleep under the same roof with them." He abruptly turned his attention to the stiffly erect soldier at Garrett's side. "Your name, sergeant," he demanded.

"Sergeant Fletcher, sir!" he answered briskly.

"Well, Sergeant Fletcher. Take this prisoner from Captain Marshall and see that she and her surly kinsmen are locked up in the stable under full guard," he commanded, then added dryly, "I'll have one of my surgeons sent over to attend to their wounds. I'd like a full complement of criminals to face the king's justice, if possible." His eyes shifted to Garrett. "Meanwhile, the good captain will kindly accompany my officers and myself to Mhor Manor where we'll discuss his notable accomplishment over a glass of wine or two."

General Hawley kicked his horse with his brightly polished boots. The animal was clearly straining as it walked past them, then stopped once again in the road. "Captain Marshall?" the general said without turning his head.

Sergeant Fletcher turned to Garrett. "I should take her, captain," he said anxiously. "I'll see to it that she's well tended, with warm blankets and the like. She did the same for you once . . ." His voice trailed off, and he looked momentarily flustered.

Garrett could empathize with his sergeant's confusion. He reluctantly handed Madeleine over to him, his hand brushing against her cheek. "Thank you, Fletcher."

He turned and mounted his bay, which had been brought to him by one of his soldiers. He drew up alongside General Hawley, who was staring toward the south end of the village, glints of fire reflected in his hooded eyes.

Garrett felt a chill cut through him at the pleased smile on the general's face. "General Hawley, I took the liberty of ordering your men to stay their torches, seeing that I've captured Black Jack—"

"So I've just been informed," General Hawley interrupted bluntly, without taking his gaze from the burning cottages. A long, uncomfortable silence settled between them until the general spoke up excitedly. "Look there." He pointed with his horsewhip. "What a magnificent sight."

Garrett followed his gaze to a cottage only fifty feet away, one of the last to have been torched before he called a halt to the destruction. A ball of flame shot up high into the inky black sky as the roof suddenly gave way, crashing into the fire-gutted interior with a roaring whoosh.

"I would like to see that happen to every cottage in the Highlands," General Hawley said acidly. "These Jacobite bastards will never survive the winter without roofs over their treasonous heads. When they're freezing and starving to death, they'll wish a thousand times I hadn't spared their miserable lives tonight." He looked sharply at Garrett. "My order stands, Captain Marshall. Farraline is to be burned to the ground as a warning to any other villages in Strathherrick who might harbor an enemy of the Crown." He dug his boots into his stallion's flanks. "I've acquired quite a thirst from this night's work, captain. Lead on."

Garrett felt as if he had been slammed violently in the chest. He could scarcely breathe, and he could not think. He could only act.

Gripped by stark despair he urged his bay into a trot, riding side by side with a man from whom he could expect no pity.

Behind them the night once again resounded with screams as General Hawley's soldiers set about their task with renewed vengeance, cottage after cottage falling to the twisting flames.

Chapter 23

It was almost noon the next day when Garrett and his soldiers prepared to leave Mhor Manor, ordered by General Hawley to rejoin Colonel Wolfe's regiment at Fort Augustus.

"Your mission is completed to the satisfaction of your superiors. You are dismissed, Major Marshall!" General Hawley's second-in-command shouted, with a final salute after the brief promotion ceremony.

Garrett stonily acknowledged the officer, then turned to Sergeant Fletcher. "Give the order, sergeant," he said tersely.

"Step lively, men. We're on to Fort Augustus!"

Garrett was consumed by fury as his men began to march in solemn double lines down the dirt drive, his prancing bay bringing up the rear. He felt as if he were living a nightmare. The events of the past hours played relentlessly in his mind . . .

Last night after a few brimming goblets of wine, General Hawley had soon tired of asking questions about Black Jack and had insisted upon viewing the secret tunnel. Axes had made short work of the planked floor in the drawing room closet, exposing the gaping black hole.

It had been a terrible revelation, and had confirmed everything Glenis had told him. Yet it was no more terrible than the general's disclosure of his plans for Madeleine and her kinsmen amid a celebration which was fueled by copious quantities of red wine.

253

"First we'll have a day's respite after the rigors of this evening," General Hawley had stated drunkenly, his strident laughter echoing about the room, "then we're off to my new headquarters in Edinburgh and the triumphant task of delivering our Jacobite dogs to the castle gaol. Within a fortnight, the wench and her traitor friends will be tried for treason and hanged!"

Garrett grimaced at the awful memory, his knuckles white as he clutched the reins. He had known at that moment there was no use in making a plea for Madeleine's life and the lives of her kinsmen. After what he had witnessed in Farraline he could expect no mercy from General Henry Hawley.

No, he had decided to wait. Another idea was forming in his mind. It was a desperate plan, but it was his only hope.

Garrett turned in his saddle, hoping to catch one last glimpse of Mhor Manor and the stable just beyond the house. His heart thudded dully. But it was too late. The buildings were already hidden behind a thick copse of fir trees.

He twisted back around, wondering how Madeleine was faring that morning, wondering if she was well. Thanks to Hawley, he had not seen her since he had handed her over to Sergeant Fletcher last night. The general had forbidden any access to the prisoners because he feared an escape attempt.

At first Garrett thought he could get around the order because his men were serving as guards. He had gone to the stable after Hawley and his commanders had finally retired to their rooms, only to discover that Sergeant Fletcher and his men had been replaced by some of General Hawley's own troops.

His request to enter had been denied. Frustrated and angered, he had returned to Glenis's room, his assigned sleeping quarters since the rooms upstairs were occupied by Hawley's officers. There he had spent a sleepless night, his mind in anguish.

The worst part of this endless nightmare was the

sickening feeling that he might never see Madeleine again.

"Dammit, man, you will see her again!" Garrett whispered fiercely to himself.

"What was that, Captain Marshall . . . uh . . . I mean Major Marshall?" Sergeant Fletcher asked, dropping his position at the back of the line to walk beside Garrett's horse.

Garrett sighed. "Nothing, Fletcher. I was merely . . ." He paused, struck by a sudden idea. "I've decided to ride on ahead, sergeant," he continued evenly, masking his impatience. "Colonel Wolfe should be informed of our successful mission and Black Jack's capture as soon as possible. I'd like you to take charge of the men and see them to Fort Augustus in my stead."

"No trouble at all, major," Sergeant Fletcher replied, slinging his musket more comfortably over his shoulder. "You're right about Colonel Wolfe. He'd be more than interested in the news."

"Good," Garrett responded, scarcely hearing him. "I'll expect you and the men sometime later this evening. It shouldn't be too hard a march without the wagons."

He didn't wait for a reply but spurred the bay into a fast gallop. The massive animal seemed to sense his urgency, and his forceful strides rapidly lengthened the distance between Garrett and his startled soldiers.

Garrett's thoughts whirled as he sped along, the wild scenery around him fading into a blur of color.

As soon as he reached Fort Augustus, he would explain everything to Colonel Wolfe. He could trust the colonel to understand. He would ask for immediate leave, then set out at once for London.

His brother Gordon was his only chance. As a respected court minister, he had the ear of King George. Nothing less than a king's pardon would rescue Madeleine from the gallows, and Garrett must somehow persuade Gordon to request one—in time to save her.

Garrett clenched this teeth as a wave of bitterness

gripped him. How humiliating that he should have to entrust his fragile dream, his very soul, to a brother who had always hated him.

He only hoped Gordon still wanted to possess Rosemoor. It was his only means of bargaining for Madeleine's life.

Biting tears suddenly clouded his vision, choking off his last thought. He was shaken by the intensity of his emotion.

"No, this fight isn't over yet," Garrett vowed defiantly.

He thought of Madeleine's wild beauty, her kiss, her laughter, her smiles, and her touch. The vivid memories spurred him on and he raced across the purple heather, thinking only of when he would see her again.

"They're gone, Maddie," Angus reported. "Major Marshall and his soldiers are gone."

He turned stiffly from the high stable window where he had watched the past half hour's proceedings: the promotion ceremony, the curt farewells, the march from Mhor Manor. His gaze met Madeleine's. "They must be on their way back to Fort Augustus. They dinna take the road into Farraline but turned south toward Aberchalder."

"Aye, 'tis probably so," Madeleine said tonelessly. She looked away, leaning her head against the stall. She winced from a sudden, throbbing ache but chose to ignore it. At least it had dulled from the piercing pain that had plagued her until a few hours ago.

She glanced back at Angus. He was staring at her strangely, as if he was surprised she hadn't thrown some sharp-tongued barb to send Garrett and his men on their way. She couldn't tell him she felt too numb and paralyzed by Garrett's betrayal even to mention his name.

Angus would never understand. He had no idea of what had passed between herself and Garrett—nor would he. It was her own private pain, her well-deserved punishment for having trusted a redcoat, for having ever entertained the notion that she loved him. Aye, she was truly a fool.

"I dinna care where the major is bound, Angus," she said dully. "I think we should be more concerned with what's to happen to us now."

It was true enough, she thought, pushing the dirty straw on the floor with her boot. She didn't want to think about Garrett any longer. He had gotten what he had come for, and left. It was as simple as could be. He was gone from her life forever.

"I heard the guards talking outside the window," Angus said, easing himself down beside her. He grimaced, his body bruised and sore from last night's ambush. "They said something about Edinburgh Castle."

Madeleine nodded slowly. "Ye know what that means, Angus. There's a prison in the castle. 'Tis where our Lord Lovat's son, Master Simon, is being held." She smiled grimly. " 'Twould not be so bad to share a cell with our future chief."

When Angus did not readily answer, Madeleine turned slightly to look at him. He was staring straight ahead, deep concern etched on his ruddy face. She followed his gaze to where Ewen sat, his eyes closed, Duncan sleeping beside him, then over to Allan, who was wiping the feverish sweat from his younger brother's brow.

She sighed heavily, besieged by despair. Kenneth was very ill, maybe dying. It was not so much the bullet that had felled him, but the surgeon's disinterested and incompetent care afterward which placed his life in jeopardy.

It had been a terrible scene. Kenneth's agonized screams were the first thing she had heard when she regained consciousness. The removal of the ball from Kenneth's thigh had been accompanied by a great loss of blood, the surgeon's clumsy knife having only made things worse. Kenneth had fainted from the pain, his hands still desperately clutching his brother's.

After the surgeon had staunched the bleeding and

bandaged the ravaged leg, he had left the stable and never returned. The others could only tend to Kenneth as best they could, tearing strips of their clothing into rags which they soaked into their drinking water to soothe his raging fever.

Now it was clear their efforts had been in vain. Kenneth was deathly pale, his breathing raspy and shallow. Madeleine feared he would not survive the journey to Edinburgh, or even the next few hours. Dear God, when would the horrors end?

She was suddenly overcome by everything that had happened and by her own wretched helplessness. Her chin trembled, tears tumbling down her cheeks. She could not have stopped them if she tried, and she was forced to break her vow that she would never let her kinsmen see her cry.

"Och, Maddie," Angus crooned gently when he heard her sobbing. He put his arm around her shaking shoulders. " 'Tis not yer fault, if that's what ye're thinking. Kenneth knew the dangers when he chose to ride with us. We all did." He hugged her tightly. "We fought a good battle, Maddie Fraser. For a few months we helped our kin to survive."

"Farraline is gone, Angus!" Madeleine cried, her tears flowing unchecked. "Burned to the ground!" She shuddered, remembering last night's flames and the curling black smoke she had seen that morning when she peered from the stable window. She could well imagine the smoldering ruins. "How can ye say we've helped our kin when we brought this upon them? Now they've no homes, and the winter is coming—"

"Hush with ye!" Angus chided, giving her a firm shake. "Think, Maddie. Think of all ye've done! Aye, ye gave them food, but dinna forget ye gave them hope, too. Do ye think 'twill die so easily in their hearts?"

She sniffed, not answering him.

"Clan Fraser is a hardy lot, lass," he continued fervently. "They'll rebuild long before winter, ye can be sure. And there's food on Beinn Dubhcharaidh, plenty of food to last the winter. Ewen saw to it last night that his good wife knows where to find the cave, and so does Flora Chrystie. Ye dinna have to worry for the Frasers of Strathherrick, Maddie. Ye saw to that.'' He swore under his breath. ''They'll prove that Hawley wrong. A Fraser wishing himself dead—'twill never happen!''

Madeleine sobs gradually quieted. She found comfort in Angus's words, though she had no idea what he'd meant by his last statement. She rested her head on his broad shoulder, wiping her face with her jacket sleeve. ''Aye, I told Glenis to let Meg Blair's father know about the cave, too,'' she said. ''I hope she's all right.''

Angus's tone was reassuring, though his expression was somber. ''Dinna fear for yer Glenis,'' he replied. ''I'm sure she had the good sense to take refuge on the moor when she saw the redcoats coming. Remember what I told ye last night, soon after ye came out of yer faint?''

''Aye,'' Madeleine said softly. ''Ye said ye had overheard General Hawley talking to Major Marshall, telling him he would spare the villagers' lives.''

''That I did,'' Angus said, nodding gravely. ''I thought 'twas important ye knew that, so ye wouldna worry. 'Twas bad enough ye were in such pain yerself, without fearing what was happening to yer kin. And ye shouldna fear for them now. Ye accomplished what ye set out to do.'' He paused, drawing a deep breath. ''I was close enough to General Hawley to overhear a few other things, Maddie, but I wanted to wait 'til ye were feeling better to tell ye the rest.''

Madeleine looked up at him. ''What did ye hear, Angus?'' she asked, puzzled.

''I believe I misjudged Major Marshall,'' he said quietly. ''Ye were right to trust him, Maddie. I've never seen a more coldhearted bastard than General Hawley. He came to Farraline looking for Black Jack, just as Major Marshall warned he might. 'Twas by divine chance we came along when we did. If we hadna, 'twould not have been enough for Hawley to burn the village. He would have taken every life in Farraline without blinking an eye.'' He shuddered visibly. ''I dinna think that bodes well for us in Edinburgh, lass.''

Madeleine was shaken by his admission. She'd never have dreamed Angus Ramsay would ever say a good word about an Englishman. Sudden indignation seized her, sweeping away her chilling numbness.

''Aye, I trusted him, Angus,'' she said heatedly. ''But Major Marshall lied to me. He said Hawley wouldna come to our village at all if Black Jack was found—''

''I think 'twas as much of a surprise for him to find General Hawley in Farraline as 'twas for us, Maddie,'' Angus interjected. ''Major Marshall received quite a tongue-lashing for saying the whole matter could have ended peacefully, if only Hawley had been more patient.''

Madeleine stared at him openmouthed, too stunned to speak.

''Major Marshall ordered the soldiers to stay the torches, Maddie. I heard him admit as much to the general. 'Twas Hawley who set his men upon the village once more, saying 'twould be a lesson for the rest of Strathherrick.''

''Why are ye telling me this, Angus?'' Madeleine demanded hoarsely, finding her voice at last. ''We're on our way to prison in Edinburgh Castle, and the major,'' she hissed, ''with his fine promotion, is on his way back to Fort Augustus. What does it matter?'' She rose abruptly to her feet, but Angus caught her sleeve.

''I'm sorry, lass. We—we face such troubles ahead,'' he said falteringly, as if unsure how to express what he was feeling. ''Last night, well, I've never seen ye so distraught. Ye're like a daughter to me, Maddie. I thought ye'd want to know what Major Marshall had done to help your kin, that's all . . . I dinna want ye to go on thinking he lied to ye, after ye trusted him so.''

Madeleine broke away from him and hurried to the high window, wrapping her arms tightly about herself. She rested her forehead upon the sill, her thoughts a tangled confusion.

Garrett hadn't lied to her. She would never have believed it but for her Angus telling her it was so. Garrett had tried to stop the destruction . . .

She inhaled sharply as vivid memories of the night before flooded her mind. The flames, the raucous laughter, the screaming. Garrett's anxious voice, imploring her to drop the pistol.

Madeleine rubbed her temples, her head beginning to pound. Garrett's words came back to her in a rush. *You can still trust me, Maddie . . . I told you the truth . . . You must believe me . . .*

Yet she hadn't believed him. She would have shot him dead if that other officer—

A ragged moan broke from her throat, and she covered her face with her hands. Other memories, other words, crowded in upon her: Foyer's Falls, their night together, his fierce embrace, his words—his words! Garrett had said nothing would happen to her, not if he could prevent it.

Madeleine slowly lifted her head, her eyes blurred with fresh tears as she gazed searchingly out the window. There were redcoats all around, marching along the drive, walking in and out of her home, camped upon the back lawn, in the orchard, laughing and talking. Yet none of them was Garrett.

He was gone.

The awful finality of it struck her with resounding force, echoing in her mind. Garrett was gone. He had spoken those words before he knew she was Black Jack. She could expect nothing from him now. Nothing.

Shattering heartache suddenly gripped her, far worse than anything she could have imagined. She trembled uncontrollably, her hands curled into tight fists.

How she wished she still believed Garrett had betrayed her, if only to dull the pain tormenting her now.

That he had forsaken her was more than she could bear.

"It doesna matter," she whispered fiercely, wiping angrily at her tears. "It doesna matter!"

Yet deep in her heart, it did matter. She could not deny it. She cared, and deep down she had begun to believe Garrett might care, too. Until now.

Chapter 24

London, England

Garrett yanked at his waistcoat in irritation, the stiff fabric driving him mad. He had become so accustomed to wearing a military uniform he had almost forgotten what it was like to dress in formal civilian clothes.

He tugged at the white muslin stock tied tightly around his neck, his fingers brushing against the frothy lace jabot. He winced uncomfortably. He couldn't say he had missed them. He felt like a preening peacock in his borrowed clothes, the pleated outer coat and breeches of plum velvet, the gold brocade waistcoat, the cream silk stockings and red-heeled shoes.

Either London fashions had become more outrageous, Garrett thought dryly, or his brother was stretching the limits of good taste. He sensed it was a bit of both. He had finally drawn the line at the curled tie-wig his brother's dresser had insisted he wear. He had no time or inclination for such frippery. It was enough he had agreed to Gordon's insistence that he change out of his travel-stained clothes the minute he walked in the door.

Garrett smiled thinly, recalling his brother's expression when he had entered the plush salon where Garrett was waiting for him. He was a study of unruffled composure, though Gordon's eyes had reflected his shock. And how like Gordon to demand Garrett change before they discussed his matter of great urgency, so that his stink and his mud-splattered clothes would not offend the household.

Garrett glanced about the library, which was clearly his brother's private domain. Well-dusted tomes stretched from floor to painted ceiling, a goodly portion of them from their late father's collection. The room was dominated by a massive desk placed near the high, arched windows overlooking the fashionable street. Garrett could well imagine his brother sitting there, poring over letters and papers dealing with the king's business.

His eyes strayed to the crystal decanter on the mantelpiece. He could use a tumbler of brandy right now. He started to rise, then changed his mind and sat back down. He wanted to be completely clearheaded for the important discussion which lay ahead.

Garrett drummed his fingers impatiently on the stuffed armrest, wondering what was keeping his brother. He had journeyed at a devil's pace to get to London, the exhausting trip taking him just over four days with stops for fresh horses and brief respites for sleep. A few moments' wait might be trivial, but to him it seemed unbearable. Every instant that passed brought Madeleine closer to—

"So, Garrett, what is this urgent matter which has brought you so unexpectedly to London?" a deep, resonant voice sounded from the doorway, startling him.

Garrett stood up and turned to face his brother. "Gordon," he acknowledged stiffly, though he did not cross the floor to greet him. He thought fleetingly how little Gordon had changed in the two long years since he had last seen him.

His older brother was nearly as tall as he and slightly broader, with the same gray-green eyes as his own, but the resemblance ended there.

Gordon took after their father's side of the family, with his pale coloring and dark brown hair barely visible beneath his full powdered wig. He was probably

considered handsome, with narrow, patrician features
that had a somewhat hawkish look about them.

An undeniable air of authority clung to Gordon,
tinged with studied restraint. He had a fearsome temper, which Garrett had witnessed on numerous occasions when it had usually been directed at him. The
last occasion had been two years ago, just before Garrett left London to fulfill his commission. Their parting
had been anything but convivial.

"You look well, brother," Gordon said, looking him
over as he walked to stand by his desk. He smiled
tightly. "The military seems to have agreed with you.
You look hale and healthy, though a bit weary from
your journey."

"Sorry to disappoint you," Garrett replied, attempting to keep the bitterness from creeping into his voice.
By his brother's raised eyebrow, he knew he had failed
utterly.

"Ah," Gordon murmured. "So the tone is set." He
moved purposefully to the mantelpiece. "A brandy,
Garrett?" he asked over his shoulder. He poured two
tumblers without waiting for a reply, returning to hand
one to Garrett. "Here, you seem tense. This might help
you relax." He clinked his glass to Garrett's, then took
a good swallow. "Go on, drink up. It's the best quality, I can assure you. You probably haven't tasted good
brandy in some time."

Garrett set the untouched glass on the table next to
his chair. "I'd rather talk first, Gordon. Perhaps I'll
share a drink with you later."

"As you wish," Gordon said lightly, sitting down at
his desk. "Dammit, man, at least take a seat. And you
might cease that glowering." He chuckled wryly. "I've
already surmised this isn't purely a social call or nec-
essarily a friendly one."

Garrett resumed his chair, not taking his eyes from
his brother. "It's a personal matter, Gordon, and I'll
come right to the point. I take it you're still interested
in possessing Rosemoor?"

Gordon's gaze widened slightly, his expression

tightening. "An unexpected question, Garrett, I must admit," he said, leaning back in his chair. He swirled the amber liquid around in his glass, studying Garrett thoughtfully. "I'm sure you can guess my answer. Why do you ask?"

Garrett felt an oppressive weight lift from his chest, though he knew the battle was not won yet. "I may be interested in parting with it—for a small price, of course." He watched Gordon's face, gauging his reaction. He could see his brother was stunned, though he was trying hard not to show it.

"What has brought about this change of heart?" Gordon inquired shrewdly. "Gambling debts, perhaps? I've been told military officers spend much of their leisure in such idle diversion. Have you gotten yourself into a bit of financial trouble, Garrett?"

"Again, sorry to disappoint you," Garrett responded with a short laugh. "My finances are secure." He sobered quickly. "My price is this. I have a friend, a young woman I met in Scotland, who desperately needs my help. Unfortunately, I cannot help her without your assistance, Gordon."

"Have I heard you correctly?" he asked, leaning forward to rest his elbows on the desk. "You puzzle me, Garrett. You speak of Rosemoor in one breath and a mysterious Scotswoman in the next."

"Exactly. They are intertwined, Gordon. If you are able to assist me in this matter to my full satisfaction, I shall present you with Rosemoor. Then we shall both have what we want."

Gordon did not reply for several long moments, his eyes boring into Garrett's. His voice was barely above a whisper when at last he spoke. "You have captured my full attention, Garrett. Now, what has this woman done? It must be something serious for you to consider striking such a rare and priceless bargain." His gaze narrowed knowingly as Garrett sharply exhaled. "Ah, so it is just as I thought."

Garrett was not surprised by his brother's astuteness. "Her name is Madeleine Fraser," he began.

"She's the daughter of a baronet who was killed at Culloden—"

"A Jabobite?" Gordon interjected archly. "I'm sure you can hear Father spinning in his grave. You and he were always far apart politically, but this . . ." At Garrett's frown he hastily apologized. "Go on. I'll not interrupt you again."

Garrett quickly recounted the entire story, doing his best to ignore Gordon's changing expressions: incredulity, contemplation, and grim humor. Finally a serious look settled on his countenance as Garrett relayed General Hawley's plans for his prisoners.

When Garrett finished, a weighty silence fell over the room. It seemed to stretch interminably, filling him with dread. He felt an added chill when Gordon tossed his head back and downed the fiery contents of his glass in one draft, then rose to refill it once again. He returned slowly, stopping in front of Garrett's chair. He lifted the tumbler as if in salute.

"I applaud you, Garrett," he said sarcastically, shattering the grim silence. "You could not have presented me with a more difficult task. A king's pardon, and the restoration of an estate, for a Highland wench nicknamed Black Jack who will shortly be tried for treason against the Crown, if she hasn't been already." He laughed under his breath. "If you were not dangling Rosemoor before me, I would have told you right out I could not help you." He paused, taking a quick sip. "Even so, I cannot guarantee my efforts will prove successful. You may find yourself alone and growing old in Rosemoor."

"What the hell does that mean?" Garrett shouted angrily, jumping to his feet. "Either you can help me or you can't!"

Gordon grabbed the glass on the table, sloshing some of the brandy onto the carpet. He shoved the glass at Garrett. "Drink this," he demanded between clenched teeth. "When you're calmer, we'll talk." He walked around the desk, pausing to peer out the window as a glossy black carriage clattered to a halt near the front door. His tone softened somewhat. "Ah, Celinda must have completed her afternoon calls." He turned around just as Garrett slammed his empty tumbler on the table.

"There, I feel better," Garrett said, his throat burning. "Do we have an agreement, Lord Kemsley?"

Gordon nodded, eyeing Garrett steadily. "I will draft a petition of pardon and present it to the king tomorrow morning. I well understand the need for haste in this matter."

"What will you tell him?"

Gordon impatiently waved off Garrett's question. "Leave the particulars to me, Garrett. I know the king's mind. His Highness has an intense dislike for Jacobites, as you've seen displayed in the duke of Cumberland's and Hawley's recent behavior, both being sons after his own heart."

"I'd call them butchers," Garrett spat.

"Now, now, brother, you'd best be careful what you say, or you might find yourself being tried for treason," Gordon warned, throwing him a dark look.

Garrett's jaw tightened, his eyes flaring. "Don't even think of it. You know such a scheme would only drag you down with me, blackening your name along with mine."

"Believe me, Garrett, I realized long ago that that idea lacked potential," Gordon commented dryly. He began to pace behind his desk, idly playing with the frothy white lace at his throat. "A young woman stealing food to save her starving people . . . Well, even if she is a Jacobite the story does have a decided touch of pathos."

"Pathos?" Garrett snorted. "You have a gift for reducing brave and desperate acts to a matter of little consequence, Gordon. You should see what's been done to the Highlands, see the innocent people struggling to survive on what little we've left to them."

Gordon pointedly ignored his outburst. "Yes, it just might sway the king," he considered aloud. "After all, the Highland Scots are his subjects as well, though they'd be the last to admit it. King George has already effected pardons for some of the misguided fools who participated in the uprising. Why not pardon a woman who has wisely seen fit to charm an English officer?'' Suddenly he stopped pacing to stare at Garrett.

"What?" Garrett snapped, glaring back at him.

"You said you love this wench?" Gordon queried. "Perhaps, then, you're even considering a marriage?"

"Her name is Madeleine," Garrett corrected him, "and yes, that is my hope, if she'll have me. After what Hawley did the other night, she's more likely to spit in my face."

"It's perfect," Gordon said to himself. "That might be exactly the point to sway him."

"What are you talking about?"

Gordon set down his glass and came around the desk to stand in front of Garrett. "You're a fool if you think the king will restore a forfeited estate to a pardoned criminal," he said harshly. "What guarantee does King George have that she won't begin her disruptive activities again?"

Garrett shook his head, unable to answer.

"Exactly. So what I propose is this. Offer the wench a choice. If she agrees to marry you, she'll be granted the king's pardon and the estate will be restored in your name. You'll be stationed permanently in Strath-herrick, where you'll complete your commission, and King George will rest easy knowing she's wed to an Englishman who will keep her under firm control."

"And if she doesn't agree to marry me?" Garrett asked grimly, though he already sensed the answer.

Gordon shrugged. "Then she chooses her own death sentence."

Furious, Garrett grabbed Gordon's velvet coat, wrenching his brother to within inches of his face. "That's not good enough, Gordon," he grated, his voice dangerously low. "Either she lives or you've lost Rosemoor forever. I'd burn it down rather than have you ever set foot in it again."

Gordon's face was ashen, though he didn't flinch.

"Let go of me," he demanded quietly, belying his barely controlled rage. "Don't threaten me again, Garrett. I'm your only hope, and you damn well know it. Do you think I'd rest this entire agreement on the fickle whims of a woman?"

He staggered back as Garrett roughly released him. His expression was grim as he straightened his coat, his gray-green eyes darkened to the same hard slate as his younger brother's. "You said she has five kinsmen who were captured with her."

Garrett nodded, too angry to speak.

"It's simple, Garrett. Tell Mistress Fraser that if she doesn't agree, her kinsmen will share the same fate as her own. Do you think she will so wantonly throw away their lives? I doubt it. From the way you've described her, she'd do anything to save them."

Gordon moved away at the sound of tapping footsteps in the outer hall. "I share the same Scots blood as you, Garrett," he added quickly. "I've heard grandmother's countless stories of clan loyalty. If Mistress Fraser knows her kinsmen will also be pardoned if she agrees to a marriage, then you'll have a wife before the day is out." He threw back the last of his brandy. "I only hope she's worth it to you."

Suddenly the door swung open, and a tall, blond woman in a beribboned gown of rose satin walked gracefully into the room.

"Oh, forgive me, darling," she said, stopping abruptly. "I didn't know you had a visitor."

Garrett turned around, his gaze meeting cool ice-blue eyes in an exquisite porcelain face. "Celinda," he said, swallowing his ire. "It's good to see you again."

"Garrett," Celinda said, clearly stunned. She walked stiffly toward him. "What a surprise." She cast a look at her husband as Garrett kissed her hand lightly. "Gordon, you didn't tell me your brother was due in London. I would have planned a dinner, made arrangements—"

"It was as much of a surprise to me, my dear."

"It's only a short visit, Celinda," Garrett replied,

seeking to ease some of the tension in the room. "I trust I will be on my way back to Scotland tomorrow, after my business here has been completed." He glanced meaningfully at Gordon, who slightly inclined his head.

"Well, I hope you'll share supper with us," Celinda said graciously, having recovered herself and her impeccable manners. She accepted Garrett's proffered arm. "Do you have lodging? If not, we'd be delighted to have you stay with us, wouldn't we, Gordon?"

Garrett found himself smiling. Celinda was as beautiful and imperturbable as ever. He had long ago forgiven her for her slight, realizing she had meant him no ill will. She had evidently always wanted to be the wife of a member of the House of Lords, something Garrett could never have offered her.

He walked with her from the library, thinking how fortunate he was that Celinda had chosen Gordon instead. It had left his heart free to love his wild Highland beauty.

Garrett felt his heart lurch in his chest at the thought of Madeleine in a cold prison cell.

God willing, he prayed fervently, King George would sign the pardon, and he would arrive in Edinburgh in time to save her from the gallows by making her his bride.

It was three days before the precious document was placed in Garrett's hands, three days that had passed like the slowest torture.

"His highness was reluctant to sign," Gordon stated matter-of-factly, "no doubt anticipating Hawley's displeasure. It was his high regard for my good judgment and the marriage clause that finally convinced him, though he quipped that you must be mad to take on a Highlander as a wife. He trusts you'll keep her well in hand." He sighed meaningfully. "I hope the delay does not prove costly to us."

Garrett made no comment as he read every word carefully, at the bottom of the page tracing his finger over the king's florid signature and the royal seal. His blood roared in his veins and he felt light-headed with relief, scarcely believing it. Madeleine's pardon.

"Satisfied?"

Garrett glanced at his brother across the desk. "Yes," he acknowledged. "Everything seems to be in order." He quickly rolled up the document and slipped it inside his heavy riding coat. "You've reviewed the papers drawn up by my solicitor?"

Gordon nodded tersely.

"Good. I have retained a quarter interest in the property's income and the monetary inheritance I received from Father, for which you receive full deed and title to Rosemoor and the remaining yearly income. Are you agreeable to this arrangement?"

"I have signed it," Gordon answered, arching a dark brow. "You strike a hard bargain, Garrett. I look forward to hearing from you posthaste concerning the outcome. I trust it will prove profitable for both of us."

Garrett was already striding to the door. As an afterthought he stopped and turned around, his gaze meeting his brother's. "I thank you, Gordon," he said, the words not leaping easily from his tongue. He knew if not for Rosemoor, the priceless parchment next to his heart would never have come to pass. Yet he meant it all the same, for what it was worth.

"Don't thank me yet, brother," Gordon replied. "You've a long ride ahead of you. You don't want to tempt the devil." He glanced out the window, then back to Garrett. "I've given you the best charger I own to start you on your way. Arabian bloodlines."

Garrett swallowed hard, not missing the hint of understanding in Gordon's eyes. It was the first warmth he had seen there in years. "Lord Kemsley," he said with a short bow, then turned to go.

"She must be truly extraordinary."

Garrett started, glancing back at his brother. He smiled faintly, then walked through the door.

Chapter 25

Edinburgh, Scotland

Madeleine sank into a crouching position against the rough stone wall and pressed her hands over her ears in a futile attempt to drown out the piteous moans of the prisoner in the adjoining cell, a Highlander who had lost his mind after Culloden.

Or so the surly guards had told her. More likely he had gone mad from torture and abuse. She had seen and heard enough misery during the past five days of imprisonment in Edinburgh Castle to last a lifetime, and her life was becoming very short indeed.

Her public execution was slated for tomorrow afternoon, on Castle Hill at the same site where scores of criminals convicted for treason, heresy, and sorcery had met their end. She was almost thankful the wretched ordeal would soon be over.

The trial had come soon after she and her kinsmen arrived in Edinburgh, a hasty affair that had taken no more than an hour from beginning to end. She, Angus Ramsay, Ewen and Duncan Burke, and Allan Fraser had been found guilty of high treason against the Crown and sentenced to be hanged until dead. Their bodies would then be drawn, quartered, and consumed by fire, their heads displayed prominently on iron spikes to the curious citizenry of Edinburgh.

At least Kenneth Fraser would not share their grisly

fate, she thought. He had died on the first day of their week-long march to Edinburgh, and his body was quickly buried beneath a cairn of stones along the steep Corrieyairack Pass.

She had shed no tears. They had all been spent. She and her kinsmen were given barely a moment beside the grave before they were shoved back into line, flanked by soldiers on every side who taunted and jeered.

It had been a nightmare. Her only consolation was that she had been spared from rape. It was as if her filthy man's garb somehow protected her, making her appear less a woman in the eyes of the soldiers.

Madeleine sat cross-legged on the floor, worn smooth by countless prisoners before her. She massaged her bare feet. The painful blisters were almost healed, enabling her to walk with only a slight limp.

The soles of her feet had been bleeding and raw by the time they had reached Edinburgh, her leather boots no match for the long march. She had collapsed on the edge of town and been roughly dumped into a wagon for the last leg of their journey, her eyes staring hopelessly into those of her kinsmen, who had trudged close behind.

Madeleine forced the bitter memory from her mind and rose stiffly, steadying herself against the wall. She had never felt so weak, and she knew it was from lack of nourishing food. The stale bread and tepid tea was hardly the fare she needed to keep up her strength.

She laughed grimly, the sound echoing about the low-ceilinged chamber. Keep up her strength—for what? So she might swing more vigorously from the gallows, fighting for breath even as the noose tightened inexorably around her neck?

Banishing the morbid thought, Madeleine limped to the narrow window and stood up on tiptoe, peering outside.

The stone ledge was slanted upward so sharply she could see nothing but an overcast sky, but she didn't care. She felt her spirits lighten despite her limited view. She was thankful she had not been thrown into a dark hole without windows. This small patch of sky had been her one link to sanity; an occasional shaft of sunlight was like a welcome friend.

She inhaled deeply, savoring the fresh air which did much to diminish the fetid stench of her cell. The steady breeze was scented with rain, and she could hear thunder rumbling in the distance.

Madeleine thought of Strathherrick and the wild thunderstorms that rolled over the mountains from spring until late autumn, when the wind whistled and howled and the rain lashed the earth. She stood before the window with her eyes closed, her hands planted on the graded ledge, the cool draft blowing through her hair, imagining she was there. She imagined she was a child again, playing in the puddles, giggling happily, evading both her father and Glenis—

A loud, jarring noise startled her, shattering her daydream. She spun around as the heavy iron bar was lifted on the other side of the door, the screeching sound causing her to grit her teeth. The door was pulled back, revealing a group of six armed guards. The closest one ducked his head and entered the small chamber.

Madeleine backed up against the wall, cold fear flooding her body. The guard was so solemn—dear God, had she miscounted the days? Was it Saturday after all, the day of her execution? Her throat was constricted so tightly she could scarcely draw breath.

"Wh-what?" she choked, her eyes wide with fright.

"You must come with me, Mistress Fraser," the guard muttered, grabbing her arm. When she recoiled, he gave her a hard push and she stumbled forward, almost falling. He caught her in time, but she yanked away from him.

"Where—where are ye taking me?" she stammered, seeking refuge in a corner. She gasped when another guard entered the cell. Her eyes darted desperately from one man to the other. She felt trapped, like a hunted animal, as they advanced upon her, seizing her arms. "No!" she cried, her feet slipping on the stone floor as they propelled her toward the door. "No!"

Outside in the dim corridor, she found herself surrounded by guards, two in front and two in back of her, besides the soldiers gripping her arms. The presence of so many guards checked her futile cries, and she fell silent, overcome with dread.

This was not how she had planned to act at all, Madeleine thought wildly, limping between her captors as they hurried her along the corridor and up a long flight of winding stairs. Where had her courage flown? Her resolve to face her death bravely? She was so frightened she feared she might wet her clothes and humiliate herself before these English soldiers. She could never have anticipated the stark terror gripping her now.

Madeleine panted, fast losing her battle to retain any semblance of reason and her ability to place one foot before the other. If not for the guards supporting her arms and forcing her along, she would have collapsed altogether. They walked through an empty room, then a wide studded door swung open and they were outside in a square courtyard flanked on all sides by two-story buildings.

Madeleine blinked, shielding her eyes. Despite the dense clouds, the daylight was much more intense than anything she had experienced for five days. She hazarded a glance around her, fearing to find a wagon which would carry her to the execution site.

There was no wagon, and as the guards marched across the courtyard, she thought fleetingly that they were going to make her walk the entire way. She could not have been more stunned when they entered another building and proceeded down a wide hallway, stopping abruptly before an ornately carved door. The guard on her left knocked loudly, then lifted the brass latch and pushed open the door.

Madeleine was ushered into a large room spartanly furnished with a long, polished table at one end and a single upholstered chair in the center of the floor. While the four guards who had flanked her waited by the door, the two men holding her arms pushed her forward and shoved her into the chair, snapping to attention as a side door creaked open.

Breathless and totally bewildered, Madeleine gasped as General Hawley lumbered into the room, scarcely acknowledging her presence. He was followed by the prison sheriff and the judge who had tried and pronounced sentence on her and her kinsmen the day after they had arrived at Edinburgh Castle.

What was going on? she wondered crazily, not even venturing to guess why she had been brought to this room. She was so intent on watching them take their places at the table that she did not notice the last man enter and remain standing near the wall. She only glanced at him when she heard his boots scraping on the wooden floor. Her heart stopped.

Garrett.

She was so stunned that the earth could have dropped from beneath her and she would never have known it. She stared at him and he stared back, his eyes filled with familiar warmth.

All she could think was that he was surely a phantom; her mind must be playing tricks. She had gone mad; the terrible strain had broken her at last. She probably would have fainted if General Hawley's booming voice had not shattered the room's silence. Blood rushed to her face as he addressed her.

"Mistress Madeleine Fraser, if you would kindly direct your attention this way," he commanded, pounding his huge fist on the table.

She jumped, her gaze riveted on the corpulent general, certain if she looked back at the wall, Garrett would be gone.

Unwittingly, her eyes darted back. He was still there, the faintest smile on his lips. How strange such a phantom had been sent to her, the image of a man she had thought she would never see again. She glanced back at General Hawley, who was scowling, his face a mottled shade of red.

"Mistress Fraser, I shall be brief," he began, shooting a furious look at Garrett. He took a rolled parchment from the somber-faced judge and held it in his hand, pointing it at her as he spoke. "His Majesty King George has seen fit to take a personal interest in your situation and has offered you the chance of a pardon, upon certain conditions to which you must agree."

Madeleine was not sure she had heard him correctly. For an instant she thought she might be dreaming, and she sank her thumbnail into her palm. She blinked at the stinging pain, but the room did not disappear. It was real, God help her. Then Garrett must be real.

"A-a pardon?" she asked.

"That's exactly what I said, wench," General Hawley spat. He leaned forward, the chair creaking ominously under his weight. "I'll tell you this, Mistress Fraser. Your pardon has come as a total surprise to me, brought forward only within the last hour by Major Marshall here. I would like nothing more than to see you hang, along with your Jacobite friends, but I am compelled to offer you a chance to redeem your miserable life." He sat back, his eyes narrowing shrewdly. "Upon certain conditions, of course."

General Hawley's words were slowly sinking into Madeleine's brain. Garrett had brought a pardon from King George himself. She felt a tiny glimmer of hope flare within her, and she glanced at him, but he was staring at the rolled parchment in the general's hand.

"What conditions?" she inquired, the timbre of her voice gaining strength. Aye, she would gladly agree to give up her raiding, she found herself thinking, if that was the condition. She would swear to it!

"Tell her, Major Marshall," General Hawley demanded heatedly, "as it seems this is your personal quest as well. But pray keep it short."

Madeleine slowly drew in her breath as Garrett took a few steps toward her.

"Madeleine, you must listen carefully," he began, his familiar deep voice sending a shiver coursing through her. "You will only be pardoned from your crime of treason, and the sentence of death, if you agree to a certain proposal."

She nodded her understanding.

"Get on with it, man, we haven't got all afternoon!" General Hawley shouted impatiently. Suddenly he changed his mind. "Back off, major. I'll tell the wench the choice she must make."

Madeleine watched silently as Garrett's jaw tightened, but he nodded, acquiescing to his commander.

"The conditions are these, Mistress Fraser," General Hawley muttered, clutching the document. "To receive his majesty's pardon, you must agree to marry Major Garrett Marshall, who shall then become the sole proprietor of the estate known as Mhor Manor in Strathherrick, Inverness-shire."

Madeleine felt as if she had been struck. She had never expected this! Her mind reeled in a confusing dance of thoughts and racing emotions. She swallowed hard, her gaze meeting Garrett's. "Marry an Englishman?" she asked incredulously.

The question came from her lips so suddenly she was barely aware she had said it. Yet it sprang from a part of her that was so ingrained she could not have responded otherwise, despite everything Angus had told her, despite the secret feelings she held so deeply within her.

Desperate wishes, vain hopes, and dreams were one thing. Reality was quite another. There was only one answer, nurtured by hundreds of years of hatred and mistrust between neighboring peoples, reinforced all the more by the recent brutality she had witnessed, even if she knew Garrett had no part in it.

She looked down at her folded hands. "I canna marry Major Marshall," she stated evenly, knowing she was choosing death. "I'll not be a traitor to my people."

"There. She has made her choice," General Hawley said, a pleased expression on his fleshy face as he sat back in his chair. "The execution will go forward as planned."

"No!" Garrett shouted vehemently, striding to the table. "You have not given her the full conditions." He glared at the judge. "You know the law. The prisoner must know every condition before the choice can be made."

The judge turned to General Hawley and whispered to him almost apologetically. "The major is correct, general. A king's pardon is not to be taken so lightly." He nodded to Garrett. "You may continue, Major Marshall."

Madeleine gasped as Garrett whirled around, his eyes blazing into her own.

"It's not so simple, Madeleine," he said, advancing on her. "There are other lives involved here besides your own, which the general has neglected to tell you. If you agree to marry me, you will not only save your life but your kinsmen's as well."

Her eyes widened, her mind spinning once again. Garrett's voice was harsh, grating into her jumbled thoughts.

"You've always claimed to put your kin before yourself, Madeleine. Will you let them die horribly—Angus, Ewen—knowing you have it in your power to spare their lives? Marriage to an Englishman seems a small price to pay for those you hold so dear. The estate may no longer be in your name, but you would be living there as before, with your kin around you—"

"That's it, isn't it, Garrett?" Madeleine accused him suddenly, jumping up from her chair. She was shaking from the anger possessing her, shaking from the cruel realization ringing in her mind. "Ye dinna care about me or my kinsmen. 'Tis the land ye want, Mhor Manor, so ye threaten me with my kin as ye've done before to get what ye want. Do ye have lands in England, an estate of yer own?"

Garrett shook his head. "No," he said quietly. "I have nothing in England."

"Aye, so I'm right, then!" Madeleine exclaimed. "Ye're landless, and ye saw yer chance to grab something for yerself when ye discovered I was Black Jack, knowing my lands would be forfeit once I was tried for treason.''

"Madeleine," Garrett began, only to be cut off as she rushed on, her voice becoming more shrill.

"Yet ye knew if ye dinna have me by yer side ye'd never be able to make a go of it among the Frasers of Strathherrick. So ye went to London quick as ye could and acquired a pardon for me so ye could do just that!'' She drew a ragged breath. "Did ye bribe yer way to the king? Obviously ye convinced him 'twould be worth a pardon and a grant of land to have an Englishman living among the Highlanders. The better to spy on them, aye, Garrett? Keeping the peace for the Crown on yer ill-gotten estate?''

"Enough!'' roared General Hawley, heaving his massive bulk up from his chair. "Stand away, Major Marshall!'' As Garrett reluctantly obeyed him, the general pointed threateningly at Madeleine.

"State your choice, wench,'' he ordered, his face bright red and sweating. "I'll not listen to any more of your treasonous talk. Either wed the major or hang with your kin. Now choose!''

Madeleine's chest rose and fell rapidly, her heart pounding furiously against her ribs. Her gaze shifted from the general's enraged face to Garrett. His face was ashen despite his bronzed coloring, and his eyes bored into hers. She heard her own voice as if from far away, answering the general, sealing her fate.

"I will wed Major Marshall, if only to spare my kin.''

She heard Garrett's breath escape in a rush, saw the flicker of relief in his eyes. She had never felt such crushing bitterness in her life.

Aye, ye've won yer fine estate, she thought fiercely, and yer Highland bride. But ye'll rue this day, Garrett. I swear it. Ye'll rue this day.

"So be it,'' the judge proclaimed, rising to stand beside General Hawley. The sheriff quickly followed his lead. "The prisoner has accepted his majesty's benevolent pardon. The sentence of death upon Mistress

Madeleine Fraser and her four kinsmen is hereby re-
voked.''

"Four kinsmen?'' Garrett queried, glancing at Madeleine. She ignored him, staring stonily at the general.

"One of the bastards saw fit to expire on the way to
Edinburgh,'' General Hawley answered for her.
"There is some justice.'' He turned to the sheriff. "Accompany the major and his lovely bride-to-be''—he
spat distastefully, appraising her dirty feet and bedraggled appearance—"to Saint Margaret's Chapel. When
they are properly wed, her four kinsmen may be released.''

"Yes, sir,'' the sheriff said, nodding briskly.

General Hawley leveled his hooded gaze upon
Garrett. "See that you're on your way back to the Highlands by tomorrow morning, Major Marshall. If I might
remind you, you still have duties to fulfill in Strathherrick. Your commission does not expire until next
summer. You will have a full company of my soldiers
to assist you until you may summon your own men
from Fort Augustus.''

With a last surly glance at Madeleine, he stormed
from the room, the judge close upon his heels. The
door slammed shut behind them.

"Let's go, major,'' the sheriff said, waving to the
guards. They immediately surrounded Madeleine.

"That will not be necessary, sheriff,'' Garrett said
grimly. "Mistress Fraser will not try to escape.'' He
glared at the nearest guard, who quickly moved aside,
then he reached out and took Madeleine's arm.

"Dinna touch me!'' Madeleine blurted in a vehement whisper, jerking her arm away. "I'll walk with
the guards, if ye dinna mind. They're far better company.'' She heard Garrett sigh heavily, but he gave no
reply as he stepped back.

Madeleine walked from the room surrounded by her
silent escort. She could sense Garrett's gaze on her as
they stepped out into the courtyard, could feel it searing into her all the way to the stone chapel.

She entered the dim interior, knowing that when she next saw the light of day she would be wife to an Englishman, wife to Major Garrett Marshall. Her life had been spared, yet it would never, never be the same.

Chapter 26

Madeleine laid her head back against the copper tub, luxuriating in the delicious warmth of her bath.

She hadn't known what she wanted to do first when she entered the well-appointed suite on the second story of this comfortable inn, eat or bathe. Now she was glad she had opted for the tub, despite her gnawing hunger. It felt so wonderful to be clean again!

She sighed, breathing in the heady fragrance of the rose-scented bath oil the maidservant had poured into the water. She had never smelled such sweetness. She began to work her fingers through her wet, tangled hair, smiling in spite of herself.

When the innkeeper's stout wife had showed her to these rooms less than an hour ago, it had been like walking into a vision of unexpected luxury, especially after the days Madeleine had spent in her bleak prison cell.

A fire burned cheerily in the sitting room hearth, and thick tallow candles were aglow on the mantelpiece and in ornate wall sconces. A cloth-covered table, laden with all manner of savory dishes beneath domed silver lids, was set near the latticed windows and flanked by two stuffed armchairs. In the large bedchamber, a gleaming copper tub was placed near the fireplace, already filled with steaming hot water, as if they had known she was coming.

She remembered gasping in surprise, and the

friendly Lowland Scotswoman had laughed heartily, urging her to make herself at home. The woman's last words before she closed the door had stunned Madeleine and still echoed in her mind.

"If there is anything else ye need, Lady Marshall, ye have only to ask my daughter, Clara. She'll be serving as yer maid during yer stay with us tonight. Yer fine husband said ye must have whatever yer heart desires."

Madeleine frowned. Lady Marshall. It felt so strange to be called by that name. And as far as having whatever her heart desired, she could see very well through Garrett's ploy. Already he was trying to curry favor with her to mask his treachery. Well, she would have none of it, and she would tell him as much when next she saw him.

Which she hoped wouldn't be tonight, she thought nervously, hugging her knees to her chest. She hadn't seen Garrett since they had arrived at the inn on the outskirts of Edinburgh. He'd ushered her in the front door and handed her over with a few short words to the innkeeper's wife, who had then whisked her up the stairs.

She was grateful the kindly woman had said nothing about her bare feet and disheveled appearance, covered somewhat by the heavy riding coat Garrett had insisted she wear. Nor had Clara, who had gathered the soiled clothes with only the faintest look of disgust and quickly left the room with them while Madeleine stepped gingerly into the tub.

Perhaps Garrett was seeing after her kinsmen, Madeleine considered, her mood darkening.

She had already been seated in the carriage when they were brought stumbling and limping from the prison, their whiskered faces haggard and pale in the gathering dusk. She had shrunk back from the window, hiding behind the velvet curtains, afraid even to face them, ashamed for what Garrett must already have told them.

Her kinsmen had been assisted into the black coach

directly behind hers, a half dozen mounted soldiers flanking the doors. Garrett had then climbed into the carriage with her and told her that the remainder of Hawley's soldiers would meet them in the morning before they set out for Strathherrick.

Those had been his only words during the entire journey to the inn. He had sat directly across from her, his handsome face cloaked in shadow, a tense silence filling the dark interior of the swaying carriage. She had held on tightly to the leather strap, pretending interest in the sights as the coach rumbled through the forbidding gatehouse of Edinburgh Castle and down the steep hill into the city.

Actually she remembered little of the journey. The countless cobbled squares and narrow wynds, Edinburgh's famed alleyways, were all a blur. Only the memory of Garrett's leg occasionally brushing against hers whenever they hit a bump stood out in her mind, unnerving her all the more.

She had never felt so uncomfortable in her life. The day's unsettling events were still difficult to comprehend, and the brief wedding ceremony was something she did not want to contemplate. It had been the greatest relief to arrive at the inn, the greatest relief to find herself alone in these rooms, at least so far.

Madeleine's gaze darted over to the canopied bed, apprehension filling her. It was so huge, so empty. Would Garrett demand to share it with her? Would he claim his rights as her husband? Surely he wouldn't force her—

A soft knock at the bedchamber door startled Madeleine, intruding into her uneasy thoughts. She sank lower in the tub and crossed her arms over her breasts, which were barely submerged beneath the water's surface.

"Who is it?" she called out, her gaze darting frantically about the candlelit room. Three thick towels were draped over a low sitting stool, well out of arm's reach. She would never make it to them in time to cover herself.

'' 'Tis Clara,'' a cheerful voice replied. The door opened wide to reveal a trim, dark-haired young woman who was deftly balancing an odd assortment of wrapped packages and boxes in her arms.

Clara smiled brightly as she bumped the door with her hip, closing it. ''Sorry for the draft, m'lady,'' she apologized, setting her bundles on a table placed against the wall. ''How's yer bath? Still warm?'' Without waiting for an answer she hurried over and dipped her fingers into the tub. ''Och, 'tis grown a bit tepid, m'lady. Would ye like some more hot water?''

''No, thank ye, Clara,'' Madeleine said, feeling the tension ease from her body. ''I've soaked enough for one night.''

''Very well, m'lady,'' Clara replied briskly, wrapping a huge towel around Madeleine's shoulders as she rose wet and dripping from the tub. Clara flung another towel on the rug, waiting patiently with the last towel in her hands while Madeleine stepped over the rim.

Madeleine's eyes widened as Clara sank to her knees and began toweling her legs. ''Clara, 'tisn't necessary,'' she said with embarrassment, wholly unused to such attention. ''I'm able to dry m'self.'' She gently took the towel from the startled maidservant. ''Perhaps ye've a robe I might wear when I'm finished? I dinna have any other clothes with me.''

Clara quickly recovered herself, a wide grin breaking across her pert features. ''Aye, there's probably a robe, m'lady, and more,'' she said mysteriously, glancing at the packages on the table. ''May I open them for ye?''

Madeleine nodded, quickly buffing herself dry. She wrapped the towel snugly around herself, watching curiously as Clara tore through the pretty floral wrappings on the largest package, string and tissue paper fluttering to the floor. She gasped as the maidservant whirled around, shaking out a lustrous blue silk wrapping gown.

''Isn't it lovely?'' Clara breathed, laying it out on the bed. Soon the bedspread was covered with delicate lace undergarments, a quilted robe in apricot satin, several sets of silk slippers, a pair of shoes with elegantly curved heels, two light woolen traveling gowns, soft leather riding boots, even a silver hairbrush, as box after box was unwrapped.

Madeleine could only stare at all the finery, her ire rising. Was Garrett attempting to bribe her with these gifts? she wondered heatedly. He would find himself sadly mistaken if he thought he could soften the edges of his selfish deceit and make her more amenable to his marriage of convenience with such a ruse.

She shivered suddenly, feeling a chill despite the warm fire at her back. Her skin rippled with goosebumps. She couldn't remain wrapped in this damp towel forever.

Clara must have read her mind, for she quickly scurried toward her with the quilted robe. ''Och, I'm sorry, m'lady. I was so busy unwrapping the packages I almost forgot ye were waiting for yer robe.''

'' 'Tis no matter, Clara,'' Madeleine said, dropping the towel and easing into the satin garment. At once she was warmed, the light padding chasing away her goosebumps. She walked over to the bed and chose a pair of slippers lined with down, sliding them onto her feet. They fit perfectly.

''Would ye like me to comb out yer hair, m'lady?'' Clara asked. '' 'Tis such a pretty color, now that the dirt's been washed away—'' She clapped her hand over her mouth.

Madeleine could not help laughing. ''Aye, I suppose I was a fine sight to behold,'' she admitted lightly. She crossed to the dressing table and sat on the brocade stool. ''Ye may try to tackle this mess if ye wish, Clara. Ye might find it more trouble than it's worth.''

As Clara picked up a comb and began working expertly through the wet, tangled snarls, Madeleine stared at her reflection in the mirror. She was shocked by the dark circles beneath her eyes and the hollowness of her cheeks, her image a weary shadow of her former self.

She sighed softly. The strain of the past few weeks had taken its toll upon her. She thought of her kinsmen, recalling their gaunt faces. If only she knew how they were faring tonight.

"Clara," she said, glancing up at the young woman. "Do ye know what's become of the four men who arrived at the inn shortly after my husband and m'self?"

"Oh, aye, they're fine," Clara answered, smiling as she combed out a glistening lock. "They've nice rooms on the third floor, along with the soldiers. Yer husband bought new clothes for them, too, m'lady. He's up there right now, seeing that they have everything they need." Her gaze met Madeleine's in the mirror. "If ye dinna mind me saying so, Lady Marshall, yer husband is a most generous man. He told my parents to spare no expense in making this a comfortable ev'ning for ye and yer kin."

Madeleine did not answer, her temper flaring anew. She was grateful her kinsmen were being well treated, but it irked her that Garrett was putting on such a grand show. For what? She was not fooled. It was all part of his plan.

If Garrett won some small modicum of her kinsmen's favor, it would only make it that much easier for him to spy on them when they returned to Strathherrick. Perhaps he was even telling them he possessed a bit of Scots blood to ease their minds and gain their trust. She couldn't wait to inform them it was Sutherland blood, the traitorous clan that would sooner lick King Geordie's boots than aid their Highland brothers in placing a Stuart on Britain's throne.

"There now, m'lady," Clara said, sweeping Madeleine's thick hair back from her forehead with the silver brush. She stepped away from the stool, surveying Madeleine's image with obvious pleasure. "Ye look beautiful, m'lady, as ye should for yer wedding night."

Madeleine started, twisting around on the stool. "Who told ye 'twas my wedding night?" she blurted.

"Why, yer husband, m'lady," Clara said, looking at

her strangely. Then a slow smile spread over her face.
"Och, I know just what ye must be feeling, Lady Marshall," she said with understanding. "I was so nervous on my wedding night only a few months past that
I locked my poor Jamie out of my room!" She blushed,
giggling. " 'Twas only later I discovered what fun I'd
missed." She sobered suddenly. "Ye're as white as a
sheet, m'lady. Let me fetch ye some wine."

Madeleine caught her frilled sleeve, fighting her
sense of light-headedness. "No, I'm all right, Clara. I
think I could use a bit of food, though." As if to emphasize her words, her stomach rumbled loudly. She
forced a smile to her lips. "Aye, perhaps some food
and a glass of wine. For my nerves, as ye say."

Clara held on to her arm as they walked into the
sitting room, not letting go until Madeleine was seated
comfortably at the table.

"Mama's an excellent cook," Clara said, lifting the
silver lids one by one. Aromatic steam wafted up from
the white, oval plates, making Madeleine's mouth water. "Ye'll feel better in no time once ye taste some of
her rabbit pie and thyme-roasted chicken.'Tis the best
in Edinburgh town, I'd swear."

Madeleine nodded, her eyes agape at all the food.

Besides the two main dishes Clara had mentioned,
there were cheese tartlets, tiny crescent-shaped meat
pies, and fresh-baked scones accompanied by pots of
golden butter and dark heather honey. A wheel of Stil-
ton cheese was surrounded by sliced apples and pears,
and for dessert, a light ginger pudding studded with
plump raisins was accompanied by a small pitcher of
lemon sauce.

Clara handed Madeleine a crystal goblet brimming
with red wine. "Shall I fill ye a plate, m'lady?" she
queried kindly, a look of concern still on her face as
Madeleine took a small sip.

"I'll see to her now," a deep, male voice answered
for her. "Thank you, Clara."

Madeleine almost choked on her wine. She looked
beyond Clara to Garrett, whose broad shoulders

seemed to fill the door frame, and she felt a nervous
rush of excitement. He stepped into the room, his eyes
warmly appraising her.

Clara bobbed a curtsy. "Of course, Major Marshall."
She flashed a reassuring smile at Madeleine, then hurried out, closing the door quietly behind her.

Silence fell over the room, broken only by the clock
ticking on the mantelpiece. Madeleine dropped her
gaze and tightly gripped her goblet, staring into the
wine's deep red depths.

She tensed as Garrett's footsteps moved toward her,
Clara's words resounding in her mind. Tonight was
her wedding night. Tonight was her wedding night . . .

She continued to stare blindly at the wine, afraid to
look up, afraid of what she might read in his eyes, and
afraid of what he might find in hers. No matter what
she thought of him, she could not slow her racing pulse
or stop the quiver of desire streaking through her.

"Mrs. Merrett said she would prepare a fine meal,
but I had no idea she meant a feast."

Madeleine blinked at the sound of a spoon hitting a
platter and looked up, hazarding a glance in Garrett's
direction. He was seated across from her now, casually
filling his plate. He smiled as he dipped the serving
spoon into the rabbit pie.

"You must be hungry, Madeleine. Please don't delay your supper on my account."

Nonplussed, she watched as he ladled a heaping
portion of every dish onto his plate, then poured
himself a goblet of wine. He began to eat, virtually
ignoring her as he savored his food.

"It's wonderful, Madeleine," he said, helping himself to a cheese tartlet. "You should eat. You'll feel
much better, and it will help you sleep tonight. We've
a long day ahead of us tomorrow."

Madeleine gaped at him, thoroughly bewildered.
Garrett seemed so nonchalant, so at ease. Hardly what
she would have expected after everything that had
happened that day. But here he was, eating his dinner
calmly, unhurriedly, and urging her to do the same!

She licked her lips, her stomach growling painfully. The heady aroma of well-prepared food was driving her mad from hunger. She quickly made up her mind. If Garrett could appear composed and unconcerned, then so could she. She set her goblet on the table and began to fill her plate.

"The meat pastries are wonderful, and the roast chicken." He spooned a few pastries onto her plate, then concentrated on his own once again.

Madeleine was so famished she immediately stuffed a pastry into her mouth, the brown gravy dribbling down her chin. Before she could catch it, Garrett reached over with his own napkin and wiped it away.

"Thank ye," she muttered, swallowing. She ate ravenously for several moments, then slowed down as the pains in her stomach subsided. She barely looked up from her plate, unaware Garrett was watching her until she took a draft of wine. His eyes were lit with amusement.

"What?" she snapped, embarrassed. She realized she must have made quite a spectacle of herself, gobbling her food like a pig at a trough. "Ye said to eat," she said defensively.

"So I did," Garrett said, sobering. "Please . . . go on."

Madeleine set down her fork. Suddenly she did not feel so hungry, and she sensed if she ate any more of the rich food, she might become ill. She plopped her napkin on the table.

"I've had enough, thank ye," she said sullenly, meeting his steady gaze. She tilted her chin defiantly. "How are my kinsmen? Do they . . . do they know about the . . ." Her voice trailed off, unable to say the word *wedding*. "Do they know what has happened?"

"Yes," Garrett answered with a touch of irritation. "They know we are husband and wife." His tone softened, though his eyes were hard. "Your kinsmen are well, Maddie, and grateful to be out of prison. Grateful to you, I should say."

A yawning silence fell between them when Madeleine did not reply to his cryptic statement. She glanced toward the bedchamber door, feeling a warmth in her cheeks as he followed her gaze, then looked back at her.

"Tired?"

Madeleine nodded, a strange feeling of breathlessness seizing her. She began to tremble, holding her hands tightly so he might not notice.

"Then I'll leave you," he said quietly.

She was stunned. "Leave?" Her response was out before she could stop it. She desperately tried to think of something to cover what she'd said, hoping she hadn't given him the wrong impression. She spied his half-empty plate. "Ye dinna finish yer supper," she said lamely.

Garrett rose from the chair, a hint of a smile on his lips. "Actually, I'm not very hungry tonight," he replied, then quickly changed the subject. "I'll have Clara come and clear away the food. She'll wake you in the morning and help you pack. I take it you opened the packages I sent up." His gaze wandered over her. "That color is lovely on you, Madeleine. It brings out your eyes as well as I thought it would."

"Aye, Clara opened them for me," Madeleine said hotly, his words pricking her temper. "If ye think to bribe me with yer gifts, Garrett—"

"Not bribes, Madeleine," he interrupted, his expression clouding. "Necessities. You didn't think you'd be traveling back to Strathherrick in those filthy black rags, did you?"

"Och, yes, forgive me," she flung at him. "My raiding clothes would hardly be suitable for the Lady Marshall. I dinna expect the fine title of lady, Garrett. I thought 'twas yer brother Gordon who had the title in the family. Or did ye acquire that from the king as well?"

Garrett seemed to flinch. "I have no title, other than 'the honorable' before my name," he explained darkly. "It's a courtesy style, as it is a courtesy for you to be addressed as Lady Marshall. And you were correct about my brother. Gordon has everything, the title, and the family—''

"Lands!" she finished for him, her eyes flashing. "So ye went after mine instead, Garrett Marshall," she spat, "Master of Farraline. I'll have ye know 'honorable' doesna suit ye at all. Try bastard, or royal spy! Aye, now that has a fine ring to it!"

It happened so fast, in a blink of an eye. One moment Madeleine was seated, then the next she was in his arms, his fingers biting cruelly into her flesh. His eyes were ablaze with fury, burning into hers. Completely stunned, she could only gape at him.

"You will not call me that again," he grated, giving her a rude shake. "I'm not the king's spy, Madeleine. Get that preposterous idea out of your mind."

"Liar! I dinna believe ye," she answered hoarsely, finding her voice. She winced at the pain in her arms. "Ye're hurting me, Garrett! Let me go!"

"Maybe you'll believe this, my lady wife," he said as his mouth suddenly came down hard on her lips.

Madeleine gasped, struggling wildly, but her strength was no match for his. He crushed her against his chest, devouring her with his kiss. She quaked from the sheer force of it. Part of her screamed to fight him, to rake her fingernails down his face, but her reeling senses demanded she surrender.

She thought no more as she felt his hand slip beneath her robe and cradle her breast, his fingers circling the hard, sensitive point—around and around—with maddening slowness until she cried out against his mouth when he tweaked her gently.

Her arms flew around his neck, and she molded herself to his powerful body, moaning with desire when his hand slid from her breast to her bare bottom. His kiss deepened as he cupped her with both hands and lifted her against the hard swelling beneath his breeches, then he abruptly tore his mouth away from hers.

"You want me, Maddie. I know you do. If you can believe in this," he breathed huskily, his hips straining forward emphatically, "in how much I want you, how much I need you, then why won't you believe I'm not a spy?"

His words pierced her passionate daze, and she froze in his arms, breathless and flushed. She was astounded her body had betrayed her so easily. Rage surged within her. Her voice rose shrilly as she tried to break free of his embrace.

"Ye're a spy, Garrett Marshall, and there's nothing ye can say or do that will ever change my mind! If ye think yer lust will sway me, ye'll do well to think again!"

She felt a flicker of fear at his thunderous look and almost regretted what she had said. God's wounds, she had never seen him so angry!

Her heart lurched in her chest when he suddenly swept her into his arms.

"No, Garrett! No! Dinna do this!" she cried, kicking and fighting him as he carried her into the bedchamber. With a heave, he tossed her onto the bed amid all the things he had bought her. She frantically pulled her robe around her exposed body and scrambled to a far corner, her eyes wide and frightened.

"Don't worry, Madeleine, I'm not going to force you, if that's what you're thinking," he said, his deep voice laden with bitterness. "I've never forced a woman before and I'm surely not going to begin with my wife." He turned and strode from the bedchamber. "We'll be leaving early in the morning. Get some rest." Then he was gone, the sitting room door slamming shut behind him.

Madeleine was so shaken that long moments passed before she ventured to draw back the covers and settle herself beneath them. She barely noticed the clothing and slippers tumbling off the bed and hitting the floor.

She brought the warm covers up to her chin, the four-poster bed seeming very large around her. She closed her eyes and placed her hand between her breasts. Her heart was still beating wildly, and her skin was ablaze from the heat of Garrett's touch.

She stared at the canopy overhead, feeling strangely alone. It was her last thought before she fell asleep.

Garrett shut the door to his bedchamber, his hand resting on the latch as he stood silently in the darkness. There were no candles lit in this room, no welcome fire blazing brightly in the hearth. It suited his black mood perfectly.

What the devil had come over him? He had only gone to Madeleine's room to see if she was well, not to force himself on her. But something had snapped inside him when she accused him of being a spy and a liar. After everything he had done for her, the hell he had gone through thinking he might be too late to save her, she wanted nothing to do with him. Even her desire was not enough to sway her!

Garrett drew a ragged breath. Fool! He should have known she would spurn any overtures he might make. He had seen the nervous defiance written plainly in those stunning blue eyes when he had first entered her room.

He had almost turned around at that moment and left, but something had stopped him. Perhaps because he hadn't seen hatred reflected there, giving him a glimmer of hope. He had decided merely to share supper with her, feigning an appetite when he had none, at least not for food.

He was grateful his charade had encouraged her to eat. He still hadn't gotten over his shock of seeing her emerge from prison so pale and thin. Yet despite her pinched appearance, her beauty had shone through with a haunting quality that had taken his breath away.

Garrett sighed heavily, his hand falling away from the latch. He turned and groped his way in the dark to the mantel, where he found a tinderbox and a piece of flint.

He lit a single candle, flooding the room with a soft glow. It reminded him of the night he had spent with Madeleine, the solitary candle burning brightly as he

held her in his arms after the passion they had shared,
spinning his dreams—

"Don't torture yourself, man," he muttered under
his breath, kicking off his boots. Madeleine was his
wife now, that much of his dream had been realized,
but it would clearly be a long time before she was convinced that he loved her more than life itself.

How desperately he had wanted to tell her that he
loved her today, in front of Hawley, during the carriage ride, just now in her rooms. Each time the words
had died in his throat.

Garrett laughed grimly. It was simple. He was terrified that she would throw his words back in his face,
just as she had done when he insisted he wasn't a spy.

Madeleine wasn't ready to hear the truth now, and
probably wouldn't want to hear it tomorrow. She was
entirely convinced he had obtained her estate and the
pardon by becoming a spy for King George. The irony
of it was almost more than he could bear. If he had
had even an inkling that this might happen, he would
have told Gordon to forget about including the title to
Mhor Manor in the bargain to free Madeleine!

Garrett stretched out on the bed with his hands behind his head. He stared at the ceiling, his mouth
drawn into a tight line.

Dammit all, what had he expected anyway? That
she'd marry him and they'd live happily ever after,
that tonight he'd be making love to the woman who
inflamed him more than any other, the mere sight of
whom set his blood on fire? He was in agony from their
brief encounter, his loins aching with frustrated desire!

He gritted his teeth, forcing his mind from his discomfort.

He hadn't expected Madeleine to turn down the pardon outright, saying she couldn't marry him because
of her people. Especially after what he had learned by
speaking with her kinsmen. Madeleine knew he hadn't
betrayed her the night Hawley torched Farraline. Angus Ramsay had told him as much, and had even

thanked him for trying to sway Hawley from his cruel purpose.

Seized by frustration, Garrett banged his fist into the headboard. If he could have half the love Madeleine reserved for her people, he would be a happy man. He would settle for a third, even a quarter!

He rolled over and brought himself up on his elbow, mulling over his last thought.

"Maybe that's it," Garrett said aloud. Maybe the way to Madeleine's heart was through her people.

She believed only the worst of him now, but it was clear he had already made some slight inroads with her kinsmen. They were still wary of him—Allan Fraser looked at him with downright hatred—but given some time, hard work, and patience, he might just have a chance to earn their grudging approval and a measure of their trust. Then Madeleine's affection must surely follow.

Garrett got out of bed and quickly pulled on his boots. It was late, but if he was going to set his plan quickly into motion, he had to accomplish a few things before leaving Edinburgh in the morning.

He blew out the candle, plunging the room into darkness, then moved swiftly to the door. His footsteps were determined as he strode down the silent hallway, a resurgence of hope spurring him along. He took the steps two at a time and was almost to the front door when Clara rounded the corner from the kitchen and nearly bumped into him.

"Och, Major Marshall, ye frightened me," she exclaimed, stepping back.

"Clara, could you see that the meal is cleared away in Lady Marshall's room?" Garrett requested. "She might be sleeping, so be careful not to wake her."

"Aye, I'll be quiet as a mouse," she replied. She studied him strangely, no doubt wondering where he was off to on his wedding night.

Garrett suppressed a smile and opened the heavy oak door. "Oh, yes," he added as an afterthought. "Lady Marshall should be awakened at sunrise and her things packed. We'll be departing early, no later than eight o'clock.'' He ignored her startled look as he walked out into the narrow street.

"But—but Major Marshall, we lock this door at midnight. Will ye be back by then?'' she called after him.

"Depends if I complete my shopping, Clara. I'll pound on the door if it's locked against me.''

"Shopping?'' Garrett heard the young woman mutter incredulously as she closed the door.

He chuckled under his breath. Yes, shopping.

Chapter 27

T he cobbled street was awash in bright morning
sunlight when Madeleine stepped from the inn
and was helped into the carriage by her silent husband. When Garrett closed the door behind her and
climbed atop with the driver, she knew she would be
riding alone. She was relieved she had been spared his
company. His light touch on her arm had flustered her
altogether.

"A good journey to ye!" the Merretts cried out as
the two shining black coaches jerked forward, the second surrounded by its somber guard.

"God's blessings to ye and yer husband!" Clara
called to her, waving her apron gaily.

Madeleine forced a smile, waving back, then settled
against the plush seat as the inn disappeared from
view.

She yawned drowsily. She had been awakened so
early, just after dawn, that she was still tired. She
closed her eyes, her head bumping upon the cushion,
but the carriage was swaying so much she knew she
would never be able to sleep. Instead, she watched as
the cluttered houses and narrow streets of Edinburgh
swiftly gave way to rolling hills and trees aflame with
vibrant, autumn color.

They had journeyed no more than a quarter hour
when the carriage rumbled to a stop.

Madeleine leaned curiously out the window, wondering what had caused their delay. She was stunned

to see a long line of loaded wagons waiting beside the road, and even more surprised by the anxious lowing of cattle filling the air.

She shielded her eyes from the sun. There were soldiers everywhere—Hawley's troops. Garrett had said they would be meeting their escort on the road leading out of the city. But why so many wagons? She counted quickly. There were twenty-six in all and a herd of Highland cattle, including a bull. She had never seen such a cavalcade!

Her attention was diverted as Garrett jumped down from the driver's seat and mounted a beautiful dappled-gray stallion brought to him by one of the soldiers.

"Garrett, what's going on?" she asked loudly, raising her voice so she might be heard above the din. "Are all of these wagons bound for Strathherrick?"

He reined in beside her window, an enigmatic smile on his face as he nodded.

"Will ye kindly tell me what's in them?"

"Supplies for the long winter ahead," he said, looking at her warmly.

"What kind of supplies? And what of the cattle?"

"A herd for Mhor Manor. If you'll excuse me, Madeleine, there's work to be done."

Before she could reply, he veered the restless stallion sharply around and rode into the midst of the soldiers. She could hear him issuing commands, and the confusion began anew as wagons were brought into line behind the carriages, the cattle bringing up the rear.

Exasperated, Madeleine fell back against the cushion. His short answers had hardly satisfied her curiosity. Surely Garrett realized the stable at Mhor Manor couldn't possibly hold so many animals. And twenty-six wagons full of supplies? Was he thinking to use part of the manor house for storage? Where would they find room for everything?

She gasped as the carriage suddenly lurched forward, and she had no choice but to resign herself to her questions remaining unanswered, at least for now.

If Garrett wouldn't tell her, she would just have to discover for herself exactly what was in those wagons.

The hours passed slowly as they journeyed through the beautiful Lowland hills. A few times Madeleine managed to doze fitfully, other times she was lost to introspection, but mostly she gave her mind a rest and simply gazed at the passing scenery.

It was near nightfall when the carriage finally drew to a halt outside a rustic country inn. Weary and rumpled from the constant jostling, Madeleine was more than grateful when Garrett lifted her from the carriage and she set her feet upon firm ground.

It was only when he led her through the inn's front door that her apprehension swelled anew. Would tonight be a repeat of last night? she wondered nervously, not daring to look up at him.

"We'll need two rooms," Garrett said to the stooped innkeeper, quickly dispelling her fears. "One for the lady, and one for myself." He turned to her, his eyes gleaming in the dim candlelight. She could not fathom what he was thinking. "I'll have your supper sent up to you. We'll be rising at dawn again, so you'd do well to retire early. Sleep well, Madeleine."

"What of my kinsmen?" she called out to him just before he walked out the door.

"They'll be camping outside with the soldiers. Don't worry, Maddie. They'll be fine." The door slammed shut, and he was gone.

Madeleine's knees fairly wobbled with the relief as she followed the innkeeper up the stairs to her chamber. She waited while the old man lit several candles and opened the shutters to allow fresh air into the room, then she sank unsteadily against the door when he left her to her privacy.

Her gaze swept the tidy chamber, falling on the large bed in the corner, a bed she would thankfully sleep in alone. It was clear Garrett realized from their unsettling encounter the night before that she had no wish to share his bed. She frowned as she pulled off her traveling coat. She did feel a bit cheated that she hadn't gotten the chance to tell him so again.

A sudden rap at the door startled her and made her heart pound furiously. Dear God, had Garrett reconsidered?

"Who's there?" she said, retreating to the window.

"I've brought yer supper, m'lady."

Madeleine ran back to the door and opened it, but only wide enough to take the tray from the old man.

"Thank ye," she said as he closed the door for her. She carried the tray to the bedside table, her hands shaking as she made short work of the steaming barley soup and brown bread.

With her stomach warm and full she felt even wearier. She undressed quickly and climbed into the bed, delighting in the clean linen sheets and down coverlet. She fell asleep immediately. She did not hear the door open quietly, nor the soft footsteps fall across the rug.

"Good night, sweet Madeleine," Garrett whispered, smoothing a silken chestnut curl from her cheek. He thought to climb in beside her, craving the warmth and feel of her lithe body next to his. He could be gone from her room well before she awoke.

With great reluctance he decided against it. He gazed at her for several long moments, then left as quietly as he had come.

A few nights later, Garrett was not feeling so charitable. He threw a stick into the blazing campfire, but his eyes were not on the flames. He was mesmerized by Madeleine's enticing silhouette on the tent wall, her every movement played out for him in the golden radiance of an oil lamp he had lit for her use.

He was glad he had ordered the soldiers to set up his and Madeleine's tent well away from the rest. He could not bear the thought that someone else might be watching her now, as he was. Madeleine was his wife, and her beauty existed for his eyes alone.

This was the first time there had been no inn to be found when the cavalcade halted for the night, and it would probably happen again before they reached Strathherrick. As they approached the Highlands, congenial inns were becoming harder to find. The cruel ravages of the past months had stamped out this means of livelihood as well.

Tonight he was almost grateful for the failure to find an inn. He was growing tired of sleeping in a separate bedchamber, knowing that a few strides, even a splintered door, would take him to her side.

Garrett sucked in his breath as Madeleine began to brush her hair, the sight of the langourous strokes fueling the rising heat in his body. He counted the strokes, imagining what that slim hand might do to his flesh in such a slow, languid fashion, and he had to force the compelling thought away as he felt himself grow hard.

He clenched his jaw, thinking instead of the journey. Each day's routine had been much like that of the last. He had hardly seen Madeleine, except for the times he would ride up beside her carriage and inquire after her well-being. They hadn't even shared a single supper after the first night. Earlier that evening she had claimed she wasn't hungry, despite the meal he had prepared. He could well imagine the reason behind her lack of appetite.

The only difference in their routine would come tomorrow, when the carriages were abandoned because of the steeper terrain. He would see much of Madeleine then when she would be riding the fine roan mare he had bought for her.

Garrett's thoughts faded as Madeleine stood up and began to remove her clothing. He could see her fingers unfasten each button on her riding coat, and then she began to pull it from her shoulders. He envisioned the lacy chemise he had bought her, molded to her breasts—

Suddenly she bent and doused the light, as if she sensed he was watching her.

"Damn!" Garrett swore heatedly, rising to his feet. He tossed the last of his brandy into the hissing flames and looked up into the night sky. Stars glittered as far as he could see against a canopy of blue-black emptiness. He stood a moment, drawing deep breaths of the brisk air, then resolutely made his way to the tent.

When he lifted the flap, he was greeted by a tense silence.

"Madeleine?" he said, stepping inside the tent.

He heard only silence at first, then the sound of gentle breathing.

So she was feigning sleep, he thought angrily, moving to the pallet he had set aside for himself. Feigning sleep for fear he would touch her, hold her, make love to her. Dammit, she was his wife!

He shed his clothing in the darkness and lay down on the pallet. He lay perfectly still, listening to her as she breathed in and out, so softly, so convincingly. How he ached to span the small distance between them and feel that warm breath against his skin, his mouth. How he longed to hear her moans, her sighs, her gasps of pleasure.

Garrett threw his arm over his head, imagining her outburst if he so much as made a movement toward her. Her screams would surely bring the rest of the camp to her rescue, thinking the tent they shared was being attacked by fugitive Highlanders.

He closed his eyes, willing himself to relax, to sleep. It seemed impossible!

He could not hold his desire in check much longer, that much he knew. He had already decided that when they returned to Mhor Manor, Madeleine would share his bed.

They were husband and wife. He would not suffer being apart from her within their home. And if they slept together, perhaps she might surrender at last to the desire he had drawn from her in Edinburgh, the desire he remembered so vividly from their one night of passion. He could only hope.

Madeleine cursed to herself as she strained to catch a glimpse of Mhor Manor in the distance, and beyond that, Farraline. After journeying for ten long days, she could barely contain her excitement. She had thought she would never see her home again. Yet her anticipation was tempered by frustration at the traveling outfit Garrett had given her. Frowning, she gave the riding coat a sharp tug.

The narrow woolen skirt forced her to ride sidesaddle, a ladylike mode she was not only unaccustomed to but disliked intensely. If she were astride her mount instead of sitting so awkwardly in the saddle, she could be standing in the stirrups, affording her a better view.

As it was she had to content herself to wait until their long procession drew closer to the estate. They were moving at such a snail's pace that it would be another half hour before they reached Mhor Manor!

Madeleine flicked the reins impatiently. She yearned to see what condition her home was in after that fat swine's brief stay. She hoped it wasn't a gutted shell like so many of the abandoned manor houses she had seen along the way, the former homes of Jacobites less fortunate than herself. Hawley had told Garrett Mhor Manor was still standing, nothing more.

She also wanted to see if the villagers had begun to rebuild Farraline, as Angus said they would. She desperately hoped that they had. Already there was a sharp snap in the air. Her people would need snug, sturdy roofs over their heads to keep out the cold winds and damp mists the autumn always brought to the Highlands.

Madeleine took a deep breath, inhaling the pungent scents of moss and heather. The heather was in full bloom, covering the rolling moor like a purple mantle, and dotted here and there with rare patches of lucky white blossoms. The scattered groves of trees were ablaze with color, especially her favorite, the beech, with its fire-bronze leaves. Another wave of excitement gripped her. She could scarcely believe she was home!

She glanced over her shoulder at the winding cavalcade stretching behind her, grateful she was not bringing up the rear along with her kinsmen and a dozen mounted soldiers. She would have been doubly frustrated. It was all those lumbering wagons that had slowed their progress in the first place.

Her forehead puckered in a frown. She still didn't know what was in the wagons. Every time she had ventured to peek beneath the canvas coverings, Garrett had suddenly been behind her, inquiring why she was snooping about where she didn't belong. That accusation had never failed to infuriate her, as did most of what Garrett said to her.

Even his apology over what had happened to Kenneth had angered her. It was Garrett's soldier who had shot her kinsman, though deep down she knew she couldn't really blame him. The surgeon's cruel treatment, after all, had caused Kenneth's death.

Madeleine sighed, her eyes unwittingly seeking out Garrett at the front of the calvacade, riding astride his prancing gray stallion. His broad back was to her, his hair shining like honeyed gold in the sun. She could not deny she found him to be the most handsome of men.

Her heart beat a little faster as Garrett turned suddenly to find her studying him. When he flashed her a smile, she quickly looked away, flustered, her anger piqued more at herself than at him. It never failed to amaze her how his slightest attention set her pulse racing. It seemed her senses were determined to thwart her best efforts to despise him.

At least Garrett had left her alone through much of the journey, she thought gratefully. Especially the nights they had shared a tent. With him lying so close to her, she had been unable to sleep until sheer exhaustion had swept over her.

She had also seen little of her kinsmen. She simply could not face them. It was enough that they presumed she slept each night with a redcoat. She knew she would have to speak to them eventually, but for now she just couldn't bring herself to do it.

"Och, Maddie, ye canna run away from them forever," she chided herself, chagrined by her fears.

Maybe her kinsmen didn't think so badly of her after
all, despite what she believed. Garrett had said they
were grateful to her.

Aye, then, she decided. After her kinsmen were re-
united with their families and friends and things had
settled down a bit, she would meet with them and explain everything.

She could only guess what lies Garrett had already
told them. Her kinsmen needed to hear from her own
lips what had actually happened and the truth behind
her pardon. She had to warn them not to be swayed
by any attempts Garrett might make to gain their acceptance, either by his words or actions—

"What are you thinking?" a familiar voice asked
lightly, startling Madeleine from her determined reverie. She glared at Garrett, who had suddenly ridden
up beside her.

"My thoughts are none of yer concern," she
snapped, sweeping a loose chestnut lock from her face.
She could see his warm smile tighten, but other than
that he appeared unperturbed by her churlish reply.

"Would you like to ride ahead with me?" he offered.
"You must be eager to see your home again."

A tart response flew to Madeleine's lips, but she bit
it back. Garrett knew well enough how she felt when
it came to Mhor Manor and his ownership of her land.
There was no sense in beating it into the ground.

"Aye, I'd like to see what's left of it," she replied
evenly, ignoring his look of mild surprise. She followed his lead, urging her roan mare into a gallop beside his powerful stallion. They quickly left the
plodding cavalcade far behind them.

Madeleine felt a wild sense of exhilaration as they
raced along and a gladness that she was still alive. In
her heart she was grateful to Garrett for saving her life,
regardless of his method. Perhaps one day she might
even thank him.

No, 'twas unlikely, she told herself, dismissing the
thought. Her exhilaration swiftly became apprehension
as they neared Mhor Manor from the south.

She spied the manor house through the spreading fir trees, standing stark and silent against the backdrop of soaring mountains. Even from this distance she could see several windows had been shattered on the first floor, the empty window frames like black holes gaping from the whitewashed exterior. Yet the house itself appeared intact, with no evidence of fire.

She anxiously flicked the reins across the mare's rump. The startled animal surged forward, outdistancing Garrett's stallion and cantering at a breakneck speed down the last stretch of road and into the drive. She drew up the reins sharply and slid off the lathered horse a few feet from the front door.

Without waiting for Garrett, Madeleine rushed inside. She stopped abruptly in the main hallway, her eyes widening, her heart sinking into her boots. She felt as if she was reliving the first time the soldiers had ravaged her home.

She turned around slowly, looking first at the dining room; the polished table was split down the center as if it had been hewn in two, wine stains were splashed on the walls, chairs were overturned. She held her breath as she glanced into the drawing room. The furniture was intact, but the glass from her mother's cabinet lay shattered on the floor, and the brocade padding on the armchairs was slashed and mutilated.

She walked into the room, staring numbly at the closet door, nearly ripped off its hinges. There was nothing left of the planked floor inside the closet, the entrance to the secret tunnel clearly revealed. Angus had told her that Garrett had said something to General Hawley about the tunnel, yet she couldn't imagine how he had found it.

"It looks like the celebration continued long after I left Mhor Manor," Garrett said behind her, cutting into her thoughts.

Madeleine turned to face him. "Celebration?"

He nodded. "Of Black Jack's capture." He quickly changed the subject. "Do you want to look upstairs?"

She shook her head. "No, not yet." She walked past

him and into the dining room, aware that he was following her.

She righted a chair near one of the shattered windows, staring dazedly at the water-damaged sill and the mildewed rug beneath her feet. Rain must have poured in through the empty frames during numerous thunderstorms like the ones she had imagined from her prison cell.

"I'll board up these windows until we can have new glass brought from Inverness," Garrett said quietly. "If there's anything else you want replaced immediately, Madeleine, you must let me know."

She didn't answer him but moved toward the door leading into the kitchen. Her nostrils flared, and her stomach flipflopped. There was a putrid stench coming from the kitchen. She paled, afraid to think of what she might find.

"Don't, Madeleine. Wait here," Garrett bid her, catching her arm. He pulled his cravat from around his neck and covered his mouth with it, then opened the door and disappeared into the kitchen.

She heard him cough and curse loudly, then listened to the outer kitchen door opening and closing and the long shut windows squeaking in protest as they were hastily raised. Finally Garrett strode back into the dining room and slammed the door behind him.

"You don't want to go in there for a while, not until the place airs out," Garrett said, his eyes watering.

"What was it?"

Garrett grimaced, slightly pale himself. "Hawley's cooks left a sheep's carcass to rot on the kitchen table. I'll have it buried right away and the kitchen scrubbed down." He shuddered visibly. "I think it will be a long time before I'm able to eat lamb again." He took her arm and escorted her back toward the main hallway. "The upstairs is probably much the same as down here. Would you rather we ride into Farraline?"

Madeleine started, his question piercing the dazed fog that had settled over her. "Why do ye want to go into Farraline?'' she asked suspiciously, jerking her arm away.

Garrett sighed heavily. ''I'd like to see the extent of the damage, if you don't mind, Madeleine. As soon as my own soldiers arrive from Fort Augustus, we're going to help rebuild the village. We'll have to work fast if we're to beat the snow.''

Stunned, Madeleine turned on him, his words confirming what she had thought all along. ''Part of yer grand plan, aye, Garrett?'' she accused loudly, her voice reverberating throughout the silent house. ''Well, I'll tell ye this. I'll not be a part of it!''

''Maddie—''

''No, ye'll hear me out,'' she silenced him. ''If ye think to use me to sway my kin to yer favor, or to influence them in any way, perhaps to accept the tyranny of King Geordie, ye're wrong. I'm yer wife by law, I canna deny it. But I winna play the wife, Garrett, nor support yer actions. Ye'll soon find out the Frasers of Strathherrick want none of yer help, nor will they want an English spy in their midst, once they discover yer true purpose.''

Garrett stared at her, his eyes darkening though his expression was inscrutable. ''It's not my plan to use you, Madeleine, as you so put it,'' he said grimly, ''or to act as a spy, as you so firmly believe. I only seek to right some of the damage done.'' He strode to the door, calling out over his shoulder. ''Either come with me or stay here. It's up to you.''

Madeleine was tempted to tell him exactly where he should go and slam the door in his face, but she wanted desperately to see for herself how the villagers were faring. She swallowed a good part of her ire, knowing she didn't want to wait and hear the news secondhand from Garrett. She ran out the door and quickly mounted her mare, cursing again the skirt that so constricted her movement.

Neither of them spoke as they rode toward Farraline, the strained silence that was becoming so familiar settling between them once more.

Madeleine felt her throat tighten as they drew closer, fearing the worse, yet she could already see white smoke curling into the air just beyond the low rise, a very good sign. She nearly shouted for joy as the entire village came into view.

Many of the cottages had already been rebuilt on the scorched earth where they had stood before, the same stones, now blackened with soot, forming the low walls. She was pleased to see even their small church had been rebuilt.

Yet it was clear there was still much work to be done. Nothing was left of those poorer cottages built entirely of turf walls and thatched heather roofs. Makeshift hovels abounded where the cottages had once stood, some propped up by charred tree trunks while others leaned against the sturdier stone cottages.

Madeleine took heart in the amount of activity in the village—children were playing, men were clambering atop newly thatched roofs and weighting them with stones to fend off the wind, women were busily sweeping streets or laboring over communal black pots set upon tripods.

She inhaled deeply of the aroma of food cooking in the air. She heard laughter and friendly shouting, calls for more stones to finish a wall or more turnips for the stew. She even heard Flora Chrystie calling for her boy Neil somewhere in the village. Her kinswoman's voice carried to her like the sweetest music.

Angus had been right, Madeleine thought, smiling as she remembered his words of comfort the morning after their capture. Her people's hope had not died that horrible night. She had accomplished what she'd set out to do.

Thanks to Garrett Marshall, she found herself thinking.

Aye, she could admit it. Garrett had played a part in this as much as she. This scene would have been far different if it hadn't been for his warning about Hawley's impending threat. She could at least thank him for forcing her into a decision that had spared her people's lives.

Madeleine turned to him, words of gratitude upon her lips, only to discover he was no longer at her side. She twisted around in the saddle, looking for him. He was riding back toward Mhor Manor. She could barely hear him calling out to the driver of the first wagon just now turning into the estate.

The moment was gone. Once again she felt her anger swiftly returning as she finally guessed what was in those wagons.

This was all part of Garrett's plan.

It had become very plain that he possessed a sizable income, no doubt his inheritance. The extravagant night at the Edinburgh inn attested to that, along with the beautiful clothes he had bought her, the finely bred mare, and even the herd of cattle.

The wagons were probably filled with things he knew her people needed, things they had lost in the flames that could not be made easily or replaced without money. Precious items he could use to win their favor and acceptance and make his task of keeping the peace for King George all the easier.

Yet if Garrett had such an inheritance, why hadn't he simply bought himself an estate in England? she wondered, perplexed. Why had he chosen her land instead, forcing her to become his bride so he might live among Highlanders who were hostile at best to any English presence?

It was beyond reasoning, unless . . .

No, she hadn't misjudged him, Madeleine decided heatedly, forcing the disturbing thought from her mind. 'Twas easy enough to explain. Whatever Garrett's inheritance, it was probably not enough to buy himself an English estate as fine as Mhor Manor, yet it was sufficient to cover his bribes and afford him a comfortable living on Fraser lands. Bastard!

Madeleine tugged sharply on the reins, veering the mare hard about. Aye, she would personally see that her kin had nothing to do with Garrett and his wagons full of winter supplies!

"Maddie Fraser!"

Startled, she spun the horse back around to find Meg Blair running toward her, waving her hand frantically.

"Maddie, I canna believe 'tis ye!" the plump young woman cried, tears swimming in her eyes. "I thought for a moment I might be seeing a ghost."

Madeleine cringed inside. She wasn't prepared to greet anyone yet, especially not Meg, whose tongue was apparently looser than Madeleine had thought. It was Meg, after all, who had spread the news about Glenis and herself tending to Garrett after he had been injured. She watched as the young woman slowed her pace and stopped, her chest heaving.

"We've been so worried about ye, Maddie," Meg gasped, her chubby face flushed pink with exertion. "Ever since we saw the redcoats taking ye and Angus and the others away that night."

She drew a ragged breath. "They told us ye were the outlaw who'd been raiding the English. Is that true, Maddie? They said ye were going to hang, but here ye are!"

Madeleine quickly thought of a way to dodge Meg's breathless questions. "'Tis I, safe and sound," she replied, forcing a smile, "but we'll have to talk later, Meg. First, ye must go and tell Agnes Burke that Ewen and Duncan are well and coming home, as are Angus and Allan Fraser."

Meg's eyes grew round. "But how, Maddie? 'Tis a miracle, to be sure—"

"Later, Meg," she repeated firmly. "Go on with ye now, and hurry. Ye mustna keep such good news to yerself."

As the young woman nodded excitedly, Madeleine suddenly remembered something. "Meg, did Glenis get off all right to Tullich?" she asked, her voice tinged with concern.

Meg's smile faded, and she looked at Madeleine blankly. "Glenis?"

"Aye, dinna she tell ye that's where she was heading after staying with ye? I've been so worried about her. What did she do after the soldiers came? Was she able to save the cart?"

Meg seemed totally confused. "Maddie, I dinna know what ye're talking about."

Madeleine felt a twinge of fear. "I sent Glenis to yer house hours before the soldiers—"

"Glenis ne'er came to our house," Meg interrupted quietly. "I ne'er saw her that night, Maddie. We've been wondering what became of her, and we checked yer house as soon as the soldiers left, but 'twas empty."

Madeleine's throat tightened painfully, her hands twisting the reins. "Are ye sure? No one's seen her?"

Meg studied her helplessly. "Aye, she's not been heard of since that night."

"Dear God," Madeleine said, her mind racing.

No, dinna think the worse 'til ye know for sure, she told herself. Glenis might have gone directly to Tullich. Aye, that made sense.

"Maddie, are ye all right?"

Madeleine blinked, meeting Meg's worried gaze. "Aye, I'll be fine," she said faintly. "Go on now, Meg. I have to get back."

"If ye'd like, Maddie, I'll come to the house in the morning and help ye clean up," Meg offered. "Those redcoats left the place in a fine mess. Shall I bring Kitty Dods with me? 'Twould be a lot of work for just the two of us, now that Glenis is g—" She bit her lip as if she just realized what she was saying.

Madeleine nodded numbly. "Aye, ye may bring Kitty."

Meg said no more but turned and scurried away as Madeleine wheeled her horse around and set off at a wild gallop toward Mhor Manor.

Chapter 28

Madeleine dodged the wagons choking the drive and dismounted near the front door. Her gaze frantically swept the estate grounds, but there was no sign of Garrett. He had probably gone up the road to direct the rest of the cavalcade.

She dashed into the house and up the stairs, deciding to share her unsettling news with him after she had changed. If she didn't find him then, he would have to wait until she returned. She took only an instant to glance in each room as she passed, relieved to see that the upstairs had been left remarkably untouched.

No doubt because Hawley's pompous commanding officers had enjoyed these rooms, she surmised with disgust, hurrying down the hall to her own chamber.

She pushed open the door, stunned to find everything exactly as she had left it but for the unmade bed. She did not waste time contemplating who might have slept there. She rushed to the wardrobe, her hands shaking as she unbuttoned her riding coat and whisked it from her shoulders.

If she left for Tullich immediately, Madeleine thought as she twisted out of her skirt, she would be at least halfway there before dark. The road was clearly marked. She would have no trouble finding the village nestled on Loch Ruthven's western shore.

She quickly dressed in a frayed fustian gown, reveling in the freedom of the wide skirt, then kicked off her riding boots. She replaced her silk stockings with thick, woolen ones and donned a pair of sturdy brogues. Lastly she fastened a heavy tartan shawl around her shoulders for added warmth.

It felt so good to be dressed in her old clothes, she thought, flying to the door. With a last glance at her room, she sped across the hall and down the side stairs. Glass crunched beneath her shoes as she walked through the drawing room to the front door, but she gave it little heed. She stepped outside into the fading afternoon sunshine, searching for her mare.

She spied the animal munching contentedly in the tall grass just beyond the drive, a soldier holding the reins. Her eyes widened as the young man clucked his tongue and began to lead the horse toward the stable.

Madeleine ran after him, shouting above the din of rumbling wagon wheels, bellowing cattle, and neighing horses.

"Hold on with ye!" she cried, catching up to him. "Where are ye taking my horse?"

"I've orders from Major Marshall to brush her down, m'lady," the soldier answered, still walking.

"I'll take care of it," she said, yanking the reins from his hand. "'Tis my mount, after all." Before he could stop her she had hoisted herself into the saddle and swerved the mare around, only to find herself suddenly yanked out of the saddle from behind and enveloped in a strong pair of arms.

"What!" she gasped, struggling to wrench herself free from whoever was holding her around the waist. "How dare ye! Let go!"

The arms only tightened, drawing her closer. Warm breath fanned her neck, and she shivered, tensing at the familiar voice which was just above a whisper.

"You must realize I can't have you stealing out by yourself, Madeleine, not with so many of Hawley's soldiers about. As your husband, I'm determined to protect you, yet I can't be everywhere at once. I'd rather you remain here with me, at least until my own soldiers arrive from Fort Augustus."

Madeleine twisted in Garrett's arms and glared at

him over her shoulder. "I believe I have more to fear from ye than from Hawley's soldiers," she said angrily. "Let go of me, Garrett." To her surprise he did, though he still stood very close to her. Too close. She stepped back, hugging her arms to her chest in a vain attempt to quiet her trembling.

"Where were you going?" he asked, his eyes staring into hers in a manner which never failed to disconcert her.

"I think ye must mean where *am* I going," she responded tartly, trying to compensate for what he was doing to her senses. She fought to keep her voice steady, her words spilling forth in a rush. "I just spoke with Meg Blair, and she told me Glenis never arrived at her home the night ye discovered I was Black Jack. I sent Glenis to Meg's, thinking 'twould be safer, then the next morning she was to set off for her sister's in Tullich." She paused to catch her breath, wondering why Garrett was looking at her so strangely. "No one's seen her since that night," she continued, "not here or in the village, so I'm going to Tullich to see if she's there—"

"Glenis didn't stop at Meg's," Garrett interjected quietly. "You don't have to worry after her, Maddie. She's fine."

Astonished, Madeleine could only stare at him.

"Glenis is at her sister's in Tullich, just as you wanted her to be."

"How . . . how do ye know?" she asked hoarsely, her mind racing. Why hadn't Glenis gone to Meg's? Surely she must have realized it was dangerous for her to be on the roads so late at night, considering what was to happen.

"Perhaps we should go inside to discuss this, where it's quiet," Garrett suggested, glancing at the commotion around them. He took her by the elbow before she could protest and steered her toward the front door.

Madeleine had to half run to keep up with his determined strides. She stumbled over the threshold but he caught her, supporting her with his arm until they were in the drawing room. He practically forced her down into an armchair, then stood in front of her so she could not rise.

"You're not going to appreciate what I have to tell you," he said cryptically, "so I'll stand here until you hear me out."

"What?" she demanded loudly, her temper kindled by his rough handling.

"Glenis didn't stop at Meg's because she went to find me," he said slowly, watching her face. "And she did, on the road to Inverfarigaig. She told me you were Black Jack, Madeleine, and she told me where we could find you and your kinsmen, at the yew tree near Errogie."

"Ye're lying," Madeleine said in disbelief. "Glenis would never have betrayed me—"

"She didn't betray you," Garrett cut in harshly. "Glenis saved your life, Maddie, the lives of your kinsmen, and the lives of my soldiers as well. If she hadn't found us there would have been a bloodbath, and all because you had some idea I wouldn't believe you were Black Jack if you simply gave yourself up."

"Would ye have believed it, Garrett?" she said bitterly.

"I don't know," he answered, heaving a sigh. "It doesn't matter now."

"Aye, ye're right," Madeleine said, staring past him and out the grimy window. "It doesna matter."

She felt numb. Never in a thousand years would she ever have imagined Glenis would play the traitor. She could hardly comprehend it. Her dear Glenis, the woman who had cared for her since she was a babe. She was her confidante, her friend, and a traitor.

Madeleine swallowed against the tears welling up in her eyes. "What else did Glenis tell ye?"

"She told me why you began raiding, to keep your people from starving," Garrett related, his voice very low, "and she explained how you managed to sneak from the house without anyone noticing, through the secret tunnel." He smiled wryly, glancing at the drawing room closet behind her chair. "I could scarcely believe it when she told me you were the one who nailed me on the head."

Madeleine said nothing, still staring into the distance. She remained silent even as Garrett gently tilted her chin upward so she was looking into his eyes.

"Glenis said she could not return to Mhor Manor, Maddie," he said quietly. "She thought you wouldn't want her around because she'd betrayed you. I wanted to argue with her and tell her it wasn't so, that you wouldn't think she was a traitor since she had saved your life—"

"Ah, but ye're wrong, Garrett," Madeleine interrupted him vehemently. "Glenis Simpson *is* a traitor. I never want to see her again." She jerked her head back, and his hand fell away from her chin. "Are ye finished? If so, I'd like to retire to my room."

Garrett seemed stunned by her bitter words. As he moved away from the chair, she stood up and walked woodenly to the archway. She leaned on the wall, needing the support.

"If ye were thinking ye might fetch Glenis from Tullich, save yerself the trip, Garrett," Madeleine barely managed, tears threatening to overwhelm her at any moment. "She's never to set foot in this house again. Not if ye want to have any peace at all." She started toward the stairway, then paused, meeting his gaze once more. "I take it I'm restricted to Mhor Manor 'til yer soldiers arrive, if I heard ye correctly?"

Garrett nodded. "It's for your own safety, Madeleine. I don't trust Hawley's men. My soldiers should be here within a few days, Sergeant Fletcher and the others, the same men who were here before, except for Rob Tyler. Then you may go where you wish—within reason."

Madeleine smiled weakly. "Funny," she said. "Ye dinna trust yer own kind and I dinna trust you and Glenis . . ." She paused, nearly choking. "Glenis betrayed my trust." Her voice fell to a ragged whisper, her eyes misting over. ''There seems to be a dearth of trust these days, wouldna ye say, Garrett? And there doesna seem to be any help for it.''

She turned and fled up the stairs, barely making it inside her room before she doubled over, her body wracked by silent sobs. She slammed the door shut and sank to the floor with the corner of her shawl over her mouth, crying as if her heart was breaking.

Her world was so completely torn apart, so upside down, she didn't know if she would ever make sense of it again.

First she had lost her father, now Glenis. Her final bond with the past was irretrievably broken. Her future loomed before her, bleak and bereft of any hope for happiness. All she had left was Garrett, a man who had usurped her land, a man who saved her life and married her because she was useful to him. And she had once believed she loved him.

The sad songs were true, she thought dazedly when her tears were finally spent and she lay exhausted on the floor, wrapped in her shawl.

Love, even at its most fleeting, brought nothing but heartbreak and sorrow. She must have been mad to think Garrett Marshall ever cared.

Madeleine awoke hours later to the sensation of being lifted from the floor where she had fallen asleep. Her eyes fluttered open, but she could see nothing in the pitch darkness. She tensed as powerful arms enveloped her, holding her close with aching familiarity, and she knew at once that it was Garrett.

''Wh—what do ye think ye're doing? Where are ye taking me?'' she cried frantically, the mists of slumber still clinging to her thoughts as he carried her down the hallway.

''Our room,'' Garrett said, hugging her tightly to his chest. ''I'll not have my wife sleeping on the floor, nor will you sleep any longer in a bed other than mine.''

His words chased the haze from her mind as if he had slapped her.

"No! Ye canna force me to share yer bed!" she exclaimed shrilly, wriggling in his arms.

"In this you have no choice," he replied firmly. "We are husband and wife, Madeleine. From this night on, we sleep together."

Garrett kicked the door open and strode into the firelit room, where he set her down so abruptly she almost lost her footing. He turned and shut the door, drawing the bolt into place, then faced her once more.

"I took the liberty of bringing some of your things in here," he began, walking toward her. "You can move the rest of your belongings tomorrow."

She shook her head slowly from side to side, retreating backward as he advanced closer and closer. "No, I dinna want to stay here," she objected nervously, flustered by the way he was looking at her. "Ye've no right."

"I've made it my right," he insisted quietly. When she took another step backward, he suddenly reached out to her, grabbing for her arm. "Madeleine, stop, there's a tub just behind—"

"No! Dinna touch me!" She jerked away from him and spun around, screaming as she toppled into a enormous wooden tub filled with steaming water. In the next instant Garrett leaned into the tub, catching her about the waist and lifting her to her feet as she sputtered and coughed, her wet hair hanging down over her face, her gown plastered to her body.

"Ye—ye bastard!" Madeleine gasped, parting her hair to glare at him.

"I tried to stop you, Maddie," he said with a low chuckle, appraising her sodden appearance. "I thought you might want to bathe tonight, so I brought up the tub for your use."

Madeleine swept her hair back from her forehead, wringing some of the water out with her fingers. She had never felt so foolish before, standing fully clothed in a tub. She glanced down, surprised by its wide dimensions.

"I bought it in Edinburgh," Garrett said, as if he

read her thoughts. "I wasn't sure if you had a tub here at the manor house or not."

"Aye, but not as large," Madeleine said almost to herself. " 'Tis big enough for two." She blushed suddenly and looked up to find him studying her most intently.

"Exactly," he said.

Madeleine inhaled sharply, acutely aware of the desire flaring in those startling gray-green eyes and even more aware of her own racing senses. She heaved up her soaked skirt and was out of the tub in a flash.

"Good night to ye, Garrett," she said angrily as she sloshed and squished her way to the door. "Enjoy yer fine tub. I'll not be swimming in it with ye, if that's what ye were thinking."

"Touch that latch and I promise you will find yourself back in this tub, but with me," Garrett threatened softly. "I mean that, Madeleine. This is now your room as much as mine. Ours. We will share it together. Do you understand me?"

Madeleine flinched at his tone and drew back her hand from the bolt. She turned away slowly and met his steely gaze. "As always, Garrett, ye must threaten to have yer way."

He did not reply. He began to undo the buttons of his shirt, revealing the golden hair on his chest.

"What are ye doing?" she asked shakily, her eyes widening.

"Undressing. If you have no plans for this bath, then I'd like to avail myself of its comfort while the water is still hot." He stripped off the shirt, baring his muscular upper body to her stunned gaze. "I've set up a screen over there for your privacy, Madeleine," he said dryly, nodding to the far corner of the room. "You'll find your travel trunk behind it." His belt fell to the floor with a thud. "Oh, yes. There's some food and mulled wine on the bedside table. Help yourself."

"I'm not hungry," she said. She glanced over to the screen, delicately painted with vines and flowers, and back to Garrett, who was pulling off his breeches. At the sight of his lean buttocks, she gasped and scurried to the other side of the room, ducking behind the screen. She plopped down on the trunk, her heart pounding furiously. She heard a splash as Garrett stepped into the tub, then his long, contented sigh as he settled himself in the water.

Madeleine's teeth began to chatter, and she felt chilled to the bone in her sopping wet gown. She was so far away from the fireplace there was little warmth in this corner.

"Ye'll surely catch yer death if ye sit here like this," she muttered under her breath, shivering uncontrollably.

"Did you say something?"

"No!" she responded tartly, his deep voice eliciting a tremor of excitement within her. She jumped off the trunk and threw open the lid, rummaging through the neatly folded clothes until she found her apricot robe. She quickly changed out of her wet things and gratefully donned the padded robe and a pair of down-lined slippers. She felt warmed immediately.

"There are some towels on the bed if you care to dry your hair," Garrett called out.

Madeleine wanted to ignore his offer, hoping there were some towels in her trunk, but after a quick search she found none. She sighed with exasperation. If she didn't dry her hair, the back of her robe would soon be soaked.

She drew a deep breath as she tied the sash securely around her waist, then stepped from behind the screen. She kept her eyes lowered as she hurried over to the bed, where she grabbed a towel and whisked it around her head.

As she began to retreat toward the screen, she hazarded a glance in Garrett's direction. Her heart stopped at the striking picture he made, his bronzed shoulders and chest gleaming wet, his dark blond hair slicked back. He looked her over as if he could see right through her satin robe.

"Are you sure you won't join me?" he asked softly, smiling at her with open invitation.

"Quite sure!" she snapped, though inside she wasn't so sure anymore. She turned away, blotting her hair with trembling hands.

"Then could I ask you a favor, Madeleine?"

She swung around, looking at him suspiciously. "What favor?"

"Would you mind handing me the soap? It's there on the mantel, a bit out of my reach, unless I stand up—"

"No, no! I'll get it for ye," she said uncomfortably. Taking a wide path around the tub, she snatched the thick bar from the mantelpiece. "Here." She handed it to him, his wet fingers caressing hers. She pulled her hand away as if stung and darted away from him, taking refuge behind the screen, amazed at what his simple touch could do to her.

She chewed her lip as she dried her hair, attempting in vain to blot out the sounds of Garrett bathing. She was startled by his sudden groan of pain. She dropped the towel and quickly peeked out at him. He was attempting to soap his back, but he grimaced, groaning again as he slowly eased his right arm into the water.

"What's wrong?" she asked, feeling more than a twinge of concern at his evident discomfort.

"It's nothing. I pulled something in my shoulder today. It was rolling this blasted tub up the stairs, I think."

She absorbed this, watching as he lifted his arm again and sought to scrub his back. He sighed irritably, his efforts thwarted.

"If—if ye'd like, I can help ye with that," she offered, venturing out from the screen. She shrugged slightly at his stunned expression. " 'Tis plain to see ye're hurt, Garrett. I dinna mind, unless ye'd rather not."

"No, I mean yes, that would be nice," he said, watching her as she walked to the tub. "That's very kind of you, Madeleine."

She said nothing and avoided his eyes as she took the soap from him. She lathered it between her hands, then dropped the bar into the water with a plunk and bent over him, massaging the rugged breadth of his shoulders. She could feel him tense beneath her touch, but gradually he relaxed, leaning forward.

Madeleine concentrated on her task, inwardly thrilled by the rippling muscles beneath her fingertips. She could feel the overwhelming strength of his body in his slightest movement, and she felt her skin tingle with fiery warmth, not knowing if it came from the rising steam or her aroused senses. Her soapy hands plied his neck, then slid down his broad back, following the curve of his spine to just below the water's surface.

"Garrett," she murmured, "could ye pull away from the side a bit more so I might reach yer lower back?" He did as she bade him and came up on his haunches, his arms braced against the wooden rim as she washed him.

She sharply drew in her breath, mesmerized by the powerful lines of his body and oblivious to her wandering hands which had strayed from his back. She caressed his tapered hips and sinewed upper thighs, then his taut buttocks, closing her eyes as she delighted in the smooth texture of his skin. She felt him shudder and heard him groan, but this time it was not a cry of pain.

She started at the sound, becoming aware of what she was doing at the same moment he stood up in a spray of warm water and faced her, his body wet and glistening in the firelight. She stepped back, her gaze falling upon his full arousal, and she gasped aloud, thinking only to flee.

Garrett was too fast for her. As she spun on her heel, he grabbed her around the waist and in one easy movement swept her into the tub with him. His arms locked around her, imprisoning her. She was so shocked she could only stare at him, her hands braced against his chest. She could feel his heart thundering beneath her fingertips, matching her own rampant heartbeat.

"You have sorely tempted me, Madeleine," he whispered hoarsely, nibbling her soft earlobe while he deftly untied her sash with one hand and slipped the satin robe from her shoulders. He nuzzled her neck as he tossed the wet garment onto the floor. "You have gone too far, I fear."

"What do ye mean? What are ye going to do?" she said breathlessly, her knees weak from the sensation of his mouth upon her skin.

"Only what you want me to do, my lady wife," he replied huskily, lifting her in his arms and sinking into the warm water with her. "I told you before I would never force you, though you've tested my limits this night." His lips trailed a searing path down her throat. "I want you to know the pleasure that you just gave me, Madeleine. If you don't soon feel as I do now, I swear I will let you go. Now lean back and close your eyes."

She did not protest as he turned her around and cradled her in his lap, her slim back against his chest, her head leaning on his shoulder. She was already lost. Any thoughts of defying her body's wanton betrayal had long since vanished. All she knew was Garrett's burning heat and the delicious warmth of the bathwater, like a cocoon enveloping her . . . then she knew no more as his large, soapy hands began to caress her.

"Do you like this?" he asked softly, cupping her breasts, his fingers gliding over her skin and teasing her slippery nipples.

"Aye," she breathed, writhing and moaning in his lap.

"And this?" His hands slid down and stroked her belly, her curved hips, then dipped between her slick thighs, creeping ever higher until his fingers were entwined in her woman's hair. "Does this give you pleasure?"

"Aye, Garrett!" she cried out hoarsely, parting her

legs for him as he plied her secret heart until she was shaking with desire.

"Tell me, sweet Madeleine," he demanded thickly, lightly biting her shoulder. "Do you want me to stop?"

"No, dinna stop." Her words died on her parted lips, all conscious thought lost to the liquid sensations rippling over her. Garrett's hands were everywhere, her wet skin ablaze from his caress.

"How do you like this?" he groaned against her ear as he lifted her up and filled her with his body.

Madeleine gave out a cry of intense pleasure, the urgent pressure of his hand, his fingers, too much for her. She bore down upon him even as his deep thrusts heightened to a fever pitch. Their release came so suddenly, so swiftly, she thought for sure she would die from the shuddering force of it.

She collapsed against him, her head lolling to one side as she fought to catch her breath. She could not have been more startled when he lifted her from him and rose with her from the tub, her body still weak and trembling from her climax.

He carried her to the bed, taking a brief moment to dry their flushed limbs with the soft towels piled there, then he fell back upon the mattress with her on top of him, her silky thighs straddling his hips. She gasped when he entered her, his body hard and aroused.

"How?" she asked breathlessly, her eyes wide as he began to move slowly within her, her pleasure building anew.

Garrett's eyes burned into hers with a passion hardly sated.

"I will never have enough of you, Maddie Fraser," he said vehemently. "Never."

He pulled her to him and seized her lips, pouring out all his inexpressible love for her in his kiss. He would never give up until she believed in him. He would make her believe that he loved her!

Chapter 29

When Madeleine awoke the next morning she was alone in the huge bed, and for that she was more than grateful. She sat up slowly, her muscles somewhat sore. Her cheeks fired with shame at the rumpled condition of the bedding. She could not believe how easily she had surrendered to Garrett, their impassioned lovemaking carrying them far into the night.

"Love had nothing to do with it," she said heatedly, throwing off the heavy tartan bedspread. " 'Twas lust, pure and simple."

She swung her legs over the side of the bed, her gaze falling on the large wooden tub and her robe lying crumpled on the floor beside it. The telling scene only heightened her chagrin. She padded over and picked up the robe to shake it out. The apricot satin was stained from its unexpected soaking and probably ruined.

Serves ye right, she scolded herself, whisking the damp garment about her shoulders and hurrying to the door. All she wanted to do right now was get dressed, and her everyday clothes were in the other room.

Madeleine held her breath as she peered out into the silent hallway, finding it empty. She dashed to her chamber, her bare feet making little sound, and bolted the door once she was inside. She leaned against it, reveling in her familiar surroundings.

At least she would have some privacy this morning,

she thought with relief. Once her things were moved into Garrett's room, she would no longer have any excuse to seek the refuge of her chamber. And he would be coming and going as he pleased, whether she was dressing or not!

She jumped at the sudden knock on the door, darting away when the outer latch was rattled.

"Madeleine, are you in there?" Garrett's deep voice called out to her. "Open the door."

She swept back her tousled hair and moved reluctantly to the door, unbolting it and lifting the latch. She cracked it, peeking out at him warily.

"What are you doing?" he asked softly, pushing the door open a little wider with his shoulder. "I was thinking to wake you, but you weren't in bed—"

"I came in here to change," she interrupted him, meeting his probing eyes. "My everyday gowns are in this wardrobe." She felt her heart beat faster as he smiled in understanding, but she tried to ignore it. "I was going to move them into our room"—she flushed at the intimate memories those two words provoked—"after I changed."

"You might have to wait until later for that," he replied. "Meg Blair and Kitty Dods are downstairs. They said you had asked them to come and help clean up the house."

"Aye, that I did," she said, remembering her brief encounter with Meg the day before. "If ye'll have them wait for me in the dining room, Garrett, I'll be there shortly."

He nodded, glancing down at the steaming pitcher of water he was holding. "I brought this for you, but be careful. The water's quite hot."

Madeleine took the pitcher from him, her hands brushing against his. She started, shocked by their warmth when hers were so cold.

"Thank ye," she said shakily, avoiding his eyes as she quickly shut the door. She sensed him lingering in the hall for a moment, and she found it difficult to

breathe normally until his footsteps sounded on the
side stairs.

How could he have such power over her. How could
he unnerve her so easily, now more than ever, she
wondered, walking to the washstand. Nothing had
changed. He was King George's spy, and she was his
unwilling wife.

Not so unwilling, she mused darkly, setting down
the heavy pitcher. Aye, that much had changed. Last
evening her desire for him had blazed like a wildfire
out of control, a fire she feared could easily flare again.

Och, dinna think of it! she bade herself, but her fingers trembled as she slid the robe from her shoulders.
She tied back her hair, then poured the hot water into
the washbasin and bent over it. She plunged in her
hands to warm them, splashing her face again and
again.

She bathed and dried herself quickly, shivering from
head to toe, her breath hanging in the air like a misty
vapor. It was plain she would have to light a fire in
every fireplace from now on to ward off the evening
chill. Glenis had always seen to that before—

Madeleine's mouth drew into a tight line as she
pulled a simple woolen gown from the wardrobe and
dressed hurriedly.

Glenis was gone, never to return. The fireplaces were
her responsibility now, as was everything in the
household, including the kitchen. Meg and Kitty would
probably agree to stay on and help her, yet it was her
duty to see that things ran smoothly.

After all, she thought grimly as she stepped out into
the hallway, she was no longer an outlaw. She had to
find something to keep herself busy until Garrett's soldiers arrived from Fort Augustus. At least then she
would be able to visit her kin in Farraline and around
the valley.

She walked down the main staircase, thinking of the
days that stretched ahead. What with her numerous
household duties and paying calls in Strathherrick, she

and Garrett would see very little of each other, except at night.

Keen anticipation coursed through her at the thought, shocking her with its bold intensity. Angrily she forced it away, a new resolve burning within her. Her lust had clearly overcome her better judgment once, but she would not allow it to happen again. Perhaps if she went to bed late enough this evening, he would already be asleep.

Aye, that's exactly what she would do, she decided, turning into the dining room. She stopped in her tracks as Meg and Kitty jumped up from their chairs and curtsied clumsily.

"What are ye doing?" she asked incredulously. "Get up, the both of ye." She immediately sensed that their awkward behavior had something to do with her being the wife to an Englishman. " 'Tis me, yer Maddie Fraser. I havna changed, nor grown two heads, no matter what ye might have heard."

Usually so lively, Meg was strangely subdued. "Should Kitty and I call ye Lady Marshall," she mumbled, glancing at the pretty, red-haired girl beside her, "now that ye're married to the major?"

Madeleine swallowed hard, her cheeks burning. So she was right, she thought. The word was already out. "Ye'll do no such thing," she replied firmly. "Ye'll call me Maddie, just as ye've always done. And ye must tell everyone in Farraline to do the same, in case they're wondering."

The two young women visibly relaxed, even venturing smiles that clearly showed their relief.

"There, that's much better," Madeleine said, smiling back. Yet she quickly sobered, waving them into their chairs. She sat down next to them, her voice falling to a whisper. "Now, before we set to work, I want ye to tell me exactly what ye've heard in the village. Was it Angus who told ye I was wed?"

Meg nodded, opening her mouth to speak, but Kitty piped up before she could say a word.

"There was a ceilidh last night, Maddie, and everyone came, even the bairns. Angus said ye saved their lives by agreeing to marry Major Marshall the day before ye were all to hang!'' she blurted in one breath, her eyes shining with awe.

"Aye," Meg added, "they're more than grateful to ye, Maddie, saying ye're the bravest Fraser lass Strathherrick has ever known."

"So they dinna think I'm a traitor?" Madeleine said quietly, her heart pounding in her chest.

"Ye—a traitor?" Meg exclaimed. "I canna believe ye would say such a thing after all ye've done for us, Maddie. Aye, we know about the raids and ye giving yerself up to protect Strathherrick from Butcher Cumberland's bastard brother. And we know ye married the major to spare yer kinsmen the hangman's noose. Major Marshall admitted as much to Angus."

"What exactly did the major say?" Madeleine asked, her temper flaring.

"He told Angus the only way he could secure King Geordie's pardon for ye was to wed ye, Maddie, but that ye dinna agree to it at first, saying ye wouldna be a traitor to yer kin," Kitty quickly recounted. " 'Twas only when ye discovered ye would save Angus and the others that ye finally agreed."

"Aye, much of that is true, but 'tis a lie about why he married me," Madeleine said, her eyes flashing indignantly. "Did the major explain to Angus why he went through such trouble to obtain a king's pardon?"

Meg and Kitty glanced uncomfortably at each other, Meg speaking at last. "Angus asked him, Maddie, but Major Marshall said 'twas between ye and him alone."

"Now there's an evasive answer for ye," she said through clenched teeth. "And a lie as well. There's nothing between the major and m'self. Nothing."

Strangely, her words seemed hollow to her. Had last night truly been nothing? With great effort she drove the disturbing thought from her mind, reaching a sudden decision as the young women stared at her silently.

Since she wouldn't be able to visit Farraline for several days, she might as well pass on her warning about Garrett through Kitty and Meg. She could be assured her kinsmen would hear of it before the night was out with these two chatterboxes serving as her messengers.

She was stunned by her unexpected stab of guilt, accompanied by a most unsettling sense of betrayal. She was hardly betraying Garrett, she reasoned with herself, irritated by her prickly conscience. She was protecting her people!

"I want ye both to listen carefully," she began, leaning toward them. "When ye go back into the village, I want ye to let everyone know what I'm telling ye now. 'Tis the truth behind my marriage to Major Marshall, and a warning to our kin not to be swayed by anything he might say or do." She lowered her voice, hastily relaying what she believed were Garrett's true motives in acquiring the king's pardon.

"He offered to spy on us if King Geordie granted him yer lands and a pardon for ye?" Kitty said with a gasp when Madeleine had finished.

"Aye."

"And he married ye thinking ye would smooth the way for him with the Frasers of Strathherrick?" Meg asked, stunned.

"He believes I'll be useful to him, nothing more," Madeleine said quietly, almost to herself. "Well, he'll soon realize he's sadly mistaken." She glanced from Kitty to Meg. "I've changed my mind about ye helping me with the cleaning, at least for a few hours. I'd rather ye go back into Farraline right now and pass along what I've told ye. Will ye do that for me?"

"Oh, aye, Maddie," Meg said somberly, her eyes wide and round. Kitty bobbed her head, her red curls bouncing.

"Good," Madeleine said, walking with them to the front door. "When ye've finished, come back to the house, but not if it takes ye 'til well in the afternoon. The days are so short now, and the nights fall early. I dinna want to worry for ye with these redcoats about Mhor Manor. They're some of Hawley's foul jackals."

The young women nodded as they stepped outside, glancing fearfully at the soldiers who seemed to be everywhere; sitting on the grounds eating their breakfast, leading horses from the stable, talking and joking among themselves.

"There's so many more now than we saw earlier this morning," Kitty breathed nervously.

"I'll watch ye walk down the road," Madeleine assured them softly. "Remember, if it's grown too late stay home, and see that ye have yer fathers escort ye when ye do return."

"Aye, Maddie," Meg called out as she and Kitty walked very close together down the drive, holding hands and looking neither left nor right. When they came to the road, they set off at a run, their skirts and aprons flapping about their legs.

Madeleine kept her eyes trained on them until they reached Farraline, then slammed the door against the soldiers' crude laughter. Bastards! At least she had no doubt that Garrett would keep his own soldiers well in line.

She stood in the hallway, her hands on her hips as she surveyed first the dining room, then the drawing room. The place was in such a shambles she didn't know where to begin—

She jumped as a loud crash sounded from the kitchen, followed by a blustered oath.

"What in the blazes?" she whispered to herself, wondering who might be causing such a ruckus. She moved cautiously through the dining room. Surely Hawley's soldiers had enough food in their supply wagons that they wouldn't be rummaging around her kitchen.

Madeleine pushed lightly on the door, opening it just a crack. She peeked into the sunlit room, laughter unwittingly bubbling in her throat. Before she could stop it, she was chuckling aloud. She had never seen a more incongruous sight!

Garrett was standing over the raised hearth, his face
and the front of his scarlet uniform covered with a
dusting of white flour. He was plopping large lumps
of dough onto the sizzling griddle while behind him
the kitchen appeared to be the scene of a disaster. Flour
was everywhere, and an overturned sugar canister was
lying on the floor. Its fall no doubt had caused the crash
she had heard a moment ago.

"Damn!" Garrett cursed suddenly, dropping the
wooden spatula. He brought his hand to his mouth,
sucking a scorched knuckle, heedless to the odor of
burning dough wafting from the overheated griddle.

Madeleine clapped her hand over her mouth, but it
did little good. Laughter erupted from her throat in
hearty peals as she stumbled into the kitchen.

Garrett wheeled around, clearly startled. "What are
you laughing at?" he asked defensively, hastily wiping
the flour from his face and brushing the front of his
uniform. "I thought you might like some breakfast."
He picked up the sugar canister and placed it on the
table. "I'm baking scones from my grandmother's rec-
ipe."

"Ye mean ye're burning the scones." Madeleine hiccoughed, giggling helplessly. She pointed to the
hearth. "Look!"

Garrett glanced over his shoulder, his eyes widening
at the black smoke rising from the griddle. He rushed
over to the hearth, obviously uncertain about what he
should do. Madeleine could not believe her eyes when
he grabbed two thick tea towels from the cupboard and
lifted the griddle from the hearth, chucking the whole
smoking mess out the nearest window.

She gaped at him, flabbergasted, tears of laughter
running down her cheeks. He smiled sheepishly, shaking his head and chuckling to himself. Suddenly he
began to laugh, a rich sound that echoed about the
kitchen.

"Ye dinna have to do that," Madeleine said at last,
regaining some measure of her composure. She walked

to the hearth and picked up the spatula, smiling at him.
"This would have worked nicely."

Garrett's laughter abruptly quieted, his eyes staring
into hers. "You have such a beautiful smile, Maddie,"
he said, reaching out to smooth a tangled chestnut lock.
"I'd burn a thousand scones each morning just to have
you share it with me again."

Madeleine felt her breath catch in her throat as his
finger brushed against her cheek, a tingle of excitement
streaking through her. He moved closer, and she
thought to turn and run, but her feet seemed rooted to
the floor.

She felt caught in some mystical spell, bewitched by
the expression in his eyes. It was a look of such potent
intensity that her body flushed with stirring warmth,
divining its meaning. He had looked at her in the same
way the night before.

Unbidden, she lifted her face to him, closing her eyes
as he bent over her, their lips touching so lightly at
first it could have been his breath on her. She gasped
against his mouth when he deepened his kiss, feeling
suddenly dizzy and drunk within his tightening embrace.

She leaned into him, her arms straying around his
neck, overwhelmed by the sheer power and the heady
sweetness of his kiss. She could almost taste the rapture beckoning to her, luring her on, as seductive
memories flickered through her dazed mind.

Madeleine blinked, the spell shattered by the sound
of the spatula clattering onto the hearth. She pushed
against Garrett with all her might, breaking free of his
embrace.

"How dare ye!" she cried, slapping his face before
she even thought about what she was doing. She was
as surprised by her action as Garrett appeared to be.
His expression clouded, then became inscrutable, only
his eyes reflecting his turmoil.

"That's strange, Madeleine," he replied darkly. "I
didn't think you minded. Last night you surely
didn't."

She blushed hotly. His words filled her with anger, mostly directed at herself, because she knew they were true. She vowed then and there to stay well out of his way as much as possible. It was obvious she had little control over her senses when she let down her guard around him, whether in daytime or at night!

She stepped away from him, grabbing the broom propped against the wall. "If ye'll excuse me, Garrett, I have a great deal of work to do."

"You don't have to bother with the kitchen, in case you hadn't noticed," he said. "The few willing soldiers I could find helped me scrub it down late yesterday afternoon." He paused, then added dryly. "Well, the kitchen was clean before I set foot in it. It's obvious my expertise does not lie in cooking."

Madeleine's cheeks fired at the sensuous thoughts his innocent statement conjured in her mind.

What was coming over her? she wondered wildly. She noticed a glint of amusement in his eyes. Could the man read her every thought? She had to get out of this kitchen!

Madeleine backed up, knocking into the door. "I'm— I'm sure Meg and Kitty will have time to see to the kitchen, Garrett, when they return from Farraline. Dinna trouble yerself. I'll fix m'self something to eat later."

"Did they just leave?" he asked, mild confusion lighting his features. "I heard you talking with them in the dining room only a few moments ago—"

"Ye heard us in the dining room?" Madeleine blurted uncomfortably, her mind spinning. God's wounds, had Garrett heard everything she had said to her young kinswomen?

"I heard your voices, Madeleine," he answered, studying her quizzically. "I was a bit too wrapped up in my project in here to pay much attention to what you were saying. Why, did I miss some interesting village gossip?"

Madeleine gulped, forcing a light laugh. "Gossip? Och, if ye mean Kitty's discussion of her latest beau, aye, then ye missed some fine gossip. She's spurned two young lads since I've been gone, or so she told me.'' She fumbled for the latch, swinging the door closed behind her.

''But I thought the girls were to help you today?''

She froze, her retreat stayed once more. ''Ye know these lassies,'' she said over her shoulder, feigning a nonchalant tone. ''They decided they'd best go bramble picking this morning before a frost kills the berries. They might be back in the afternoon if they're able to fill their baskets by then.''

Madeleine quickly closed the door without waiting for a reply and hurried into the drawing room.

A half truth was better than none, she thought as she began to sweep furiously. She only hoped she would be able to keep all of her stories straight and warn Kitty and Meg in time so they wouldn't give her away if they did return to help her in the afternoon.

Beaus and brambles indeed. How did she think up such things?

Garrett stood in the midst of the floury mess he'd created, thoughtfully rubbing his left cheek. It still stung, but the unexpected kiss he and Madeleine had shared had been well worth the slap.

Just as last evening had been well worth the frustrating nights spent alone in country inns and chasing sleep in a tent. Both were welcome signs that her defenses against him were crumbling and that he had a fighting chance to win her love.

Maddie Fraser. His beautiful, defiant, and reluctant bride.

How long would it take him to find some measure of acceptance with her people, and, he hoped, favor and acceptance in her own heart? How long would it take before he would hear words of love mingling with her sweet cries of passion? Weeks? Months?

''Patience, man,'' Garrett said under his breath, the recent memory of her kiss etched indelibly in his mind. ''It's the only way you'll win her. You must have patience.'' It was enough for now that they were sleeping together, enough that she was yielding at last to her desire. Perhaps tonight she might surrender again . . .

He walked silently to the window and gazed outside at the double row of wagons, filled with every manner of household goods he had thought Madeleine's people might need after their recent devastation. He glanced beyond the wagons to the makeshift corral where the cattle were confined. He could hardly wait until his men arrived from Fort Augustus, so that he could set his plan into motion.

Yes, he had a grand plan, but it was far different than the one of which Madeleine had accused him. He would prove to the Frasers of Strathherrick an Englishman could be trusted, on his own and without any help from her. He was committed to this plan with his whole heart and soul. So much depended on its success.

Garrett clenched his fist against the window frame.

However long it took him, Madeleine was worth it. Her rare smiles were worth it, as was her laughter, her kiss, and her love.

Late that night, Madeleine crept quietly into the dark bedchamber, her heart fluttering madly within her breast.

Was Garrett asleep? She stopped and listened for a moment, relieved to hear him breathing evenly. Aye.

As she stole across the floor to the screen, she glanced at the hearth. Only faintly glowing embers remained of the fire she had stoked there after supper, hours ago. She had purposely kept herself busy with other household tasks since then, and she wasn't even sure when Garrett had retired for the night.

Madeleine quickly changed into her cambric nightdress, then walked silently toward the bed. She held her breath while she lifted the covers and climbed in next to him, fearful of the rustling sounds she was making. She started when her fingers accidentally brushed against his muscled thigh, her blood thundering through her veins as she realized he was naked.

She began to roll over onto her side, thinking to sleep as far away from him as possible, when his arm caught her around the waist and pulled her back. She gasped, struggling, but he held her so tightly she could not escape him.

"You're not the only one accomplished at feigning sleep," he said, nuzzling her nape. He pushed away her hair and kissed the hollow at the base of her throat. "I've been waiting for you, sweet Madeleine."

She gave a small cry as his hand found her breast, his fingertip stroking her through the thin nightdress. She felt the wildfire ignite within her, melting her resolve in a blaze of heat and desire. He captured her lips, and she was lost. . . .

Chapter 30

∽⊙∽

Madeleine whisked the crisp linen sheet over the aired mattress, and Meg caught it on the other side.

"So ye're saying Major Marshall and his soldiers finished two more stone cottages yesterday, and none of the villagers will claim them?" she asked as she deftly smoothed and tucked in the clean sheet.

"Aye, Maddie," Meg replied, finishing a corner. Flushed with exertion, the plump maidservant stood upright and caught her end of the thick tartan blanket. "And they'll stay empty, too, along with the other twelve. We'll have nothing to do with the major's handiwork. My da says he'd rather live in a drafty hovel 'til he can finish his own cottage than dwell in one built by King Geordie's spy."

"And what of the wagons Major Marshall left by the church?" Madeleine queried. "Has anyone taken any of the things he brought from Edinburgh yet?"

Meg shook her head. "Not a butter churn, not a spinning wheel, not even a pot. There's even been talk of setting a torch to the wagons. 'Twould make a fine ceilidh fire, dinna ye think?"

"Aye," Madeleine said quietly, though deep down she wasn't sure if she truly agreed.

Why did she feel so guilty at this latest bit of news? she wondered, tucking in the blanket. She should be elated her kin had heeded her warning about Garrett, yet she wasn't.

Instead her emotions were becoming increasingly confused, as if half of her wanted things one way while the other half yearned for something else, something she was afraid even to dwell upon. Frustrated by her thoughts, she tossed two down pillows onto the bed and plumped them vigorously.

She had been so busy she hadn't gone into Farraline yet to see for herself how Garrett was faring, though it made no difference. Kitty and Meg had kept her up on what was happening in the village, especially since Garrett's soldiers had arrived at Mhor Manor over a week ago.

The Frasers of Farraline had confounded Garrett's every effort to gain their favor. They'd even loosed the cattle he'd given them out onto the moor. Garrett and his men had spent a full day searching for the beasts and corraling them at the estate, his plan thwarted again.

No doubt that was why he'd grown so moody and sullen, she thought, pulling the down coverlet over the freshly made bed. Garrett had said little last night when he and his exhausted soldiers had returned for supper, and later she had felt a palpable desperation in his caresses, almost like anger. His fierce passion had left her wholly breathless and spent, and feeling even more guilty than before.

Madeleine sighed heavily. If today went much as she imagined, she could probably expect the same from him this evening. Yet why did it bother her so, like a twisting pain in her heart? He was a spy. He deserved such treatment, didn't he?

"There now, Meg," she said, forcing her mind from such troubling questions. She tucked the coverlet between the mattress and the carved headboard. "We've done a fine job in here."

She stood up, her gaze sweeping the immaculate guest room from the scrubbed floors and clean woolen rugs to the dusted furniture. She had saved the two upstairs guest rooms for last, seeing to the rest of the house first. After this morning's work, everything was finally in order. No trace remained of Hawley's unwelcome visit.

Even the ruined furnishings and shattered windows had been replaced, Madeleine mused, raising another window to further air out the room.

Garrett had wasted no time in sending several of his men to Inverness with a long list of things to buy. They had returned with more wagons carrying a mahogany dining table, armchairs, a china cabinet, a gleaming silver service, bottles of fine brandy, a mantel clock, and many other items too numerous to contemplate. It was hard for her to admit, but Garrett had made Mhor Manor feel like a real home again.

"Are ye ready for some lunch, Maddie?" Meg asked, startling her from her reverie. "I know I am." The maidservant giggled when her stomach growled loudly, but she didn't seem embarrassed in the least. "Kitty said she was preparing a steak and game pie for us and apple fool for dessert."

"Aye, I suppose," Madeleine said. She smiled weakly, though not at the thought of Kitty's cooking.

Kitty possessed quite a flair in the kitchen, surprising in one so young. Then again, her mother was a renowned cook and had obviously taught her daughter well. Kitty had gone out of her way to prepare tempting meals since she'd taken over the kitchen.

Yet Kitty's recent efforts had been lost on Madeleine. She hadn't had much of an appetite lately. She knew she wasn't pregnant. Her monthly flow had come while she was in prison. And it was much too soon yet to feel any ill effects if she had been with child. At the rate she and Garrett were going, however, she would be pregnant in no time at all!

A bairn. She flushed warmly at the unsettling notion. If it happened, they would become a family, with a new life between them. It struck her that she would not love their child any less, despite what she thought about its father.

Och, 'tis exhaustion ye suffer, she told herself, following Meg from the room. She had been working very hard. Perhaps now that she had finished the bulk of the cleaning, she could afford some extra rest.

Madeleine paused briefly to pick up a small embroidered pillow that the maidservant had unknowingly knocked from a chair near the foot of the bed. She straightened, almost collapsing to the floor as a sudden wave of dizziness gripped her.

"Meg," she called weakly, hanging on desperately to the chair.

"What's wrong?" Meg cried, rushing back into the room. She took one look at Madeleine's ashen pallor and immediately helped her sit down. "Och, ye're ill, Maddie. What can I bring ye? What should I do?"

Madeleine waved away Meg's frantic barrage of questions, feeling her sense of equilibrium gradually returning. "I'm fine," she insisted, though she could tell by Meg's worried expression that her young kinswoman was not convinced. "I'll just sit here for a moment. I'm sure the faintness will soon pass. Do ye think ye might fetch me a glass of water?"

"Ye've been working far too hard, Maddie," Meg chided, wringing her apron. "I hope ye're not coming down with a sickness from pushing yerself so. Now dinna move from the chair, ye hear? I'll be right back."

Madeleine leaned her head back and closed her eyes as Meg bustled from the room. She forced herself to breathe slowly and steadily, despite the rapid beating of her heart. She licked her lips, hoping Meg was hurrying back with her water.

At last she heard footsteps in the hall, though they sounded oddly different than Meg's. She shrugged, thinking perhaps she only imagined it. She opened her eyes, gasping when Glenis suddenly walked through the door.

"Glenis! What are ye doing here?"

"I came for a wee visit," the old woman stated matter-of-factly. "I only got here a few minutes ago. I was on my way up from the kitchen when I ran into Meg. She says ye're not feelin' well." She pulled up a stool beside Madeleine's chair and sat down. "Here's yer water, lass, but dinna take more than a sip at a time.''

Madeleine gaped at Glenis, so stunned she couldn't speak. The glass shook in her hand, water sloshing through her fingers and into her lap. She barely noticed when Glenis took the glass and held it to her lips.

''Drink, Maddie,'' she commanded briskly, smiling faintly when Madeleine did as she bade her. ''Kitty tells me ye've been pickin' at yer food like a bird, despite her fine cooking,'' she continued. '' 'Tisn't like ye, Maddie. Ye've ne'er lacked for a good appetite. Then Meg rushes in, sayin' ye look as white as a sheet and that ye're feelin' faint.'' She paused, sighing. ''What's ailin' ye, lass? Is there a chance ye're carryin' a bairn?''

''No, I dinna think so,'' Madeleine replied, pushing away the half-empty glass. ''Not yet, anyway.'' At Glenis's shrewd look, she added uncomfortably, ''I'm tired, that's all.''

''Aye, ye've done wonders with the house,'' Glenis remarked, glancing around the room. She turned back to Madeleine, studying her face. ''What's truly ailin' ye, Maddie? A heartache, perhaps? Tell yer Glenis.''

''Ye're not my Glenis!'' Madeleine snapped indignantly, her light-headedness swept away by Glenis's words. ''Not anymore! Surely ye must know I've long since heard of yer deceit from Major Marshall.''

''Major Marshall, is it?'' the old woman commented with unusual sarcasm. ''Is that how ye refer to yer husband, Maddie, or do ye deign to call him by his first name when it suits ye? Perhaps when he takes ye in his arms?''

Madeleine felt a surge of outrage that Glenis was asking her such questions, or even sitting here in her house for that matter!

''I dinna know why ye took it into yer mind to visit Mhor Manor,'' she said unkindly. ''Ye must know ye're no longer welcome here.''

Glenis rose from the stool so abruptly it toppled over, hitting the floor with a thud. Her dark eyes flashed with temper, the expression on her wrinkled face sterner than Madeleine had ever seen it before. For a moment she feared Glenis would slap her, but instead the stooped woman drew herself up and rested her hands on her narrow hips.

"I'll tell ye why I've come back to Mhor Manor, Madeleine Elisabeth Fraser," Glenis said, her voice crackling with anger. "To set ye straight! Ye're makin' a fool of yerself and ye dinna even know it!"

"What do ye mean?" Madeleine sputtered, her hands tightly gripping the chair.

"Garrett Marshall loves ye, ye foolish lass! Loves ye! He told me so when I found him on the road to Inverfarigaig, and thank God I got there when I did. If I hadna, ye would likely have been killed along with yer kin. Ye went to prison instead, Maddie, buying Garrett some time so he might help ye—"

"Ye're mad, Glenis," Madeleine accused vehemently, cutting her off. She rose shakily from her chair. "Ye dinna know what ye're saying."

"Aye, I know exactly what I'm sayin'," Glenis countered, staring up at her boldly. "Ye're so ready to think the worst, Maddie, just because Garrett's an Englishman. A redcoat. Ye havna given him a chance to explain, have ye? Did ye ne'er think to ask him how he was granted a king's pardon for ye, before ye came to yer own conclusions? Ye've always been a good storyteller, lass, and I swear ye've outdone yerself this time!"

Madeleine found that she could barely swallow, her throat was constricted so tightly. Her head was beginning to pound. "No, I dinna ask him," she said through clenched teeth. "I dinna have to ask him."

"Well, ye might!" Glenis said heatedly. "Ye might be surprised to find his answer is far different than yer own fanciful version. Such nonsense about spies and Garrett wantin' yer land, and him usin' ye to ease his way with Clan Fraser."

"How have ye heard all this?" Madeleine demanded shakily.

"The story has traveled up to Tullich, and well be-yond Strathherrick, I'll warrant. 'Tisn't ev'ryday an Englishman takes a Highland lass for a bride to save her from a hangman's rope. Yer warning has traveled as well, which is why I decided to come here and risk yer fond greeting. Ye've done a terrible thing, Maddie. Ye've set yer kin against Garrett before ye even knew the truth."

"I dinna want to hear any more of yer wild talk, Glenis," Madeleine said angrily, brushing past her to the door. She was stunned when Glenis caught her arm, the old woman's gnarled fingers gripping her like talons.

"Aye, then, if ye tell me ye have no feelings for Gar-rett, none at all, I'll ne'er say another word!" Glenis challenged her. "I believe 'tis a heartache that's been plaguin' ye, Maddie, because ye know deep in yer heart what I'm tellin' ye is true. Ye're lovesick, and ye winna admit it, not even to yerself! Well, if ye swear to me now I dinna know what I'm sayin', I'll leave this house and ye'll have seen the last of yer Glenis Simp-son."

Madeleine stared at her, a fierce denial on the tip of her tongue. Strangely, she could not say it, nor could she find it within herself to lie. She heaved a ragged sigh, her tormented expression revealing to Glenis more than words could have ever expressed.

" 'Tis so plain, Maddie, ye havna been able to see it," Glenis said fervently. "Garrett told me he loved ye, and I believe him. He promised me he'd help ye, lass, and not let anything happen to ye." She released Madeleine's arm, her tone almost pleading. "Garrett saved yer life because he loves ye. He helped yer kin before, and he's tryin' to help them now because he loves ye. However it came to pass, Maddie, he's yer husband. Someday ye'll carry his bairn. Ye must ask him for yerself if my words are true."

"If 'tis so, why hasn't he said something to me al-ready?" Madeleine asked quietly, tears glistening in her eyes.

"Ye're one to ask me that?" Glenis scoffed lightly. "Ye've made no secret of yer hatred for the English. Garrett might be afraid ye'll spit in his face, seein' as ye believe he forced ye into a marriage to suit his own ends. Perhaps he's tryin' to show ye by his actions how much he cares for ye, hopin' 'twill soften yer heart a bit so he might tell ye, except ye're thwartin' him ev'ry step of the way."

When Madeleine did not reply, Glenis sighed wearily. The strain of their encounter was clearly etched on her wizened face.

"I'll leave ye now, Maddie," she said. "Ye must decide for yerself if ye'll accept what I've told ye. If ye love him, as I believe ye do, ye'll ask Garrett if 'tis the truth. Then ye'd best undo the damage ye've caused between him and yer kin. No good will come of things as they are, Maddie. I only hope 'tis not too late."

"Too late?" Madeleine breathed, searching Glenis's eyes.

"Aye," she replied gravely. "Yer kin believe ye're unhappy, married to an Englishman ye've branded as a spy. Did ye ne'er think they might somehow rid ye of yer husband, believin' 'tis what ye want? Or did ye think Garrett would simply become discouraged and leave for England?" Glenis shook her head slowly. " 'Tis more likely yer kinsmen will seek to end yer problems long before Garrett would ever leave ye, lass."

Madeleine sank into the chair, completely overwhelmed.

Garrett loved her. Could it really be true? So many thoughts, so many sensuous memories, so many things Garrett had said to her swirled in her mind that she scarcely noticed Glenis quietly leaving the room. It was the door clicking shut that pierced her unsettling reverie.

"Glenis!" Madeleine jumped up and raced to the door, flinging it open. She dashed into the hall. "Glenis! Wait!"

Glenis turned around, her face cloaked in shadow. "What is it, hinny?" she asked gently.

"When I said ye were no longer welcome here," Madeleine began, her voice catching, "I dinna mean it, Glenis. 'Twas the hurt in me, after what ye did."

"I know. Ye thought I betrayed ye, and in a sense I did. 'Twas the only thing I could think of to save ye, lass. I took a chance Garrett might care about ye, even as I care about ye. 'Twas worth it to me, though I knew ye'd hate me for it—"

"I dinna hate ye," Madeleine interjected fiercely, tears tightening her throat. "I want ye to stay here, Glenis. Ye belong at Mhor Manor. 'Tis not the same without ye."

Glenis did not answer for a long moment, a weighty silence filling the hall. At last she spoke, her voice breaking with emotion.

"No, Maddie, I canna. Ye've much to sort out for yerself. Ye dinna need me here right now. I'll know when 'tis the right time to return again to Mhor Manor."

Madeleine didn't know what to say. Tears filled her eyes and tumbled down her cheeks as Glenis turned and walked down the stairs, leaving her alone in the hall.

She stood there a long time, dazed and uncertain while one thought rang in her mind.

Tonight, when Garrett returned from Farraline, she would ask him if what Glenis had told her was true. She had to know. Until then she would not even dare to hope.

Chapter 31

 I t was near nightfall when Garrett settled one of the last stones on the newly thatched roof, then climbed down the rough-hewn ladder.

"That's it, Fletcher," he shouted, rubbing his chafed hands together as he surveyed the two cottages they had finished that day. "Call off the men. It's growing too dark to continue, and too cold, for that matter."

"I'll agree with you there, major," Sergeant Fletcher replied heartily from the other roof, his breath hanging like a mist upon the brisk air. "I hope Jeremy has a nice hot supper waiting for us."

"I'm sure he does," Garrett said, thinking about his own supper. He only hoped some of Kitty's wonderful cooking would soothe his foul mood, along with a snifter of good brandy and Madeleine's company. During the past few days her behavior had somehow softened toward him, which was more than he could say for these stubborn villagers.

He glanced at a group of men gathered up the street. They stared back at him sullenly, then turned and walked into the nearest cottage, but it was not one that he had built. Those cottages were still standing silent and empty, as if they were tainted with the plague. As these two would no doubt stand empty, he thought grimly, their efforts wasted once again.

Garrett was frowning as he sought out Corporal Sims in the gathering dusk.

"Sims, ride over and tell the men clearing the eastern fields that we're finished for the day."

"Yes, sir, Major Marshall."

As the young man rode away, Garrett untethered his dappled stallion. "Let's ride by the church first, Fletcher, then make our way back to Mhor Manor. I want to see if anything's been taken from the wagons today."

He mounted, grimacing at the soreness in his limbs, and noted how Sergeant Fletcher was hauling himself into the saddle. The older man caught his look and grinned tiredly.

"Building that last wall today really took the wind out of me. Those damn stones seem to get heavier all the time."

"I know what you mean," Garrett said dryly, urging his stallion into a trot as the sergeant rode alongside him and the rest of his weary soldiers brought up the rear. "I'm beginning to wonder what the devil we're trying to prove in the first place." He glanced at the grizzled soldier, noting the deep lines in his face. "What *I'm* trying to prove," he amended, his tone laced with bitterness. "You're just following my orders, and very well, I might add."

"I didn't mean the work was bothering me, major," Sergeant Fletcher replied. "It's just we've been pushing so hard. We've done a lot since we got here, and the men haven't complained, but they need a break. A day's rest would suffice."

Garrett sighed heavily, knowing the sergeant was right. "Granted, Fletcher. Tell them they've earned my highest compliments for their efforts and a well-deserved day off. You might also say they'll receive an extra reward when their pay arrives from Fort Augustus."

"That's not necessary, Major Marshall," the sergeant insisted gruffly. "We're here to follow your orders. You don't need to compensate us for doing our duty, especially from your own pocket."

"Enough said, Fletcher. It's what I want to do. I'm

sure the men have wondered often enough why they're building cottages and clearing fields, which is not your typical military duty. Yet they haven't questioned my orders once. I've you to thank for that. Perhaps sometime I'll offer all of you an explanation.''

"You don't have to explain your motives to me, sir," Sergeant Fletcher said, lowering his voice. "I can well imagine the task you've set for yourself. I only wish these Highlanders might show some appreciation for what you're doing for them. I get the strong impression they don't want our help. Don't even want us around, for that matter."

"So do I, Fletcher. So do I," Garrett said, watching as suspicious faces appeared behind cracked doors or peered out at them from windows as he and his men rode along the main street.

He drew up on the reins when they reached the reconstructed church, his mood darkening even more. The fully loaded wagons he had left there days ago were still untouched, further proof that his plan was failing miserably.

He shot a glance over at Angus Ramsay's cottage across the street. His worst moment had come yesterday when Angus turned his back on him, refusing even to speak with him. Whatever inroads he thought he had made with the burly Highlander had vanished.

Thoroughly disgruntled, Garrett was about to veer his horse around when he spied movement beneath the protective covering on one of the wagons. He dismounted quickly, leaving Sergeant Fletcher and his soldiers staring after him. He strode over to the wagon and threw back the canvas, starting in surprise when a small red-haired boy jumped up and scrambled over the side.

"Hold on there," Garrett said, catching the boy by the collar of his jacket.

"Let me go!" the boy cried desperately, his short legs pumping uselessly. "Let me go!"

Garrett grabbed the child's narrow shoulders and

turned him around gently. "It's all right, boy. I'm not going to hurt you. Tell me your name."

"Neil, Neil Chrystie," the boy stammered, looking up at him with wide, frightened eyes.

"Well, Neil Chrystie, my name is Garrett Marsh—"

"I know who ye are," the youngster blurted with astounding bravado, his fear clearly forgotten. "Ye married our Maddie!"

"So I did," Garrett said, somewhat nonplussed. "Tell me Neil. What were you doing in the wagon? Choosing something for your mother, I hope. Do you need some help?"

Neil shook his head vigorously, shrugging away from Garrett's loosened grasp. "There's nothing my mama would want from those wagons!" he shouted, clenching his small fists and shaking them at Garrett. "We Frasers dinna want a thing from King Geordie's spy!"

Completely stunned by this belligerent outburst, Garrett caught the boy's sleeve. "Spy? Where did you hear such nonsense, Neil?" he asked tightly, but before the child could answer another voice sounded behind him.

"Let the boy go, if ye will, Major Marshall."

Garrett released him and spun around to find Angus Ramsay staring at him stonily, the man's huge arms crossed over his chest.

"Angus," he said in a greeting as he straightened up, but he received no response.

"Go on home with ye, Neil," Angus commanded the astonished boy, who was looking from Garrett back to his towering kinsman. "Dinna be playing 'round the wagons anymore, do ye hear?"

"Aye!" Neil took off like a frightened rabbit and didn't look back.

"A good ev'ning to ye, then, Major Marshall," Angus muttered with the slightest nod.

Garrett said nothing as Angus turned abruptly and strode back to his cottage, the door held open for him by a strapping dark-haired man Garrett had never seen before. Then the door slammed shut, leaving Garrett to his simmering fury, young Neil Chrystie's words ringing in his ears. Suddenly everything was clear to him, painfully clear.

Spy! So that was it. The villagers truly believed he was a spy for King George. That would explain everything: the spurned cottages, household goods, and cattle, and Angus's surly behavior yesterday and just now. Somehow they must have gotten the word from Madeleine, even though she had never left Mhor Manor since returning from Edinburgh. Somehow . . .

It must have been through Meg and Kitty, Garrett surmised grimly, walking back to his stallion. Madeleine must have filled their ears with every manner of accusation—probably the same farfetched story she had flung at him at Edinburgh Castle—and told them to pass it along to the villagers in Farraline.

Perhaps she had even done so that morning the two young women had come to help her with the cleaning, he thought incredulously, amazed that he hadn't considered the possibility sooner. They had suddenly disappeared to go—bramble picking! On top of her betrayal, Madeleine had lied to him. How many more of her lies had he unwittingly swallowed?

Such anger burned inside him, his hands were shaking as he seized the reins and hoisted himself into the saddle. Yet it was nothing compared to the fierce resolve burning in his heart.

Dammit, he had taken enough abuse! Madeleine had obviously turned her kin against him, so his plan had been doomed from the start. Well, the devil take his plan and the hell with patience!

"I'll see you at the house," he said tersely, veering his stallion sharply around. Sergeant Fletcher's words were lost to him as he set out at a full gallop through the village and onto the road to Mhor Manor. The wind whistled wildly around him, fueling his racing thoughts.

It was time Madeleine knew exactly how he felt about her, whether she wanted to hear it or not. He would not keep his feelings to himself any longer, nor would he tolerate any more of her irrational lies and accusations. She would know the truth behind King George's pardon once and for all!

Vibrant memories crowded in upon him as he sped toward the manor house. He could remember so clearly that sunny afternoon when he first set eyes on the mistress of Farraline, Madeleine Fraser, the fairest woman he had ever seen. It could have been yesterday, the recollection was so vivid.

Yet it was hard to believe that just over two months had elapsed since that day. It felt as if he had lived a lifetime since then, as if he had exhausted a lifetime of emotion ranging from the sweetest joy to the most heartrending despair. All condensed into nine turbulent weeks.

Garrett scarcely waited for his powerful stallion to come to a stop before he jumped from the saddle and ran to the kitchen door. At this time of night, Madeleine was usually helping Kitty by setting the dining table. He burst in the door, a loud gasp and a crash of china greeting his stormy entrance.

"M-major Marshall!" Kitty cried, a puddle of brown gravy and broken china at her feet.

Garrett glanced into the dining room, but there was no sign of Madeleine. "Where is she?" he asked impatiently.

"Who?"

"Maddie, wench! Who do you think?" he responded angrily, then softened his tone at her stricken look. "I'm sorry, Kitty. Isn't she helping you tonight?"

"No, I believe she's lying down," the maidservant said shakily. "At least she was a while ago. She wasna feeling herself today. She's been working far too hard, we think."

That news gave Garrett pause, but he quickly shrugged it off. Exhausted from the web of lies she's spun around herself, he thought darkly, rushing through the dining room. He took the stairs three at a time and strode to their room, his blood roaring in his ears.

He pushed open the door, stunned to find the bed-chamber dark and silent, without even a low fire burning in the hearth. He moved toward her side of the bed, his heart beating fiercely against his chest. He reached out his hand and found nothing. The bed was empty, the covers drawn, as if no one had slept there for hours.

His startled gaze swept the shadowed corners. He even went so far as to check behind the screen, but to no avail. Madeleine was not there. He strode from the room, angrily slamming the door.

Myriad unpleasant possibilities flashed through his mind as he checked every room on the second floor, only to find them all empty. Dammit, where could she be? he wondered wildly. Where could she have gone? Farraline? Surely she hadn't ventured out on another raid . . .

That unsettling thought filled him with cold fury. As soon as he grabbed his heavy coat from the drawing room closet, he would set out to look for her and not rest until he found her. Enough was enough!

Garrett ran down the stairs, almost bumping into Madeleine as she rounded the corner from the dining room.

"Madeleine!"

"G-Garrett," she stammered, spots of high color appearing on her cheeks. "Kitty just told me ye were looking for me upstairs. I was on my way to find ye. I must have been in the dancing room when ye came in. I put some extra blankets in there for yer men. 'Twill be a cold night, I think."

Garrett pulled her into the drawing room, his gaze swiftly raking over her. She was wearing the wrapping gown he had given her in Edinburgh, the shimmering blue silk matching the vivid azure of her eyes. Her chestnut hair flowed freely down her back and softly framed her lovely features, the thick tresses gleaming with gold in the firelight.

He found himself thinking he had never seen her so bewitchingly beautiful. But why was she looking at him so strangely, as if she were seeing him for the first time?

"I was just coming in here to get my coat," he said distractedly, glancing at the closet door.

"Are ye going out again? I've been waiting for ye, hoping we might talk. Could we—before ye go?"

Garrett stared at her, confused. "I'm not going any-where. I was setting out to look for you. You weren't in our room, you weren't in any of the rooms, and I thought . . ." His voice trailed off, and he sighed heavily, looking down at his dusty boots. "Who the hell cares what I thought," he said to himself, running his fingers through his hair. "It seems I was wrong."

"I dinna understand," Madeleine said softly.

Garrett met her eyes. "It was nothing, Maddie." He exhaled sharply. "I want to talk to you—" His words died on his lips, suddenly realizing what she had just said. "You want to talk with me?"

"Aye," she said, shifting nervously. "But if ye have something to say first, Garrett . . ."

"No, you go ahead," he replied evenly, belying his own fierce impatience. He drew her further into the room to afford them some privacy, then abruptly changed his mind just as she opened her mouth. Dammit all, what he had to say wouldn't wait!

"Glenis was here today, Garrett," she blurted. "She claims—she claims ye love me."

"I've had enough, Maddie!" he exclaimed at the same time. "When are you going to realize that I love you?"

The room echoed with their voices, followed by a stunned silence.

Madeleine's knees felt so weak she thought for sure they would buckle beneath her. God's wounds, he had said it. 'Twas true. She stared at Garrett, her heart in her throat. His eyes were boring into hers. He had never looked so shaken.

"Glenis told you what?" he asked at last, his voice low and intense.

"She said ye admitted ye loved me when she found

ye on the road to Inverfarigaig the night I was captured."

"When was she here?"

"This morning," Madeleine answered softly, trembling from head to foot. "But she's gone back to Tullich. She only came to tell me I was a fool." She saw the barest trace of a smile touch Garrett's mouth, and she rushed on. "That's why I wanted to talk with ye. I want ye to tell me for yerself how ye gained King Geordie's pardon." She paused, blushing warmly. Her voice fell to a whisper. "Glenis claimed if I knew yer side of the story, I'd understand how much ye care."

Garrett sobered, his expression deadly serious. "This is quite a turnaround, Madeleine. Does it matter that much to you to hear the truth?" he asked, studying her face intently.

"Aye, it matters, Garrett," she breathed. "I must know."

"Very well," he replied, moving closer to her. He stopped within arm's reach, though he did not touch her. "You accused me of being landless," he began, "which was true when I came to get you out of prison. I bargained away my estate in Sussex, Rosemoor, to obtain your pardon, Madeleine."

"Yer estate?" she said incredulously. "But ye're a second son. I assumed ye dinna have . . ." She faltered, at a loss.

"Rosemoor first belonged to my grandmother, a gift from her English husband," Garrett explained, "then it was my mother's, and she left it to me. Fortunately my brother, Gordon, wanted Rosemoor so badly he was willing to do almost anything for it," he continued, "and fortunately he was in a position to help me."

Madeleine listened breathlessly as he recounted his story, his words confirming what Glenis had told her and more.

How cruelly she had misjudged him, she thought dazedly, believing only the worst of everything he had done for her and her people. The truth had been plainly before her, yet she had refused to see it. She had been blinded by her prejudice and fears, instead of trusting her deepest feelings. She had sensed all along he cared, just as she did.

"I'm not the king's spy," Garrett finished, his eyes darkened to slate as he stared into hers. "I gained your pardon for only one reason. I love you, Maddie. You're everything to me. I would have given my life to save you."

Madeleine gasped softly but kept silent, overwhelmed. Her mind spun; her blood raced in her veins. He reached out and gently caressed her cheek, sending shivers streaking along her spine.

"You said it mattered," he said, his voice dropping to an insistent whisper. His gaze was desperate, searching, as if he could divine the hidden secrets of her soul. "Why? Is there a chance you might care, Madeleine?"

All was suddenly still within her, a joy like none she had ever known unfolding. She trembled from its awakened power. It surged and swelled, sweeping away all fears, all mistrust, leaving nothing behind but the secret she had held for so long in her heart. Aye, she loved him! How she loved him!

Madeleine gazed at Garrett, so overcome she could not speak. There were no words to express the wonder she felt, no words to describe the tumult of emotion that enveloped her so completely.

She flew to him suddenly, and he opened his arms to her, shattering forever the bitter void that had separated them. She had made her choice. She would never turn back.

"Maddie," Garrett whispered hoarsely against her hair, hugging her as fiercely as she embraced him. Time was lost while they held each other, sharing an infinite moment of radiant happiness.

It was Garrett who pulled away at last, smiling through the tears in his eyes. He tenderly kissed her face, her throat, her eyelids. His lips brushed against her damp lashes, then sought her mouth. She tasted the salt of her own tears as he kissed her until she was breathless.

"To think I had stormed around looking for you, and you were waiting for me all along," Garrett said, holding her close once more. "Waiting with such news." He swept back her hair and nuzzled her neck, kissing a delicate earlobe. "I owe everything to Glenis. Everything. Without her I might never have fulfilled my dream."

"Yer dream?" Madeleine asked softly, delighting in the delicious sensations his touch aroused in her.

"You are my dream, Maddie," he replied, his words punctuated by fervent kisses. "My wife—my love—my life." He abruptly drew away from her, searching her face, his eyes full of concern. "Kitty said you weren't feeling well today—"

"I'm fine," Madeleine insisted gently, smiling up at him. "Glenis was right. 'Twas a malady easily cured, by a kiss." As she stood on tiptoe and did just that, a small, embarrassed cough sounded from the archway. They both turned to find Kitty standing there, looking at them strangely.

"Supper is ready, Maddie," she said. "Major Marshall."

"Ye must be famished," Madeleine said as Kitty turned and walked back into the dining room.

"Yes, I am," Garrett answered, a rakish smile lighting his handsome face. "Ravenous." He swept her so suddenly in his arms she gasped aloud.

"Garrett!"

He chuckled deeply, raising his voice as he carried her up the stairs. "We'll dine later, Kitty. Have Sergeant Fletcher escort you home. Oh, yes, and tell him everything is fine! Couldn't be better!"

Madeleine felt his body tense as they neared their bedchamber, and she felt a wild tremor of excitement.

"If you'll kindly open the door for us, m'lady," Garrett said playfully, his warm breath tickling her ear.

She did as he asked and they entered the darkened room, then she swung the door closed behind them.

"Well done." He set her down gently, cradling her face as he kissed her fervently. "Just a moment, love, while I light the fire," he said, moving away from her.

Madeleine stood there shivering, missing him terribly even though he was so close. In a few moments a bright fire was blazing in the hearth. She rushed forward, holding out her hands to warm them.

" 'Tis grown so cold in here," she said through chattering teeth, watching as he shoved the large tub into a corner.

"It will heat up soon enough," Garrett said huskily, returning to embrace her. Then he was gone from her again, wrenching pillows, the tartan blanket, and the heavy bedspread off the bed. He quickly arranged them on the floor in front of the fireplace, then grabbed her hand and pulled her down beside him.

"How do you like our bower?" he said softly, running his fingers through her lustrous hair as they lay together before the fire. "Do you think it will do for our wedding night?"

Madeleine's heart seemed to skip a beat, and she blushed in confusion. "Wedding night? But we've already—"

He silenced her with a lingering kiss, then drew back, staring into her eyes. "This is our wedding night, sweet Madeleine. From this night we start anew, you and I. Love has made it so."

"Aye, love has made it so," she repeated softly, tracing the sensuous curve of his mouth with her fingers. " 'Tis a fine wedding bower, Garrett." She thought she might faint when he took her hand and tenderly kissed each fingertip in turn, his tongue teasing the hollow of her curved palm.

"I would that my hunger be sated, my lady wife," he said, a wicked glint burning in his eyes.

A seductive smile played about her lips as she gazed at him boldly, his words filling her with daring. She wound her arms about his neck. "Yer bride is willing and awaits yer pleasure," she said saucily, pressing her mouth to his.

Garrett groaned against her lips, his arms tightening around her like strong bands. For a long time they were lost in the glory of their shared kiss, and it was with great reluctance that he pulled away from her and stood up. His movements were impatient as he kicked off his boots and worked at the buttons on his shirt.

Madeleine rose to her knees, staying his hands. "No, husband, allow me," she insisted brazenly, smiling at his startled expression. "Come." She drew him down to kneel in front of her.

One by one she slowly undid the buttons, revealing his bronzed chest with its sprinkling of blond curls. She gently pushed the shirt from his broad shoulders, her hands caressing and exploring the rugged breadth of him, as if touching him for the first time.

"Never before was a man as beautiful as ye, Garrett," she whispered, her desire making her even bolder. She wanted to please him, wanted desperately to make up for everything that had gone before.

She reveled in the hard strength of the muscles that bulged as his arms reached out for her. She ran her hands down his chest, delighting in the sinewy power beneath her fingertips and the smooth, supple texture of his skin. Her hands strayed lower, over a taut abdomen ridged with muscle, until her fingers found his leather belt.

"You're a wanton lass," Garrett said, his eyes searing into hers as he allowed her to unbuckle the belt and slide it from his waist.

"Only with ye, my love," Madeleine replied, tossing the belt aside. Her fingers wandered to the vertical row of buttons at the front of his breeches. Garrett moaned and caught her hand. "Would ye have me stop, then, husband?" she asked, taunting him provocatively. When he did not answer, she undid the first three buttons, blushing when she encountered the hard swelling beneath the fabric. Anticipation streaked through her, her skin dimpling with goosebumps, and she dared to caress him.

"Enough!" Garrett commanded thickly, rising and yanking off his breeches.

Madeleine had barely an instant to feast her eyes on his glorious nakedness before he was pushing her down on the soft blankets. He stretched his long length atop her, supporting his weight with his elbows.

"It's my turn to play the wanton, my lady wife," he said, his narrowed eyes glinting with heat and fire. He traced his finger along her lace-edged bodice, just grazing the lush curve of her breasts. "Though I promise I will not dally as long as you."

Garrett drew himself up and knelt over her, his powerful thighs straddling her hips. He deftly untied the sash securing her gown. "I like these wrapping gowns best of all," he murmured, chuckling deep in his throat as the lustrous silk fell away from her body. "I'll see that you have dozens. They reveal your hidden treasures so easily." He slid his hand under the hem of her chemise. "And as for this," he whispered roguishly, "the seamstresses shall be kept busy stitching these as well."

Madeleine cried out in surprise when a tearing sound suddenly rent the air as her chemise ripped in two. She felt her exposed nipples grow taut, and she arched her back when Garrett bent over her suddenly and captured a rosy peak in his mouth.

She moaned aloud, thrusting her fingers through his hair as he suckled hungrily and lightly nipped the swollen nubs with his teeth. She was so lost in the dizzying sensations she scarcely realized he had divested her of the last of her clothing, revealing her lithe body.

"There's never been a woman fashioned more beautifully than you, Madeleine," Garrett said thickly, echoing her words to him. His lips found hers, drawing jagged breaths from her as he kissed her with impassioned fervor, a kiss that claimed her once and for all as his own.

His hands, his mouth, and his tongue raced up her writhing body and down again, caressing, teasing, as if he had to touch every inch of her and savor every silken secret she possessed. She opened herself to him, freely, gladly, urging him on with frantic whispers and pleading sighs.

Madeleine heard herself cry out his name as he entered her at last, sheathing himself within the softness and warmth of her body. She eagerly arched her hips to meet his thrusts and wrapped her arms tightly around his back. She rejoiced in the wondrous sensation of his desire throbbing within her, the friction of their skin like a searing mantle of flame between them.

She hurtled wildly toward rapture, oblivious to all else but panting breaths, frenzied kisses, and Garrett's ragged whispers, urging her on.

Suddenly he seized her tightly and rolled over onto his back, carrying her with him. She was astride him now, bracing her hands against his glistening chest as she met the urgent fierceness of his movements, his strong hands grasping her hips as they strove to become one.

"Come with me, Maddie," Garrett demanded huskily. His eyes blazed into hers, his powerful body shaking with passion. "Come with me—now!"

He pulled her to him, capturing her in his arms, his body driving upward within her even as she cried out her piercing pleasure; she, a part of him, he, a part of her . . . one at last in the blinding rapture surrounding them.

Late in the night Madeleine awoke to the dull thud of a charred log falling through the grate. She rose slightly from the bed and glanced drowsily at the hearth. Only faintly glowing embers remained of the roaring fire Garrett had stoked there earlier.

She sighed, pulling the blanket up to her chin and snuggling closer against his warm length. She marveled at how well they fit together, as if the contours of their bodies were especially made for each other. One of his arms was hugging her protectively, and she marveled at that, too, how he held her so closely even in sleep.

She peeked at him over her shoulder. His handsome features were lost in shadow, but his beloved face was etched forever in her mind. She rested her head on the pillow, smiling softly to herself as she thought back on their long night of passion. She could hardly wait for the morning, when they might love again.

Desirous warmth flooded her body as she blushed at her newfound wantonness. It was Garrett, after all, who had teased her just before they slept by whispering that he planned to keep her in bed with him throughout the next day. He had claimed a wedding night was hardly enough to satisfy him. He wanted a wedding week, a wedding month!

Madeleine shivered at the provocative thought. She had to admit that the notion thrilled her.

A darker thought suddenly pressed in upon her, clutching at her heart. Glenis's dire warning echoed in her mind, and it chilled her despite the comforting warmth of Garrett's body.

No, tomorrow she would not be able to spend the day in bed. Glenis had judged her well. She'd done a terrible thing, and only she could set it to rights. Tomorrow she would go into Farraline and speak with her kinsmen, alone. She only hoped Garrett would understand and not insist on accompanying her.

It was going to be hard enough to admit to him the accusations she had spread throughout the valley, even though she had believed it was the truth at the time. To have to tell Garrett she had endangered his life was a most unsettling prospect. She would rather die herself than have anything happen to him!

Madeleine's heart thudded painfully. Garrett would have to remain at Mhor Manor. There was no other way. He would be far safer at the estate than riding into Farraline with her.

She closed her eyes, knowing sleep would most likely elude her for the rest of the night. Maybe it was just as well. She needed time to think.

God help her find the right words to sway whatever plans her kinsmen might have made, she prayed fervently. If they branded her a traitor after they knew her change of heart, her brief happiness would be lost.

Chapter 32

"**W**ake up, Maddie. Please wake up!"
Madeleine's eyes blinked open at the
rude jarring. She was stunned to find Meg bending
over her, roughly shaking her shoulder.

"Meg, what are ye doing here?" she said, sleep
muddling her thoughts. "Quiet with ye now or ye'll
wake Garrett."

Meg's expression was guarded as she shook her
blond head. "Major Marshall is gone, Maddie. He's
ridden out with his men."

"Gone?" Madeleine's heart lurched in her throat,
and she rolled over, wide awake. It was true. The bed
was empty but for herself, and the sheets were cold
where Garrett had slept. She glanced back at Meg, a
blush burning her cheeks. She had always made it a
point to be well out of bed before the girls arrived in
the morning.

"What's going on?" she asked, clutching the covers
beneath her chin to hide her nakedness. "Where's
Gar—Where's Major Marshall?"

"He's gone in search of two of his soldiers," Meg
replied, shifting uneasily. "Seems they went out early
this morning to hunt for grouse and never came back.
Their horses returned almost an hour past without
them."

Madeleine could hardly believe she had slept so
soundly that she hadn't felt Garrett rise from the bed

or heard him leave the room for that matter. Perhaps he hadn't wanted to wake her.

The last thing she remembered was falling asleep sometime near dawn after lying awake for several hours. She must have been more exhausted from their lovemaking than she realized, despite the worries that she had thought would prevent her from sleeping.

"When did he leave?"

"Only a short while ago, just as Kitty and I arrived at the house. He said to tell ye what had happened and that he'd be back when he found his men."

Madeleine raised herself on one elbow. "Meg, kindly hand me my dress, if ye would," she said, nodding to the blue gown lying crumpled on the floor near the fireplace. She winced, rubbing her aching shoulder. "Why did ye have to wake me so roughly?"

Meg picked up the dress, but she did not readily hand it over, nor did she answer Madeleine's question. Instead she drew a folded piece of paper from her apron pocket and held it out to her.

Madeleine took the paper, noticing that Meg's hand was trembling. "What's this?"

" 'Tis from Angus," Meg said. She suddenly turned on her heel and bustled across the room to the massive wardrobe. "I'll fetch ye one of yer riding gowns, Maddie."

Madeleine stared after her, completely bewildered. Meg was acting so strangely, so unlike herself. Something odd was going on. She could sense it.

She unfolded the letter, quickly perusing Angus's stilted handwriting. Her brow knit in confusion.

" 'Ride as quick as you can to the fork of Aberchalder Burn, Maddie,' " she read aloud. " 'You've an old friend waiting there to see you. Do not worry, you will not be followed. We're leading the major and his men on a merry chase this morning. 'Twill keep them busy 'til you return. Angus Ramsay.' "

What was going on? she wondered wildly, reading the note again. She started when Meg rushed back to

her, a pile of clothing draped over her arm, topped by
a pair of brogues.

"What do ye know of this, Meg?" she asked sharply.
She sat up, still clutching the bedspread over her
breasts.

"I'm only doing what I was told, Maddie," the
young woman replied evasively. "Angus said to give
ye the note as soon as Major Marshall and his soldiers
were gone from the house."

"Surely ye must have read it," she accused. "Why'd
ye have known to fetch my riding clothes?"

"I dinna read it. Angus told me to see that ye were
dressed and sent quickly on yer way, that's all."

"Very well, Meg," Madeleine said, throwing back
the covers. "I can dress m'self, thank ye."

Affronted by her brisk tone, Meg set the clothing on
the bed and left the room without another word.

Madeleine dressed hurriedly, her mind in a total
quandary.

What should she do? Her first instinct was to try to
find Garrett, despite the urgent note. She didn't like
the idea that he was being led on some mysterious
chase through Strathherrick, knowing his danger as she
did.

It was clear to her that his two missing soldiers had
unwittingly become part of this ruse, probably trussed
up at this moment and hidden where Garrett would
never find them. For what purpose? So she might meet
an old friend at Aberchalder Burn? Who could it possibly be?

Madeleine suddenly thought of Lord Lovat. He was
an old friend, nearly eighty years old. Had he perhaps
decided to remain in the Highlands rather than take a
ship to France? Since he was a hunted fugitive with a
price on his head, it would make sense he would not
want to risk having Garrett and his soldiers following
her to their meeting place.

She felt a rush of excitement and quickly came to a
decision. What better person to help influence her kin
than the chief of Clan Fraser himself? Once Lord Lovat

knew the truth behind everything Garrett had done for his clansmen, and for her, surely he would persuade the Frasers of Strathherrick to accept Garrett's presence among them.

Madeleine threw the tartan shawl around her shoulders and ran to the door. Perhaps she could venture to hope that everything was going to work out after all.

Madeleine shivered as she veered her restless mare onto the leaf-strewn footpath that ran alongside Aberchalder Burn.

The fir trees were dense here, interspersed with Scots pine and naked beech trees that choked out what little sun there was on this cloudy autumn day. The air was chill and damp, indicating that there would be a frost that night if it grew cold enough.

She drew her tartan shawl more tightly around her, wishing she had worn something with more warmth, such as trousers and a heavy jacket. Too bad she hadn't thought of it before she left. She still possessed a set of black clothes, hidden deep in one of the drawers in her old room. She simply hadn't gotten rid of them yet.

Madeleine ducked her head, dodging a branch. The fork in this swiftly running stream lay beyond the next thick clump of firs. She listened carefully for any voices but heard nothing except trilling larks and crossbills piercing the sound of rushing water.

As she followed the narrow path down a slight decline, Madeleine trained her eyes on the fork clearly visible ahead. There was no one standing there waiting for her, nor did she see any movement in the dense green foliage surrounding her on all sides.

At last she drew up on the reins, bringing her horse to a halt. She sat quietly in the saddle for a moment, looking around her again, then cautiously dismounted.

She tensed as twigs and dried pine needles rustled and snapped close behind her. She turned around slowly. Her eyes widened at the sight of seven ragged Highlanders emerging from behind trees and thick hedges. They were bearded and unkempt, rough-looking men she had never seen before. She doubted they even belonged to Clan Fraser.

Surely Lord Lovat would have his own clansmen for an escort, she thought fleetingly, feeling the slightest quiver of fear. Men he could trust without question. Who were these—?

"Mistress Madeleine Fraser?" one of the men asked gruffly, breaking into her anxious thoughts.

"Aye," she said, holding her ground. She expected him to say more, perhaps explain their presence here, but instead he looked away from her.

Madeleine followed his gaze, her breath catching in her throat as another man stepped from the dense wood, a big man with dark hair and deep-set hazel eyes that caught and held her own. She watched, paralyzed, as he drew closer, not stopping until he loomed in front of her. His massive frame blocked out all else.

"Maddie," he breathed, his voice rough, deep, and hauntingly familiar.

"Dougald," Madeleine whispered hoarsely, staring at his bearded face. "I canna believe 'tis ye. Some fugitive kinsmen told me ye were dead, that the redcoats had hanged you at Inverness in the town square, not long after Culloden." Her voice quavered and died away, her stricken expression registering her shock.

"Ye were told wrong, love," Dougald said, taking a step closer. "I was taken prisoner and held in a stinking Inverness gaol, but they dinna hang yer Dougald. 'Twas another poor wretch they must have seen at the noose." He gestured to the men who were watching them silently. "We escaped from that gaol only two days past, six Camerons, one Macdonald, and I. We're on our way to Glasgow, where we'll catch a ship to France."

"Ye're sailing to France?" she said numbly, her mind barely registering his words. " 'Tis where our Lord Lovat was bound, or so I believed 'til today. The note from Angus said an old friend was waiting here. I thought perhaps 'twas Simon Fraser having changed his mind to stay in the Highlands.''

Dougald's expression was grim. ''Lord Lovat was captured by the redcoats almost a month ago, Maddie.''

''No!''

''Aye, I only heard it m'self the day before we broke from the gaol. They found him hiding in a hollow tree trunk on an isle in the middle of Loch Morar.'' He clenched his teeth, his tone dripping with bitterness. ''Lord Lovat was almost to the sea and they caught him, the bastards. He's in the Tower of London, lass, awaiting trial for high treason.''

''God save him,'' Madeleine whispered, completely stunned. Lord Lovat was in the infamous Tower! He would not be able to help her now. She would have to plead for Garrett alone.

''I've come to take ye away with me, Maddie, to take ye to France,'' Dougald said in a rush, shattering her dark reverie. His tone grew harsh, his eyes burning into hers. ''Ye'll be glad to know ye'll not have to spend another night with that English swine ye wed to save yer kin. Nor will ye have a lawful husband when the sun rises in the morn. Ye'll be free to wed yer Dougald Fraser.''

She gasped as he reached out suddenly and enfolded her in his brawny arms, a huge hand stroking her hair.

''I've more good news for ye, love. Our bonnie prince escaped to France a few weeks ago, and we're following him there. He'll soon make another bid for the throne of Britain, and this time we'll prove the victors. Ye'll have yer lands restored, Maddie, and I'll be the master of Farraline, just as yer father intended.''

Madeleine could scarcely breathe for the icy fear gripping her heart, a sense of foreboding striking into the depths of her soul. At that moment she did not care about the prince. She could only think of Garrett.

Dear God, what were her kinsmen plotting to do with him? she wondered desperately. She had to know before she could even begin to plan how to protect him.

She wrenched away from Dougald, ignoring his startled look. "What do ye mean?" she rasped in disbelief. "Stop talking to me as if I were a child! Ye speak as if I'll be a widow by morning."

"So ye will, my darlin' Maddie," Dougald said soothingly. " 'Tis all arranged. Our kinsmen were having the devil of a time trying to decide how to rid ye of the major 'til I came along unexpectedly. Back from the dead, ye might say."

Madeleine winced as he laughed hollowly, a dry echo of the hearty laugh he had once possessed. It chilled her to the bone.

"Angus and I spent last night devising our plan, so 'twill appear to be an accident," he continued, sobering. "We canna risk the redcoats venting their wrath on Farraline once more. But we'll need yer help."

Madeleine tried to speak steadily though she felt her world was crumbling around her. "What plan, Dougald?" she asked, glimpsing the flare of intense hatred in his eyes.

"Once the redcoats have bedded down for the night, ye're to give us a signal. We'll creep in and capture them, tie them up, then burn Mhor Manor down about their heads. 'Twill be a ceilidh fire like none other, Maddie! And the English authorities will ne'er question what happened, since ye'll supposedly have perished, too. 'Twill seem an unfortunate accident, and there'll be nothing left to prove otherwise—"

"Ye would burn them alive?" Madeleine cut him off, gaping at him in horror.

"Aye, and gladly!" Dougald spat, his ruddy skin flushed with fury. "They did the same to us at Culloden. Surely ye heard that story from the hunted clansmen passing through Farraline. I was hiding in a ditch and heard the terrible screams when the redcoats set the barn afire, with the wounded Highlanders inside."

He paused, his face twisting in torment at the awful memory, then continued, eyeing her grimly. "If 'tis

yer house ye're worried after, Maddie, I'll build ye a
far grander one when we return with our prince to
claim Britain's throne for the Stuarts. But dinna let me
think ye're balking because ye might harbor some bit
of affection for these bastards, or yer English husband,
I should say.''

Madeleine backed away from him, terrified by the
dark threat in his voice, terrified by the change the ill-
fated rebellion had wrought in him. The Dougald she
had known since childhood was gone, the same as if
he had died. This cruel man was a stranger to her,
hardened by all the brutality he had witnessed, embit-
tered and hell-bent on revenge.

Only such a man could have conceived this gruesome plan, and her kinsmen were influenced enough
by her false accusations and the thought of her unhap-
piness to go along with it. She doubted Dougald would
let her leave the glen if he knew where her true feelings lay. She would be a fool if she made even the
slightest mention of it.

She forced a smile. "Of course I'll help ye with yer
plan," she said, hoping her trembling would not give
her away. "I hate these redcoats as much as ye. What
signal shall I use?''

"When all is quiet, wave an oil lamp in the kitchen
window," Dougald replied, studying her strangely. He
moved toward her. His voice was eerily quiet. "Ye're
shaking so, Maddie? Why?''

" 'Tis—'tis such a shock to see ye again, Dougald,''
she said truthfully, staring into his eyes. "I'm so
happy, that's all. So glad that ye're alive.''

Madeleine swallowed hard, hoping her last words
had convinced him. She was grateful Dougald had
been spared the noose. She had cared for him, after
all. But now she felt more wretched than she ever had
before.

She loved a man she had once hated, and hated this
man for threatening her newfound love. And Dougald
was the man her father had chosen for her . . .

No, dinna think of it! she berated herself, stifling her

twinge of guilt. If loving Garrett made her a traitor, so be it. She would do anything to protect him, to protect their love—

Madeleine started as Dougald's hands easily circled her waist. She didn't dare protest as he pulled her against his powerful chest.

" 'Twas only my dreams of ye that kept me going during those long months in that filthy gaol, Maddie Fraser," he said thickly. "I stayed alive for ye, finally broke out of prison for ye. When I heard ye were married to a redcoat I would have come for ye then and strangled him with my bare hands if Angus hadna stopped me." His arms tightened around her, and he sank his fingers into her hair, drawing her head back roughly. "This Major Garrett Marshall, he's tasted yer charms before me, hasna he, Maddie?"

Madeleine said nothing, not wanting to goad his rage any further.

"I know he has, and for that he will die," Dougald said bitterly.

She closed her eyes as his mouth found hers, possessive and brutally demanding. He was hurting her, and tears welled beneath her lashes. She choked them back, even as she fought against the wave of nausea assailing her senses. She only hoped he would not discern that she felt nothing for him now—nothing.

When he finally released her, she felt defiled by the man who had once been her betrothed—a man who was no more than a shell of his former self, a man from whom she had everything to fear.

"I—I should get back," Madeleine stammered, glancing behind her for her horse. One of the other Highlanders was holding the mare for her, and she quickly thanked him as she took the reins. She winced as Dougald gave her a lift into the saddle, hardly able to bear his touch on her.

"We'll watch for yer signal, Maddie," Dougald said, his hazel eyes boring into hers curiously. "Dinna forget."

Her throat was constricted so tightly she could not

reply. She merely nodded, a fixed smile on her face as she sharply turned the horse around and galloped back along the shaded path, putting as much space between herself and Dougald Fraser as possible.

Tears ran unchecked down her face; sobs of disbelief tore at her throat. Her desperate thoughts spurred her on, even as she broke from the trees and raced toward Mhor Manor.

As soon as Garrett returned to the estate, they would ride into Farraline and face Angus together.

Next to herself, Angus spoke for the entire village, and his word was respected throughout Strathherrick. He had believed in Garrett once, before her wild accusations had poisoned his mind against him.

If Angus accepted the truth, there was still a chance that he might be able to sway her kinsmen against Dougald's hideous plan.

She cried out her anguish at the darker thought that he might not be able to convince them.

If so, she would flee her beloved Highlands with Garrett and never return. Aye, she would do it gladly. She would do anything to save his life and their future together.

Chapter 33

⌒~⌒⌒~

Almost two hours passed before Garrett's soldiers thundered up the dirt drive, Sergeant Fletcher in the lead.

Madeleine flew from the drawing room where she'd been anxiously waiting and met them just outside the front door. Her gaze scanned the entire group, her heart lurching in her breast. Garrett was not among them.

"Where's Major Marshall?" she blurted as Sergeant Fletcher dismounted. He appeared startled by her question.

"The major's not here?" he asked as she rushed up to him.

"No," she replied, searching his face. "I've been standing by the window, watching, and ye're the first to come back."

"That's odd," the sergeant said, clearly perplexed. "As soon as we found our missing men, Major Marshall took off across the moor." He cleared his throat, glancing at her somewhat sheepishly. "Don't think me too bold, m'lady, but he said his beautiful bride was waiting for him."

"But if he left before ye, he should have been here by now," Madeleine insisted, too worried even to smile at the sergeant's statement. "How far away were ye? Where did ye find yer two soldiers?"

"That's another strange thing," Sergeant Fletcher related. "I doubt we'd ever have found them if we hadn't given chase after a Highlander who fired a pistol at us—"

"Ye were shot at?" she interrupted him, horrified.

"Over our heads, m'lady," the sergeant continued. "We set off after him and stumbled upon our men, tied and blindfolded beneath a tree along the banks of Loch Mhor, almost four miles directly to the south." He shook his head. "It was almost as if we were led to that spot, as if this whole escapade was planned, though the major and I had no clue as to why."

"Did ye catch the man who fired upon ye?"

"No. A few of us went after the bloke, but we lost him in the woods. Major Marshall decided as long as we'd found our men, we should head back. He mentioned that he was going to discuss it with you later, since you know these people so well. What do you think, m'lady?"

Madeleine didn't reply, her mind racing. If Garrett and his men had ridden to the south, then they surely would have forded Aberchalder Burn. Was it possible that Garrett might have been apprehended on his way back because he was alone?

Raw fear shot through her. Had she given herself away to Dougald after all? Had he possibly sensed the truth of her feelings for Garrett? Was he planning his own personal revenge rather than waiting for this evening?

She blanched, remembering Dougald's ominous words. He had said he wanted to strangle Garrett with his bare hands—

"Lady Marshall, are you all right?" Sergeant Fletcher asked, startling her. He took her arm. "You look ill. Let me help you inside."

"No, I'm fine, sergeant. But thank ye," she said, forcing herself to think rationally and calmly. Hysterics would do neither her nor Garrett any good and would only stir the sergeant's suspicions. She had to act, and quickly, but she couldn't involve Garrett's soldiers.

If he had been taken captive by Dougald and his renegade Highlanders, they'd probably kill him at the first sign of any redcoats, if they hadn't already.

Sickened by the thought, Madeleine banished it from her mind. She would not give up hope so easily. She couldn't. She began to walk into the house, Sergeant Fletcher at her side, still holding her arm.

"I'm sure my husband will return shortly," she said to him at the foot of the stairs, affecting a light tone. "Thank ye for yer kind attention, sergeant. In truth, I have been feeling a bit tired of late. I think I'll go lie down for a while. When Major Marshall arrives, ye might tell him I'm waiting for him in our room."

Sergeant Fletcher nodded, smiling at her. She had no idea what Garrett might have told him, but obviously it was enough that the sergeant surmised all was well between them. She smiled back at him warmly, then turned and hurried up the stairs.

Once in the hallway, Madeleine rushed right past their bedchamber and into her former room. She closed the door quietly and hurried over to the armoire, pulling out the bottom drawer. She dug beneath piles of linen bedding to find what she was looking for. She drew out the last set of black clothes she possessed and carried them to the bed.

She changed quickly, grateful she still had a pair of trousers to wear instead of skirts which would only slow her down. Her thoughts turned to what lay ahead.

She had to get to Farraline at once and find Angus. She held no illusions that she would be able to persuade Dougald on her own to spare Garrett's life: Dougald would laugh in her face. She needed Angus by her side, and as many of her kinsmen as would follow her to Aberchalder Burn. But first she would need to convince them Garrett was not the king's spy.

Madeleine shook out the black jacket, her dirk falling onto the floor. She picked it up, testing its familiar weight in her hand. The silver hilt had tarnished since she had seen it last, the night she was captured as Black Jack. How long ago it all seemed.

She hadn't taken the dirk with her that night but had

hidden it instead, not wanting her father's prized gift to fall into her captors' hands. She slid it into the leather sheath at her belt, knowing she might very well need a weapon.

After slipping her brogues back on her feet, Madeleine was ready. She left her chamber and sneaked silently down the side stairs, heading for the drawing room. She had never thought she would use the secret tunnel again, until a few moments ago.

If Sergeant Fletcher knew she was going into Farraline, he'd insist she have an escort. That was the last thing she wanted. The only problem was that she wouldn't have a horse, but that could not be helped. She would never make it to the stable without being seen. 'Twas almost impossible in the full light of day with so many soldiers around. She would have to borrow a horse in the village.

Madeleine peeked into the drawing room, not surprised to see it was empty. Garrett had insisted that the main part of the house was to be restricted for their private use alone, unless by invitation. Yet she had to be careful nonetheless.

She darted into the closet, fumbling with the newly repaired trap door, which was slightly different than the last. Finally she got it open. She clambered down the ladder, realizing she had forgotten a flint and candle.

There was no time to go back. With her arms held out in front of her, she ran through the pitch-dark tunnel, gasping as invisible spiderwebs swept across her face. Her hands broke her impact as she hit the far wall with a thud.

She cursed loudly, her voice echoing eerily in the dark. She could not scramble up the ladder fast enough. She pushed against the heavy trap door until it gave way, blinking as daylight flooded the tunnel.

In an instant she was out, heaving in great gulps of fresh air. She began to race toward Farraline, hiding behind the trees as long as she could, then broke into a dead run across the rolling moor.

She was astounded when she reached the southern edge of the village, thinking how much it resembled the Farraline that had stood there before Hawley had burned it down. She hadn't been there since the day she returned from Edinburgh. It was amazing how much had been accomplished in so short a period of time, thanks in large part to the labor of Garrett and his men.

Madeleine slowed her pace only slightly when she came upon the main street. It was freshly swept, neat and deathly quiet. No children shrieked and played in the streets, no feminine laughter filtered from the cottages, no male voices rang out, no horses neighed, nothing. Only silence and the sighing wind.

She rushed up to the nearest cottage and peered inside the door, which had been left standing ajar, but it was empty. So were the next three she visited. She dashed down the street to Angus's house, built exactly on the spot where his cottage had stood before. She entered only to find that it was empty, too.

Madeleine hastened back into the street and ran up and down its length, calling out to anyone who might be there. Her cries carried back to her, muffled by the brisk wind. She had never encountered a stranger scene. The village was completely deserted.

She stood there a moment, not knowing quite what to do. If she did not find Angus, she would have to face Dougald alone. A daunting thought, but if that was all that was left to her . . .

A distant rumbling sound suddenly caught her attention, and she stiffened, listening. Had she only imagined it? No, there it was again, louder this time—and it was coming from the direction of Loch Mhor.

Madeleine began to run toward the sound, leaving the village behind her. What had been a rumbling to her ears in Farraline become raised voices, shouting in anger. She could see them now, a large group of people, some on horseback, some standing, all of them gathered around a tall beech tree with thick branches overhanging the dark water.

She ran faster, her breath ripping at her throat, her lungs on fire. She began to make out faces: Allan Fraser; Flora Chrystie holding her wriggling babe in her arms, her three boys at her skirts; Ewen Burke and Agnes, his wife; Meg and her parents; Kitty; and so many others. They were all the villagers of Farraline.

What could they possibly be doing? she wondered, dazed and light-headed from her exertion. Why were they assembled here, so far from their homes?

Then she saw him, his head towering above the crowd, and she felt as if she were choking, unable to draw breath.

Dougald.

He yelled out something, and the villagers responded by shouting back at him. She caught words, phrases, each one a death knell pounding into her brain.

"Hang the English bastard!"

"We dinna want King Geordie's spy in our midst. Do away with him now, with our blessing!"

"Ye'll not torment our Maddie Fraser any longer, ye devil!"

"Aye, hang him and throw his corpse into the loch. 'Twill appear he drowned, and good riddance!"

"No! Garrett," she gasped in disbelief, fearing she might collapse at any moment. She no longer felt her legs pumping beneath her, and she was terrified she might lose consciousness before she reached them. "Please, God, dinna let me faint," she prayed breathlessly. She was almost there. "He needs me . . . he needs me . . . grant me courage—"

Madeleine burst upon them so suddenly the villagers jumped back in surprise. She stumbled, but no one was close enough to break her fall. She sprawled face-down in the heather, the wind knocked out of her, too exhausted even to lift her head.

" 'Tis Maddie!" the villagers echoed throughout their ranks, astonished.

In the next instant she was dragged to her feet, a

strong arm supporting her around the waist. She looked up, meeting Angus's concerned gaze.

"Ye must stop this," she rasped, fighting to catch her breath, fighting the numbness in her limbs. " 'Tis not right! I love him—I love him."

"Hush, lass. Be careful what ye're saying," Angus warned, keeping his voice low, aware that everyone was staring at them.

Madeleine did not answer, her gaze falling on the man lying crumpled at the base of the tree. His dark blond hair was matted with blood.

"Garrett," she whispered, tears spilling down her cheeks.

His face was turned toward her, battered and bruised, one eye swollen shut. She could tell he had been severely beaten. He was stripped to the waist, his broad back marred by bloodied strap marks. His breathing was shallow, precious evidence that he was alive. Then she saw the noose dangling six feet above him. It was hovering, waiting.

Madeleine pushed away from Angus and staggered toward Garrett, her legs wooden yet gradually regaining strength. She was stayed suddenly by a massive hand on her elbow. She wheeled on her huge captor, her blue eyes ablaze.

"Take yer hands from me!" she railed at Dougald, who towered above her. "Ye've done this deed, haven't ye?"

"Someone take her. Let's be on with this hanging," he said, shoving her back into Angus's outstretched arms. "She's been so bewitched by this bastard she no longer knows what she says."

"Be still, lass, there's nothing ye can do," Angus whispered in her ear. " 'Tis been decided by one and all. Yer love winna save a king's spy, Maddie."

"He's not a spy, Angus, ye must believe me!" she said frantically. Her words spilled forth in a wild torrent, loud enough so everyone could hear. "I asked Meg and Kitty to fill yer heads with false accusations, thinking 'twas the truth. But I was wrong, just as ye're wrong now. 'Twas Glenis who set me to rights yesterday, when she came to Mhor Manor. She swore Garrett loved me. 'Twas so plain, but I couldna see it m'self. 'Tis why he won a pardon for me. He bargained away his estate in England for it! 'Tis why he saved my life and yers as well! 'Tis why he's been trying to help us. He loves me, Angus, as I love him. I tell ye he's not a spy!''

Angus's hands gripped her arms tightly, his expression grim. "Ye would swear to this, Maddie?"

"Aye, on my life. I swear it. 'Tis the truth, and I've never lied to ye, Angus," she declared vehemently. "Ye once told me ye'd misjudged him. Ye saw for yerself what Garrett did to help our kin. He's been trying to help us since we got back from Edinburgh, but I turned ye against him with my foolish charges."

Madeleine wrenched free of his grasp, her gaze settling on one somber-faced villager after the other. "Major Marshall's a good man," she said, her voice pleading for reason. "A man ye can trust, no matter that he's English and a redcoat. None of ye would be alive today if not for him! He wants to live among us in peace, as I want to live in peace. I canna bear any more senseless bloodshed and warring."

"Aye, he wants his peace so badly he took my brother's life to have it!" Allan Fraser exclaimed, pushing forward from the crowd.

"Ye know 'twas Hawley's surgeon who caused Kenneth's death," Madeleine objected. "Ye cannà blame Major Marshall for that."

"Aye, 'tis true," Angus added, silencing him. "Kenneth was felled by the surgeon's knife, and well ye know it, Allan."

"Dinna ye see?" Madeleine continued desperately, glancing gratefully at Angus and then back to the villagers. "If ye hang him, or go through with yer barbaric plan to burn Mhor Manor, 'twill only bring more horrors down upon us. Ye're fools if ye think the Crown authorities will believe 'twas an accident! And Dougald here," she flung at her scowling kinsman, "will be safe in France where the redcoats canna find him. Ye'll be suffering while he enjoys his freedom and dreams of a Stuart conquest that might never come."

This declaration elicited a low buzz of discussion among the villagers, some casting suspicious looks at Dougald.

Madeleine approached him, her eyes flashing angrily. "Ye've not given much thought to what will surely happen to yer kinsmen, have ye, Dougald? All ye care about is venting yer rage and yer hatred on this one man because he has been given what fate decreed ye'll never have. Ye're only concerned for yer own selfish desires!"

"I will have ye for my wife by sunset, Maddie," Dougald growled, "and yer land one day."

"Never," she said fiercely. "I'll never be yers, Dougald. I'd die first."

"Enough with such talk!" he roared, striding over to Garrett and roughly pulling him to his feet. " 'Twas decided this redcoat should hang, and by God, he will!" Two of the other renegade Highlanders grabbed Garrett by the shoulders while Dougald began to settle the noose around his neck.

"No!" Madeleine screamed, rushing forward. She pulled her dirk from its sheath and brandished it at Dougald. "Ye'll have to kill me first, Dougald Fraser. I'll die before I see my husband hang!"

A stunned silence fell over the villagers, broken suddenly by Dougald's uproarious laughter.

"Ye threaten me, ye slip of a lass?" he mocked her, baring his wide chest to her dirk and advancing on her. "Go on with ye, then. See what damage ye can do before I wrest yer knife away and stick it between yer fine husband's ribs," he spat derisively. "When he's dead and ye're my wife, ye'll ne'er raise yer voice to me again, Maddie. That I promise ye."

"Garrett Marshall is the only husband I will ever know," she countered defiantly, shifting her feet to better her stance.

"Aye, and ye'll have to fight me, too," Angus said

suddenly, walking up beside her. "Next to ye, Dougald, I'm an old man, but I'll fight ye to the death for my Maddie Fraser. We'll have no more bloodshed in this valley, not if I can help it—unless 'tis yer own that is spilled."

Madeleine glanced at him, tears brimming in her eyes, but she quickly wiped them away and faced Dougald once more.

"And me, Dougald," Ewen Burke said quietly, flanking her other side. "Ye must fight me as well. I stand with the mistress of Farraline, and her husband."

"Aye, and me!" Duncan cried, joining them. He was followed by more villagers, men, women, and wide-eyed children, until there was no one left standing behind them but Allan Fraser.

"I'll not join with ye, Maddie," he said, walking over to Dougald's side. "But I'll not fight against ye."

" 'Tis been decided, Dougald, and well ye can see it," Angus stated clearly. "Garrett Marshall shall go free. Take yer hands from him now—or forever know the scorn of yer clan."

Madeleine held her breath as Dougald stared at them for a long, long moment. His eyes were full of fury, the battle he was waging between his own will and the stronger will of the clan evident in his face. Finally he stepped back, gesturing to the two men who were holding Garrett.

"Release him," he said.

As the noose was lifted over Garrett's head, Madeleine sheathed her knife and ran to catch him, shouldering his weight while Ewen rushed over to support his other side.

"Stand away, Dougald," Angus commanded. "If there comes a time when all fugitives are pardoned and ye may return to the Highlands, ye'll come in peace or else ne'er set foot in Strathherrick again. Do ye swear on yer fealty to Clan Fraser?"

"Aye."

"Allan Fraser?"

"Aye, I swear."

"Men of Clan Cameron and Clan Macdonald. Do ye swear as brothers of our clan?"

"Aye," they said.

"So be it," Angus said evenly. " 'Tis witnessed. Godspeed to all of ye on yer way to France."

Dougald said no more as he mounted his horse, followed by the seven Highlanders and Allan Fraser. They set out at a gallop across the rugged, heather-clad moor, never once looking back.

"Garrett," Madeleine said, stroking his bloodied hair and bruised face with tender, trembling fingers. "Ye're safe, my love. We're taking ye home, to Mhor Manor."

Garrett smiled faintly, hearing her words through the swamping pain that gripped him.

"Yes, take me home, Maddie," he whispered weakly, feeling her lips lightly brush his mouth.

It was the sweetest kiss he had ever known.

Epilogue

Mhor Manor
September 1747

Madeleine smiled softly as the light breeze fanned the chestnut tendrils framing her face. She breathed in the fragrant air, scented with wildflowers and sweet heather.

Aye, 'twas a most special day, she thought happily. Bright with warm sunshine and bright with promise and hope.

Her heart overflowed with love as she gazed at Garrett. He was standing beside Master Simon Fraser, eldest son of their late chief, Lord Lovat. The two men faced the assembled Frasers of Strathherrick, and she thrilled to the rich timbre of Garrett's voice as he addressed the attentive crowd, over three hundred strong.

"As Master Simon has claimed, the time for reconciliation is upon us. There is much hurt to heal between our two peoples, and perhaps a prejudice that will never be overcome. Yet whatever has gone before, we must not forget we are a united land serving the same king . . ."

Madeleine grew pensive as she listened to him, her musing inspired by his heartfelt words.

They had come so far since that afternoon last autumn when the villagers of Farraline had joined with her to save Garrett's life. Each passing day had brought with it new triumphs and small successes, a slow, steady building of trust between Garrett and her people that had grown stronger and flourished before her eyes.

So had their love flourished and strengthened, she thought warmly, cementing a bond of respect and trust between herself and Garrett that could never be broken. She had been so happy these past months, her days spent building a life with the man she loved and her nights spent in his impassioned embrace, sharing dreams, laughter, love.

Madeleine glanced tenderly at their infant son, slumbering so peacefully in Glenis's arms. Her happiness had been made complete at his birth only two weeks ago. They had named him Hugh Geoffrey Marshall, after her father and Garrett's. Their little son was beautiful, with golden curls and bonnie blue eyes.

Her gaze sought Garrett once more. He looked so handsome in his forest-green coat and breeches. He was no longer a soldier since his military commission had expired. He stood before Clan Fraser not as a conqueror but as a man who wanted only peace and prosperity for the valley he loved almost as well as she did. He had not turned his back on England. He had simply adopted Strathherrick as his own, a part of him as surely as the Scots blood coursing through his veins.

Madeleine's eyes strayed to her cousin Simon, the young chief of Clan Fraser, recently released from an Edinburgh gaol. His strong profile and stout stature echoed so clearly the features of his father.

She sighed faintly, feeling a rush of sadness as she recalled the mournful day in April when they received news that their Lord Lovat, Simon the Fox, had been beheaded on Tower Hill for his involvement in the Jacobite rebellion. His death had led to an understandable setback in Garrett's efforts with her people, yet gradually the pain and bitterness had eased, and progress had begun anew. Especially when word came that Master Simon had been pardoned by King George.

She and Garrett had rejoiced in Master Simon's letter, filled with his plans to visit Strathherrick and his former holdings in the Aird before taking up residence in Edinburgh. It was Simon's intent to encourage reconciliation among his clansmen, hoping that through his efforts he might one day regain his titles and lands. There was even talk of his forming a regiment of fighting men for the king, who would be known as the Fraser Highlanders.

Madeleine's reverie faded as Garrett's words filled her with quiet joy.

". . . It is time to set aside the hatred of the past and rebuild, for the future of Scotland, for the future of Great Britain. I swear on my love for everything I hold dear that I will continue to help Clan Fraser in this worthy task."

Garrett turned and held out his hand to her, his eyes smiling into hers. Madeleine clasped his hand proudly and took her place by his side.

"As my husband has sworn to ye," she stated loudly, her gaze sweeping her kinsmen, "so do I swear."

Rousing cheers of approval met her declaration, heightening as Master Simon Fraser gathered their young son gently into his arms and held him up for all to see.

"This wee babe will grow to manhood among ye," he shouted, his voice booming out over the din. "He's one of yer own, a symbol of the blood tie between ourselves and our English countrymen. In him we'll see our hopes for the future, that we might live in peace. I give ye Hugh Geoffrey Marshall, heir to Mhor Manor and one day master of Farraline!"

Garrett squeezed Madeleine's hand, his dream fulfilled more completely than he ever could have imagined. He stared into her stunning eyes, seeing a fierce love shining there that burned as brightly as his own.

"I will love ye forever, Garrett Marshall," she said softly.

His heart was full. He bent and kissed her smiling lips, oblivious to all else, including his son's lusty cries.

"Aye, that's my fine Highland laddie," Glenis crooned to the howling infant as Master Simon placed him in her arms again. She glanced at Madeleine and Garrett, her dark eyes twinkling. "Let 'em know ye're in Scotland!"